Made in Goatswood

A Celebration of Ramsey Campbell

GOATSWOOD
ALLEN K. '95

CALL OF CTHULHU® FICTION

Made in Goatswood

A CELEBRATION OF RAMSEY CAMPBELL

new tales of horror
set in the Goatswood region of the Severn Valley
by

RAMSEY CAMPBELL

A. A. ATTANASIO
FRED BEHRENDT
DONALD BURLESON
PETER CANNON
C. J. HENDERSON
KEITH HERBER
J. TODD KINGREA
PENELOPE LOVE
RICHARD A. LUPOFF
ROBERT M. PRICE
KEVIN A. ROSS
DIANE SAMMARCO
GARY SUMPTER
MICHAEL G. SZYMANSKI
JOHN TYNES
RICHARD WATTS

SCOTT DAVID ANIOLOWSKI

Selected and edited by SCOTT DAVID ANIOLOWSKI

A Chaosium Book

1995

Made in Goatswood is published by Chaosium, Inc.

Cover artwork by H. E. Fassl. Severn Valley map by J. Todd Kingrea. Ramsey Campbell portrait by Allen Koszowski. Chapter decorations by Earl Geier. Cover layout by Eric Vogt. Editing and layout by Janice Sellers. Proofreading by James Naureckas and Linda J. Short.

Please address questions and comments concerning this book, as well as requests for free notices of Chaosium publications, by mail to: Chaosium, Inc., 950-A 56th Street, Oakland, CA 94608-3129, U.S.A.

FIRST EDITION
1 2 3 4 5 6 7 8 9 10

Chaosium Publication 6009. Published in July 1995.
ISBN 0-56882-046-1.
Printed in the United States of America.

CONTENTS

INTRODUCTION *Scott David Aniolowski* vii

A PRIESTESS OF NODENS *A. A. Attanasio* 1

GHOST LAKE *Donald R. Burleson* 9

BEAUTY *Fred Behrendt* 21

UNSEEN *Penelope Love* 35

FORTUNES *Keith "Doc" Herber* 51

CROSS MY HEART, HOPE TO DIE *J. Todd Kingrea* 57

I DREAM OF WIRES *Scott David Aniolowski* 75

THE TURRET *Richard A. Lupoff* 91

THE SECOND EFFORT *John Tynes* 125

THE QUEEN *Diane Sammarco* 131

THE UNDERCLIFFE SENTENCES *Peter Cannon* 143

THE AWAKENING *Gary Sumpter* 161

RANDOM ACCESS *Michael G. Szymanski* 175

FREE THE OLD ONES *C. J. Henderson* 189

THE MUSIC OF THE SPHERES *Kevin A. Ross* 211

GROWING PAINS *Richard Watts* 223

THE BEARD OF BYATIS *Robert M. Price* 233

THE HORROR UNDER WARRENDOWN *Ramsey Campbell* 255

Needing Ghosts And Ancient Images

"Those stories had been products of his own mind, yet he couldn't shake them off except by writing—but now he was suffering nightmares on behalf of the world."

— Ramsey Campbell, "The Depths"

Welcome to *Made in Goatswood*, and the nightmare-haunted world of Ramsey Campbell.

Ramsey Campbell's career began back in 1962 when August Derleth published "The Church in High Street" in the Arkham House collection *Dark Mind, Dark Heart*. He was sixteen at the time. Two years later Derleth published the seventy-ninth book under the Arkham House imprint, Campbell's *The Inhabitant of the Lake and Less Welcome Tenants*.

Although the influence of Lovecraft is painfully obvious in those early *The Inhabitant of the Lake* stories, Campbell's unique style was already beginning to peek out from behind the shroud of Cthulhu Mythos pastiche. In 1968 the transitional tale, "Cold Print", appeared in *Tales of the Cthulhu Mythos*. With this story Campbell was truly trying on his own style in lieu of cheap Lovecraftian imitation. By the 1973 *Demons by Daylight* he had successfully broken away from HPL and was on his own in the dark realms of the weird tale. The rest, as they say, is history.

At the behest of August Derleth, Campbell rewrote his early stories and set them in more familiar British surroundings. Instead of Lovecraft's Arkham, Kingsport, Dunwich, and Innsmouth, he dropped his ill-fated protagonists into the equally-haunted Severn Valley towns of Severnford, Brichester, Camside, Clotton, and Goatswood. After *The Inhabitant of the Lake* and *Demons by Daylight*, he would return to his ancient and shadowy Severn Valley settings only rarely with such offerings as "Dolls" (from *Scared Stiff*), "The Tugging" (from *The Disciples of Cthulhu*), and a few others. Ramsey Campbell's Cthulhu Mythos tales have since been collected in the complete British edition of *Cold Print*.

It has now been more than thirty years since Ramsey Campbell first created those strange British towns and villages to use as a backdrop for his Cthulhu Mythos stories. Today he is among the leading modern authors of the weird tale and has influenced a generation of writers. It is the intent of this collection to return to the Severn Valley and to pay homage to the man who has influenced so many of us, who has filled so many nights with twisted nightmares.

I am very proud of the diversity of authors presented herein. Voices both new and old, from small press to established pros, are collected here to share their visions of the Severn Valley. I am especially proud to present a brand new Severn Valley/Cthulhu Mythos story written by Mr. Campbell especially for this book, the first he has written in almost a decade.

These stories run from subtle to sublime, from innovative to imitative, from haunting to hushed. We have returned to the Valley to explore what ancient evils lurk there. The result is this book of collected tales by diverse voices: stories of corruption of the mind, the heart, and the soul. The outer forces of the Mythos linger at the fringes of some of these tales, and spill full force into others. Presented are glimpses into the past, visions of the future, and horrors of today. But fear and horror and cosmic evil are timeless forces, and will lurk at the thresholds, stalk shadows in lonely streets, and rap at darkened windows long after you and I are gone. Such is their power, and it is this power that we savor.

I hope you enjoy these little glimpses into the dark as much as I, and there is something here for every taste. So board that train bound for Goatswood, or take a drive along the A.38 to Brichester, and experience for yourself these tales that were *Made in Goatswood*! Unpleasant dreams ...

A number of people were instrumental in the creation of this anthology, and I wish to thank them for all the help. Thanks to my publisher Greg Stafford for making this book a reality; to Andrea Sammarco for invaluable legal advice and assistance; to Robert M. Price and Edward P. Berglund for supplying addresses and leads on interested authors; to Lynn Willis of Chaosium for his invaluable assistance and feedback; to Tracy Sammarco for more legal advice and support; to artists H. E. Fassl, Allen Koszowski, J. Todd Kingrea, and Earl Geier for making the book look good; and to all of the talented authors who took the time to tell their twisted little tales for me. No words can express my gratitude to my mother, Linda Short: It is undoubtedly from her that I inherited my love of horror films and literature—what a gift, indeed. My own story in this collection was inspired by the lyrics of British musician Gary Numan, and I thank him for so graciously allowing me to weave bits of his work into my own, and for the original inspiration. But most of all I thank Ramsey Campbell, without whom this anthology would not exist. A million thanks!

— Scott David Aniolowski
Lockport, NY
October 31, 1994

"The boys were running; the light congealed about them, the ceiling descended, threads of cobweb drifted down. A turn, an alcove, webs. Another. Glancing sideways, John was chilled by a formless horror; the cobwebs in the alcove suggested a shape which he should be able to distinguish."

— Ramsey Campbell, "The Interloper"

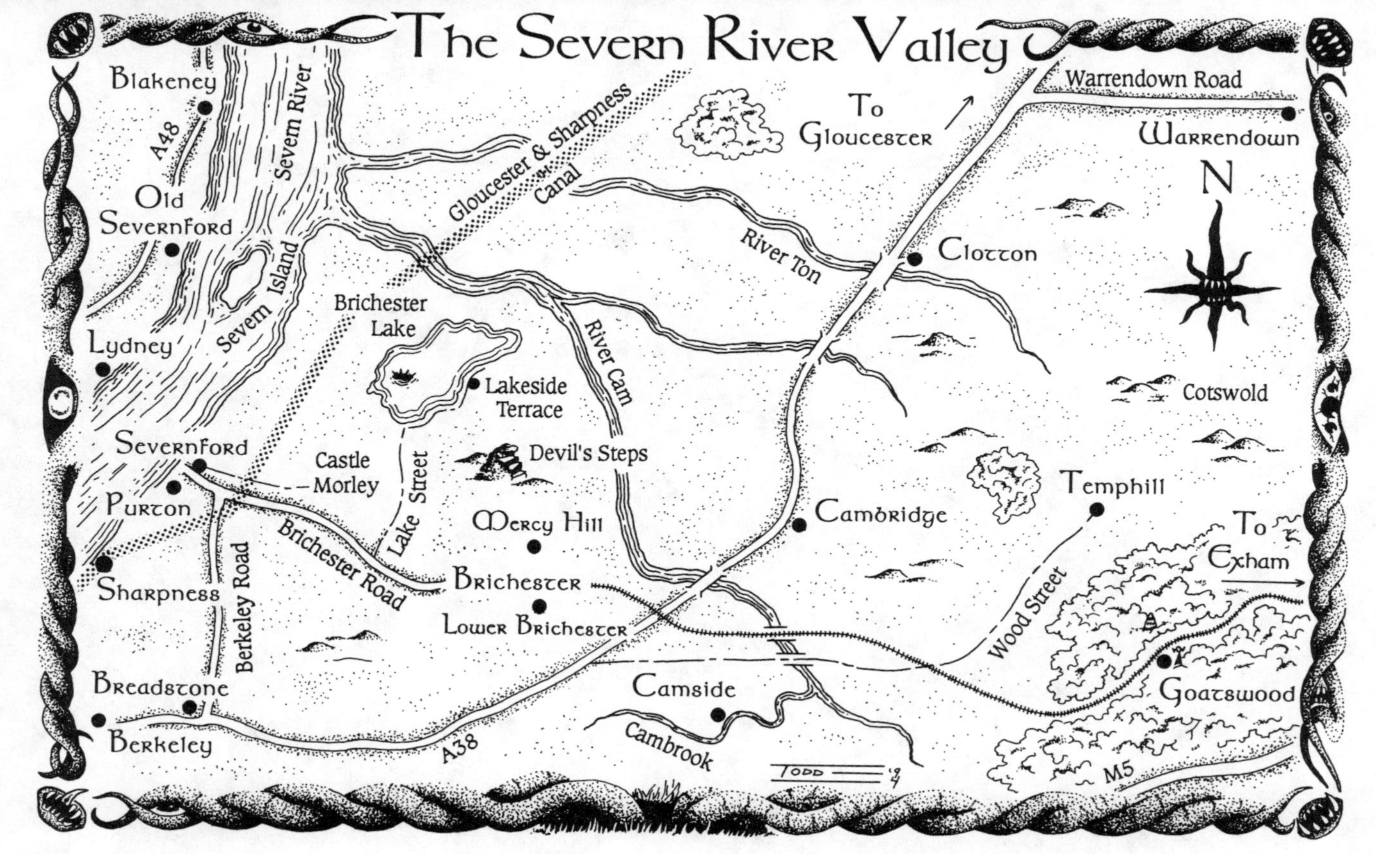
The Severn River Valley
Blakeney
A48
Severn River
Old Severnford
Severn Island
Lydney
Severnford
Purton
Sharpness
Breadstone
Berkeley
Berkeley Road
Brichester Road
Castle Morley
Brichester Lake
Lakeside Terrace
Lake Street
Devil's Steps
Mercy Hill
Brichester
Lower Brichester
A38
Gloucester & Sharpness Canal
River Cam
River Ton
To Gloucester
Clotton
Cambridge
Camside
Cambrook
Warrendown Road
Warrendown
N
Cotswold
Temphill
Wood Street
To Exham
Goatswood
M5
TODD

DEDICATION

Karl Edward Wagner was a true craftsman of the macabre. Perhaps best know as the editor of the annual *The Year's Best Horror Stories* series, he had an encyclopedic knowledge of the field and a writing style all his own. He was also a dear friend of Ramsey Campbell and an "adopted uncle" to Campbell's children. Karl was eager to contribute a tale to this very collection but never got the chance to write it. Sadly, he died on October 15, 1994. This anthology is dedicated to him: The realms of horror and dark fantasy won't be the same without Karl Edward Wagner.

A Priestess of Nodens

by A. A. Attanasio

Twilight shrouds the Cotswolds. Laggard hills and autumn trees sink slowly into blue mist, and the sky slants toward night. On a slope of elm, six naked couples walk single file through the woods, hands interlocked. The wind burns with cold, and they move quickly among the wrangling branches. Even the oldest ones, their flesh fluttering, march spryly.

At the spur of a hill they come to a glade of whispering alders where split cherry logs and crowns of dried roots have been stacked for a bonfire. The cadence of the march slows and takes on the float of a dance as the twelve circle the wood pile. Sunlight stands like smoke among the great trees, and the air is filled with what the leaves can no longer hold.

After three rounds, the couples stop their dance, spread out into a circle, and sit down in the resinous grass facing the unlit pyre. Their minds are quiet. Personal thoughts have been left behind, back at the camp with everybody's clothes. Now they are naked of body and mind, skyclad, waiting for the priestess. The cold deepens with their stillness, and several begin to hum softly to themselves.

As the sun sets, the air goes glassy. Night flexes around them, and everyone aches in their ribcages with shivering. The oldest among them is Violet, a tarnish-skinned crone with a flat stump of a head and neck muscles taut as roots. She is the coven's priestess, intimate with the Goddess, the spirit of life they have gathered to worship. Unlike the others, Violet does not shiver. She is in a rapture, feeling the close presence of the Goddess. Warmth radiates through her with the excitement she feels for this ritual. Her earliest memories are just like this: sitting in the forest with others who, like her, are willing to abandon hope and all its separations and sit naked as the woods. The Goddess is not a world away but right here under them in the one Earth broken into trees, leaves, wind, and them. The purpose of the ritual is to acknowledge the reality of this unity. And, if the conditions have the precision of luck, they might move a little bit out of their lives toward life and waver inside the transparent vision of an awakened mind before surging back into their individual dreams.

The whistle of a morning bird trips out of the gloaming, and everyone's breathing tightens. The priestess is coming. Twelve faces peer into the darkness between the powerful trees, hoping to catch an early glimpse of her.

Violet smiles a little hook of sadness. Tonight is Samhain, year's end, the Night of the Dead. For over fifty years on this night she has presided as priestess, using her apprehensions of the Divine to guide the others into reverie. Now on this Hallowed Eve, maybe her last, the Goddess has sent someone else, a stranger. She is a guest to the coven, a traveler passing through. But they have heard of her months before from a fen meeting at Stonebench where she healed a deaf and dumb boy. And that group heard of her from a river commune outside Gloucester where she had danced with an autistic girl and left her speaking and laughing, for the first time a normal child. Intrigued by the miraculous, the coven passed word on to her, not at all certain of receiving a reply.

When the reply came by phone call and Violet had a chance to speak with the slow voice at the other end, she learned to her disappointment that she knew the stranger. Her name was Dana Largo, and she had belonged with the Coven of the Shining Face in Lydney. Violet remembered her as a pale, vaporous-looking woman with lank red hair and a squinted face. Something was wrong with her. Bad blood or cancer. And she had looked it: Her arms had been thin and white as fluorescent tubes and the sheen of her skull had glowed through the flesh at her temples. She had not been expected to live long.

The bad blood or the cancer eventually got worse, and she disappeared. Violet's friends in the Coven of the Shining Face had told her she had gone off to die alone. So Violet was surprised to find out that not only was Dana Largo alive, but she had somehow been empowered by her dying. At least so the other covens reported. Violet and all those of her circle, the Mulch Coven, who recalled seeing her at the big festival in the Forest of Dean more than seven years ago, could not imagine such a wastrel conducting a strenuous year's end ritual. But when she came to them, quiet-eyed, with cheeks lean as a deer's and nettle burrs snagged in her red hair, they sensed at once her change.

On the phone she had instructed them to meet her in an area none in the coven had visited before, a forested enclave called Goatswood. She had arrived at the camp strolling out of the wooded pass that led through dense tree haunts to the railway, her handstitched backpack laced with vine and flowers. She had said little, but her demeanor had been playful as she passed out posies of fire-colored leaves to the coveners. Judging by her bright rag travelcoat, cloth boots, and the trim black bush hat she wore, Violet had thought she was a hippie revenant.

Afternoon had been low in the trees when she arrived, and meditation for that evening's ceremony had already begun, leaving Violet time for only a brief exchange with Dana. They had wandered to the edge of the camp where a field of thistle grass clicked with the wind. "This coven is your family," Dana told Violet, speaking gently and personally, dispelling the old woman's disappointment. "I was invited as a priestess, but I'd be just as happy to join the circle and follow you tonight. You see, my devotion has gone somewhat beyond the Goddess to an elder god, an Old One, whose temple in Lydney has become my home. I'm afraid you'll find my practice unorthodox."

Violet had been tempted to accept the leadership for herself again. She was feeling very close to the autumn earth, her old age a consummated decay celebrated in the leaves. Myriads of them, she had daydreamed all day, like thin flames shedding no light. Yet because she was so borne away with the power of the season, she felt close to the Goddess, and she was clear. A mood of luck urged her to trust this young wanderer, to see for herself how unorthodox she was. And also, on a more mischievous level, she wanted to be compared.

After sharing the traditional mulled cider with the coven, Dana Largo had taken her crude backpack and had hiked out toward the ceremonial clearing. Beneath a hedge of hawthorn bracken, whose glossy leaves shed rain, she hid her large overcoat, hat, and backpack.

Alone with autumn's imagination, she circled the glade of leafless trees a dozen times counterclockwise to unwind the tight feelings in herself. She forgot her journey in the relentless erasures of twilight. That is her great strength: She learned early and well how to forget.

Her personal memories faded, and she unwrapped her boots and let her strong, callus-toughened feet dance through the fallen leaves. A deer stared at her from among the last stairways of sunlight, and an owl hooted from another room in the forest.

Blood drummed through her muscles as she removed her sweater and the cold touched her flesh. In the space of her forgetfulness, she was lucent with emotion. She untied the long braids that held her hair back. A dance unfolded through her, and she moved in a twirling step around the foot of an eel-branched hazel.

Nodens drew close to her, and Dana entered a state of terror and love. Terror as the cold sharpened with the wind and she became her true littleness. And love as a giant of feeling began to rise out of the loam of the earth.

Darkness thickened, and she pulled off her trousers to stand naked in the Presence of her elder god and the forest. She forgot the dangers of the world. She was a sacrifice to Nodens, trusting in the Old One's meaning. Standing perfectly still in the night, she was with all that trembles, all that hides.

* * *

The naked circle-sitters shiver only a short time before a morning bird calls out of the east where no morning is. All twelve stare in that direction.

Silence, while a fragment of moon appears over the shoulder of a cloud. All senses strain toward where the bird has sounded, and no one sees her until she is among them. She glides into the circle from the west, the direction of the dead, the moon's wraith-light shining blue off her pale skin. Her red hair gleams purple with night, and she has weighted strands of it with snailshells so that it moves like seaweed.

Her voice penetrates: "This is the night of darkness. Year's end. Between worlds. Life and death open into each other tonight. The dead walk and the living are a Dance of Shadows, meeting here and there, everywhere and nowhere, as us." A spark flares between her cupped hands and steadies to the calm flame of a taper. Radiance underlights her face, revealing a sapience in her slender eyes that shines green in the burning. She throws the taper onto the wood, and, with a startling flap of heat and refulgence, the pile roars into flames.

She's treated the wood, Violet reasons in the face of her excitement. Sparks crawl up the wind like spirochetes, and as the night folds back, the nakedness of the priestess seems to expand. Her white flesh glows with the fire's sheen, and the six men feel lust and mother-awe mix like pigments; the six women watch and watch, for what they see is more ancient than anything they have known. The priestess dances orgasm and birth-rack simultaneously. She dances more lewdly than the flames, and she suffers more cruelly than the twisting wood.

One by one, she pulls them to their feet and charms them with moving. They circle among the fireshadows, bouncing like a fountain to the unheard music of their lives, following the cadence of the flames and the wind.

Dana Largo shares the dance with each of the twelve. She shawls herself in their movements. She mimes them. And her awareness, streaming off of her into the beard of the wind and its sparks and stars and flying darkness, slows to match their motions. The moment flutters and cramps, and within her mime she sees the vagaries and misdirections of each of their lives.

Between warming dances, the circle sits close to the flames, and the coven does the new year scrying. All look ahead into the future together, some silently and some saying what they see. Usually, the scrying is uncertain as smoke, more self-reflection than prophecy.

But on this night, the visions are as majestically clear and unique as gems. The priestess tells each of them something about their doom in such a way that they are braver for it. And, in turn, Nodens speaks to Dana Largo: Violet stares through the priestess' hair into the flames. "I see the blood tree inside you—and the spiders of blood eating you! And an old tower—an old tower on a dark shore lit by the bright hair of angels. Astral voices—I hear them singing, singing sorrows of the other world. They sing of the mercy of darkness. And there you are again—but not you, yet you—your blood tree chewed to a lace of decay by the blood spiders. It's horrid! Your decayed body dancing with spiders in shadows under the purple sun ... ."

Violet jerks back, her sinuses aching with the red smell of danger.

The priestess gazes at her with a rictus grin, her skull in the firelight shining through her waxy flesh. "You have seen the truth of me, Violet."

Violet blinks, but the skeletal visage does not pass. "I don't know what I've seen."

"Then, I will tell you." The priestess leans closer, her face a fossil. "I am dead. The spiders in my blood have devoured me. But the Old One—Nodens—has restored me to a life. A life like no other life. You know of Nodens?"

Violet looks to the other coveners, but they stand about embedded in the darkness, inert as tree boles.

"Nodens," the priestess repeats, and something inside Violet leans forward with all its weight and pulls her attention into the firepoints that are the priestess' eyes.

"The ancient Romans worshiped him."

"Oh, yes—they worshiped him." Flames seem to sit inside the priestess' head. "The Roman station at Lydney has a temple to the elder god Nodens. That is the old tower on the dark shore. You must be half dead now and faithless to this world to find it. I went there when I was far into my dying, when the Goddess could not, would not, stop my dying, for death is but the flip side of life to Her, a dazzling impermanence. That is the truth we celebrate tonight, isn't it? But Nodens took me beyond life and death, to the other world, to the light of the purple sun."

"Why?" Violet's words cake like cinders in her throat, yet she must know. "Why would an elder god take mercy on us?"

"For a dark purpose, Violet. I must serve him." The incandescent skullbones darken behind the priestess' swollen face, and her sadly wrung features become luminous and full of pity. "For this life he has given me, I must serve him, from the dark to the dark. Inside my cage of bone, I am a slave to the elder gods, on the dark shore where the dead eat their unspeakable meals. But I have nothing to say about the company of the dead. I serve the Old Ones well, and occasionally, as on this night, they allow me to walk again among the living and use the elder powers at my whim. That assuages a little the insufferable strangeness of my fate." The embers of her eyes flare hotter. "Tonight, I would use those powers for you."

A charge of fright sparks down the knuckles of Violet's spine. "Leave me be, weird sister! I belong to the Goddess."

"And the Goddess belongs to the Old Ones!" Dana's arms open to the night, and the flametips of her fingers illuminate the bronchial branchings of the trees. "We are as sparks, Violet. We blow like pieces of burning ash over the sour weeds, and we are consumed in the wind under an empty sky. Our lives are as nothing to the elder gods. So, let me do a thing for you before I return to the dark shore, for it pleases me to please the living."

Before Violet can protest again, the priestess rises. Her fiery hair spreads into the sudden wind, her radiant tresses braiding into the ropes of stars that blaze lucently in the cope of heaven. She holds the massive night between her burning hands, and Violet feels the spiders that web their threads in her lungs shrivel. Cool, sweet air fills the hollows of her chest, and the pain in her joints unknits. The cracked coat of lacquer on her skin softens and glimmers with a magnetic tingle, and the gnarled boniness of her hands unlocks, relaxes, and smooths into the tapered fingers of her youth.

"What have you done to me?" Violet cries, and her voice has lost all the smoke of her weary years. "What have you done?"

But the priestess is not listening. She is dancing. And the others are dancing with her, their joyful faces bright as apricots in the fire's light. The priestess beckons, and Violet's numb shock vanishes, replaced by a jubilation that lifts her to her feet and sweeps her into the circle dance with the others. And they dance and they dance until the empty sleeve of dawn drags its pastels across the sky.

The fire slows, and the priestess calls the coveners closer and has everyone lie down head to foot in a circle. She covers their bodies with leaves and feeds the fire with slow-burning root-burls so they will be warm. Then, wonderfully clarion, she begins to chant: "As your thoughts are like a flight of birds, be the sky, wide as all there is and open to everything. As your body is like the slow burn of a fire, be the light in the flame, cleanly burning earth and air. As your life is like a river, be the course of the water, one moment flowing the whole length of your being."

Some slumber. And long after Dana Largo finishes, some lay awake hearing her voice in the thin scream of the dying fire. A few see the shape of their lives, clear as teardrops, and are changed forever.

As the sun crests the treetops of Goatswood, Violet smiles awake, more alive in her bones than she has ever been. She wakes the others, and none of them recognizes the young, sable-haired woman standing over them, the pale, perfect, white violin of her body lovely as the Goddess Herself. They want to know where Violet has gone, and she laughs so deeply she cries.

Together they look for the priestess. But there is no sign of her anywhere in the clearing or in the surrounding woods. Back at the camp, they find a pomegranate she has left on a stump. It is cleaved open with the ritual cut that reveals the star formed by the seeds.

Ghost Lake

by Donald R. Burleson

The country beyond Brichester is desolate and lonely. After the garish bustle and clamor of the city with its regal university towers and its pressing crowds, the outer reaches of Bold Street seem uncannily quiet, as if in leaving the city behind and winding into the wilder expanses of the Severn River Valley the road traces a pathway to another world where the prosaic concerns of urban life may never extend. The landscape here becomes more densely wooded, more closely crowded by gnarled trees standing sentry on the sides of the little-traveled road like brooding gargoyles, until the very light of day is unable to penetrate the general air of gray gloom that these arboreal wraiths seem to clutch about them.

So it seemed, at least, to Roger Barton on the late autumn day when he went into the valley, rucksack on his back, pipe in his mouth, strange thoughts in his head.

It was, after all, a strange cycle of legend that had brought him out here to Gloucestershire from London. The Severn region had long fascinated him, with its folktales of oddly surviving ancient religions and furtive races of beings peering out of shadowed recesses, watching the unwary traveler with faces that were not human. There were the stories of Temphill with its morbid old church and the abominations dwelling beneath it. There were the stories of Clotton on the Severn, with its demon-haunted bridge. There were the stories of Goatswood and of what lurked behind the great door in the hill overlooking the town. But of all the bizarre places chronicled in the folk legendry of the region there was none so intriguing as the ill-regarded lake of which the aged innkeeper in Brichester had spoken; here, only a few miles' walk out from the city, was a locale more darkly fascinating even than those repositories of rumor in quest of which Roger had taken the train from London.

Stopping at the university library to examine their collection on local folklore he had noticed, under glass in a securely locked display case, a nine-volume set of books described as exceedingly rare on the explanatory sign beside the case, a sign which identified the multivolume work as *The Revelations of Glaaki*. Roger had heard of the work before, in connection with his readings in obscure lore, but remembered no particulars, and the library staff had enlightened him very little, remarking only that the *Glaaki*, as they called it, was the product of several anonymous members of a defunct cult formerly living near the infamous lake. They would tell him no more, and it remained for the old innkeeper to relate to him what little else he was to glean.

"A long way out on the lake road," the old man had said, "a few miles past the hospital at Mercy Hill, out where the land's all woods, the road turns into a little street at the shore of the lake, just enough for a string of six old houses that faced the water."

"Faced? You mean the houses aren't there any more?"

"Well, yes," the innkeeper had said, lighting a cigarette, "they say the houses are still standing, about to fall down, maybe, but they're still there. It's the lake that isn't."

"The lake?"

"Oh, it was drained years ago. Bloody hard job, but the authorities pumped it dry as a bone. Nothing there now but a crater where it used to be."

"Why in the world did they do that?"

"Well, there'd never been nothing but trouble reported from out there. Those houses were built back in the late 1700's, nobody even knows by who, and a whole series of tenants rented 'em over the years through the estate agent in town here that used to handle the property. Heaven only knows how many complaints the police received, from people saying that their family members had gone out there for one reason or another and never come back. Folks in town started calling the place Ghost Lake, and rumors started going around that this cult out there worshiped some—thing—that was supposed to live in the lake, as crazy as that sounds. Some people said there was a stone city down there under the water. Them rare old books at the university are supposed to tell about it, but they don't let nobody read 'em, I guess because they're supposed to be valuable, though I wouldn't give you twopence for 'em myself. Well, anyway, the whole area's deserted now. Gradually all the people out there in those houses by the water disappeared and the houses went empty and the estate agent didn't even bother with 'em any more because they were rotting away anyhow. But the complaints about people missing kept on coming in from time to time, 'til first the police tried dragging the lake for bodies and then just decided to drain it altogether. Even then they didn't find nothing. That was all years ago, but people around here still don't care for the place."

"Really?"

"To this day. There's a popular writer, mystical sort of chap named Khem-Bei Ramses, even wrote a story about it; my granddaughter reads that sort of thing. Me, I'd rather forget all about the whole affair. But just two years ago a couple of kids went out there and didn't come back. I wouldn't muck about there if I was you. Course, you bein' young, Mister Barton, you're going to do what you want."

And indeed these scraps of hinted lore had only fueled his desire to see the locale, however disappointing it was to hear that the lake itself was no longer extant. Walking along the lonely road now, past Mercy Hill and the outermost traces of the city, his pipe smoke rising to hold counsel with the twisted tree limbs that overhung the road like the roof of a tunnel, Roger wondered what sort of mental extravagances could account for such legends—a city under the water, a creature living there, a cult worshiping it, people disappearing. As a student of dark folklore he well knew that even the strangest legend could have some remote source in fact, however embellished or distorted, and with this thought came a growing feeling that perhaps in the old innkeeper's warning there had been, even if for the wrong reasons, a modicum of truth—maybe the place really was unhealthy, maybe he ought to have stayed away.

But by the time he had formulated this thought, the seemingly endless road had come out into a sort of clearing, and he could see that it skirted the rim of what must at one time have been the infamous lake, now a bleak crater ulcerating the earth; and across on the other side—the lake, if deep, had not been wide—he could see the land clear for a little distance near the erstwhile shore, with woods beyond.

What really took his attention, though, was on this side, a short way ahead, where the tar road became a cobbled street whose smooth stones even now were only partly grown over with weeds, as if plants disliked to grow there. Along this short stretch of cobblestones the rotting bulks of six old three-story houses stood, broken-paned and half fallen in and morosely silent in the gathering dusk.

Somehow the scene filled him with repugnance, a reaction he was hard put to justify even considering the fragments of folklore he had heard; he was a student of such lore, after all, and shouldn't be repelled by a strange local story about which he should in fact be able to be objective and dispassionate. But the feeling was there; this spot was distinctly eerie, especially with evening coming on.

A few straggling remnants of daylight illumined the great crater that marked where the lake had been, and walking to its edge, only a few yards off the cobblestone, he saw that the pit was cup-shaped, deep in the middle, perhaps only two hundred yards across to the opposite shore, where a narrow clearing soon gave itself over to trees. The bottom of the pit was only a mess of dry but porous-looking earth and pale, twisted weeds—certainly no "stone city", no monster lurking in the gathering shadows, since so far as Roger could see there was no place for it to hide. Odd, catching himself thinking this way—hadn't he outgrown monsters and hobgoblins?

He was going to have to decide, fairly soon, about spending the night—would he stay in one of those half-tumbled-down houses standing here so unaccountably, or would he sleep in the open, making a campfire? In any case it was too far and too late to walk back to Brichester. At length he decided against investigating the ruins of those houses 'til morning light; old houses could be structurally unsafe. Gathering some firewood from the deadfall beneath the trees just short of the little stretch of cobbled street, he prepared his campfire between the nearest cobbles and the point at which the land dropped away into the dusky pit that was once a lake. Down there, in the bottom of the crater, the darkness was nearly total now, the choppy earth and wild tufts of weeds lost in shadow. Before long night had fallen, with only the flickering of the little fire to hold it at bay.

Sitting on the edge of his sleeping bag beside the crackling flames, he ate some strips of dried beef and drank a little water from his canteen and tried to feel good about being here, but felt instead a growing unease. The moon had not yet risen, and it was hellishly dark; he could see nothing at all but the wavering glow of his fire. In his mind's eye the fire was a little island of light and warmth floating in a murky sea of darkness, as if the lakebed were welling over with inky black night instead of the water it must once have brimmed with. And somewhere nearby, out there in impenetrable shadow, the six gaunt old houses stood in a row, ghastly and silent, and Roger felt almost as if they leaned and whispered to each other, conspiratorial in the night. If the darkness were dispelled right now, would they stand in their original spots beside the cobbles, or would they have subtly shifted, moved?

These thoughts were insane; he had to get hold of himself. Smoothing out his sleeping bag, he made ready to turn in; it had been a long day with all this walking, and he was tired. A chill breeze had sprung up, and he zipped the bag nearly up to his chin for warmth. The dry snapping of twigs in the fire was soothing, comfortable, and he began to doze.

And woke with a sense that something was wrong.

He blinked, staring into the shadowy realm beyond the dying fire. The darkness was not quite so profound out there now, around the great dry pit, because a wan gibbous moon had risen; it hung sickly-looking in the sky, as if having second thoughts.

But what was wrong was that somewhere below the moon, out there in the blackness of the dry lakebed, a second pale moon shimmered, like a reflection. How this could be, Roger was at a loss to say, because he had seen for himself that there was nothing in the pit to reflect light, nothing there at all but dirt and weeds. Yet this second moon was out there, floating and shifting and uncertain in the diffuse light of its more substantial counterpart in the sky.

It was as if—but no, the thought was truly preposterous.

Still, he wriggled part way out of the sleeping bag and, without getting up—somehow he felt safer down low, near the fire—he stretched his arm out on some nameless impulse and grabbed up a fist-sized rock and tossed it over the campfire, far out into the dark in the direction of what seemed to be the reflection of the moon. A gust of wind came up, stirring the remnants of the fire into popping sparks and animating the unseen treetops behind him, and surely it was only this confusion of impressions that made it seem to his troubled ear as if he had heard, from out there in the shadows of the pit, a splashing sound. Involuntarily he closed his eyes, and from sheer fatigue he must have dozed again, for when he next lifted his head and peered out over the embers, a veil of iron gray clouds had been drawn across the sky, and both the moon and its strange reflection were gone. At some point a fitful sleep overtook him yet again, and then it was dawn.

* * *

He rekindled the fire enough to make some rather wretched coffee and sat chewing a bit of dried fruit from his pack and sipping the coffee from a tin cup and thinking. His eyes felt raw, swollen, and he was a little ashamed that he had let a scrap of local legendry make him so distraught as to sleep badly, even if he had slept long at last; the sun was rather high, and he glanced at his watch to see that it was nearly eleven o'clock. Standing up and kicking some loose dirt over the fire, he looked out across the great crater of a lakebed and found it empty and dry as before. But then what had he expected it to be? It had been a disturbing series of impressions he had had during the night, but by daylight everything was normal.

At least, everything was as normal as it could be in such a place. One had to admit that when one had a stretch of cobblestone sprouting six old houses beside the shore of a lake that was no longer there—well, it was all fairly peculiar, and no wonder if odd stories did abound.

In any case it was time to examine what was left of the houses, not that he expected to find much. On reflection he rather wondered what he had hoped to learn by coming out here, but perhaps the houses would prove to be of some interest.

There was scarcely enough left of the first two of them to bother with. Walking along the smooth cobbles, he could see that these structures were almost entirely tumbled down; huge holes gaped in the few ragged walls that remained standing, and both roofs had mostly collapsed into the spaces below. The third house appeared to be a little better preserved, though still nothing an estate agent would want to have anything to do with. As the houses further on appeared to be little more than tumuli of formless wreckage, he ascended the shaky steps to the third house and bent down and peered through a filthy broken window to form the impression that most of the inner walls were more or less intact, though he could actually see only a litter-strewn front room with a doorway leading to some darker region beyond. The whole air of the place was bleak, desolate, depressing in the extreme, and he had to overcome considerable repugnance to push the door open with a rusty creak of hinges and step inside.

Such of the windows as still had glass were so befouled that little sunlight filtered through, and in the dimness it took a moment of readjustment of his eyes to see that whole sections of plaster had come away from the walls to leave great leprous-looking sores, with mounds of dusty debris underfoot. No recognizable furnishings survived, beyond what appeared to be the shattered remains of a table in one corner, an angular obtrusion festooned with spiderwebs. Stepping over fallen plaster and brittle curls of fallen wallpaper, he ventured into the rooms beyond, finding them in similar disrepair. When he returned to the front room his eyes were well enough adjusted to the gloom that he spotted something he had missed before: On one relatively intact wall, to the left as one entered the house, someone had left a considerable quantity of writing, and a bit of artwork besides.

The writing, rust brown in color and covering nearly the entire wall, seemed to have been done with some sort of small brush. The characters were somehow frenetic in appearance, almost deranged-looking in their flourishes; they put Roger in mind of the odd cult that was said to have lived here. He squinted to read what was written.

First a patch of wholly illegible symbols, then: ... *from before all time, from beyond all space, corporeal yet more than substance, striding unbridled in the very marrow of the mind. When He pours forth His desire, the summons can in no way be denied, nor is there any furthest corner of concealment not open to the relentless probing of His will. The very lines of space and time bend themselves to His purposes. In corridors of black stone beneath the waves He lurks dark and eternal, for He is Glaaki, the Inhabitant of the Lake, the Lord of All Existence, to Whom all praise is due. O ancient and terrible One, O Glaaki, Thou Who seeped down from the icy stars, bend us to Thy will, and look with favor upon these, our sacrifices.* And there followed, in the lower right corner, a crude drawing of what appeared to be a sort of face, bloated and repellent, with tiny dull eyes spaced far apart and, for a mouth, a kind of thin slash that seemed to run around the entire circumference of the pulpy head. Even as apparently simpleminded as the execution of the drawing was, Roger found it profoundly disturbing, and he felt better only when he was back outside on the cobbles, lighting his pipe and trying to assess his reactions to what he had seen.

How many cult fetishes like this had come and gone in the long history of human folly? There should be nothing really startling in this particular instance. What did it amount to, really? Some fanatic cultists had lived out here, formulating a system of fantasy, inventing their repulsive god of the lake, perhaps luring innocent people out here and sacrificing them. The celebrants of this weird religion had chosen to see themselves and others as drawn here by the will of the thing in the lake. Serious pathology, to be sure, but nothing more, and all bygone now anyway with the dispersal of the cult. Bizarre, yes, but fairly well in keeping with the whole tradition of cultism and fetishism. In terms of that tradition, nothing out of the ordinary.

But then why did that inscription, that drawing, linger in his mind with such force?

Whatever the reasons, the inscription was not going to change his mind about a decision already made: He would spend the night tonight in the third house, not outdoors. The place seemed fairly free of vermin, and he would be comfortable stretching his sleeping bag out on the floor. Meanwhile he amused himself by walking completely around the dry lakebed a couple of times, puffing his pipe, snacking on some trail mix from his pack, and roughly measuring the crater at perhaps a third of a mile around. The pit was uniform in appearance from whatever viewpoint, its bottom a featureless plain of dirt and weeds sloping gradually down as one looked farther out; the lake would have been perhaps sixty or seventy feet deep in the middle by all appearances. Evidently it had not been spring-fed, or the source had been plugged, for it was dusty-dry now. Actually the pit looked rather more like a meteor crater than an ordinary lakebed. In any case, as he pondered these things the day wore on toward evening, and again he saw the bottom of the pit thicken up with shadows. As the sun set, he had a simple dinner beside his old campfire, briefly rekindled, and moved his belongings inside—none too soon, either, it would seem, for a grumble of thunder came across the land, and the air felt like impending rain. In the last remaining light he unrolled his sleeping bag on a clear spot on the floor in the front room, fished his flashlight out and placed it nearby in case he needed it, and crawled into the sleeping bag, not zipping it up since even these splintered walls offered some protection from the chill air.

He was almost asleep when a clap of thunder and the sound of light rain on the roof brought him fully awake, and he lay open-eyed in the dark and listened to the rain and to the wind that sighed around the creaking old rafters. Fortunately the ancient roof seemed to be proof against the onslaught of rain, but he still felt ill at ease, and finally switched the flashlight on and played it over the inscription on the wall. *The Inhabitant of the Lake ... ancient and terrible One ... seeped down from the icy stars. ...* It was astonishing, the extent to which these fetish groups could carry their obsession. He lay listening to the dark. Outside the thunder muttered off over the horizon, taking the rain with it, and all was silence.

Well, not quite all.

He lay very still, listening.

An occasional gust of wind still ruffled the trees out there, and beneath this sound of the wind whispering in the leaves there seemed to be another, less accountable sound.

It was very much like water lapping against a shore.

He was up on his feet, flashlight in hand, heading for the door, feeling more angry than anything else, annoyed that he had let the place, the situation, prey on his nerves like this. Outside on the cobblestones it took him a minute to notice that he didn't need the flashlight, because the moon, brighter now than before, had risen to send a shimmering ribbon of reflected light across what should have been the empty lakebed. His breath caught in his throat when he realized the significance of this reflection, and realized that with the faint soughing of the wind, black ripples of water were washing against the crumbling shore near his feet.

And God in heaven, what was this?

Stepping a little closer to the edge of the water—the water that shouldn't be there, couldn't be there—he strained to see the surface of the lake in the moonlight. Though dark on first glance,the water was remarkably translucent, for he could discern, starting perhaps fifty feet out, the submerged corners and edges of what looked like great sable blocks of stone, as if some cluster of basalt towers stretched their unyielding fingers nearly to the surface of the water. This was madness, for such structures to be here only by the light of the moon. What depths their foundations might be mired in he could scarcely imagine, but he had little time to wonder about that, because now a sort of pale scum seemed to have passed over the underwater stones, a layer of lighter color floating just beneath the surface and undulating there as if the ooze had risen from the bottom and were still rising.

It was only the sheer size of the thing that kept him from understanding, at first, what he was seeing. By the time it had risen, pallid and pulpy, a few feet above the water, Roger realized that it was a face, though only the tiny baleful eyes, set far, far apart on thick and quivering little stalks, would even remotely have suggested a face, because no face should be a hundred feet across. When the mouth opened as a noxious wound running the full width of the face, it was as if the head had split itself apart like a rotten melon, and the odor that came forth was unthinkable. Roger was running before he even began to choke.

Darkness enveloped him as he left the clearing behind, plunging along the road through the woods. He fled blindly, mindlessly, scraping his face on tree limbs that extended into the roadway, falling, getting up disoriented and dizzy, running, falling again, running. At some point a corner of his mind registered that the moon in front of him over the encroaching trees should have been behind him. Gasping for breath, he came back out into the clearing and stopped running when he felt cobblestones beneath his feet.

There was no more time, anyway, for running. With an overwhelming sense of resignation, and the beginnings of an understanding, he sat down upon the cobbles, his back to the decrepit houses, his face toward the lake and toward the thing whose stony will must have drawn him here. How long had it been drawing him here, through subtle channels of influence?

For weeks? Years? His whole life? It scarcely mattered, after all, for the being before him had all the time in the world. Filling his vision, the face rose above the black water like a pale and bloated fungus, the dull little eyes dead upon him, the foetid mouth opening, closing, opening in the moonlight, closer, closer. Roger clasped his hands together and closed his eyes, and took a deep breath, and just waited.

Beauty

by Fred Behrendt

One evening I seated Beauty on my knees. And I found her bitter. And I cursed her.

— Arthur Rimbaud

Brichester Road twists recklessly through Severn Valley and through the tumbled recollections of my childhood. Each turn in the road, each suddenly remembered landmark, was painted inside my skull like a Parrish illustration—unnaturally and vibrantly clear, and lit by alien color.

My feelings were as twisted as the road I followed with automatic surety. This was the first time I had returned to my youthful stomping grounds since I had gone away to university. My absence had not been accidental. I pondered the invitation to my ten-year secondary school reunion for a long time before submitting to its compelling call. I could not hide from the painful moments of my past any longer. They had to be excised like winter weeds pulled from the garden. I claimed to seek wholeness within myself—it was time to act upon my convictions and overcome old demons.

Still, I was filled with reluctance. I had convinced myself the reunion was destined to be a crashing bore. A pale shadow of amusement compared it to a weekend at home with Lucy; but I had made my decision, and I intended to stick with it.

I curved past a well remembered oak—Lucy's brother (and my best friend) Harry had dashed his brains against it on what was to be my last night in the valley. That had been August of 1960. Harry had collided with the tree while grappling with his two favorite demons: marijuana and bourbon.

Harry's face swam before me briefly. I thought of the funeral, and the open grave took shape in my mind. And Lucy—with a pang I remembered her standing aside as they lowered the coffin. Her bright eyes streamed tears. I knew she would never return here.

Light from the descending sun struck the tree's leaves and the glow quaked like disembodied eyes above me. I shifted low, edged the wheel around and left the tree behind.

I came upon Brichester before nightfall. Damp shadows sought me at day's end, enfolding me with a smothering embrace I could not shiver off.

Brichester's worn buildings rose about me.

I parked at a curb near the center of town. In a few ways the old town had remade itself during the years of my absence. A pub calling itself the "Blooded Tangerine" spilled unpleasant rock and roll music into the street—even at this early hour. Three large American motorcycles stood propped on the walk, blocking pedestrian traffic. An older denizen of the town, a white-haired man in tweeds using a cane to walk, struggled around the vehicles while muttering ferociously and directing icy glances at the open door of the pub.

In some ways, it seemed, Brichester's citizenry was unchanged.

I scented an acrid odor, like burning leaves. Then glimpsed ragged, brightly dyed cotton. Holed denim. A military officer's raincoat, stitched across the back with a design like a distorted, inverted cross. Young women and men I would have assumed to be American hippies straggled in and out of the Tangerine and along the ancient flagstone walk. Their north country accents belied their local origins, however. I was surprised to see such a recent American phenomenon represented so strongly in isolated, legend-wracked Brichester.

Harry, if he had been alive to see this new addition to our reviled old home, would have declared himself a kindred soul of these rebels—though these children could hardly have matched my late brother-in-law's rebellion. How I wished I had not been the first one upon him that evening, there under the tree—

I still had not moved from the seat of my car when she separated herself from the crowd outside the Tangerine. Her body was a cipher of extremity, reflecting the sparse crowd around us. Her legs were bare except for a pair of tight black vinyl boots. She wore a black leather skirt with a hemline well above mid-thigh, and a crimson blouse of threadbare cotton. Her hair was a dark, curly cloud displaying a single hint of gray above her left temple. Her eyes hid behind a band of wide wrap-around smoked plastic. Her lips and nails were painted a red so deep that as she passed into shadow they appeared black. She swung a multi-colored bead bag by a thin strap.

She stood above me at the side of my car, and looked down through smoky plastic into my face. The burnt-leaf odor clung to her.

"Groovy car. 'Ow about a ride?" She said.

"I'm not going anywhere," I said nervously. To prove my point, I put up the convertible roof, got out and stood by the car. I turned from her and surveyed the street. I anticipated the dwindling rap of her boot heels on the flagstones, but it did not come.

"All right then, a walk." I heard her strike a match. The acrid, burning leaf smell suddenly intensified. "Have a puff?"

The woman extended two fingers, and between them a slim, hand-rolled cigarette. The unburning end was twisted closed. Smoke drew a line between her smiling dark lips.

I opened my mouth, said nothing, shook my head.

"Suit yourself," she said through a blue-white mouthful. She drew with great effort on the cigarette, and I started off down the uneven walk; the heavy-looking motorcycles loomed ahead.

The sound of her boot heels came up beside me. She exhaled an immense pungent blue cloud that momentarily enveloped me.

She extended her hand and the cigarette to me again; I shook my head silently. I noticed a plain white ring, ivory perhaps, on her middle finger.

"Let's slip into the Tangerine for a pint, and talk over old times." Her voice recalled summer nights a dozen years behind me. Could I possibly know her?

It grew darker and the damp chill clung tighter at my fingers and toes. Her pale-skinned face, with its blackening lips and glasses, resolved into bands of light and dark in the shadows lengthening over us.

My hotel and the reunion was forgotten for the moment; suddenly getting out of the damp evening was the most important thing on my mind. Putting away thoughts of tomorrow's gathering also allowed me a respite from my thoughts of Harry.

"All right then. Just one drink." I pursued a sudden feeling. "You remind me of someone. Should I know you?"

She continued smiling, but said nothing.

As we crossed the portal into the Tangerine, blaring music intensified, falling upon me like a physical force. Something large moved into the corner of my sight. A burly arm snatched in and caught the girl by the wrist, elevating the hand bearing the burning cigarette.

"'Ere now, Beauty. That's enuff a' that. You want John L. Law climbin' our arse?"

The girl's smile grew wicked. And despite that—I then knew her. Angela. Her name was Angela Hotchkiss. She and Harry—her hair had been bobbed, her features delicate—almost perfect—and she had been demure, an incongruous balance to Harry's excesses. Apparently in ten years that had changed. Changed very much.

The bouncer was wide and round, fat and bristling hair over muscle. His squat hand plucked the cigarette from her outstretched, acquiescent fingers, then popped it burning into his mouth. After a single grinding mastication, he swallowed, then waved us along into the din.

We found isolation at an empty table in one corner. The distraction of music and mini-skirts swirled around us while we placed an order with a pale skinny girl with dark circles beneath her eyes and mouth, a bare midriff and dirty white vinyl boots constricting her calves. The girl seemed to know my companion, and said "Thank you, Beauty." after bringing us two pints on her dripping tray.

"I haven't heard from Lucy in an age. How's she doing?" The dark band of plastic was still across her eyes, hiding any subtlety of expression. Did I detect irony in her tone?

"She's fine. Fine." Thinking, *She blames you for it all, you know.*

"She was the envy of the class. Success, stability, a way out of this vile valley—all those things—had their mark on you. And she had you and we all knew it." Her face changed beneath its black bands of disguise. "The only mark on Harry was one of this valley."

"There's no fence around this land. You can drive to London in a few hours. Leaving this place behind is up to you, you know."

A rueful smile twisted her lips and she mumbled something in the blasting music. I thought she said, *Not any more*, and then, perhaps, *I hurt*.

"Are you ill?" I tried to be concerned. In the din of blaring music it was difficult to be anything but impatient. Perhaps Angela could come to London and stay with us for a time until she got on her feet. Then I thought of Lucy and the quiet order of our apartment and said nothing.

"Nothing is holding you here," I repeated.

Her face changed again.

"No one ever asked me about that black book Harry stole, but the library was after his parents for the longest time."

Threatening a suit at one time, I recalled. I did not want to think about Harry and his earnest predilections for trouble.

I was increasingly awed and fascinated, however, by Angela's transformation. The last time I saw her her hair was neatly bobbed close to her skull, and she wore no makeup. Her eyes were bright and searched each room she entered eagerly. Her unpainted lips smiled openly, easily, often. This girl hid behind whatever smile stretched her lips. But the shape of her nose, her cheekbones, everything belonged, including a small mole on the back of her hand, several inches from the plain white band of bone around her finger.

"I always have a bit of Harry with me you know, even now." She held up her hand and displayed the bone ring.

"Harry gave you the ring?"

The smile again.

"Yes, he gave it to me."

She leaned around the table close to me.

"I have something for you. Something I have saved a long time."

Her mouth tried to find mine, but I pulled back a hand's breadth. I inhaled her marijuana aura. A pungent reminder of Harry's days in the woods out by Temphill where we would walk while he smoked and talked of things I found both horrible and fascinating. He seemed to know everything that had gone on in those woods in years long gone by. He even implied that spaces under the ground had not been as quiet as we would like to think. I had only wondered what he had done and to whom he had spoken to to learn these hidden "truths." In the last year of his life, Harry spoke of making a deal, a "bargain" he called it, with some all-knowing source of blasted information. He never elaborated, however, and I never pressed him for details. Growing up in Brichester, I had never doubted that some truth abided in Harry's words. And when I came upon his body that last night—my last night in this cursed valley—I knew what truth abided in Harry's words. In what I saw there among the car's twisted metal and blood and shredded flesh that had once been a man's body—

Angela's face was still close to my own, almost touching, but she no longer smiled. I pulled the dark plastic band from across her eyes. She blinked back tears against the brightness, even in this dim light. A network of wrinkles fractured the thick make-up at the corners of her eyes, belying her carefully made illusion of youth. I had a glimpse of some part of her I had not yet seen in the flicker of muscles around her eyes. I thought her smiles had been somehow cold, and now I knew they were, as she tried to rally under my new scrutiny.

Before I could frame a new question, however, our corner grew darker as shadows of big men crowded in around us.

"Well if it isn't the best fuckin' bird in Brichester." A tall, solid man wearing an olive-colored wool sweater leaned in and took Angela roughly by the chin.

"Or just the bird fucked the most." He squeezed her chin, scraping away make-up with his glove's thumb. "Aren't ya, Beauty?"

Heavy features darkly lined by dark strokes of uncombed beard, his lips smiled palely with anger.

Another man with a protruding stomach turned to me, his hands dropped loosely, but threateningly, level with his hips. I was paralyzed with indecision and fear. Waves of cold and hot fear surged against one another in my body. I shifted in my chair, facing away from the fat man, trying to discount his jarring presence in my life.

A balding, older man behind the bar stood straight and tense, looking at us, perhaps waiting for some unknown signal to interfere or call for help. The girl with the dark circles of eyes and dripping tray stood a few steps away studying the damage to Angela's black and white mask.

A black and sliver knife, a shard of night and light, opened in the tall man's hand, unheard amidst the diminishing sound from the band in the corner that had finally noticed the moment of violence unfolding in our corner. Until it was quiet everywhere and everywhere in the room the eyes looked at us.

"Where's Jeddy, Beauty bitch? His bike was outside when we came and everyone we talked to said you and him were gropin' here at this table earlier." He touched the knife to her below her left breast.

I cleared my throat.

The fat man seized me and pushed me against the wall; red and purple streaks flashed behind my eyes. The bearded man looked away from Angela to us. A crescent of water droplets glittered for a moment in a strobe of light as the girl with circles under her eyes swung her wet tray into the back of the bearded man's head. Undamaged but distracted, he released Angela and turned to the other girl—who was fleeing through the silent bodies turned to watch us. As the fat one released me to turn to his friend (I seemed unthreatening, I suppose), I kicked the table into the back of the bearded man's legs, who folded down in surprise. The balding older man from the bar appeared beside me, cracking a thick, rectangular bottle against the fat man's head. The latter slumped. I took Beauty across me in my arms and pushed through the kitchen door.

The smell of hot grease overcame Beauty's aura of burnt marijuana. I ran without thinking, dimly hoping that Angela would do the same, though I was not sure how much I cared if the men caught her. Except for that strand of connection to Harry I was unsure what she meant to me—except that she meant something to me suddenly, suddenly enough to make me kick that table in the bar. Regardless, however, I ran, my feet squirming on the greasy floor.

The lights went out. I believed it was the work of the balding man from behind the bar.

Angela vanished by the time I had entered the alley and shut the door. In one end of the alley was light; the other dwindled away into total blackness. I opted for the cover of night and headed for blackness. I did not hear Angela moving around anywhere.

I seized upon a certain irony—if Lucy knew that I had just rescued the one person in the world she blamed most for Harry's death, she would never forgive me. I had always thought Lucy's connection to Harry had been pretty tenuous, nothing more than a family commitment. The two were so different. Lucy was quite conventional, and Harry a wild man on the fringe. But after his death, Lucy took hold of the irrational notion that Angela was at the heart of it, and never let it go. Now if the old Angela had just been a mask over the new one, perhaps there was something in Lucy's belief. But even in light of this night's events, I doubted it.

My hunch had been that Angela would run in the direction of greater darkness, but I did not hear her, even though I thought I caught a scent of marijuana. Was that her shape ahead of me in the dark? The curly mass of her hair? I took a step toward the shadowy mass.

"I never thought you'd sneak around behind my sister's back. That's what you said, anyway: 'I'll never be unfaithful.' Now here you are thinking about being unfaithful to both of us. Lucy is your wife, and Angela's my girl, and she always will be." A libidinous chuckle came from the darkness. "She has turned out to be quite a 'beauty' now, hasn't she?"

The voice. It was distorted, pitched too high; but the phrasing and modulation were Harry's. It could not be Harry, not after—that thing emerging from him in the twisted metal—

"You had your hand on me for a moment," the voice continued. But no one had known that; I had told no one I had touched Harry. "Why didn't you pull me free? You could have pulled me free, but you left me for John Law. At least you could have kept me from them. You could have taken me in your innocent hands and buried me in the woods. You could have washed the blood away."

The voice became more and more like Harry's with every word. Or my memory adjusted to the subtle differences. I was no longer sure that long-ago coffin had borne my best friend into the ground.

An acrid, unfamiliar odor wafted up around me. Sour and bitter, it brought tears to my eyes, and those tears merged with sweat that stood out on me like icy beads.

"You could have washed the blood away!"

I was no longer confused—now the voice was harboring a threat, and I heard a step taken toward me on the soft alley floor.

I turned and fled.

The wan moon cast pale light in the other end of the alley. Another shape loomed before me—a stripe of pale light painted itself across a balding human pate.

"What are ye runnin' at me for, man?" His dense hand pressed on my chest, and I stopped. It was the barman. "Where's the girl? She get loose, too?"

"I don't know," I said through hard breaths. We were silent a moment as I let fear and over exertion drain from me. I could hear the unpleasant rock and roll music resume its throbbing within the pub.

I moved further toward the moonlit end of the alley, away from the dark mystery and the chilling voice. The barman followed. When we reached the street he took my arm and we stopped.

"Why did those toughs pull a knife on Angela? She's no threat to them."

He turned away. He became a shadow and receded. I waiting for some answer or dismissal.

"Some people wonder about Beauty. About Angela. She hangs about and gets it on with blokes who drift through here. Guess some people think it strange that no one ever sees them again before they drift on. Like they meet her, something happens, and they're gone. You know people—they have nothin' to do, they talk instead."

He paused.

"Guess people are afraid of Beauty, 'cause she's a loner and does what she wants. I haven't lived here my whole life like some has, but I hear tell there was something about an old boyfriend smashed 'is fuckin' 'ead on a tree outside of town. She's been all screwed up since that."

Another pause.

"Least that's what they say."

Harry, I thought, when I found you in the dark—I heard movement and looked in with you and the torn metal of your car, hoping for an instant you had somehow survived in the carnage—until I saw what lay in there with you—

The barman spoke again. "Not a bad idea to stay shy of her, though. Who knows what kind of trouble she'll bring. But if you see her, tell her to stay clear of the Tangerine, until things settle a bit."

I thanked the barman and tried to press a pound note on him, but he rebuffed it, and disappeared down the alley way. When he opened the door, momentary light flooded the alley and my eyes.

I stood blinking, waiting for my eyes to readjust, thinking the barman and I had not exchanged names, when Angela's aroma of burnt leaves returned.

"Angela," I said into the darkness, "are you hurt?"

"I hurt," she said, "but not from them." She pressed the palm of her hand against the back of mine. I felt the band of her white ring press into my cold flesh.

"We can't go back inside," I said. "He said *you* couldn't go back inside."

Something covered the moon and I was glad, as I remembered the damage to her face where the biker had smeared away the make-up. Then her face was on my shoulder and I felt also the black band of her sunglasses. Everything as it was, I could see nothing in the darkness.

"There is a another thing about Harry," she said, her voice quavering. "Can we go somewhere and I can tell you one last thing about our old friend Harry?"

I thought to just nod but realized she could not see my gesture in the darkness.

"Yes," I said flatly. Questions clamored up within me, but I smothered each and every one. Desire and reluctance boiled within me and, tossed between extremes, I could say nothing.

Angela finally pulled away, wavering on her feet. The smell of her was pungent, nearly overpowering me in a clasp of second-hand marijuana smoke.

I beat away the cloying sensation, and rebuilt a picture of Lucy within my mind. *I am faithful*, I thought. Her light hair and open round features rose in contrast to Angela's mask-like face. I tried to take strength from the internal exercise.

"Where do you want to go, Angela?" I asked.

"You have to call me 'Beauty'," she said in a small voice. "That's what you have to call me. I don't like Angela." Whether she meant the name, or a former self, I could not determine.

"If that's what you like," I said, "I'll call you Beauty, then."

You swore never to be unfaithful, said the voice

"Thank you," she said. "You were always the kind one." Her voice faltered. "Let's go to my place. No one will bother us there with unimportant questions."

"Yes," I said again.

My unfaithful voice.

Her place turned out to be a shack at the end of a dismal street not far away. A bare bulb burned in the window facing the street. Angela pulled on the door. It resisted a moment, then (after a second, harder, tug) scudded open. We entered. Another light came on. A single bulb on the ceiling, shaded by a handmade lens consisting of variously colored plastic sheets, cast uneven red, blue, green and orange light into a single room. A high, unmade bed with a metal, black-painted frame dominated the room. A narrow table cluttered with untidy make-up pots was pushed against one wall. A large mirror with dirty glass hung on the wall behind the table. The wall was also halfheartedly decorated with several garish posters of rock musicians. A wooden-backed chair with a broken-down seat was positioned at the table; another chair in similar condition stood in a corner. Newspapers and wadded clothing lay everywhere.

A choking miasma of marijuana, burned food and something else, something bitter, choked the room with an almost visible cloud of odor.

Beauty went to the bed and sat on its edge. I took a chair as she worked off her tight plastic boots. Her toes nails were painted the same dark red as her finger nails. She had taken time in the darkness of the alleyway to repair her face. She still wore her sunglasses.

"What did you want to tell me about Harry?"

When she gestured for me to take a seat with her on the bed, I did.

Again her mouth moved toward mine, and this time I did not pull away.

Never unfaithful.

Beauty's mouth was bitter with smoke. The smoke of her indulgence. She was my indulgence. I was not her indulgence. I was her revenge. Revenge against Lucy's hatred. Against Lucy's cold heart. Beauty did not make Harry die; Beauty did not force the bourbon flask to his lips that final night. That final night we enjoyed life without a weight of black guilt.

Beauty's soft skin under my hand was cool and dry, like a smooth stone from the Severn River bank. When I was a boy I spent afternoons turning those same cool, smooth stones out of the riverbank—often revealing bristling brown-haired spiders with legs long enough to span the back of my hand. I drew my hand off hers.

She plucked at the buttons of my shirt and trousers. Part of me protested, and another part of me looked into the doorway of my flat and in at Lucy frying up dinner and I said to myself, *Give me just this one moment of release.* Just this one time, then I could pass on like all the other one night stands in Beauty's life and return to London and my flat and my life as unchanging as an insect trapped in amber.

I assisted her with removing her clothes.

She ran her arched palm and the white ring over my face. I teased at the band with my teeth.

Unfaithful.

I tore away her sunglasses so I could punish myself with her ruined eyes.

Her body was smooth and round, but cool and dry like her hand's flesh had been. Curiously she was not a very good lover—her body grew unyielding, almost stiff; and when I withdrew from her I felt a painful pinch at my groin as a fold of my flesh seemed to adhere to Beauty's pudenda. Jerking away and standing I saw a spot of blood, about the diameter of a fingertip, a hand's span above my genitals. As I watched, the blood beaded until its natural cohesion failed and a thin trail of blood ran down into my pubic hair.

Anger gathered on my brow. I looked in Beauty's hand for a knife, but there was none. Her thin arms and legs lay slightly bent, emaciated upon the bed. No longer rounded, her breasts were tiny withered mounds, her ribs pressed upward through tautly stretched flesh, striped dark and purple, and Beauty's pelvic bones jutted like knives.

"You should not have been unfaithful," said Harry's distorted voice. It came from Beauty's bitter mouth, as I knew it would. Gasping horrible laughter choked in her throat.

Beauty's head turned in its stiff cloud of dark hair. A dry tongue, like a dry brown worm, probed at her stiff, horn-like lips.

"I think he's done now," came Beauty's thin voice, returned. "And you have your last answer about Harry. The thing in me and now in you came to me in the night after Harry died and told me it could bring him back to life inside me if I'd accept a bargain. If I'd allow it to come in. Harry would be alive inside me, but there would be a price." She coughed lightly as a white serum erupted from her mouth and nose. "But I can't feed on them anymore. You're the last one—I can't feed on them anymore. They've taken all my memories and all Harry's into you."

Her back arched, heaving her purple and pink striated belly off the bed. Something brittle cracked.

"Tell Lucy—"

The taut skin clinging to her bones split at the stomach and thighs. The bitter odor washed from her body and overcame every other stench in the room. My throat constricted and I gagged, but I could not move. White bead-like shapes the size of thimbles squeezed from her rent skin, scurried to the edge of the bed, and dropped to the floor.

Beauty's lips cracked at the corners as she spoke.

"Tell Lucy I always loved Harry. I never would hurt him. For anything. And you see. I tried to make him live on inside me. But now! Now he's in you and so am I and so are they! Oh yes! It is done."

Her eyes had collapsed in their pits, but she turned toward me once again as if she could see.

"Yes, I hort. It is done."

Then she fell apart, bloodlessly, like a poorly sewn doll. And I fell, hot with pain, into night's dark, unending hole.

Unseen

by Penelope Love

Not in the spaces that we know, but "between" them, they walk, serene and primal, undimensioned and to us unseen.

— H. P. Lovecraft

Josephine stumbled through the dusk, trying to shield her load from the worst rain. She scrambled up over the last of the rough ground radiating from the excavation, tripped over the spoil heap, and stumbled into the closed door of the site hut.

"Open up," she shouted, and hammered at the door, water gushing in torrents around her. Morley's Mound was a bleak, looming hulk on her right, the rain rattling on the streaming canvas that protected the bites torn out of its flanks by bulldozers. Andrew opened the door.

"Inside, inside," he said, his mild face surprised.

"Thank Christ!" Josephine gasped fervently at the sight of the bright, crowded cramped space within. She slid past Andrew's elongated frame, and into the warmth.

"You're wet through," Carol exclaimed from the warmest niche. Carol, golden hair soft lapping the curve of her cheek; Carol, the bold, the laughing, the generous. She dumped Diane into Bruce's lap, and jumped up to remove Josephine's dripping coat. Josephine laughed helplessly at herself, standing still under the other's attentions. Her wet run turned from irritant to an amusement as water streamed from her to soak the dirt-caked boards. Baz, Gaz, Spiro, and Kev, big lads all, gawped companionably over steaming mugs of tea; Bruce, the wiry, the sharp-eyed, grappled with the baby. Diane's blue gaze followed her mother with the wise fixedness of six months old.

"Who would have expected this weather, after such a string of nice days?" Andrew said, hovering, the awkward host. He squinted at his watch. "And it's so dark, for only five past five."

"Too late to get back to work, eh, after the rain?" Gaz said, and all his road workers laughed uproariously. The A.38 bypass around Berkeley, a wet, black-ribboned road ending in a churned morass of mud, was fast receding in their memories. Morley's Mound was to be swept aside by metaled industry, rescue archeology only interesting to them because it provided a snug hut and friendly company. All five were outsiders to this county. The locals were so sunk in apathy that not one of the myriad unemployed took up the job. And there was no friendly company in town. They'd been harassed by a slab-faced police sergeant. In the pub they had seen the girls making signs at them, to avert the evil eye. Gaz took a reflective swig of warm, sweet tea. Andrew took Josephine's coat from Carol, and carefully, precisely arranged it to dry.

Josephine unwrapped and flourished aloft her prize.

"Champagne?" Carol exclaimed. The laborers grinned.

"I've sold the story to the *Sunday Express* weekend magazine!" Josephine crowed. "Four-page spread, color pictures! Andrew, you'll be a six-by-four glossy in the dead center. The photographer will be down on Sunday."

"Comb your beard," advised Carol.

"Oh, er, gosh," Andrew said. He sat suddenly and reached for his tea. A stiff man in his early forties, still bewildered at the ridiculous luck of his marriage. Carol grinned and teased him, imagining headlines, her hair gleaming as she turned. Gold. "DIG LEADER TURNS RED," she said, "REMAINS COLOR OF BEETROOT FOR WEEKS ON END." Kev, Gaz, Spiro, Baz, and Bruce roared in appreciation.

Josephine struggled a moment with cork and wires, and then gave it to Carol, who gave it to one of the eagerly competing men. Andrew gathered tea cups and poured their contents into the bin. The emptied mugs were presented for the champagne, and Carol foraged for the disposable plastic cup that was the only other clean receptacle the dig possessed. She presented this to Josephine, as if it were the choicest crystal.

"Cheers," said the laborers, gleefully raising their filled mugs.

"Next step the world!" Carol said, knowing from confidences Josephine's painful ambition. The job accepted at a country paper as a stepping stone, but the next step never came. Bad luck? Ill-timed reserve? Or the general backwardness of the Camside area, that meant no spectacular stories to splash across a front cover, or at least none fit to be published in a family newspaper. Next step the world! Josephine, short, plump and pink with exhilaration, bowed.

"Speech, speech," they all called to Andrew, they all laughed, they all jeered. The younger road workers furiously drummed their heels, Baz and Kev and callow, keen Bruce. Diane crowed.

"Oh, er, gosh," Andrew said, shoved to his feet unwillingly, tall length bowed beneath the hut's low beam. One sip of the champagne and the room was swirling. He blushed painfully, "I suppose—"

* * *

The next morning the door of the dig opened to the din of the bulldozers on the road, closer every day now, from a distant, intermittent call two weeks ago to a constant cacophony. Gaz, Baz, Spiro, Kev and Bruce hard at work, all big men. The sun risen in a sky from which the rains had swept away.

"Blue as Diane's eyes," Carol cooed, as she twiddled her daughter's toes, fresh from a night's sleep at the local inn. Josephine, armed with notebook and a tape recorder, had a reason to be here now. She was not just goofing off work with a vague promise of a story to the *Camside Observer*. She followed Carol importantly round the hut, and got out her life's history. How dropping her grandmother's Wedgewood at age six led to a life-long interest in pottery shards. How she met Andrew on a dig in Greece. Solemn, defensive: "Underneath that reserve he's very sweet." Diane waved her chubby arms and urgently demanded kisses.

Outside in the muffled distance, they heard Andrew using the full range of his small store of swear words. They looked at each other, ducked their heads beneath the weight and the stench of the wet canvas, and went into the dig.

Morley's Mound was a long barrow named after its discoverer, Sir Gilbert Morley, a local eccentric who had fancied himself an antiquarian. Andrew had researched Morley's notes in the British library during his initial survey, for archeological interests in the Camside area were few and far-between. He had since discovered, to his horror, that the notes detailed all archeological sites of significance from Goatswood to Severnford. Morley had gutted the lot.

"The one other knowledge-seeker a ham-fisted amateur," Andrew had mourned, surveying ruined site after ruined site as Carol cursed the relentless zeal of the Victorian era. That Morley had left this one surprised them, for the first survey had revealed a site apparently intact and undisturbed.

"He wants to make it as difficult as possible for us. He foresaw the motorway and knew we'd have to rush," Carol guessed at the time. "Spiteful old goat." Carol, eight months pregnant and in the depths of winter, was given to odd fancies. Mocked her fiance's insistence on sensible knitwear but finally succumbed to the lure of one of his old cardigans. Hunched on the couch and in the car, hair golden, awkward girth sensibly brown, curled like a broody hen around her unborn child. Carol, too unwieldy for fieldwork, read up on the local folklore. Was given a fat, leather-bound, pleasingly dusty second edition of A. B. Wilshire's *The Vale of Berkeley*. After reading that Carol did not like Sir Gilbert Morley.

In the race against the motorway they had torn out the side of the mound until they reached the barrow walls, and there they made the unwelcome discovery. Morley had dug into the mound from the side, dug a tunnel almost the length of the site, and then retreated, carefully filling in the earth behind him, concealing his original entry.

"Why didn't he just gut it like the rest, and have done with it? Carol had many times cried, trying to find a pattern in pottery shards centuries distant from one another, but found randomly, gloriously jumbled together.

Morley's name featured large in Andrew's renewed curses.

"What's he done now?" Carol said, ducking her head under the lip of the earth. Resigned. As if she had known all along Morley still had the power to thwart them. Andrew backed out of the narrow tunnel of earth. He turned when he was under the canvas, at the dig table amid the shovels, the string, the site map and grid markers, the stacks of dirt-clogged brushes and mud-covered boots, the sifters of earth, the careful shelves of pottery. He was clutching an object the size of a telephone directory, seemingly made of caked earth.

"He put something in," he cried in despair. "Look at this, right in the middle of the earliest grave. He's ruined it. Then he filled it in again. It's insane."

"Witchcraft," Carol said, Diane at her hip, finding in this somehow a source of morose cheer. Andrew glared at her with the scientist's disdain. She went back into the hut and returned with her latest read, picked up at a second-hand bookshop during a rainy day visit to town. Red leather spine stamped, "Property of Berkeley University Library. Do Not Remove."

"How's this for a snappy title?" she said, seeing Josephine's tape recorder. She read aloud, obligingly, "*Notes on Witchcraft in Monmouthshire, Gloucestershire, and the Berkeley Region*, by A. V. Sangster, Complete and Unabridged with Foreword by the Author."

Her husband managed a derisive snort as he fetched a wire brush and started removing the dirt. She flipped the book one-handed at him. Its yellow pages flurried in the draft the movement raised.

"Hey, Morley believed in all this stuff," she said. "That's the reason why he did all his investigation, trying to find proof." Andrew, busy brushing, gave vent to a second derisive snort.

"The Witch of Berkeley," Carol read, flipping, "who three times broke the chains on her coffin. Serpent-bearded Byatis—gave me bad dreams for a week—here! The local people told Sangster that who raised up the Berkeley Toad." She gave a cheerful haps he was doing witch-work at the mound."

"I'm not going to reread his notes just to check for occult significance in dates," Andrew said, teeth gritted, glasses glinting, with the wire brush removing the earth. Mourning the ruin to his work.

"Late October?" Josephine guessed, hopefully. Halloween was the only occult date she knew.

Andrew treated her comment with the same seriousness as he had his wife's jest. "Hardly. Frosts," he explained.

"It's a box," Carol said, the wire brush now showing the outline clearly. Andrew shifted to a softer bristle. A locked case, dull-heavy colored, obviously machine-turned.

"I would guess less than two centuries old," Andrew said, heavily.

"Don't get too carried away with dates until you've done the carbon 14 test, darling, you know the dangers of guesswork," Carol joked. She reached over Diane's down-soft head and kissed her husband's brown beard. "Poor Andrew," she said.

He smiled wanly as he continued with his examination, speaking aloud for the benefit of Josephine's winding cassette. "Made of lead." With a screwdriver he wrenched open the lid.

Within a circle, as startling as Diane's eyes and almost as blue. A moment later and a mask took shape, of glazed ceramic. A man's face bearded and smiling. Vivid. The three stared. Then Andrew grunted and with one hand traced first the way the beard writhed to rounded, raised heads, and then to a line of script around the mask's brink.

"What's that?" Josephine said, virgin to the thrill of discovery, and succumbing entirely.

"Greek?" Carol said. Andrew shrugged.

"Antique?" asked Josephine.

"Fake," Carol guessed.

"You've heard of dog-Latin?" Andrew said. A frown creased his bristled cheek. "Morley was not as learned as he liked to think." A moment more, and he recited, head tilted to follow the angle of the writing, eyes fixed. "'Serpent-bearded Byatis, god of forgetfulness, who as Hypnos, god of dreams, is worshipped amongst the Greeks.'"

* * *

Josephine and Carol, girded with baby Diane, walking along the green brow of Morley's Mound, towards the stink of bitumen, the scar of brown earth, the grumbling machines mowing through the wildflower speckled meadows. The dig hut and the eaten earth behind them were clearly visible, and the snub shape of Andrew's car. A mere half-mile now separated the dig and the advancing work. The rain had been burned off by the late afternoon sun, leaving a light haze, a mist that never lifted. All around was the flat rim of the world, a grey and undulating plain. To the left was the pointing black thread strung with bright car-jewels that was the A.38. The wind snatched at the edges of their words, spun them in a haze of sun-blur.

"Are these things meant to happen?" Josephine asked Carol.

"What things?"

"Finds—like that," Josephine said, meaning the mask, strung up on the wall of the dig hut as a souvenir.

"You'd be surprised at the things archaeologists find," said Carol.

"I had a dream," Josephine confessed, as shy as Andrew. They arrived at the foot of the hill.

"Look at the pretty flowers," Carol said to Diane. Diane burbled. Carol knelt carefully and spread her hands, graceful and long-fingered, amid the low-growing soft-furred leaves. Within a few minutes she collected a softly scented handful. In the protected hollow at the base of the mound violets bloomed in countless number, and another, long-stalked, white-blossomed, solitary.

"Heavenly!" exclaimed Josephine as its elusive scent welled up in the still air. She bent to pluck it.

"Goodness," said Carol, staring as Josephine turned with the flower, Carol and her baby curled together in a violet hollow. "That's an asphodel."

"Asphodel?"

"A lily. It carpeted Elysium," Carol said. She took the fragrant flower, and sniffed delightedly. "I didn't even know they grew in Britain."

"Elysium?" Josephine said, meekly, feeling to the full her journalist's ignorance.

"The Heaven of the ancient Greeks," Carol said, and slower, reciting, "The scent of asphodel renders immortal the blessed dead."

"We should really be getting on," said practical Josephine.

"We won't be welcome visitors until knock-off time," Carol said, "Half an hour yet." Bruce had seen a flint with a chipped edge and given them a call from the pub to come over and collect it. Bruce had spotted this tiny, fragile thing in the turning earth, from the seat of a moving bulldozer. Bruce the eagle-eyed, who had in one Saturday afternoon of voluntary work at the dig found a record fifty-eight pottery shards in the sifting dirt.

"I worship at Bruce's feet," Andrew had said that night, wiping gravy from his beard, giving Bruce a steak and chips feast. He promised Bruce an expenses-paid holiday in Greece.

"Can't leave the wife and kid," Bruce had said, grinning and flushed with triumph, that something so useless should be so important to anybody. He was given the next day a full inspection of the dig finds. Andrew opened the cases of bones and flints, the tarnished brooch-pins and the solitary, rusted, iron knife.

"A robust people," Andrew said, showing the thickness of the bones.

"Like Gaz?" Bruce said.

"Not exactly"—a pained wince. Andrew continued, "You'd be a giant among them. Thick-boned. It's a classification. Robust versus gracile." He stopped and frowned. "Gracile. An ugly word." He lifted, by way of explanation, the next tray, where lay a fragile handful topped with a tiny skull. "A skylark," he said, "found near the hand of a buried child. Was it a pet? Food? Or were its wings to lift that small soul to the gods in the western sky? We know they are truly human, when they care about their dead."

"To bury them, to heap over them the sheltering earth," over the head of her own small daughter, Carol had softly said. Bruce had nodded, understood none of this, found a steady stream of flints and bone fragments in the roadwork since. Proud. Felt his bones grow thick and dense.

"People come here to bury their dead, makes sense. There's bound to be other sites around," Andrew had said. Accepted the found with a gratitude equal to the pain with which he thought of the unfound, being so swiftly buried beneath the advancing road.

Carol lay back amid the violets, holding the pale, slender lily, hugged Diane, then fed her, the child nuzzling to her breast. Perfume blossomed everywhere. "What dream was this?"

"Dream?" Josephine said, then recollected and blushed, "Oh nothing really." Carol raised her brows.

"I dreamed I was looking for you in a mist, but I could not call for you because I had forgotten your name," Josephine said.

Carol grinned, and closed her eyes. Invoked drowsily the name of Byatis. "Although I looked him up in Sangster last night," she said, "and *Vale of Berkeley*." Speaking severely. Disappointed. "Byatis turns up glowing green on hilltops. People who touch him go mad and start beating drums in the woods at night. Nothing poetic. And so silly. Would you touch a glowing green serpent-draped idol at midnight?"

"Not likely," Josephine giggled.

"I had a dream too," Carol said, brimming with confidences. "Do you want to hear?" She half opened her eyes to catch the response. Josephine leant forwards to hear Carol's hushed voice. She caught the asphodel's elusive scent, and felt the sun warm on her back.

"Andrew was kissing me, but his beard was moving," Carol whispered, eyes closing again. "Like snakes."

* * *

Silence filled the hollow where they sat. Josephine realized the machines were still with the day's end. Looked up, then turned back to hurry her friend along. But time had passed without recollection, the sweet, painful time of holidays and dreams. Carol and Diane, pillowed in violets, were asleep. Clasped in Diane's infant hand, and arched over their heads, nodded the asphodel, the lily whose fragrance renders immortal the blessed dead.

* * *

The next day the photographer arrived. Andrew, startled and shy, bolted into his mound like a rabbit. Carol and the baby got the lion's share of the pictures. The charmed photographer reluctantly departed at dusk, promising to send back a sheaf of proofs. Josephine got down to work, and in one night and one day pounded out a satisfactory first draft. She found also in her researches a battered copy of *Legendry and Customs of the Severn Valley* by A. P. Hill. The index listed Byatis, although she had no time to read further. She walked up to the dig at five o'clock Monday to present it, and invite everyone to the pub for fish and chips. Andrew, earth-spattered and diligent, came out of the tent at her hail, under the sardonic blue stare of the mask. Andrew actually smiled at the prospect of a drink.

"Carol started walking back. She's going to check with Bruce, and Diane wanted violets," he said. He looked at his watch and clucked, then turned and closed and locked the hut. He tested the door for firmness and checked he had all the keys, methodical as always.

"I said I'd pick her up at the roadwork. Give you a lift?"

"Yes please."

* * *

They drew up as the men were knocking off. The bright day was cooling as a wind blew across the plain from the lake.

"Where's Carol?" Josephine asked, getting out of the car. She drew surprised stares.

"She supposed to be here?" asked Gaz.

"I saw her," Bruce volunteered. "Walking down the mound with the kiddy." He pointed, then reckoned at Andrew's inquiring stare, "About a half hour back."

"They're asleep in the violets," Josephine said. She shook her head. Gaz shouted robustly that Bruce had something for Show and Tell, for the teacher. Andrew got out of the car. Bruce flushed and fumbled with his overall pocket. The men laughed as they started for the mini-bus for the trip to town.

"Wait," Andrew called to Josephine. He went back to his car and leant in the open door, fished out a cardigan, ancient and brown. Feeling for his wife the change in the weather.

Josephine walked back towards the mound, well lit in the hazy weather. She rubbed her hands to her arms, so the cardigan wool scratched her. The plain was an undulation all around. She topped the last rise and saw the nest of violets. She saw Carol, a curve of hip, swell of breast, a gleam of golden hair. She saw Diane, asleep against her chest. She expected to see them so much that she saw, for one moment glimmering, mirages in the clear evening. Then sight re-established itself over memory. There was only a hollow of violets blooming, empty and bare, the lone stalk of asphodel nodding gently in the fragrant air.

"Carol," she called. She folded the thick stuff of the cardigan in her hands, and scrambled to the crest of the mound. She could see on one side the dig hut, door firmly closed, and on the other the roadwork, the men milling, reluctant to go home. She could see for miles. Nothing moved except cars.

"Carol," she called. The wind tugged the word from her mouth.

* * *

First their own search, confused, methodless. The trip to the inn to see if Carol had walked the whole way, the return to the site, the search of the barrow, the absurd unlocking of the dig hut door. The slow car-crawl up and down the road, stopping as every hitcher, every hiker flashed a momentary beacon of hope into the dimming air. The searching through evening into dusk and night. The men striding, turning wide swaths of light in every direction. Voices blare. The calling, "Carol", over and over; as night went on the calls interspersed with others, for "Diane."

* * *

The police arriving. The vividness of the blue light above the car. The sergeant's slab-faced stare. The ceaseless, fruitless quest into the night. Nothing. No one. No answering cries. A woman and a child into misty air. A half mile between a hut and a road, both places at all times clearly visible and within hail. The surroundings a flat plain with no deep water, no treacherous ground.

* * *

At dawn, the sergeant again.

"What was she wearing?" Andrew and Josephine staring at each other. Something so familiar. Impossible to remember. Someone clearing his throat. The turning to him. Bruce, the eagle-eyed, the diligent, squinting to remember. "A blue dress, with yellow flowers. Sir."

* * *

The sergeant, flint-eyed, taking Bruce in for questioning, releasing him the next morning only on heavy bail at Andrew's undertaking. Bruce in the back of Josephine's car, cursing all cops, red-eyed from lack of sleep and weeping. "My kid's just that age. The idea—"

* * *

Josephine too close to file a convincing story.

* * *

Andrew walking backwards and forwards the crest of the mound. A hundred times. Fifty miles. His ridiculous luck. The brown cardigan.

* * *

The sergeant grilling Gaz, Baz, Kev, and Spiro. Grilling everyone day after day, trying to catch them out. The sergeant hammering at every hesitation, every word-stumble, too used to local people to do anything but suspect foul play. Saying bluntly to Andrew, "They never went out of each other's sight. Or they're lying like Trojans. Nothing can stick."

* * *

Gaz, Baz and Spiro and Kev, big lads all, turning up nothing in the mist that first dawn. Coming to stand by Andrew waiting at the roadwork, and then to Josephine, alone in the dig hut, making tea. Just in case Carol walked in. The men saying to her, "If we ever get our hands on the bastard who did this—." Red eyes glinting. Hands clenched.

* * *

Forensics trampled the violets flat. Police went over the hollow a hundred times on their hands and knees, praying for an answer. The entire force suddenly composed of young fathers and wives.

* * *

After four days the sergeant was showing signs of strain, "You didn't quarrel? A domestic?" Hopeless into Andrew's shut face and shield eyes. *Too dull?* the sergeant wondered, throwing down the morning's tabloid on his desk, eyes creased: "LOST YOUNG MUM AND KID." To Andrew: "Most cases, in two-three days, they reappear. Her mother. Some town."

* * *

After a fortnight they sent Andrew away.

Josephine took his keys and went to check on the dig hut. Waited on the dusk, too afraid to tear herself away. In case Carol should reappear. In case Carol should walk out of the mist, unconcerned, Diane on her hip. She was surprised when trucks drew up instead. When Gaz, Baz, Kev, Spiro, and Bruce came crowding in, stiff-legged. They had come prepared to force the door with crowbars.

"It's that damn mask," Bruce said, curtly. "The locals reckon the only good thing Morley did was bury it."

"We're going to smash it," snarled Gaz.

"Fucking dreams. Nightmares more like," from Baz.

"A mother and kid," Spiro roared.

Was it imagination or shadows or did the mask's sardonic smile change to a cool leer? Tension rose inside the hut. The crowbar flourished.

"You can't smash that," yelled Josephine, surprised at herself, for what they were saying she had read. She had pieced together that notion herself, from Hill, Wilshire, and Sangster. Told herself again and again that it was absurd, but could not deny that the half-thought of reburial had prompted her return. She snatched the mask from the wall and clutched it to her. His find, not hers.

"He won't notice it missing," Gaz yelled.

"He wouldn't notice if a fucking elephant waltzed through this place," said Bruce, more explicit. Josephine's voice shrill above the pack's bay.

"I've volunteered to look after the dig hut. It's my responsibility. You can't smash that."

* * *

The works halted for the examiner. Into winter. Headlines: "LOST ROADWORK CONTRACT, £££."

* * *

The day after work started again, Josephine walked up through the rain to watch the road advance under a sky of freezing slate. Stood in the company of the slab-faced sergeant, for the same reason a watcher. The backhoe jerked forwards to gouge a bite from the mound to fill a potential dip in the road. They watched the machine, jaws lowered, nose at the hollow where in summer violets scented the air, and the thin thread of asphodel.

Josephine. Imagining the impossible, "YOUNG MUM AND KID FOUND SAFE AND WELL IN AUSTRALIA." She looked up and down the road. Still expected Carol and Diane to walk around a corner. Was dully surprised when Andrew did.

Andrew driving up. Getting out of his car, blank-faced, flat-eyed. He flourished in explanation yesterday's *Camside Observer*, with the renewal of work front-page news. Held in one hand the brown cardigan. A bewildering dream would have explained everything except the pain.

* * *

A dull roar, and the jaws dug. Josephine and the sergeant, alone and together. The sergeant, alert and suspicious, had driven up to the roadwork one night last summer, noting the lights streaming, the people on the side of the road, the unmistakable churning of a concrete mixer. Had arrived as Josephine, resisting outright destruction to the last, dropped the mask into a posthole half-filled with water. As Baz, Gaz, Spiro, Kev, Bruce, and Josephine craned, expecting it to disintegrate. But blue, blue sank into the black circle, water streaming through sardonic eyes. Vanishing from sight as the sergeant arrived.

They stood together and swore they were doing nothing wrong. The sergeant, too learned in local ways to interfere, supervised the pouring of the concrete. And that was the last of serpent-bearded Byatis, god of forgetfulness, who as Hypnos, god of dreams, was worshipped amongst the Greeks.

A wedge of wet mud rose in the air, above the watching huddle of people. The yellow backhoe against slate sky, streaming silver, turned and dumped its load. Andrew stared with archeologist's eyes. Brown matter showed through the mud, neither rock nor dirt nor blue cloth sprinkled with yellow flowers. He screamed a halt. Returned to his car. He fetched the wire brush, and the one with finer bristle. The roar of the machine stilled. Only the sound of the rain pattering on earth and hooded heads. Knelt in the mud and carefully worked. What thoughts behind that stiff demeanor?

"Too long in the ground," he said at last, turning the fragment in his hands. Not looking up at the circle of people, disappointment twisting the hope in their eyes to knives. At least then they would have known. Would have had something to mourn over.

"This has been a place of burial for centuries," said the sergeant, clearing his throat.

Josephine, gently, "The mound—"

"Not the barrow," Andrew said. He stood, the fragment placed delicately, precisely, in the center of his palm. Shaking his head over and over, while around him the watching circle reeled. Murmuring gently, absurdly, to himself. "They were a robust people."

* * *

Investigation unearthed the gracile skeleton of a woman, curled around the bird-bones of a child.

Fortunes

by Keith "Doc" Herber

The fun fair was one of those small affairs. A collection of "thrill rides", sideshows, and snack booths, a seedy collection of attractions toted around the countryside on the backs of lorries. You see them all the time, set up in parks, fields, anywhere they can get a permit. Or anywhere they think they can get away without one.

My friend and I—we were but eighteen at the time—stopped in at this particular fair outside Brichester one night in search of a little excitement and, hopefully, some unattached girls. The name of the show was Hodgson's.

Once inside, we discovered how small the crowd was and prospects for a having a whole lot of fun took a dismal turn. We took a crack at the shooting gallery but neither one of us could put the red star out of the target. A quick spin on the Tilt-A-Whirl convinced us the "thrill" was not so much in the ride itself but whether or not the aged and creaking equipment would suddenly let go, rocketing car and passengers off into space to crash spectacularly somewhere in the asphalt parking lot.

It was after trying the rides that we discovered the fortune teller. The shadowy tent was located off to the side, not easy to find. In fact, I didn't notice it at all; it was my friend who found it.

"C'mon," he pleaded, "let's do the fortune teller."

I didn't want to. The idea seemed silly. The thought of some old gypsy crone fingering my palm was distinctly unappealing.

"No," I answered. "Let's take off. There's got to be something else around here." I really didn't want to have my fortune told. I didn't know why at the time, but I didn't. My friend practically dragged me to the entrance.

"Know Your Future!" proclaimed the faded banners above the entrance. "Peter Tholany, Egyptian Seer of the Highest Degree, Knows All, Sees All." It cost two pounds. I had my friend go first while I waited outside.

But I only had to wait for a minute or two. He was soon back out.

"How'd it go?"

"Great!" he said, grinning from ear to ear. The grin looked a little funny though. "It's your turn. Go on in."

I tried resisting, but he was insistent. Realizing it would be easier to go through with it than try to avoid it any longer, I stepped into the darkened tent.

Inside was cramped and stuffy; the damp air smelled of stale tobacco. There were few lights and I could barely make out the dark, cowled figure sitting near the far wall, smoking a cigarette. Atop a small round table covered with a fringed cloth stood a large "crystal ball." An empty chair waited for me.

"Do you wish your fortune told?"

His voice was deep and resonant, with the trace of an accent.

"Sure." I stepped forward and sat down at the table across from him.

The man lifted his head. "It costs two quid."

His face was a surprise. Dark-skinned, olive almost, his age was difficult to guess. Maybe sixty—but a very healthy sixty. Something about his eyes was disturbing. They seemed terribly old, and terribly wise. He caught me studying his face.

"As the sign outside says," he explained, "I am Egyptian—descended in a direct line from royalty." He lifted his cigarette to his mouth and inhaled deeply. He held the smoke in his lungs for a moment, then expelled it in a swirling cloud.

I really didn't have the faintest idea of what an Egyptian should look like, but if asked to pick one out from a line-up this would have been the man. I handed over the money and waited.

"Gaze into the crystal ball," he smiled at me, stubbing out his cigarette. "Gaze deeply."

I peered at the ball, trying to see through the hazy surface. Something was moving about inside. It was difficult to be sure in the dim light but it looked to be some sort of crystal, facets constantly moving, changing and shifting shape, describing odd patterns. I remember thinking at the time that the thing inside was slowly spinning around, probably driven by a small motor and batteries.

From the corner of my eye I saw the man reach into his cloak and draw out a small card and pen. He quickly scribbled something on the card, folded it, then sealed it with a piece of gold tape.

"Here it is." He handed the card across the table.

"That's it? That's all I get?"

"This is all you'll ever need—maybe more." He thrust the card at me. "Take it."

Disgusted and feeling slightly cheated, I took the card and left. Outside my grinning friend was waiting for me.

"How'd you like it?" he asked.

"Some deal. Why didn't you warn me? I really didn't need to spend two quid on that." I looked at the card in my hand. It was heavy manila, cheaply printed with some sort of Egyptian decorations—hieroglyphs and such.

"Admit it," my friend demanded. "Just meeting that guy was worth the money. What's your fortune say?" He was already breaking his open, reading the insides.

"Whooo!" he exclaimed. "Now that's what I call a fortune."

"What is it?" I tried to peek over at it.

"Oh no," he refused, holding it away from me. "Open yours. Then I'll tell you mine."

That's when the two girls walked by. I remember slipping the card into my back pocket, and then it was forgotten. I imagine my mother found it when she washed all my clothes before I left for university. At any rate, I never saw it again and in all those years never even had occasion to think of it.

I don't recall for sure, but I don't think we got anywhere with the two girls. I do remember, however, that it was the last night out my friend and I ever spent together. School began the next week and we left for two different universities miles apart. For a time we still saw each other on holidays but gradually we drifted apart. After graduation we stayed in touch but when law school got serious, we both got too busy. We eventually lost contact and we didn't talk again for several years.

I next saw him in court. We weren't involved in the same litigation but simply ran into each other one day in the halls. We later met for lunch, had a couple drinks, and talked about old times. My friend, like me, was married, had two children, and was working as an associate with a reasonably prestigious firm. He seemed to be doing well and moving up fast—perhaps a little faster than myself. It was an enjoyable afternoon and we promised to get together again—but never did.

It was less than a year later that I heard about my old friend's suicide—or his suspected suicide. He left no note, but the head wound was typical of the self-inflicted gunshot. For a short time there was talk of a professional hit, suspicion revolving around a handwritten card found on the victim's desk. In an effort to solve the mystery the police had finally published a photo of the mysterious note in the newspapers.

It was a small card on which was handwritten: "You will die on August 24, 1994." The card was cheaply printed, decorated with Egyptian-styled hieroglyphs. My friend's death had, of course, occurred on August 24, 1994.

I never bothered to contact the police. There seemed no point in telling them what I knew about the card because none of it made any real sense. Besides, the investigation was already winding down. It had quickly become evident my friend had no underworld connections, nor any gambling or drug habits. The ink on the card had been found to be years old, eliminating the card as possible evidence of homicide. It was finally ruled a suicide.

But seeing the photo of that card in the newspaper left me uneasy, bringing back memories of that evening at the carnival, and the fortune teller's tent—the enigmatic smile of the old Egyptian, my future written on a cheaply printed card.

I asked around about the old friend and learned that his life had taken a sudden and inexplicable turn for the worse beginning just shortly after the time the two of us had lunch together. There apparently had been problems with his firm, as well as with his wife, and he had developed a drinking problem. His office eventually placed him on medical leave, his wife soon after leaving him, taking the children with her. At the time of his death, less than a year later, he was completely destitute, his creditors on the verge of suing him. It seemed to have happened all so fast. The day I'd seen him he'd been bright, positive, and overflowing with plans for the future.

It was certainly a sad story. I could see how he might have been driven to end it all—though not quite why it had all come about. Then I found *my* card.

It was in one of my mother's old books, part of a collection I'd inherited from her a few years ago, after her death. She'd apparently used the card to mark her place in a book she'd never finished. The card was waiting for me on page 198, still sealed by its piece of gold tape. No one had ever opened it. I dismissed it as coincidence. I locked the card away in my desk and tried to put it out of my mind.

But the thoughts wouldn't go away. I wondered if my friend had found his card under the same sort of chance circumstances I had? If he'd gone home that day after our lunch and discovered the card tucked away in some forgotten corner? Years ago, at the fun fair, he had opened it, read it, and laughed; then we'd forgotten about it—or at least I had.

The date on that card—the date of my friend's suicide—had been written down more than ten years earlier. My friend had read it. Was it possible that he'd kept it all this time?

But it made no difference. Mine was here in my hand, discovered as if by chance, its frightful knowledge still a secret. I wondered if it held the same fortune as his. The *ultimate fortune*—the exact day on which you would die. I thought more than once of simply throwing the card away but couldn't bring myself to do it, haunted though I was by the awful knowledge I knew it must contain.

It seemed to me a man could do a lot if he knew exactly when he would die. He would know when to invest, when to spend. He could provide properly for his family, and their future. He could make plans and do things that he couldn't possibly do otherwise. Life could be maximized, lived to the fullest. But I was too filled with fear to learn the truth.

I again tried to forget about it. I told myself that it was ridiculous to think that a carnival fortune could predict my own death, rule my life. But it stayed with me, dogging me, constantly vying for my attention. My mind began to wander and my work suffered as a result. Like my friend, I began to drink, trying to put the thoughts out of my mind. Nonetheless, I continued to brood upon the card locked in my desk, worrying about the great secret it contained, and how much it might mean to me. And I brooded on my fear of knowing.

My marriage, already rocky, crumbled; I moved out and took a lease on this small apartment. I have not been to work in six weeks and I suppose they have fired me. I have brought the card with me, as yet unopened. I am, for all intents and purposes, paralyzed. It has been two weeks since I have left this filthy room. My money is gone.

The gun lies on the table before me, next to the folded card sealed with its piece of gold tape. I will open the card soon—I can feel it. Maybe not today, but soon—perhaps tomorrow, or the next day. But very soon, at any rate. I know what it will say and then I will use the gun.

So it has been written.

Cross My Heart, Hope to Die

by J. Todd Kingrea

... Then I saw the Pale One, the Shambler Below, the God of the Labyrinth carried forth upon the backs of His children. They bore Him toward me, out of His eternal darkness and once more into the world of Light. And I watched in ecstasy as His children crawled and scuttled from every hiding place that held them, growing strong and worshipping their Master.

— *Revelations of Glaaki,* Volume VII

I

Jamie remembered getting sick in the loo. His stomach had felt like a twisted piece of lead, heavy and aching beneath his feverish skin. The slightest movement sent spasms of nausea through him. He had barely managed to make it to the cool porcelain rim of the commode before his stomach buckled, heaving its meager contents into the light. His head swirled like a pinwheel and he fell to the floor, unconscious.

He opened his eyes and looked up. He was back in bed. The faces of his parents and Dr. Sommerston swam into view. His mother bent close to him, the smell of fresh laundry on her. "Jamie, dear, are you all right? How do you feel?" she asked, sitting down on the edge of the bed and placing a comforting hand against his forehead.

"I feel pretty good. My tummy isn't hurting anymore. Not even a little." The doctor bent over and gently thumbed the boy's abdomen, then studied his eyes and ears.

"Well, young man," Dr. Sommerston said, "everything seems to be in order. You color's returned and your stomach isn't as tight as it was earlier. A good night's rest and you should be like new. Your left ear will likely be a bit sore for a day or two, but that's to be expected. Just have a care with it."

"Was my ear bleeding?" the boy asked, fingering his ear beneath a wing of orange hair.

"Aye." Sean Underhill scratched his heavy beard and looked inquiringly at Dr. Sommerston, as if trying to find an explanation for the boy's malady on the old physician's owlish face. Dr. Sommerston patted Jamie on the shoulder, scooped up his bag and stethoscope, and walked out of the room. Mr. Underhill hesitated long enough to smile at his son before following the doctor downstairs.

"Mum, I'm starved. Can I have something to eat?"

"Straight away," Mrs. Underhill replied, delighted to see the lad's appetite returning so quickly. He hadn't eaten much in two days. "How does hot vegetable soup sound?" she asked, smoothing the covers as she got up.

"Yum!" he answered.

"Right, I'll be back in a minute." She disappeared down the hall and Jamie leaned back on his pillow, yawning heavily. He was tired, but he did feel better. This was the first time he'd felt good since—

His eyes snapped open and he bolted upright. *Oh no, no—what have I done?* he thought. He'd told Dr. Sommerston everything, hadn't he? He remembered telling the old man all about what had happened. At least, everything he could remember about what had happened that night—

The breeze ruffling his curtains was warm for early spring, yet he shivered, his skin prickling with a chill. He clutched the blankets tightly in sweaty fists; his heart felt like a hammer in his chest. He sank back onto his shapeless pillow. *What'll they do to me? I mean, I broke the oath. I know they'll do something—no, wait. They don't know I told. Kerwin and Davey and the rest of them, they don't know. I'll just act like nothing's happened. They'll never know.*

Tossing the covers back, Jamie got up and walked to the window. The carpet felt spongy and fuzzy beneath his feet. On the lawn below Dr. Sommerston was tottering toward his automobile near the gate. Night had settled over Camside, leaving windows lit in the dull red brick cottages up and down the lane. Overhead the sky glittered with tiny sequins, winking and sparkling against the velvet emptiness. Lights from the town made a white glow just above the tree tops. He shivered again, wrapping his arms around himself and looking away from the town's halo. He'd rather not think about that glow—

Through the ebony shroud that draped Camside came the haunting, lonely bleating of a single sheep. Others responded, their distant bellowing drifting through the evening air. A lorry roared down the lane, coughing out plumes of smoke from its broken muffler. When the vehicle boomed into Hill Street it was lost from sight. The echoes from the holed muffler began to fade, and the night was still once again. Even the sheep had been silenced.

Fog curled over the lawn, milky and unformed. Below the window insects chirped and whirred, and a fat cream-colored moth smacked repeatedly into the screen, trying to get at the light. Jamie looked out at the shadowed hedges and rustling trees, and suddenly leaped away from the window. Anyone out there watching could easily see him silhouetted against the light.

Come on, stop this! he thought. *You're ten years old—quit acting like you're five! There's nobody out there spying on you. That's stupid. You act like they can read your mind or something—like they already know what you've done.* His thoughts were interrupted by his mother, bringing his supper on a tray. He was glad for the intrusion.

"Jamie Underhill! What are you doing out of bed, young man? Dr. Sommerston said you needed to get some rest." He spotted the bowl of vegetable soup and the stack of wafers beside it. The sweet aroma of roast beef and carrots filled the room; steam rising off the soup reminded him of the fog outside, the way it coiled into the air.

"Aw, Mum, I just had a peep out the window. I've been in bed for weeks!"

"Oh, you have not, you've only been in bed since yesterday. Now get back in there; I've brought your dinner." Mouth watering, he climbed into bed and adjusted the pillow behind him, then attacked the dark, heavy broth. His stomach moaned in anticipation.

As he swallowed the warm, chunky soup he watched his mother fuss about the room, tidying and straightening. The soup warmed his belly, driving away the hunger and making him lethargic. If only he could drive away his thoughts about the initiation, and about what Kerwin would do to him when he found out.

Jamie lifted a spoonful of soup to his mouth, then hesitated, noticing a white oval bean swimming in the broth. It lay there, staring up at him like a scummy, accusing eye—like Kerwin's eyes. The spoon dropped back into the soup with a plop. He looked toward the window and felt his stomach grow cold despite the soup.

* * *

Later that night he lay in bed, watching the shadows of tree limbs wiggle across the wall, thinking about what he'd told Dr. Sommerston. The old doctor had questioned him about what had happened. He'd asked gently but persistently for the whole story, and that's when Jamie broke. He remembered throwing his arms around Dr. Sommerston's neck, feeling the old man's feathery hair, smelling the mustiness of his rubbery skin. He'd cried hard, but not loud—he didn't want his parents to hear him. They didn't like Kerwin and his mates, and they had expressly forbidden him to have anything to do with them. So he had sobbed quietly on the old man's shoulder, the horror in his eyes pouring out in a cascade of tears and broken sentences.

He'd told Dr. Sommerston about a secret club, the Survivors as Kerwin called them, and the dares kids had to do to get in. After the dares there was the final initiation at the secret clubhouse. He had met Kerwin, the club leader, and Davey Nooren, his right-hand man, at the secret clubhouse; the two boys had blindfolded him, then made him repeat the Survivor's secret oath—making him swear never to reveal anything about the club.

Jamie had told Dr. Sommerston all he could remember: about the cold, dank place he went into that had a sour and unhealthy odor; about Kerwin and Davey, and the peculiar words they whispered in eerie sing-song voices. He'd told how he stumbled through the darkness, guided by the firm, chilly hands of the older boys.

Jamie wormed deeper beneath the sheets. The wind billowed his curtains, causing them to look like bloated white things. He clamped his eyes together to shut them out. "Cross my heart, hope to die," he'd said. "Hope to die."

He didn't want to die. It was just a silly oath, recounted thousands of times on playgrounds and in parks. It didn't mean anything.

So why was he trembling, buried beneath his blankets?

It wasn't until the sky looked like hazy charcoal that he fell asleep, his dreams filled with everything but color.

II

"Come on, get that little sod! Get him!"

Jamie pounded down the pavement, his shoes thudding on the smooth stones with each step. His blood thundered in his ears as he raced along Jenner's Lane, breathing furiously, sweat streaming down his cheek. Crinkly trees, brooding cottages, and crumbling stone walls watched him pass, uninterested. A small knot of kids scampered after him, yelling and screaming.

"You can't get away from us, Jamie!"

"Get him! Get him!"

Crying, gulping air, he veered left and dashed into Camside Park, his pursuers close behind. Several old men smiled toothlessly and wistfully as he sprinted by, and young mothers with prams stared impassively. No one moved to help him. To them it must look like just another game. Couldn't they see his terror? Couldn't they tell that his life was in danger?

Jamie ran across the slimy footbridge that arched over Cambrook Stream, then out through the front gate. He dashed across High

Street, amid blaring horns and the ripping squall of brakes. His legs were heavy from the flight, and his throat was a raw, aching furnace. Glancing back he saw the kids jackrabbiting through the traffic, giggling at the curses flung at them by the drivers. He fled onward, down lanes and alleys, through gardens of nodding flowers, past flocks of sheep grazing peacefully on fields and hills, all the while staying only a few steps ahead of the others.

Slowly they spread out to the left and right, paralleling him, preventing him from turning in either direction. There was only one direction for him to run: straight ahead.

"Ha ha ha, look at him go! Like a rabbit, he is!"

"Wait'll we catch you! You've had it, you little wanker!"

Tears stung his eyes as he stumbled down Fisher Hill. Kerwin had known. Somehow he had known that Jamie had broken his vow. He'd given Jamie that look this morning, the look that said, "I know what you did, and I'm going to get you for it."

He staggered to a halt, panting and wheezing; he recognized his surroundings. Terror spiked through his body.

He was in Grigsby's Field. The meeting place of the Survivors.

And Kerwin and Davey were standing by the old well, grinning.

He spun around, ready to flee once again, but found his way blocked. The other kids had caught up with him. Red-faced and sweaty, they loped up to him, grasping hands, barring his retreat. Kerwin's slow, measured voice pricked him like a pin.

"Well, well, well, my Survivors. What do we have here?" Kerwin asked, striding toward the wheezing boy. "I do believe it's our oath-breaker, our little snitch." The last word came out in a crackling hiss. Behind him Davey lit a Silk Cut, flicked the match into the well, and exhaled a vaporous cloud that did little to hide his sadistic grin.

Jamie glanced up into Kerwin's pale, watery-blue eyes as he approached. They seemed to float in their chalky sockets. Kerwin was five years older than Jamie and much taller. He looked like a lanky scarecrow from a picture book that a child had forgotten to color. His top lip peeled up in a sneer, revealing gums and long dull teeth. With a swipe of his bony hand he raked his grungy blonde hair out of his eyes and stepped closer. Without taking his eyes off Jamie—who was nervously trying to avoid the disquieting gaze—Kerwin spoke: "Survivors, Jamie Underhill has broken his oath. He has told our secrets to the grown-ups." A low murmur rippled through the assembled kids. "He has betrayed us."

Jamie glanced behind him. Several of the kids appeared worried as they watched him and Kerwin. A few, trying to be invisible, studied their feet or the bustling clouds overhead. All looked hesitant and unsure.

"Kerwin," he began, forcing a feeble smile to his lips, "I didn't—"

"SHUT UP!" the pale boy shrieked, his voice cracking from high to low. The children jumped, then stood motionless, their attention captured by the shrill sound. "Don't lie to me, you little bastard! I know you told. I know it."

"B–but how? How?"

A victorious smile spread Kerwin's puffy lips. "Jamie," he said evenly, "you're no longer a part of us, you're no longer like us. Because of that, I know." Raising his head he addressed the children: "Survivors, hear me! Because this one has broken the sacred vow, he must be punished. Let this be a lesson to you." Kerwin paused a moment, looking around the overgrown, lumpy field. Several of Grigsby's sheep in an adjacent field stared back with cool, black eyes.

Then with a smile Kerwin turned back. "As penalty for your sin, I hereby sentence you to be thrown into that well!" He jabbed a narrow finger in its direction. Davey, leaning against the well, coughed out a low chuckle of approval.

The children gasped. "Kerwin, we can't do that," a plump, shaggy-headed boy nearby replied. "That ain't—"

Kerwin's icy stare cut through the boy, silencing him instantly. The other children fidgeted beneath's Kerwin's watery gaze, like insects pinned to a corkboard.

Jamie turned and fled then, sprinting past the unprepared kids. He heard Kerwin screaming for them to catch him, but he had a strong start and fear lent wings to his feet. He scampered over the mossy stone wall at the end of the field, glancing back only to check on his pursuers. They were all standing motionless in the field. The kids had averted their gaze, but the eyes of Davey and Kerwin pierced him like icicles.

III

The shiny white light from the refrigerator seeped out into the otherwise dark kitchen. Jamie stood in his sock feet before the refrigerator, casually swinging the door back and forth as he searched for something to drink. He withdrew the milk bottle and sat it on the wooden counter beside a bag of crisps, then pulled a glass from the cupboard. He heard tapping at the front door; his father moved to answer it.

"Hello, Mr. Underhill. Can Jamie come out and play?"

Jamie jumped; fear closed around his heart like a fist. The frosty milk overflowed the glass and spattered across the counter. He recognized the voice. It was his friend, Allan Roth. They were the same age, and spent a good deal of time playing together.

Allan was also a member of the Survivors.

He quietly closed the refrigerator, throwing the kitchen into a fuzzy blackness. He tip-toed across the slick, hard wood to the front window. He could hear his father in the next room: "Hello, Allan. Won't you come in?"

Jamie felt his hands flush with the heat of terror. His eyes widened as his heart pumped faster. *He can't come in here*, he thought frantically. *He'll kill me! Kerwin's sent him to kill me, right here in my house!* His head felt light.

Then he heard Allan's voice again: "No thank you, sir. I just wanted to see if Jamie could come out and play."

"I don't think so," his father replied. "It's getting late and he'll be getting ready for bed soon. Maybe you two can play tomorrow." There was a short pause, then his father added, "Anyway, Allan, isn't it awfully late for you to be out?"

Lifting the curtain, Jamie closed one eye and peered through the window. A heavy fog blanketed everything. He could barely make out the autos parked along the street. The porch light gave off a misty, pale aura and pressed ineffectually at the drifting fog; heavy, ropy strands of mist floated past the window like restless spirits.

Mumbled words were exchanged in the next room, then the front door scraped closed. Allan stepped off the porch and walked toward the street. Jamie watched, feeling his heart slow and his body relax. Allan, now an indistinct grayness, cut toward the corner of the yard. He started to drop the curtain when a movement in the fog stopped him.

He lifted the curtain higher, squinting. A gray, shapeless blob moved on the other side of the yard. It was another kid emerging from behind a tree. The figure seemed to glide through the fog toward Allan. More shapes materialized out of the fog. Small, bobbing forms that had no substance appeared from behind trees and along hedgerows, all converging in the corner of the yard.

A pair of headlamps sliced through the fog as an auto turned onto the street. The light silhouetted the children for an instant, then swept on. Jamie gasped and dropped the curtain, his pulse quickening. He knew those kids out there were his friends—or used to be his friends. Surely Kerwin hadn't turned them all against him? What if his father had let him go out and play? He'd be dead, he was certain of that. But what if his mother and father hadn't been here tonight? What if he'd been alone?

He raced out of the kitchen and into the warmth and security of the living room where his parents were watching the telly. He snuggled up close to his mum, who put her arm around his shoulder and laughed at a silly man on the program. Jamie tried to focus on the lurid colors and blaring noise from the set, but his mind kept returning to the children in the fog.

He remembered them huddled together in the mist, the headlamps sweeping over them, turning their bodies from grayish-white to black. In that split second he'd seen the knives they were clutching, glinting wickedly in the passing light—the knives that had been meant for him. Feeling secure in his mother's presence, he looked toward the window. He watched and waited, anticipating, dreading. But there was nothing out there now. Nothing except drifting, colorless tendrils that pressed heavily against the glass.

IV

The last two days had been pure hell at school. Kerwin and his mates had harassed Jamie every chance they got. They threatened him, chased him, pranked him, hunted him. He'd made sure to stay near his teachers when moving through the halls or on the playground. He knew, however, that this was only a minor respite; Kerwin had no love for the teachers, or any authority figure for that matter. He knew it wouldn't be long before they'd catch him alone. Then they'd kill him. Of that he was certain.

Jamie had known Kerwin ever since he could remember. So had most of the other kids in Camside. They'd all grown up together. As far back as he could remember, Kerwin had always been the leader. In everything. Why, he couldn't say. Kerwin wasn't good-looking or strong; his parents didn't have a lot of money. There wasn't anything special about him. So why did everyone follow him around?

Jamie thought back to the dares he'd had to perform to be considered for Survivor membership. The dares made up and ordered by Kerwin: setting the tail of Mrs. Dandridge's cat on fire (which the yowling puss had doused by sliding around on it—much to everyone's delight); stealing three cans of lager from the market and drinking them; and having to run through the vicar's house at tea time and throw a live garden snake on his kitchen table. That was the one his dad had found out about, and he winced as he remembered the beating his arse had taken for it. And all because he wanted to be a member of the club. Just like his mates.

Almost everyone he knew was in Kerwin's secret club. And while most of them hung around with Kerwin, very few of them actually liked the creep. A handful of his mates had risked Kerwin's wrath by talking to him on occasion. He had the distinct impression that many of them didn't care for the harsh treatment he was suffering, but none had the courage to speak out against Kerwin. They went along reluctantly, ashamedly, with Kerwin and his campaign of terror. But why?

What sort of control did he have over them? Why, if they disliked him so much, did they continue to flock to his side?

And why were they getting more and more belligerent? They gleefully beat up smaller children and nicked their lunch money, or shoved them down stairs. They cursed their teachers, and threw bottles and stones at old men and women. They had even set fire to some packing crates along Grimsdyke Mews, causing considerable damage. Some of the older members were even carrying knives to school, threatening instructors and pupils alike. Their actions weren't harmless, juvenile fun anymore; their pranks no longer meant to scare or inconvenience, but hurt.

Their parents had been contacted. Curfews had been set, threats made, beatings distributed, but still the kids returned again and again to Kerwin. It was like everything they had ever believed in and participated in—school, church, family—had been abandoned.

Or more appropriately, replaced.

By Kerwin.

V

Jamie checked the time. It was 9:30 p.m. He returned quickly to his comic book, eager to finish it before his parents got back and caught him. When he came home from school he'd found a note saying that his parents wouldn't be in 'til later. He was supposed to be doing his homework, but he'd spent the whole evening watching telly and reading comics. He'd even made his own dinner—a jam sandwich, crisps, a tower of Jaffa Cakes, and pudding—even though shepherd's pie and peas had been left for him in the fridge. He smiled, pleased with his sense of independent accomplishment. Nestling back against the pillow, he continued to read.

As he flipped the page he heard the front door open. Hurriedly he flung the comics under the bed, then scattered his schoolbooks about on the covers. Sitting cross-legged, elbows on knees, chin in hands, he opened a science book and pretended to read. His mother would come in any minute now.

Footsteps thumped up the stairs. He scowled at the text, acting as if he had been studying hard for hours. He felt quite good about his deception.

The door opened. Jamie scratched his head to give the final touch of authenticity to his performance, then looked up.

Kerwin grinned demonically at him from the doorway!

Jamie let out a shriek and threw himself back against the headboard. His throat went dry and prickling ribbons of heat lanced through his body. His eyes widened as Kerwin sauntered into his room, followed closely by Davey, green-toothed Nick Selsby, and several other kids. He recognized Allan Roth and two other mates of his. His eyes pleaded with them for help, but their sinister grins showed only their allegiance to Kerwin.

He had lost three more allies to Kerwin.

The ghost-white boy walked over to him. For the first time he noticed the long coil of rope in Kerwin's spindly hand.

"How—" he began, trying to talk through a constricted throat, "how did you get in here?" Then as an afterthought, a warning: "My mum and dad'll be home any minute now. You—you better get out of here." The last sentence came out sounding flat and empty.

Kerwin's grin turned his face into a leering death's head. Several of the other children snickered and looked at each other, sharing a private joke. "Jamie," Kerwin replied, "we're not worried about your parents. As a matter of fact, they're the ones who let us in here." More giggling from the kids clumped together in the doorway.

"No!" Jamie cried out, his voice strong once again. "No, they don't even like you. They wouldn't let *you* in here."

"Oh, but they did, me lad, they did. We," he gestured to include the others in a dramatic fashion, "sort of—*bumped* into them outside tonight, didn't we fellows?" The children laughed and jabbed one another, still sharing their secret joke.

"They even let me borrow the key to get in." Kerwin held up the copper key between two spidery fingers. Jamie's heart slammed furiously in his chest. He felt his eyes beginning to water.

"Where's my mum and dad? Where are they?!" he yelled, swinging his legs off the bed. "What did you do to them, you stupid skinny bastard!?"

Kerwin's smile dropped. Jamie stood up and Kerwin motioned for Nick, who trotted forward eagerly. Spinning, he tried to scramble back onto the bed, but Nick grabbed him by the hair and yanked him hard into the air. He hit the floor with a thud. Nick laughed, an abrasive, grating sound that held little humor. "You shouldn't be so worried about what happened to your mummy and daddy. You ought to be worried about what's going to happen to you, you prissy little wanker!"

Furious, Jamie gritted his teeth and kicked upward with all his might. His foot crunched into Nick's groin. The husky boy emitted a squeal and grabbed his crotch, toppling over against the bureau. Jamie scrambled up just as the other kids grabbed him.

"Tie him up!" Kerwin yelled, tossing the rope to a freckle-faced girl beside him. "Tie him up good and tight."

Jamie was crying and screaming as the children overran him, shoving him off his feet. He was buried beneath the kicking, squirming pile of fists, teeth, legs, and knees. All he could hear was the grunts and curses of the others. He tasted his own bitter blood in his mouth as blow after blow was hammered down upon him.

After a few moments he curled up in a ball on the floor, gasping and weeping with great haggard breaths. He didn't struggle when the rope was twisted around his body and his hands were knotted behind his back.

He was hauled roughly to his feet by Nick, who was still grimacing from his sore genitals. Jamie's head spun with flecks of light and fuzzy images. He tried to look at Kerwin, but the boy's face swam in and out of focus. His ears rang, his body ached in countless places, and his nose, lips, and cheeks were bleeding. The floor tilted as his vision dimmed. As darkness swallowed him he heard Kerwin's voice, hollow and far away: "You're coming with us, Jamie. We're taking you to meet a very special friend of mine."

VI

The southern end of Grigsby's Field was a wild, overgrown tangle of ash trees, thick briars, and drooping, spiny nettles. The land hadn't been worked in generations, and had slowly given itself back to its primordial mistress. The black soil was lumpy and uneven, crisscrossed by mole tunnels and dotted with sinkholes and leathery roots.

In the corner of the field rose a low, domed hill. The undergrowth, thicker here than anywhere else, ringed its base like a wall. Jagged stones and twisted trees clung tenaciously to the hill's sloping sides. Animals and birds alike shunned the hill, leaving its surface to the pallid spiders that raced across it in the dark of the moon.

Jamie awoke beneath a creaking, naked tree at the base of the hill. Icy, black rain spattered on his bruised face.

The field was in complete darkness. Distended, angry clouds rolled overhead, blotting the moon and stars. He looked up, felt the stinging rain on his face. Lightning crackled through the soggy clouds. He struggled to his feet, remembering Kerwin's final words. His pulse quickened. He recognized the field and its sentinel hill. This was where he'd come for his initiation. He thought he saw a faint glimmer of light in the direction of the hill—

He glanced about, seeking to pierce the slashing rain, trying to locate Kerwin or any of the others. There was no sign of them. Had they perhaps brought him out here and left him, as a lesson or a warning? Maybe they weren't going to kill him? Whatever the reason, he had to get home.

Jamie stepped away from the skeletal tree and something grabbed his leg.

He screamed, jumped, and pitched forward onto the muddy soil. Thunder bellowed above, mocking him. He rolled over and tried to pull his foot loose. A hateful, wrinkled face grinned at him from the base of the tree. He screamed again and kicked fiercely. The grasp on his ankle bit deeper. Was that an evil laugh he heard or the thunder overhead?

Lightning flashed; Jamie choked off his next scream. He could see what held his leg. Kerwin's rope was knotted severely around his ankle, the other end around the base of the tree. He collected himself and crawled toward the tree. The leering face he'd imagined was just shadows clinging to the rugged bark. He shivered.

Half-laughing, half-crying, he fumbled with the wet, coarse rope, trying to free himself. He saw movement out of the corner of his eye.

Several plump, white spiders were scrambling across the ground. They were as big as a shilling and he saw at least half a dozen of the glistening things skitter past him. As he continued fumbling with the rope, he saw them crawling down the tree, emerging from cracks and crevices in the old trunk. They fell from the limbs, white pulpy drops that hit the ground with soft thumps.

Whimpering and shaking, he clawed violently at the rope, ignoring his bleeding fingernails. All around him he could hear the soft thump-thump-thump of pale spiders falling to the ground. He glanced up and saw hundreds of the things racing past him toward the lonely, silent hill and the light at its base.

Jamie froze.

His eyes bulged as he stared at the pale, shimmering circle of light. It grew brighter, brighter.

Suddenly his initiation flooded back over him. He remembered the blindfold being taken off. He had been in a cave or tunnel. It hadn't been dark—a shaggy growth of lichen on the slimy stones had given off a faint, sickly glow. He vividly remembered Davey's expectant, unflinching face as he stared into the darkness ahead. Kerwin's narrow face had reflected the strange glow like a pasty mirror.

He'd been in that cave, the one from which ghastly light even now jumped and twitched. His body tingled with the heat of fear. Sweat beaded on his face, mixing with the pelting rain. He bit his lower lip, trying to keep from remembering. But the memories came.

He'd seen the pulsating white light that had come down the tunnel. There had been something in the light, something that had squelched and bubbled, and had caused Kerwin to shriek with delight. Jamie had screamed and wet himself as he saw through the corona of sallow light to the great body within.

The light from the cave grew stronger.

Thunder pounded the sky, keeping rhythm with his frantic heart. His fingernails dug into the flesh of his leg as he tore at the unyielding rope. He remembered fleeing the icy cave and racing home, screaming and crying as he stumbled through the hateful, mocking darkness.

He looked up just in time to see the light flare, then burst forth, shaming the lightning with its whiteness.

Walking out of the pulsating light was Kerwin, arms raised high, squealing with joy. He was naked—and with the exception of his head, the rest of his body was entirely devoid of hair, even though his muscles, his voice, his sex all showed signs of pubescence.

Behind him came a bloated, quivering thing that slopped forward on thick legs that did not move. It was the thing from his initiation, the thing in the light. Gobs of white jam with quivering yellow pupils were what passed for its multiple eyes. They jerked and rolled, unblinking in the pelting rain. The thing's stench—like a hot, thick pool of vomit—threatened to choke him. Gagging, he stumbled back and collided with the weathered bark of the gnarled old tree.

The pale thing shuddered in anticipation. Its mouth separated, opening like a fissure in the earth. Milky strands of saliva dripped from its jagged, bony gums.

Jamie screamed until he could taste blood running down the back of his throat.

He watched, paralyzed by fear, as the pallid, blob-like mass moved toward him. Kerwin ran before it, capering and shouting like the Fool on May Day. Rain heaved itself down in drenching sheets. The grubby, gelatinous spiders raced along the ground, part of the hideous parade. He noticed dozens of them scuttling over the blubbery, peeling meat of the obscene creature.

Then Jamie saw the children, and he knew how the thing from the cave could move without using its legs.

All the club members—his mates—were beneath the horrid thing, carrying it upon their backs! The children slipped and stumbled as they struggled to hold the bloated pile aloft. Grubby spiders fell into the children's hair and picked their way across tiny, hysterical faces. Screams and piercing wails carried from beneath the swaying horror as the children stumbled forward, bearing their load out of its inky domain.

Kerwin, slick with rain and grinning like a skull, cavorted to a stop in front of Jamie. Behind him the children knelt crying and slid the squalid white thing off their backs. It made an anxious sucking sound from a mouth that looked like a rip across its white fat. Jamie wiped water out of his eyes and looked up at Kerwin.

Still panting, Kerwin slicked his hair back and bent over, his razor-thin nose inches away from Jamie's. The shiny, textureless skin repulsed the smaller boy, as did the stale breath. Kerwin's swashy eyes gleamed with triumph.

"The Lord of the Labyrinth! He has come for you, Jamie—FOR YOU!" Kerwin threw his head back and laughed into the flooded sky.

"You rejected my gift. You rejected Him. That cannot go unpunished." The other children were crying, frozen with horror and revulsion. Some had curled up in the mud, whimpering. "The time is now!" Kerwin screamed. "The time to accept the bargain!" Bony hands bit into the smaller boy's shoulders.

"NO!" Jamie screamed. He grabbed a smooth stone sticking out of the miry earth and with a single motion yanked it loose, slamming it against Kerwin's skull. There was a sickening crack and Kerwin's eyes went wide. He fell back, grasping his head.

For the first time in his life Kerwin Barclay screamed. Trembling, Jamie watched in disbelief as a large, mushy chunk of Kerwin's flesh fell to the ground. It hit the mud with a wet plop and immediately melted into dozens of kicking white spiders. Kerwin staggered around clasping his skull, his scream becoming an eerie, hollow wail that unnerved and agitated the globby spiders. In a few seconds his entire face and neck were covered with dozens of gutted patches where bits of his flesh had fallen away. Patches quickly spread all over his body. And as they hit the ground, each hunk separated into hundreds of individual skittering things.

Then Kerwin melted.

His entire body lost its cohesiveness and he dissolved in on himself. His face, chest, legs—every single part—liquefied into soggy mounds of writhing, shining, jellied spiders. Within a few second all that remained were the entangled blobs that had once been Kerwin.

Jamie heard the other children screaming. They were collapsing and rolling on the ground, shrieking and crying. He watched in horror as he saw blood-stained spiders wiggle out of each child's ear!

He felt his stomach churning and the acidic sting of bile climbed his throat. He hauled on the rope a final time and felt it slip from his ankle. He could see the children limping away into the darkness, clutching one another. A few still lay sobbing in the mud. He wanted to yell at them, to tell them to get away, but he couldn't. Lightning crackled. Jamie leaped to his feet—and the Pale God stood before him.

I Dream of Wires

by Scott David Aniolowski

with very special thanks to Gary Numan

The sun set pale over Brichester, dusting the city in a monochrome twilight. Sallow lights winked on towering and peaked silhouettes, throwing a glowing shroud over the jagged skyline. And with the dark descended the damp coolness of an autumn evening like a fog. Pedestrians snuggled under their coats against the damp chill air and queued for the buses to carry them to the suburbs. Offices closed, shop fronts darkened, and by the dinner hour the daylight bustling of the city melted away into eerie quiet.

Christian Barnett pulled his collar up around his neck to fend off the chill. A tram sped by, crowded with commuters fleeing Brichester for yet another day. Bits of litter and dried leaves caught up in the trail of the bus skittered around the young man's feet, taunting him with brittle laughter. A newspaper—the day's *Brichester Herald*—flapped along the sidewalk on inky wings, finally curling around the base of a lamppost. Christian glanced absently at the paper but the tiny black writing wriggled out of his sight. He continued up Brentan Street toward Ellwood Park and Brichester University.

The young man was approaching his twentieth year—his second at university. He was a slender boy with dark hair and darker eyes. The stiff black fuzz of a few days hung over his upper lip, a striking contrast against otherwise smooth alabaster skin. He wore his hair shaved close on the sides and long on top so it hung over one eye like a curtain—a narrow white streak completed the contrast. Metal glinted in both his almost-pointed ears, around his long fingers, and in spikes all over his black leather jacket. His tight jeans were battered and frayed, both knees slashed wide to the elements. His black boots were scuffed, caked with the grime of the city.

As he crossed to Orrick Road a dark figure bundled in rags passed by. Christian stopped the man and begged a cigarette. A black hand proffered the fag and then a light. The acrid burst of sulfur burned his nose, and in the momentary flare he could see the man's expressionless face, sooty and almost featureless.

"Remind me to smile," said the man.

"Sorry?"

"Cry, the clock said," the stranger replied.

"Here, what are you on about?"

The man did not respond but turned and walked away.

"Crazy bastard." He inhaled the warm tobacco smoke. A mangy beast of a dog glared at him from the corner, its eyes gleaming like headlamps through the haze of the invading dark.

"Piss off," the young man waved at the animal. Its hackles stood and it growled once before lunging past him into darkness.

By the time he'd exhausted the cigarette he was already half way through the park. He could see the shapes of the university buildings just on the other side, beyond the outline of the copse of trees. Spectral denizens haunted the park—whores and drug dealers hawking their wares, and young lovers seeking private havens for their after-dark trysts. The cool wind rustled the branches in the trees, bending and contorting the misshapen blobs set against the murky sky.

A large-breasted woman with serpentine locks approached Christian, slipping deft fingers into the waist of his jeans. He offered her a few quid and steadied himself against the smooth, straight trunk of a towering oak as she earned her wage. The ether above was veiled in flat gray bands, yet sparks flashed through in spots like fireflies. How he wished he'd gotten two cigarettes from the crazy black bastard. His body shuddered once. When she finished he zipped up his trousers, gave her the pound notes, and went on his way.

He climbed the cold stone steps to Payne Hall where he shared a claustrophobic dormitory room with another bloke. The room was a small rectangle of space with matching beds, dressers, and desks. A frayed bit of carpeting hid most of the hardwood floor, movie and rock posters most of the plastered walls. A single dim desk lamp, its shade like flesh stretched taut over a frame, cast a feeble mist of light on the room.

The blond did not look up from his desk when Christian entered the room. His roommate was a taller, muscular lad with round glasses and long hair parted down the middle and gathered into a ponytail in the back. His name was Brian.

"I've almost finished with your portrait," Brian said.

"Yeah?" He dumped his jacket on his unmade bed, its metal ornaments rattling like change. He was shirtless beneath his leather.

Brian held up a large black and white photograph of his roommate, artistically altered into a montage of images. Bits of machines and mechanical workings were grafted onto Christian's form. Gears and wires protruded from his torso and the face of a tiny clock replaced one eye. It was the portrait of a man-machine. "I call it 'The Skin Mechanic'," he said.

"Not bad, that."

"It's not done yet. Almost. If I work straight through, I ought to be able to turn it in tomorrow."

Christian nicked a cigarette from his roommate's desk and turned to the small tombstone-shaped mirror with the spidery crack in one corner that hung on the wall. It took a moment for his eyes to adjust to the artificial twilight of the room, and the face that stared back was dark and alien.

"I got me a bit in the park just now."

"You're going to get the sex skin crawl."

"I want another tattoo," he flexed his pale and poorly sculpted arm, ignoring Brian's comment. It was decorated with a serpent wrapped around a bloody cross. "Maybe on my chest," he inhaled deeply, puffing out his featureless chest.

"I was thinking about going to the literary festival in Cheltenham this weekend," Brian countered.

"Yeah," he mumbled, switching on the small black and white telly. A shaft of ghostly blue light burst from the box, turning his thin body into a cadaverous shadow. "This is the one where The Doctor kills the demon with a silver bullet. The Destroyer." A horned, demonic figure filled the screen.

"Hungry? I thought I'd get something off campus," Brian asked.

"Chinese take-away?"

"No, I'm not in the mood."

"Now what if God's dead?" came the voice from the television. The demon behind the glass turned to Christian. "Sing the new leader's song," it demanded.

He looked to Brian. He hadn't heard it—obviously didn't see it. He shook his head and stared at the glass. The demonic face stared back, a jagged grin breaking across its visage. It reached toward the screen, and then through it. A gnarled, taloned hand stretched out of the glass. It grasped him around the throat, pulling him to the box until his face was flat against the cold glass, eye to eye. "Herald the Tick Tock Man," it laughed triumphantly.

Christian gasped as though the air had been knocked out of his lungs. He pulled back from the screen in a panic. The grip extricated and he fell backwards to the floor. When he looked to the small box the program was progressing normally. The demon was gone.

Brian looked over the top of his desk.

"I tripped on the carpet," he gathered himself up.

"So, are you hungry?"

"I'm a bit peckish." A cursory examination of the glass screen indicated that all was normal. The young man told himself that he must have been hallucinating and mentally swore off cheap drugs.

A short, brisk walk brought the pair to the restaurant on Webb Street. Large smoky windows looked out onto the park. A crowd of young people—students mostly, from the university—loitered near the entrance. They looked alien bathed in the garish purple-red light from twisted neon tubes above. It burned Christian's eyes to stare into the harsh purple-red. Wisps of cigarette smoke and steam from manhole covers curled up into the odd-colored light, taking everything out of focus.

They shouldered their way through the crowd; strains of haunting synthesizer greeted them as they pulled back the heavy door. Shafts of harsh white light cut through thick smoky air. A long bar dominated one entire wall, with small, high triangular tables filling most of the rest of the area. A narrow dance floor ran the length of the back of the building; a small booth of black glass occupied a corner.

"Welcome to Zom Zoms," said a smallish figure at the door, his voice odd and almost mechanical. He was wrapped in a white tunic and pants, with high white boots. His face was as white as his clothes but his lips were deep blue: the same blue lined his dark eyes and frosted his eyebrows and short black hair. A small loop decorated each ear.

"Zom Zoms?" Christian couldn't recall having seen or heard of the place, even as close as it was to campus.

"A place to eat like it was built in one day," said the white and blue figure, like an enigma machine.

"Two, Gary," Brian gestured to himself and his roommate.

"We are here to serve you," nodded the host. He led them to a table near the front windows where the techno-pop wasn't so loud.

"This is a good table," said Brian.

"You can watch the humans trying to run," Gary replied.

"He's an odd bloke," Christian mumbled as the figure in white disappeared into the crowd. A familiar face fell into his roving gaze. She was tall, thin, and wore a snug black dress cut high up one leg. She had sharp crimson nails and eyes painted like an Egyptian queen, her auburn hair up in a hive and falling long down the back of her neck. Their eyes met, and the corners of her ruby lips curled into a delicate smile.

"Chris," she purred in his ear as she glided to the table.

"Zara," he smiled. They embraced and kissed.

Brian coughed once.

"Zara, this is my mate Brian—." He hesitated. "Brian—." A deep furrow formed in his brow, and he looked to his companion for assistance.

"Collis—Brian Collis," the blond youth interjected. He extended a hand to the young woman.

"Zara. It's very nice to meet you, Brain Collis," she took his hand. She spoke with an accent Brian didn't recognize.

A tall figure approached the table. He wore a black jumpsuit with a pair of thin red belts around his waist and another pair over one shoulder. "I'm your waiter, Jo," he said.

"Brian Collis" wasn't right. The name didn't sound familiar. He knew Brian's surname—he was sure of it—yet it wouldn't come to him. His mind raced, searching for information about Brian—memory. He found none.

Then everything began to blur. Sounds became distorted, muffled roars—slow and drawn out, like a record played at the wrong speed. Christian felt as though he was falling and reached out to steady himself, but found nothing to grasp.

A brilliant flash of whiteness, and several blurred silhouettes stood over him, their voices deep and droning. He tried to rise—to speak—but couldn't. Everything was bright and hazy and white. The alien voices buzzed like a hive of insects in his head. His eyes watered from the brightness, his ears ached from the buzzing. He could make out something—a little bit.

"Ssllleeepruumm," said one of the distorted voices.

The shapes of machines and wires began to take form. A mechanical landscape of keyboards and wires and winking circuits. And an incandescent sun.

Then his vision cleared again and he was perched on a high stool at the small triangular table with Brian. "Snap out of it," he heard Brian say.

"Dream corrosion," he mumbled.

"What?"

He was disoriented, his head spinning.

"You'll feel better once you eat," Brian insisted.

"We haven't ordered."

"We have. Don't you remember?"

"Zara?"

"Don't know," he shrugged. "She disappeared when the waiter came. Probably went back to wherever she came from."

"She's got claws."

"Quite a looker."

"Like a stormtrooper in drag."

Shortly, Jo the waiter returned with their food and drink. They ate, while searing white shafts cut through the rolling fog-like thickness and mechanical music buzzed.

As he ate, Christian watched out the long smoky window. The crowd outside thinned until only a few youths lingered beneath the burning neon. A familiar dark figure appeared at the window. He peered through the glass and smiled stiffly, teeth black and rotten. "Pray to the aliens," chuckled the figure, and he turned and walked away. A pair of hounds followed and licked his hands.

"The crazy sod," Christian blurted out.

Brian glanced over his shoulder. There was no one there.

"I saw that bloke earlier. On Orrick Road."

"Who?"

"You didn't see him? That black man in rags?"

"I didn't."

Two pairs of eyes glared back at Christian out of fog. Or maybe it was just the headlamps of passing cars.

The young men took Webb Street to Brentan Street and began the steep climb to the university.

"Where are you from, again?" Christian asked his companion.

"North, up the coast from Liverpool near Pine Dunes. You know that."

It didn't ring familiar. He felt puzzled.

"And you're studying?"

"Do you feel all right?"

"I'm confused," he hesitated. "Weird things have been happening to me all night. Now I can't remember things."

"Probably just need a good night's sleep. Feel good as new in the morning."

A crowd in formal attire queued at the Riordan Theatre to see the Brichester production of a popular musical. The theater's turn-of-the-century architecture was eerie in the shadows of the night; the marquee's lines of dazzling lights did little to dispel the oppressiveness. An enormous white mask glared down onto the slope of Brentan Street from the roof of the Riordan, mocking the rows of people in black and white.

A block up the incline stood a tuxedoed figure in silhouette. A long cloak billowed around him, and as they neared Christian could make out a white mask covering his face. He looked to Brian and they both shrugged.

"Must be from the Riordan. Probably for publicity," Brian said.

The cloaked figure spread open its arms to them. "The sleeproom still waits for you," he said.

"Who are you?" Christian shouted.

"We're dreams in cold storage," the man answered in a resonant voice. He pulled off the white half-mask and beneath was the black face of the vagrant.

"You! Bugger off, you wanker," Christian taunted.

"I die: You die," he replied.

"What do you want?"

The black figure tugged at his expressionless face, peeling back the flesh to reveal wires and gears and mechanical workings. "I close up my brain and another friend dies," he laughed.

"The Tick Tock Man," gasped Brian.

* * *

The sun cried morning, waking Christian from his sleep. All was a blur. He rubbed the sleep from his eyes and focused on an outline at the window.

"Did I wake you?" Brian asked. Morning harshness streamed in around him.

"I must have been dreaming."

"I couldn't sleep. The machmen were in the park last night chanting 'Death, death, death.' I'm surprised it didn't wake you. They didn't stop until the sun came up."

"What are you on about?" He sat up stiffly in the bed, burying his face in his hands. His head throbbed and every movement caused dizziness and nausea. "Bloody hell," he groaned.

"They were with the machines playing kill-by-numbers."

"What did we do last night?" he murmured between his fingers.

"We went to eat when you got back."

"Yeah?"

"And then we came back here. You watched the telly and I finished the portrait." Brian leaned over his desk and held up the black and white photograph. "See?"

"What about the bloke on Brentan Street?"

Brian looked at him blankly, shook his head.

"You remember–the black sod. You called him 'the Tick Tock Man.'"

"You were dreaming," Brian insisted.

"Who's the Tick Tock Man?"

"Didn't your mum or gran ever tell you stories about the Tick Tock Man?"

"No."

"He's a clockwork man—part man, part machine. The bogey man. He's called the Skin Mechanic, too. That's probably why you dreamt of him—because of your portrait. I entitled it 'The Skin Mechanic.' Remember? A man-machine?"

"Why can't I remember anything about you?"

Christian's vision clouded again. Slow, distorted roars replaced sounds. He lost his equilibrium and fell backward—or forward. His tactile senses were in chaos: Directional sense and touch were foreign. The brilliant whiteness returned, and the fuzzy silhouettes. Again he tried to move but couldn't. He screamed at the figures, but no sound came from his throat. The light bothered his eyes, like he had just come into the sun after having been in darkness for a very long time, but slowly his eyes began to adjust.

Several of the shadowy forms gathered around a machine like bees around a blossom, bathed in a sickly, flickering cathode glow. An intricate web of wires and cables sprouted from the mechanical mass, but they terminated or connected somewhere beyond his limited, hazy view. It was like some great electrical plant with vines and branches spread in all directions.

One of the shapes broke away from the swarm and bent close to him. The youth could see his own reflection in its large, unblinking glassy eyes. There were wires attached to his head, and he could barely see wires on his chest.

"Fffiivvvv," said the being in its deep drone.

"INITIATE SEARCH," came the synthetic voice. "LOCATE ERROR," it continued. It was in Christian's head. "INITIATE BARNETT PROGRAM."

And then his vision cleared and he was standing in front of the window.

" ... straight away before I'm late," Brian finished.

Christian stared at him.

"Are you coming?"

He sank back to the bed, shaking his head. "I think I'm going mad," he sobbed.

* * *

Webb Street was alive with morning traffic, business people and shoppers. Zom Zoms was silent and dark. He pressed his face to the glass. There was nothing to see, just dark emptiness. The exhaust-heavy breeze blew bits of litter around his feet.

"We take mystery to bed," came an odd, almost mechanical, yet familiar voice.

Christian saw the smallish figure standing behind him, reflected in the window. He wore a tan pinstriped suit, double-breasted jacket, and a matching fedora. His lips were silver and his eyes outlined by thick black. A single small hoop hung from each ear.

"You're the doorman," he turned, recognized the man.

"I'm an agent on the joy circuit. The 1930's rust."

"You remember me, then?"

"Steel and you."

"Then do you recall what time I left last night?"

"My brother's time."

"What does that mean?"

"Are you real?"

"Am I real? Of course I'm real!"

"Stay away from the zero bars. The dream police are looking for you," he said in his odd voice and turned.

"Wait," Christian made to grab his arm, but his hand passed through.

"Remember I was vapor. I'm off to catch a subway called 'you'," and the smallish man was gone.

He slumped to the pavement, back against the cold face of the building. Everything was coming apart, or he was going mad. He stared out onto the street where images and people faded in and out like shadows in vain. The scene began to break into tiny colored shapes and fractal bits. Mandelbrot's puzzle unraveled before his eyes.

Thunder or an explosion rumbled in the distance. A siren sounded and a voice blared: "CALL OUT THE DOGS." It was cold and mechanical, yet distinctly feminine. Somewhere, a police siren warbled and dogs howled. The sky became as coal and the wind smelled hot and electrical.

Christian was alone on the street, cast in a searing purple-red. The great tubes of scorching light wriggled like serpents. Glowing coils fell around him and with a single constriction they hoisted him up, forcing the air from his lungs. The street below melted away, replaced by gleaming metal. From out of the distance came a parade of dark, androgynous figures in black suitcoats and stiletto heels. Each was identical, with a flat-top haircut and dark almond-shaped glasses. The line of goosestepping figures was endless, the clacking of their heels like the maddening time of a metronome. Above, the sky was a circuit board full of diode stars.

He struggled against the coils, kicking and writhing. "We are glass," he screamed. "We are so fragile."

A horse-drawn coach thundered around the corner, hooves and wheels throwing off sparks. The horses exhaled clouds of roiling exhaust and their eyes shone brightly like electrical torches. A pack of yowling, snapping hounds chased behind. They were horrible clockwork beasts, as much machine as flesh.

Glass shattered and the young man fell to the ground in a heap. The horses bore down on him—the ground trembled beneath their hooves. They would be on him before he could move. The sound of his own breathing exploded in his ears. He closed his eyes and threw his hands up in a vain attempt at protection.

Silence.

Slowly, he opened his eyes. Hooves were inches from his head. He looked up into the motionless, painted face of the merry-go-round horse. There stood a black coach and four plastic horses. He pulled himself to his feet, trembling and damp with sweat. Gone were the marching clone-figures and the growling dog-machines.

"Welcome to Zom Zoms," came the now-familiar voice like a silicon dream.

He turned. It was the smallish figure in white and blue. He gestured to the young man from a crowd in front of the building with the garish purple-red neon.

A figure in a long black trench and fedora jumped from the coachman's seat. It was Brian. He tipped his hat to Christian and opened the coach door, extending a gloved hand to the passenger. A black figure stepped down. His eyes were two small clock faces.

"The life machine," snickered Brian.

Christian backed away.

"Me, I disconnect from you," said the black man with the clock eyes. He laughed.

Christian turned to run, but something had him by the arm. He struggled to pull away.

"Chris, come on." Brian shook his roommate.

He broke away and fell, damp earth and grass beneath him. They were down in the park. A warm afternoon breeze rusted nearly bare tree branches, their few remaining leaves rattling dry and dead. Brian moved to help his companion up.

"Stay away from me," he cried.

"What is it? One minute we're walking to class and the next this." Brian gestured to his friend cowering at his feet.

"You were there. With the Tick Tock Man," he choked.

"What are you talking about?"

"Your breathing haunts me."

"You're not making sense, mate." Brian squatted down near his roommate.

"No, something's not right. It's you. I'm not crazy." He fumbled to his feet.

"Then what is it?"

"I dream of wires!"

Brian just looked at him. Terror had settled into Christian's dark eyes.

"What's the sleeproom? You have to tell me!" He grabbed Brian's collar.

"I don't know, I swear." Brian pulled away.

"ERROR. PERSONALITY MALFUNCTION. LOCATE AND CORRECT," came the artificial voice in Christian's head.

"You do know. You're a part of all this."

"Steady there," Brian insisted.

"You know bloody well what's going on."

"Everything breaks down, and me, I'm trapped inside." Brian finally turned and ran through the park.

Christian followed but the wire grass tangled his feet, slowed him down. Metallic leaves rang like chimes in trees of twisted cables. Machmen in bowler hats and old school ties gathered in the park, and a rape machine prowled for victims.

"ACCESSING FILES," came the voice again. He tried to shut it out.

Brian dashed into Selby Road, his roommate close behind. A fire burned in Christian's chest and he struggled to force the voice from his head.

A tram came screeching around the corner. Christian spotted it too late. He screamed once for Brian but it all seemed like dreams in slow motion. He watched the speeding bus approach, frozen in time and space. It struck and then was gone, a huge mechanical predator hunting fleshy prey.

A crowd gathered like flies. Brian was on his back in the road, blood trickling from his mouth. Christian knelt next to him, cradling his head. Brian opened his eyes and tried to speak. "This machine runs down," he choked.

"Someone call a medic," screamed Christian.

Brian shook his head. "Time to see the God film," he coughed. He motioned for his mate to bend closer. "Five, are friends electric?" he managed to whisper. The blood thickened and turned black. The ticking stopped and he was still.

Christian sat in the street, holding the broken body of his friend while the world spun around him. A pain throbbed in his side; his leather was wet. He reached beneath his jacket to feel the warm wetness and the torn flesh. Dark, thick oil covered his hand. The ruptured flesh exposed bits of broken wire and gears.

"My dying machine." He held himself and sobbed. Faces and forms faded in and out. He heard music and screams and discordant mechanical whining: white noise. He felt faint, and reclined on the hard pavement next to Brian's motionless form.

"Fffiivvvv," said the deep and droning voice.

He looked about. He was in the bright white place. Rippled sheets of light shone down in his face. He tried to rise but something restrained his head and his wrists. He felt a chill, and metal cold against his bare back. He couldn't see beyond his chest, but felt the warmth of clothes below his waist.

There were others in his peripheral vision. Other people on metal tables, naked from the waist up. Each had straps around his wrist and forehead, and wires attached to his head and chest like a hospital patient. He couldn't tell how many others there were, but they were all asleep.

And he saw machines—or one great machine. Gurneys holding the people were arranged around an island of monitors and keyboards and cables. The filaments attached to heads and chests plugged into the computer: flies caught in the wire web of a mechanical spider. Christian was one of those flies.

The alien figures hovered about him, buzzing and droning in his ears. He closed his eyes, squeezing out the brightness, squeezing out the weird figures. Slowly, sounds cleared. Several voices chattered around him. Intelligible voices. Human voices. When he opened his eyes it was people in lab coats that stood around him, not explorers from another world.

"Subject Five is awake," said a woman, her black hair pulled back into a tight braid. She clutched a clipboard close to her.

"Check the program." A balding man with glasses peered closely at him. The man's hands were cold against his skin.

"Where am I?"

"Not to worry, Mr. Barnett. You're safe." It was the woman with the black braid.

"This is the sleeproom," Christian said.

"This is the Dughall Computer Lab. You're at the University," corrected the balding man. He flashed a tiny light first in Christian's right eye and then his left. "Subject is fully conscious."

"What are you doing to me?"

"Dream corrosion. The program has been prematurely terminated. Prepare the subject for reintroduction," the balding man continued.

"Hey, answer me." He struggled against his bonds; wires from his forehead fell loose.

"Shh, calm yourself," soothed the woman with the braid.

"You volunteered to be a test subject. Don't you remember?" said a man with a full white beard.

"No, get away from me." He bucked and squirmed. The bearded man and another woman held him down.

"Get me the gas," shouted the balding man as he replaced the disturbed wires.

Someone clamped a mask over Christian's mouth and nose. He could hear the hiss.

"THIS DARK FACADE ENDS." It was the voice from his head, only it wasn't in his head now. It came from the computer.

"You're the Tick Tock Man," the youth mumbled from beneath the mask.

"YOU STEP ON MY DREAMS," said the machine.

"You're an explorer, my boy," cooed the balding man, "among the first to make contact with artificial intelligence. It has been inside your mind and has created a whole world in your subconscious."

Images began to blur, and sounds drone. Christian's whole body tingled.

"THOUGHTS NUMBER TWO. CHECK IT. INITIATE BARNETT PROGRAM."

Sleep stalked him. He tried to resist, struggled in vain. Little remained but a hazy whiteness and a humming. And snatches of fractal images in his mind's eye. Finally, sleep swept him away and he was still, only the rythmic rising and falling of his chest.

"ASSASSINATION OF THE VOICE OF GOD," said the Tick Tock Man.

Christian Barnett slept and he dreamt—of wires.

The Turret

by Richard A. Lupoff

I was not really surprised when my employer, Alexander Myshkin, called me into his office and offered me the assignment to troubleshoot our Zeta/Zed System at the Klaus Fuchs Memorial Institute in Old Severnford. The Zeta/Zed System was Myshkin Associates' prize product, the most advanced hardware-software lashup in the world, Myshkin liked to boast, and the Fuchs Institute was to have been our showpiece installation.

Unfortunately, while the Zeta/Zed performed perfectly in the Myshkin lab in Silicon Valley, California, once it was transported to the Severn Valley in England, glitches appeared in its functioning and bugs in its programs. The customer was first distressed, then frustrated, and finally angry. Myshkin had the Fuchs Institute modem its data to California, where it ran perfectly on the in-house Zeta/Zed and was then modemed back to England. This was the only way Myshkin could placate the customer, even temporarily, but we knew that if the system in Old Severnford could not be brought on-line and into production, the Institute could order our equipment removed. They could replace it with a system from one of our competitors, and further could even sue Myshkin Associates for the lost time and expense they had put into our failed product.

"Park," Alexander Myshkin said to me as soon as I entered his office in response to his summons, "Park, the future of this company is in your hands. If we lose the Fuchs Institute, we could be out of business in six months. We're hanging onto that account by our fingernails. You've got to get that system running for the customer."

I asked Myshkin why our marketing and technical support teams in the UK had not solved the problem. "We have good people over there," I told my employer. "I know some of them, and I've seen their work."

Myshkin said, "You're right, Park." (My name is Parker Lorentzen; Lorentzen for obvious reasons, Parker in honor of a maternal ancestor who actually hailed from the Severn Valley. I had never seen the region, and was inclined to accept the assignment for that reason alone.)

"You're right," my employer repeated, "but they haven't been able to solve it. Somehow I don't think they *like* visiting this account. They don't like staying anywhere in the Severn Valley and they absolutely refuse to put up in Old Severnford itself. I've never been there myself, but I've seen the pictures, as I'm sure you have."

I admitted that I had.

"The countryside is beautiful. Rolling hills, ancient ruins, the Severn River itself and those smaller streams, the Ton and the Cam. I'll admit, a certain, well, call it *sense of gloom* seems to hang over the area, but we're modern people, enlightened technologists, not a pack of credulous rustics."

"True enough, chief. All right, no need to twist my arm." I gazed past him. Beyond the window the northern California hills rolled away, lush with greenery. I found myself unconsciously touching the little blue birthmark near my jawline. It was smaller than a dime, and oddly shaped. Some claimed that it resembled an infinity sign; others, an hourglass; still others, an ankh, the Egyptian symbol of immortality. My physician had assured me that it was not precancerous or in any other way dangerous. Nor was it particularly unsightly; women sometimes found it fascinating.

My mother had had a similar formation on her jaw. She called it a beauty mark and said that it was common among the Parkers.

"Thanks, Park," Alexander Myshkin resumed. "You're my top troubleshooter, you know. If you can't fix a problem, it can't be fixed."

Within twenty-four hours I had jetted across the country, transferred from my first-class seat in a Boeing jumbo jet to the cramped quarters of the Anglo-French Concorde, and left the western hemisphere behind for my first visit to England, the homeland of half my ancestors.

I stayed only one night in London, not sampling that city's fabled theaters or museums but simply resting up, trying to rid myself of the jetlag inherent in a body still running on California time even though it had been relocated some eight or nine time zones. I boarded a wheezing, groaning train that carried me from fabled Victoria Station through Exham and the very peculiar-looking town of Goatswood and thence to its terminus at Brichester.

My luggage consisted of a single valise. In this I had placed my warmest clothing, a tweed suit and Irish hat that I had purchased years before in an English shop in San Francisco and reserved for trips from California to areas of less salubrious climate. I carried an umbrella and, slung from my shoulder, a canvas case containing a notebook computer.

In Brichester I spent my second night in England. The inn where I lodged was old and run-down. It contained a pub on its ground floor, and I looked forward to an evening of good fellowship, a tankard of beer (perhaps more than one!), and a platter of good English beef before bed.

Alas, I was disappointed on every count. The beef was tough, stringy, and overdone. The beer was watery and flat. But most disheartening of all, the local residents, for all that they appeared just the colorful and eccentric folk that I had hoped to encounter, proved a taciturn and unforthcoming lot. They responded to my opening conversational ploys with monosyllabic grunts, and rejected my further attempts at camaraderie by pointedly turning their backs and engaging in low, muttered dialogues, casting unfriendly glances from time to time at the obviously unwelcome interloper in their midst—myself.

After chewing futilely at the beef until my jaws ached, and giving up on the poor beer that the innkeeper served, I finally retiredearly, not so much from fatigue, for my body was beginning to recover from its jetlag, but simply because I could find no comfort in the surroundings of this disappointing pub and its hostile clientele.

In the morning I was awakened by a pale wash of sunlight that seemed barely able to penetrate the gray and lowering sky that I soon learned was typical of most days in the Severn Valley. I found myself wondering why the residents of these towns remained there—why, in fact, their ancestors had ever settled in this gloomy and unpleasant region.

At first I thought it fortunate that I had brought my cellular telephone with me—my room at the inn, of course, had no such modern convenience—but of course I got nowhere with the local telephone system when I tried to place a call. Eventually I located a pay station, however, and spent most of the day conducting business. I spoke several times with Alexander Myshkin, and let me not rehearse the agonies of placing a call from a decrepit pay station in the Severn Valley town of Brichester to Myshkin Associates in Silicon Valley, California. I finally reached my employer, after being cut off several times by malign operators somewhere in the British telephone system, and at least once by Myshkin's own secretary, who apologized effusively once the connection was re-established, only to cut me off again.

Myshkin brought me up to date on further tests which were being run continuously on the Zeta/Zed System in our California laboratory. The system, of course, performed flawlessly, leaving me no less baffled than beforehand by the reported problems at the Fuchs Institute installation.

I succeeded in reaching the Institute as well, for all that I was distressed at how difficult it was to do so. Silicon Valley was some 6,000 miles from the Severn Valley. That was at least some mitigation for the difficulties in communication. But my call from Brichester to Old Severnford, a matter of a mere few miles, was interrupted several times by unexplained disconnections. Even when I was in communication with my opposite number at the Fuchs Institute, one Karolina Parker—I found myself wondering if we might be related through my mother's side of the family—conversation was not easy. There was a curious buzzing and an occasional unpleasant *scraping* sound on the wire. I asked Karolina if she was not disturbed by these noises, but she denied hearing them. She suggested that they were all at my end of the hook-up—or perhaps in my mind. The latter implication did not sit well with me, but I made no point of it at the time.

Eventually I took a late and unpleasant dinner in Brichester, in a restaurant some distance from my inn. There was not a single other customer in the establishment, and yet it took the waiter a long time to approach me. His manner was surly, and I got the feeling that the management would have been happier to forego my trade than to have it. The surroundings were stuffy and utterly devoid of decoration or distraction. As had been the case with my dinner the previous evening, the food was bland in flavor, unpleasant in texture, and served at a uniform degree of lukewarmness, whether the dish was a supposedly chilled madrilène or an allegedly freshly broiled mutton chop.

Abandoning the sorry repast after a half-hearted attempt to consume it, I paid my bill and, leaving the restaurant with a silent vow never to return, hefted my single valise and began the trek to Old Severnford. With difficulty I was able to hire a car and driver who insisted on being paid in advance for his services. I was not pleased with the arrangement, but, feeling that I had no choice, I consented.

The car was of uncertain ancestry and vintage; its transmission was badly sprung and I suspected that its heater was connected directly to its exhaust pipe—the chill of the day was dispelled, all right, but was replaced in the car by a choking unpleasantness far worse.

The afternoon had turned a dark gray, and it was impossible to tell just when the sun dropped beneath the rolling, sinister hills beyond the Severn River to the west, save for the moment when my driver switched on the car's headlamps. They cast a feeble, amber patch of light on the narrow and ill-repaired roadway ahead of us.

The driver stayed muffled deep in his sweaters and overcoat, a visored cap with furry earflaps covering most of his face. He wore a pair of mirrored eyeglasses—a peculiarly modern touch in this archaic valley—and between his upturned collar and the visor and earflaps of his headgear, all that I could see of his face was the mirrored lenses and a huge, walrus moustache, grayed with age and yellowed with I knew not what.

We reached the Severn River without incident, save for a few bicycling schoolchildren—these, among the very few children I ever saw in the Severn region—who halted their bikes and pointed as we passed them in the roadway. I thought at first that they were waving a friendly greeting and waved back at them, pleased at this sign, however slight, of cheer and goodwill.

Once more I was mistaken. Quickly I realized that their gestures were not friendly waves, but some sort of mystical sign, whether intended to ward off evil or to bring harm upon me. One boy, who seemed almost unnaturally large and muscular for his age, but whose face appeared unformed and vaguely animal-like, hurled a large rock after my car. The rock struck the rear of the car, and for a moment I thought the driver was going to stop and berate the children, but instead he pressed down on the accelerator and sped us away from there, muttering something beneath his breath that I was unable to make out.

The driver brought the car to a halt in a decrepit dockside district of Severnford. Full night had fallen by now, and the quays and piers before us seemed utterly deserted. I asked the driver if he would wait for a ferry to carry us to Old Severnford, and if he would then drive me to the Klaus Fuchs Memorial Institute.

He turned around then, gazing at me over the rear of his seat. I had switched on the cars tiny domelight, and it reflected off his mirrored glasses. "Last ferry's run, mister," he husked. "And meuns don't fancy spending no night by these docks. You get out. Get out now, and you're on your own."

I started to protest, but the driver leaped from the car with surprising agility for so bulky and aged an individual. He yanked open the door beside which I sat, caught my lapels in two thickly gloved hands, and lifted me bodily from the car, depositing me in no dignified condition on the cracked and weedy sidewalk. He hurled my valise after me, jumped back into his vehicle and sped away, leaving me angered, puzzled, and utterly uncertain as to how to resolve my predicament.

I recovered my valise and tested my notebook computer to reassure myself that it was undamaged. I then pondered my next move. If the Severn Ferry had indeed ceased its runs for the night, I could not possibly reach Old Severnford before morning. I did not know my way around the town of Severnford itself, and with a shudder of apprehension I set out to explore.

At first I walked beside the river. A moon had risen, apparently full, yet so cloaked by heavy clouds as to appear only a vague, pale disk in the sky, while furnishing the most minimal of watery illumination to the earth. But as my eyes grew accustomed to the darkness, I realized that there was another source of illumination, faint and inauspicious.

A glow seemed to come from beneath the surface of the Severn River. Seemed? No, it was there, it was all too real. I tried to make out its source, but vague shapes seemed to move, deep in the river for the most part, but darting toward the surface now and again, and then slithering away once more into the depths. And a mist arose from the sluggishly flowing water, and gave off a glow of its own, or perhaps it was that it reflected the glow of the river and the vague, luminous shapes therein. Or yet again, were there shapes *within the mist* as well, floating and darting like fairies in a garden in a child's book?

The sight should have been charming, almost pretty, but for some reason it sent a shudder down my back. With an effort I turned away and made my way up an ancient street, leading at a slight uphill slant from the river and the docks and into the heart of town.

Perhaps I had merely strayed into the wrong part of Severnford, or perhaps there was something about the town itself that set off silent shrieks of alarm within me. I could find no establishment open, no person to ask for assistance. Instead I paced darkened streets, chilled and dampened by the night. Once I thought I heard voices, rough and furtive in tone, murmuring in a language I could neither comprehend nor identify. Twice I heard scuffling footsteps, but upon whirling clumsily with my valise and computer weighing me down, I saw nothing. Thrice I thought I heard odd twitterings, but could find no source or explanations for them.

How many miles I trudged that night, finding my way from alley to courtyard to square, I can only guess. I can only say that the first pallid gray shafts of morning light were as welcome to me as any sight I had ever beheld. I was able, by heading steadily downward, to find my way back to the docks.

In the morning light the mist was lifting off the Severn, the hills on its far shore looked almost welcoming, and the disquieting shapes and lights beneath the river's surface were no longer to be seen.

I located the quay where the Severn Ferry made its stops and waited for the morning's first run. I was rewarded soon by sight of an ancient barge, something more suitable to a motion picture about nineteenth century life than to a modern enterprise. Nonetheless cheered, I climbed aboard, paid my fare, and waited with a small party of taciturn passengers until the ferryman saw fit to weigh anchor and transport us across the slowly flowing water.

I tried my cellular telephone from on board the ferry, and by some miracle of electronics managed to get through to the Fuchs Institute. I spoke with Karolina Parker, who expressed concern as to my welfare and my whereabouts. As briefly as possible, I explained my situation and she said that she would personally greet me at the pier in Old Severnford.

She proved as good as her word. I found her a delightful young woman, perhaps a few years younger than I, but showing so marked a family resemblance as to remove all doubt as to our being related. I explained to her about my Parker ancestors, and she astonished me by planting a most uncousinly kiss on my mouth, even as we sat in her modern and comfortable automobile.

I was still puzzling over this remarkable behavior when we arrived at the Klaus Fuchs Memorial Institute. Karolina Parker introduced me to the director of the institute, whose friendly greeting was tempered by his assertion that I was expected to resolve the troubles of the Zeta/Zed system post haste, if Myshkin Associates was to retain the Fuchs Institute as an account.

Without stopping to arrange lodging in the town of Old Severnford itself, I set to work on the Institute's Zeta/Zed machines. The system was taken off-line, which did not please the director, and I ran a series of diagnostic programs in turn on the mainframe processor, the satellite work stations, and the peripheral units that ran under system control.

As long as I used only sample data for testing, Zeta/Zed performed to perfection. It might be thought that I would be pleased with this result, but in fact the opposite was the case. If the system had malfunctioned, I possessed the tools (or believed that I did) to narrow down the area of malfunction until a specific site in the hardware or software remained. This could then be examined for its flaw and repaired or replaced.

When nothing went wrong, I could correct nothing.

"Very well," my hostess, Karolina Parker, suggested, "let's go back on line while you observe, Mr. Lorentzen."

I was as surprised by the coldness of her address as I had been by the warmth of her greeting in the car, but I could think of no response better than a simple, "All right."

Zeta/Zed was placed back on line. Almost at once error messages began flashing on the main monitor screen, but the system did not shut down. I permitted it to run until a batch of data had been processed, then attempted to print out the results.

The high-speed laser printer hummed, then began spitting out sheet after sheet of paper. I tried to read the top sheet, but it seemed to contain sheer gibberish. The printout comprised an almost random pattern of numbers, letters, and symbols which I knew were not part of any font supplied by Myshkin software. I asked Karolina Parker about this, but she insisted that no one had tampered with the software and no virus could have been introduced into the system as it was swept by anti-virus software regularly.

What could be the answer?

I asked Karolina Parker the source of the Institute's power supply, and was told that the Institute generated its own power, the River Severn turning a generator housed in a separate building. In this manner the Institute was independent of the vagaries of the local power system, antiquated and unreliable as it was known to be.

Furnished with a sparse cubicle from which to conduct my affairs, I soon sat alone with the enigmatic printouts. I had been furnished with a meal of sorts from the Institute's commissary, and I sat eating a stale sandwich, pausing to wash it down with occasional swigs of cold, stale coffee, trying to make head or tail of these pages.

After a while I found a passage that seemed less chaotic than what had gone before. The printing was in Roman letters, not mathematical formulas, and by concentrating on the "words" (which were in fact not any words I recognized), moving my lips like a child just learning to read, and letting the sounds that were suggested pass my lips, I realized that this was the same language I had heard the previous night as I wandered the streets of Severnford.

By quitting time I was tired, nervous, and eager to find a warm meal and a soft mattress, if such amenities even existed in this accursed Severn Valley.

To my astonishment, Karolina Parker offered me a ride home in her automobile, and even offered me room and lodging in her house. I insisted that such hospitality, while appreciated, was excessive, but she replied that everything should be done to make my visit pleasant. We were, after all, family!

Karolina Parker's home was a pleasant house set in the center of a modest but beautifully tended park-like estate. The house itself was of late Tudor style, with half-timbered beams and diamond-pane windows. There was a great fireplace in the living room, and through the front windows I could see the peculiar topiary shrubs that stood outside like unfamiliar beasts grazing an alien landscape.

My hostess explained to me that she lived alone, and showed me to a comfortable bedroom which she said would be mine during my stay in Old Severnford. She suggested that I refresh myself while she prepared dinner for us both.

An hour later I was summoned to dine in a charming informal room. Karolina apologized for her impromptu mode of entertaining, but I found both her manner and the meal which she served me the high points of my until-now dismal journey. She had decked herself out in a pair of tight-fitting blue jeans and a tee shirt with a portrait of Klaus Fuchs himself blazoned on it. Over this amazing outfit she wore a frilly apron.

She served me a delicious ratatouille accompanied by an excellent white wine (imported from northern California, I noted with some pride) and a crisp green salad. How this attractive young woman could work all day at the Institute and still entertain in such delightful fashion afterwards was quite beyond my power of comprehension.

After the meal we repaired to the living room and shared coffee (hot, fresh, and strong!) and brandy before a roaring fire. Oddly portentous selections of Carl Philip Emanuel Bach and Georg Philipp Telemann came from the speakers of a superb sound system. Karolina and I spoke of computers, of her work at the Fuchs Institute and mine at Myshkin Associates. We tried to trace our common ancestry but ran into a blank wall somewhere around the year 1665. At no time did we speak of our personal lives. I did not know whether she had ever been married, for instance, or seriously involved with a man, nor did she query me with regard to such sensitive (and for me, painful) matters.

The sound system must have been preprogrammed, for after a while I found myself drawn into a complex composition by Charles Ives, and then into one of the stranger sound pieces of Edgar Varese. Our conversation had turned to the history of the Severn Valley, its peculiar isolation from the rest of England, and the odd whispered hints that were sometimes heard regarding the dark countryside and its inhabitants.

I fear that my stressful journey and my lack of sleep the previous night caught up with me, for I caught myself yawning at one point, and Karolina Parker, gracious hostess that she was, suggested that I retire.

"I'll stay downstairs to clean up a little," she volunteered. "You can find your room again, of course?"

I thought to offer a familial hug before retiring, but instead I found Karolina returning my gesture with a fierce embrace and another of her incredible kisses. I broke away in confusion and made my way to my room without speaking another word. I locked the door and placed a chair beneath the doorknob before disrobing, then climbed gratefully into bed and fell asleep almost at once.

I do not know how much later it was that I was awakened by—*by what?*, I asked myself. Was it a careful rattling of the doorknob of my room? Was it a voice calling to me? And in words of what language—the familiar tongue which Americans and Britons have shared for centuries, or that other, stranger language that I had heard in the streets of Severnford and had myself spoken, almost involuntarily, as I struggled to decipher the peculiar printouts of the Zeta/Zed system at the Fuchs Institute?

Whatever it was—whoever it was—quickly departed from my ken, and I sought to return to sleep, but, alas, I was now too thoroughly wakened to do so easily. I did not wish to leave my room; I cannot tell you why—I simply felt that there were things, or might be things, in that pleasant, comfortable house that I would rather not encounter.

So instead I seated myself in a comfortable chair near the window of my room and gazed over the Severn landscape. I could see but little of the village of Old Severnford, for this was a community where the residents retired early and stayed in their homes, the doors securely locked and the lights turned low, perhaps for fear that they attract visitors not welcome.

Raising my eyes to the hills above, I saw their rounded forms as of ancient, sleeping beings, silhouetted in absolute blackness against the midnight blue sky. The clouds that had obscured the moon and stars earlier had dissipated and the heavens were punctuated by a magnificent scattering of stars and galaxies such as the city lights that blazed all night in the Silicon Valley could never reveal.

I permitted my gaze to drift lower, to the Severn Hills, when I was startled to perceive what appeared to be an artificial construct. This structure was in the form of a tower surmounted by a peculiarly made battlement or turret. I had thought the Severn Hills uninhabited save for a few examples of sparse and ill-nourished wildlife, hunted on occasion by locals seeking to add to their meager larders.

Even more surprising, the turret appeared to be illuminated from within. I strained my eyes to see clearly that which was before me. Yes, there were lights blazing from within the turret—if blazing is a word which may be applied to these dim, flickering, tantalizing lights. If I permitted my fancy to roam, the lights would almost form themselves into a face. Two great, hollow eyes staring blindly into the darkness, a central light like a nasal orifice, and beneath that a wide, narrow mouth grinning wickedly with teeth—surely they must be vertical dividers or braces—eager to invite—or to devour.

I stared at the turret for a long time. How long, I do not know, but eventually the night sky began to lighten, the moon and stars to fade. Were the lights in the turret extinguished, or was it the brightness of morning that made them fade?

A chill wracked my body, and I realized that I had sat for hours before the open window, clad only in thin pajamas. I climbed hastily back into bed and managed to catch a few winks before the voice of Karolina penetrated the door, summoning me to a lavish breakfast of bacon and eggs, freshly squeezed orange juice and a rich, hot mocha concoction that offered both the satisfying flavor of chocolate and the stimulation of freshly brewed coffee.

In Karolina's car, on the way to the Klaus Fuchs Memorial Institute, I sought to gain information about my peculiar experience of the night before. I realized that my suspicion of my dear, multiply distant cousin (for as such I had chosen to identify her, for my own satisfaction) had been the unjustified product of my own fatigue and depression, and the strangeness and newness of my surroundings.

Almost as if the turret had been the figment of a dream, I grappled mentally in hopes of regaining my impression of it. To a large degree it eluded me, but I was able at length to blurt some question about a turreted tower in the hills.

Karolina's answer was vague and evasive. She admitted that there were some very old structures in the region, dangerous and long abandoned. In response to my mention of the flickering lights and the face-like arrangement in the turret, Karolina became peculiarly agitated, insisting that this was utterly impossible.

I averred that I would like to visit the tower and see for myself if it were inhabited, even if only by squatters.

To this, Karolina replied that there had been an earthquake in the Severn Valley some years before. A fissure had opened in the earth, and the row of hills in which the tower was located was now totally unreachable from Old Severnford. I would have to abandon my plan and give up on my hopes of learning about the turret and its lights.

I spent the day at the Fuchs Institute working diligently on the Zeta/Zed system. Since my attempts of the day before had led me only to frustration, on this day I determined to take the problem on a smaller, more intensive basis. I powered down the entire system, disconnected all of its components from one another, and began running the most exhaustive diagnostic programs on the circuitry of the central processor.

During a luncheon break I thought to ask another employee of the Institute—*not* Karolina Parker—about my experience of the previous night. Strangely, I was unable to recall just *what* I had experienced that I wished to inquire about.

This was by far the most peculiar phenomenon I had ever encountered. I *knew* that something odd had happened to me, I *knew* that I wanted to seek an explanation for it, but I was absolutely and maddeningly unable to remember just *what* it was.

Humiliated, I terminated the conversation and returned to my assigned cubicle to study manuals and circuit diagrams associated with Zeta/Zed.

That night Karolina furnished another delicious repast, and we shared another delightful evening of conversation, coffee and brandy, and music. Karolina had attired herself in a shimmering hostess gown tonight, and I could barely draw my eyes from her flowing, raven hair, her deep blue orbs, her pale English skin and her red, generous lips.

When the time came for us to part to our rooms and retire for the night, I no longer recoiled from my cousin's ardent kiss, but luxuriated in it. As I held her, our faces close together, I saw that she, too, carried the familiar Parker mark on her chin. I placed my lips against the mark, and she sighed as if I had touched her deeply and erotically. Images and fantasies raced through my mind, but I banished them and bade her good night, and climbed the flagstone staircase to my quarters.

I wondered whether I really wanted to lock my door tonight, whether I really wanted to place a chair against it, but I finally did so and climbed into bed. This time I was not able to sleep, so I attired myself more warmly than I had the previous night, and placed myself in the comfortable chair before the window.

In the darkness of the Severn Valley my eyes soon adjusted themselves, and the utterly murky vista that greeted me at first once more resolved itself into rows of hills, clearly old hills smoothed and rounded by the passage of millennia, silhouetted against the star-dotted heavens. And as I simultaneously relaxed my body and my concentration, yet focused my eyes on the area where I had seen the turret rising the night before, once again I beheld its shape, and once again I beheld what appeared to be faint, flickering lights in its windows, making the suggestion of a face that seemed to speak to me in the peculiar tongue of the night prowlers of Severnford and of the enigmatic computer printout.

I did not fall asleep. I wish to make this very clear. What next transpired may have been a vision, a case of astral travel, a supernatural or at least supernormal experience of the most unusual and remarkable sort, but it was absolutely *not a dream*.

Some force drew me from my chair in my room in my distant cousin Karolina Parker's home. That which was drawn was my soul.

Now you may think this is a very peculiar statement for me to make. I, Parker Lorentzen, am a thoroughly modern man. I hold degrees in mathematics, linguistics, philosophy, psychology, and computer science. I could, if I chose to do so, insist upon being addressed as Dr. Lorentzen, but I prefer not to flaunt my education before others.

I opt philosophically for the kind of scientific materialism that seeks explanations for all phenomena in the world of physical reality. I know that there are great mysteries in the universe, but I think of them as the *unknown* rather than the *unknowable*. Research, careful observation and precise measurement, computation and rigorous logic will eventually deliver to inquisitive intelligence the final secrets of the universe.

Such is my philosophy. Or such it *was* until I visited the turret which my cousin Karolina claimed was unreachable.

At first I was frightened. I thought that I was being summoned to hurl myself from an upper-story window, from whence I would fall to the garden below and injure myself. I looked down and the weird topiary beasts seemed to be gesturing, urging me to fly from the house. I knew that this was impossible—in my physical being—but by relaxing ever more fully into my chair, while concentrating my vision, my mind, my whole psychic being on the distant turret in the Severn Hills, I felt my soul gradually separating from my body.

Why do I use the word "soul", you may ask? Did I not mean my mind, my consciousness? Was I not having an out-of-body experience, a controversial but nevertheless real and not necessarily supernatural phenomenon?

But no, it was more than my mind, more than my consciousness that was leaving my body. It was my whole *self*, which I choose to refer to as my soul. For all my scientific skepticism, I have been forced to the conclusion that there is some part of us that is neither material nor mortal. Just what it is, just how it came into being, I do not pretend to know. I have heard every argument, faced every scoffing comment—have made them myself, or did so when I was a younger man—but I cannot now deny the reality of this thing that I call the soul.

For a moment I was able to look back at my own body, comfortably ensconced in the chair. Then I was off, drifting at first languorously through the open window, hovering briefly above the topiary figures in my cousin's garden, then rising as if on wings of my own, high above the town of Old Severnford, and then speeding into the black night, soaring toward the hills to the west of town.

I did see the fissure that Karolina had described, a horrid rent that seemed to penetrate deep into the earth. Its walls were strewn with boulders, and brushy vegetation had made its way down the sides of the fissure, attracted, perhaps, by the heat that seemed to radiate from its depths, or from the water that I surmised would gather there.

As I approached the turret I had seen from my window, I could again perceive the flickering lights within, and the facelike formation of the illumination. From the distance of my cousin's house, and against the blackness of the Severn Hills, the tower had been of uncertain shape. Seen from a lesser distance, it assumed a clear shape and a surprisingly modern architectural aspect. It seemed to rise almost organically from its surroundings, a concept which I had come across more than once while browsing architectural journals.

Entering the largest and most brightly illuminated window, I found myself in a large room. It was unlike any I had ever seen before. As familiar as I am with every sort of modern device and scientific equipment, still I could not comprehend, or even describe, the titanic machinery that I beheld.

Figures utterly dwarfed by the machines tended them, tapping at control panels, reading indicators, adjusting conduits. Lights flashed on the machinery, and occasionally parts moved. Just as the building itself had exhibited an almost organic quality of architecture, so the machines within it seemed, in addition to their other characteristics, to be, in some subtle and incomprehensible way, *alive*.

Strangest of all was a gigantic, rectangular plane that filled an entire section of the monstrous room. Its surface was of a matte gray finish and had a peculiar look to it as if it were somehow *tacky*, as sticky as if a thin coating of honey had been spread on it, and let to stand in the sunlight until it was mostly but not entirely dry.

I approached the gray rectangle by that peculiar sort of disembodied flight that I had used since leaving my body in my cousin's house in Old Severnford, and hovered effortlessly above the gray plane. From my first vantage point at the window of the turret room the plane had looked large, but was still contained within the single, large room. If I had been forced to make an estimate of its dimensions, I would have described it as three to four yards in width, and as much as forty yards in length.

But as I hovered above it, I realized that it was incredibly larger than I had first estimated. That, or perhaps it was merely my change of perspective that gave it the appearance of great size.

Have you ever played with one of those optical illusions, in which you are asked to look at two curved rectangles, or sections of arc cut from the perimeter of a circle or torus? One may appear far larger than the other, yet the instructions that come with such games always urge you to measure the rectangles and see that they are exactly the same size.

Maybe something like that is what happened to me. I cannot testify with any degree of certainty.

But I can tell you that, as I hovered above the gray plane (perhaps I should refer to it, now, as a gray *plain*) it was gigantic. It was miles in width and hundreds of miles in length—or perhaps it was thousands or even millions of miles in each dimension. I felt myself being drawn down toward it, and feared that if I approached too close to it I would be caught in its gravity—or in the tackiness of its surface—and be unable to escape.

With a huge effort I managed to halt my descent, but already I was so close to the plain that I had lost sight of its termini. Grayness stretched to infinity in all directions. I could turn, and above me I saw only star-studded blackness. *Was the turret room open to the Severn sky?* I wondered.

Beneath me I thought I saw stirrings in the gray. At this range it was not a smooth and stationary surface, but seemed textured, as if it were of wet concrete, and tiny specks that at first seemed to be merely part of this texture could be seen to move. They reminded me of insects caught in the sweet, tacky covering of a roll of old-fashioned flypaper.

I descended farther, and realized that the moving specks were alive, and in some inexplicable way I realized just what they were: They were the souls of human beings, trapped in the hold of the gray plain, struggling futilely for their release.

How could such a thing be? I wondered. Whose souls were these? Were they the immortal parts of residents of the Severn Valley, the souls perhaps of local residents who had died, and been trapped here in this bizarre limbo, neither attaining heaven nor being consigned to hell? Had they been summoned by the shapes tending the titanic machines? And if such was the case, what mad motive had moved these weird scientists to set such a trap?

A sudden fear overcame me, lest I be drawn down into the gray plain and be trapped with the other souls, and I beat my ethereal wings with all my strength, struggling to rise above that horrid gray surface. For a time the struggle seemed hopeless, but I persevered the limits of my strength and beyond, forcing myself as great athletes are said to do, to find and call upon unknown reservoirs of determination. And at last my efforts were rewarded, for I found myself rising with painful slowness above the gray plain.

In time the laboratory, if that is what it was, reappeared around me. The gray plain was reduced to a rectangular area in the great room. The shadowy figures continued to tend their titanic machines, either unknowing or uncaring of my presence.

I struggled to the window and darted back toward my cousins house. Despite the great distance, I could see myself, that is my body, seated before the window in my bedroom. My eyes were hooded, my chin rested on my chest as if I had fallen asleep.

The turret fell behind me. I passed over the fissure in the Severn Hills, down their lower slopes and the darkling meadows that separated them from Old Severnford. I passed over the modernistic buildings of the Klaus Fuchs Memorial Institute, flashed over the topiary garden that surrounded my cousins house, and entered my bedroom.

I was able to circle the room once, gazing down with a peculiar detachment at the body that had been my residence for so many years, then slipped back into it. I rose, yawned, and climbed into my bed.

In the morning I tried to discuss the matter with my cousin as we motored to the Institute, but I found myself able to speak only in vague and indefinite terms about that which had been so concrete and specific when I experienced it during the night. Once within the confines of the Institute, even more strangely, I found that my memory of the experience deserted me altogether. I knew only that I had seen and done *something* odd during the night. Twice I fell asleep over my work, which conduct would certainly not help the standing of Myshkin Associates with this, its most valued account.

Progress on the problems with the Zeta/Zed System were small or nil. I found myself wondering if the cause of the systems failures were not external to the system itself. The old computer slogan, GIGO—Garbage In, Garbage Out—suggested itself to me. But one does well to tread carefully before suggesting such an explanation to the customer. It can be offensive, and can alienate an important executive even if it is true.

I spoke with Alexander Myshkin by telephone. He was disheartened by my lack of progress on the Zeta/Zed System problem, but urged me to pursue my theory of external sources for the failure of the system. "You're a diplomat, Park, my boy. You can handle these Brits. Be honest with 'em, be tactful but be firm."

Following another frustrating day, Karolina Parker and I returned to her house. Once away from the Institute, I was able to recall something of my strange experience. Karolina suggested that we repair to a local restaurant for dinner rather than return directly home. Astonished to learn that an establishment existed in Old Severnford which Karolina considered worth visiting, I agreed with alacrity.

The restaurant was located in a converted country manor—in another context I would even have termed the venue a chateau. Waiters in formal garb attended our every whim. The preprandial cocktails which we shared were delicious. Our table was covered with snowy linen; the silver shone, the crystal sparkled, the china was translucently thin and delicate.

The meal itself was superb: a seafood bisque, a crisp salad dressed with a tangy sauce, tiny, tender chops done to perfection and served with delicious mint jelly, baby potatoes and tiny fresh peas. For dessert a tray of napoleons and petit-fours was passed, and we ended our repast with espresso and brandy.

Our surroundings had been as splendid as our meal. We dined in a hall with vaulting ceilings, ancient stone walls and a flagged floor. A fire blazed in a huge walk-in fireplace, and suits of armor, ancient weapons and battle flags set the establishment's motif.

A single disquieting note was sounded when, in the course of my tabletalk with Karolina, I happened to mention the turret. Karolina gestured to me to drop the subject, but I realized that I had already been overheard. The table nearest ours was occupied by a dignified gentleman in dinner clothes, with snowy hair and a white moustache. His companion, a lady of similar years, was decked out in an elaborate gown and rich-appearing pearls.

The gentleman summoned the waiter, who hustled away and returned with the maitre d'hotel in tow. After a hurried conference with the elderly gentleman, the maitre d' approached our table and, bending so that his lips were close to my companion's ear, hastened to deliver a verbal message to her.

Karolina blanched, replied, then nodded reluctantly as the maitre d' took his leave.

I had not fully understood a word of their brief conversation, but I could have sworn that the language in which it was conducted was that strange tongue I had heard in the streets of Severnford, and read from the faulty computer printout at the Fuchs Institute.

In any case, Karolina immediately settled our bill—she would not permit me to spend any money—and hustled us to her automobile. She spoke not a word en route to her house, but spun the car rapidly up the driveway, jumped from her position at the wheel and hastened inside the house casting a frightened look over her shoulder at the topiary garden.

Once in the main room of her house, Karolina did an extraordinary thing. She stood close to me and reached one hand to my cheek. She moved her hand as if to caress me, but as she did so I felt a peculiar pricking at my birthmark. Karolina peered into my face while a frown passed over her own, then she stood on her toes to reach my cheek (for I am a tall man and she a woman of average stature) and pressed her lips briefly to the birthmark.

I placed my hands on her shoulders and watched as she drew back from me. She ran her tongue over her lips, and I noticed a tiny drop of brilliant scarlet which disappeared as her tongue ran over it.

What could this mean? I wondered. But I had no time to inquire, for Karolina made a brusque and perfunctory excuse and started up the stairs, headed for her room, with a succinct suggestion that I proceed to my own.

Once attired for repose, I found myself drawn to the comfortable chair which stood before the open window of my chamber. My eyes adjusted rapidly to the dim illumination of the night sky, and almost at once I found my consciousness focused on the illusion (if it was an illusion) of a face, gazing back at me from its place high in the Severn Hills.

Almost effortlessly I felt my soul take leave of my body. For the second time I flew across the topiary garden, across the village of Old Severnford, across the modernistic buildings of the Fuchs Institute. The brush-choked earthquake fissure in the Severn foothills passed beneath me and the tower loomed directly ahead.

Strangely enough, it seemed to have changed. Not greatly, of course, and in the pallid light that fell from the English sky it would have been difficult to make out architectural features in any great detail. But the tower looked both *older* and *newer* at the same time.

Hovering motionlessly in my weird ethereal flight, I studied the tower and in particular the turret which surmounted it, and I realized that the architectural *style* had been altered from that of modern, twentieth century England to the form and designs of an earlier age. As I entered the turret through its great illuminated window, I briefly noted the cyclopean machines and their scurrying attendants, but sped quickly to the gray rectangular plain I had observed the previous night.

I sank toward its surface, bringing myself to a halt just high enough above the plain to make out the struggling souls there imprisoned. They had increased in number from the night before. Further, I was able to distinguish their appearance.

Again, you may wonder at my description. If a human soul is the immortal and disembodied portion of a sentient being, it would hardly be distinguished by such minutia as clothing, whiskers, or jewelry. But in some way each soul manifested the *essence* of its owner, whether he or she be soldier or peasant, monarch or cleric, houri or drab.

And the souls which I had seen on my first visit were the souls of modern men and women, while those I beheld on this, my second visit to the turret, were clearly the souls of people of an earlier age. The men wore side-whiskers and waistcoats; the women, long dresses and high hair styles and broad hats. No, they did not wear hair or clothing—it was their essences, as of the England of a century ago, that *suggested* as much.

How they had come to the turret and how they had become entrapped on the great gray plain I could not fathom, but their agony and their despair were manifest. They seemed to reach out psychic arms beseeching me to aid them, but I was unable to do so; I was totally ignorant of any way to alter their condition.

My heart was rent by pity. I flew to the attendants of the cyclopean machines, intending to plead with them to help these poor trapped creatures, but I was unable to communicate with them in any way. I studied them, hoping to discern some way of reaching them, but without success.

At last, in a state of despair, I began to move toward the great open window. I turned for one last look back, and had the peculiar sense that the attendants of the machines were themselves not human. Instead, they resembled the vague, yellowish creatures I had seen swimming beneath the surface of the Severn River.

A shudder passed through my very soul, and I sped frantically back to Old Severnford, back to Karolina Parker's house, back to my body. I re-entered my body, dragged myself wearily to my bed, and collapsed into sleep.

Again in the morning my recollections of the strange experience were vague and uncertain. By the time I reached my cubicle at the Institute I was unable either to summon up an image of the night's activities, or to speak of them to anyone. I did, at one point, catch a glimpse of myself, reflected in the monitor screen of the computer work-station beside my desk. I must have nicked myself shaving, I thought, as a drop of blood had dried just on the blue birthmark on my jawline. I wiped it away with a moistened cloth, and was surprised at the fierceness of the sting that I felt.

Struggling to resolve the problems of the Zeta/Zed System, I had arranged an appointment with the chief engineer of the Fuchs Institute, a burly individual named Nelson MacIvar. When our meeting commenced, I surprised MacIvar by inquiring first as to why the Institute had been situated in so out-of-the-way a place as Old Severnford, and on the outskirts of the town at that.

MacIvar was blessed with a thick head of bushy red hair, a tangled beard of the same color, save that it was going to gray, and a complexion to match. He tilted his head and, as my employer Alexander Myshkin was sometimes wont to do, answered my question with one of his own.

"Why do you ask that, Mr. Lorentzen? What bearing has it on this damned Zeta/Zed machine and its funny behavior?"

I explained my theory that some exterior factor might be causing the system's problems, and reasserted my original question.

"You think this is an out-of-the-way place, do you?" MacIvar pressed. "Well, indeed it is. And that's why we chose it. I've been here for thirty-two years, Mr. Lorentzen. I was one of those who chose this spot for the Institute, and I'll tell you now, if I had it to do over, I'd have chosen a far more out-of-the-way location. The middle of the Australian desert, maybe, or better yet the farthest Antarctic glacier."

I was astounded. "Why?" I demanded again. "This location must make it hard enough to bring in supplies and equipment, not to mention the difficulties of recruiting qualified workers. The people of the Severn Valley—well, I don't mean to be offensive, Mr. MacIvar, but they don't seem to be of the highest quality."

MacIvar gave a loud, bitter laugh. "That's putting it mildly, now, Mr. Lorentzen. They're a degenerate stock, inbred and slowly sinking back toward savagery. As is all of mankind, if you ask me, and the sooner we get there, the better. This thing we call civilization has been an abomination in the eyes of God and a curse on the face of the earth."

So, I was confronted with a religious fanatic. I'd better change my tack, and fast. "The water that drives your generators," I said, "Miss Parker—" MacIvar raised a bushy eyebrow "Dr. Parker, then, tells me that you use the Severn River for that purpose."

"Yes, she is exactly right."

"Do you make any further use of its waters?"

"Oh, plenty. We drink it. We cook in it. We bathe in it. The Severn is the lifeline of this community. And we use it to cool our equipment, you know. Your wonderful Zeta/Zed machines can run very hot, Mr. Lorentzen, and they need a lot of cooling."

I shook my head. "Have you tested the river for purity? Do you have a filtering and treatment system in place?"

"Yes, and yes again. Just because we're out here in the country, Mr. American Troubleshooter, don't take us for a bunch of hicks and hayseeds. We know what we are doing, sir."

I gestured placatingly. "I didn't mean to cast aspersions. I'm merely trying to make sure that we touch every base."

"Touch every base, is it? I suppose that's one of your American sports terms, eh?"

By now I felt myself reddening. "I mean, ah, to make sure that no stone goes unturned, no, ah, possibility unexamined."

MacIvar glared at me in silence. I asked him, "What happens to the water after it's been passed through the heat-exchange tanks?"

"It goes back into the river."

"Has this had any effect on the local ecology? On the wildlife of the valley, or the aquatic forms found in the river itself?" I thought of those graceful yet oddly disquieting yellowish shapes in the river, of the glow that emanated from their curving bodies and reflected off the mist above.

"None," said MacIvar, "none whatsoever. And that is an avenue of inquiry, Mr. Troubleshooter, that I would advise you not to waste your precious time on."

With this, MacIvar pushed himself upright and strode ponderously from the office. Something had disturbed him and I felt that his suggestion—if not an actual warning—to steer clear of investigating the River Severn would have the opposite effect on my work.

At the end of the working day I feigned a migraine and asked Karolina Parker to drive me home and excuse me for the remainder of the evening. I took a small sandwich and a glass of cold milk to my room and there set them aside untouched. I changed into my sleeping garments and stationed myself at the window. At this time of year the English evening set in early, for which I thanked heaven. I located the flickering face and flew to it without hesitation.

The tower had changed its appearance again. From its Victorian fustian it had reverted to the square-cut stone configuration of a medieval battlement. Once within the great turret room I sped by the cyclopean machinery and its scurrying, yellowish attendants and headed quickly to the gray plain.

Hovering over the plain, I dropped slowly until I could make out the souls struggling and suffering there. More of them were apparent this night than had previously been the case, and from their garments and equipage I could infer their identity. They were members of Caesar's legions. Yes, these pitiable beings were the survivors—or perhaps the casualties—of the Roman occupation force that had once ruled Britain.

After a time they seemed to become aware of me and attempted variously to command or to entice me into placing myself among them. This I would not do. One legionnaire, armed with Roman shield and spear, hurled the latter upward at me. I leaped aside, not stopping to wonder what effect the weapon would have had. It was, of course, not a physical object, but a psychic one. Yet as a soul, was I not also a psychic being, and might not the spear have inflicted injury or even death upon me?

The legionnaire's conduct furnished me with a clue, however. He had seen me—that I knew because he aimed his throw with such precision that, had I not dodged successfully, I would surely have been impaled on the spear-point. Even as the legionnaire stood shouting and shaking his fist at me, I willed myself to become invisible.

The look of anger on the ancient soldier's face was replaced by one of puzzlement and he began casting his gaze in all directions as if in hopes of locating me. I knew, thus, that I was able to conceal myself from these wretched souls merely by willing myself to be unseen.

Remaining invisible, I proceeded farther along the gray plain. There were many more souls here than I had even imagined. Beyond the Romans I observed a population of early, primitive Britons. Hairy Picts dressed in crude animal skins danced and chanted as if that might do them some good. And beyond the Picts I spied—but suddenly, a sheet of panic swept over me.

How long had I been in the turret this night? I looked around, hoping to see the window through which I had entered, but I was too near the gray plain, and all I could in any horizontal direction was a series of encampments of captive souls, the ectoplasmic revenants of men, women, and children somehow drawn to the turret and captured by the gray plain over a period of hundreds or thousands of years.

I turned my gaze upward and realized that the turret room was indeed open to the sky of the Severn Valley, and that night was ending and the morning sky was beginning to turn from midnight blue to pale gray. Soon a rosy dawn would arrive, and in some incomprehensible way I knew that it would be disastrous for me still to be in the tower when daylight broke.

Thus I rose as rapidly as I could and sped over the gray plain, past the machines and their attendants, out of the turret and home to my cousin's house.

At work that day I met once again with Nelson MacIvar. He had appeared vaguely familiar to me at our first meeting, and I now realized that this burly, oversized man bore an uncanny resemblance to the great child who had thrown a rock at my car as it carried me from Brichester to Severnford. I came very near to mentioning the incident to him, but decided that no purpose would be served by raising an unpleasant issue.

Rather should I save my verbal ammunition for another attempt to get MacIvar to order tests of the River Severn water used in the Institute. By this time I had come to believe that the water was impregnated with some peculiar *force* that was interfering with the operation of the Zeta/Zed System. This force, I surmised, might be a radioactive contamination, picked up at some point in the river's course, perhaps as a result of the fissure at the foot of the Severn Hills nearby.

When I thought of that fissure and of those hills, a feeling of disquietude filled me, and I had to excuse myself and sip at a glass of water—that same damnable Severn water, I realized too late to stop myself—while I regained my composure. *Why* I should find thoughts of that fissure and of those hills so distressing, I could not recall.

This time MacIvar grudgingly yielded to my request, insisting that nothing would be found, but willing in his burly, overbearing way to humor this troublesome American. I reported this potential break to Alexander Myshkin by transatlantic telephone, and spent the remainder of the day more or less productively employed.

Again that night I feigned migraine and excused myself from my cousin's company. She expressed concern for my well-being and offered to summon a doctor to examine me, but I ran from her company and locked myself in my room. I stared into the fiery orb of the sun as it fell beneath the Severn Hills, then willed myself across the miles to the turret.

As I approached it tonight I realized that it had changed its form again, assuming the features of a style of architecture unknown and unfamiliar to me, but clearly of the most advanced and elaborate nature imaginable.

I flashed through the window, sped past the machines and their attendants, and hovered above the gray plain. I had reached a decision. Tonight I would pursue my investigation of the plain to its end! I swooped low over the plain, passed rapidly over the Victorian village—for such is the way I now labeled this assemblage of souls—over the Roman encampment, over the rough Pictish gathering, and on. What would I find, I wondered—Neanderthals?

Instead, to my astonishment, I recognized the ectoplasmic manifestation of an Egyptian pyramid. I dropped toward it, entered an opening near its base, and found myself in a hall of carven obsidian, lined with living statues of the Egyptian hybrid gods—the hawk-headed Horus, the jackal-headed Anubis, the ibis god Thoth, the crocodile god Sebek—and I knew, somehow, that these, too, were not physical representations created by some ancient sculptors, but the very *souls* of the creatures the Egyptians worshiped!

I did not stay long, although I could see that a ceremony was taking place in which worshippers prostrated themselves, making offerings and chanting in honor of their strange deities. I sped from the pyramid and continued along the plain, wondering what next I would encounter.

In Silicon Valley, Alexander Myshkin and I had spent many hours, after our day's work was completed, arguing and pondering over the many mysteries of the world, including the great mystery of Atlantis. Was it a mere legend, a Platonic metaphor for some moral paradigm, a fable concocted to amuse the childish and deceive the credulous? Myshkin was inclined to believe in the literal reality of Atlantis, while I was utterly skeptical.

Alexander Myshkin was right.

The Atlantean settlement was suffused with a blue light all its own. Yes, the Atlanteans were the precursors and the inspiration of the Egyptians. Their gods were similar but were mightier and more elegant than the Egyptians; their temples were more beautiful, their pyramids more titanic, their costumes more fantastic.

And the Atlanteans themselves—I wondered if they were truly human. They were shaped like men and women, but they were formed with such perfection as to make the statues of Praxiteles look like the fumblings of a nursery child pounding soft clay into a rough approximation of the human form.

These Atlanteans had aircraft of amazing grace and beauty, and cities that would make the fancies of Wonderland or of Oz pale by comparison.

And yet they had been captured and imprisoned on this terrible gray plain!

I sped beyond the Atlantean settlement, wondering if yet more ancient civilizations might be represented. And they were, they were. People of shapes and colors I could only have imagined, cities that soared to the heavens (or seemed to, in that strange psychic world), wonders beyond the powers of my puny mind to comprehend.

How many ancient civilizations had there been on this puny planet we call Earth? Archaeologists have found records and ruins dating back perhaps 10,000 years, 15,000 at the uttermost. Yet anthropologists tell us that humankind, *Homo sapiens* or something closely resembling him, has been on this planet for anywhere from two to five *million* years. Taking even the most conservative number, are we to believe that for 1,985,000 years our ancestors were simple fisherfolk, hunters and gatherers, living in crude villages, organized into petty tribes? And that suddenly, virtually in the wink of the cosmic eye, there sprang up the empires of Egypt and Mesopotamia, of ancient China and India, Japan and Southeast Asia and chill Tibet, the Maya and the Aztecs and the Toltecs and the great Incas, the empires of Gambia and of Ghana, the mysterious rock-painters of Australia and the carvers of the stone faces of Easter Island?

This makes little sense. No, there must have been other civilizations, hundreds of them, thousands, over the millions of years of humankind's tenancy of the planet Earth.

But even then, what is a mere 2,000,000 years, even 5,000,000 years, in the history of a planet six *billion* years of age? What mighty species might have evolved in the seas or on the continents of this world, might have learned to think and to speak, to build towering cities and construct great engines, to compose eloquent poems and paint magnificent images—and then have disappeared, leaving behind no evidence that ever they had walked this Earth—or at least, no evidence of which we are aware?

Such races did live on this planet. They had souls, yes, and so much, say I, for human arrogance. This I know because I saw their souls.

How many such races? Hundreds, I tell you. Thousands. Millions. I despaired of ever reaching the end of the gray plain, but I had vowed to fly to its end however long it took. This time, if daylight found me still in the tower, so must it be. My cousin might discover my body, seemingly deep in a normal and restorative slumber, propped up in my easy chair. But she would be unable to awaken me.

Yes, I determined that I would see this thing to its conclusion, and from this objective I would not be swayed. I saw the souls of the great segmented fire-worms who built their massive cities in the very molten mantle of the Earth; I saw submarine creatures who would make the reptilian plesiosaurs look like minnows by comparison, sporting and dancing and telling their own tales of their own watery gods; I saw the intelligent ferns and vines whose single organic network at one time covered nearly one third of the primordial continent of Gondwanaland; I saw the gossamer, feathery beings who made their nests in Earth's clouds and built their playgrounds in Luna's craters.

We humans in our conceit like to tell ourselves that we are evolution's darlings, that millennia of natural selection have led Nature to her crowning creation, *Homo sapiens*. Let me tell you that the opposite is the case. The story of life on Earth is not the story of evolution, but of *devolution*. The noblest, the most elevated and most admirable of races were the first, not the last.

But still I pursued my flight, past wonder on wonder, terror on terror, until at last I saw the gray plain, the gray *plane* curve upward, rise into the brilliant haze that I recognized as the primordial chaos from which our solar system emerged. And the souls that were captured by the turret—what was their fate? For what purpose were they caught up in every era of being, and drawn backward, backward toward that primordial haze?

A great mass of soul-force formed before my ectoplasmic eyes. A great seething ball of sheer soul-energy that accreted there in the dawn of time, now burst its bonds and rolled down that great gray plain, sweeping all before it, destroying cities as a boulder would crush an ant's nest, shaking continents to their foundations, causing the globe itself to tremble and to wobble in its orbit around the Sun.

But even this was only the beginning of the havoc wrought by this great ball of soul-energy. From the remote past to the present—our present, yours and mine—it roared, and then on into the future, sweeping planets and suns in its path.

And when the roiling concentration of soul-force reached that unimaginably distant future, when all was dim and silent in the cosmos and infinitesimal granules of existence itself floated aimless in the endless void, it reversed its course and swept backward, roiling and rolling from future to past, crushing and rending and growing, always growing, growing.

It reached its beginning point and reversed itself still again, larger and more terrible this time than it had been the first, and as it oscillated between creation and destruction, between future and past, between the beginning of the universe and its end, the very fabric of time-space began to grow weak.

What epochs of history, human and pre-human and, yes, post-human, were twisted and reformed into new and astonishing shapes. Battles were fought and unfought and then fought again with different outcomes; lovers chose one another, then made new and different choices; empires that spanned continents were wiped out as if they had never existed, then recreated in the images of bizarre deities; religions disappeared and returned, transmogrified beyond recognition; species were cut off from the stream of evolution to be replaced by others more peculiar than you can imagine.

A baby might be born, then disappear back into its mother's womb only to be born again a monstrosity unspeakable. A maddened killer might commit a crime, only to see his deed undone and himself wiped out of existence, only to reappear a saintly and benevolent friend to his onetime victim.

And what then, you might wonder, what then? I'll not deny that my own curiosity was roused. Would humankind persist forever? What supreme arrogance to think this would be the case! Mightier species than we, and nobler, had come and gone before *Homo sapiens* was so much as a gleam in Mother Nature's eye.

In iteration after iteration of the titanic story, humankind disappeared. Destroyed itself with monstrous weapons. Was wiped away by an invisible virus. Gave birth to its own successor race and lost its niche in the scheme of things. Was obliterated by a wandering asteroid, conquered and exterminated by marauding space aliens—

Oh, space aliens. Alexander Myshkin and I had debated that conundrum many a time. Myshkin believed that the universe positively *teemed* with intelligence. Creatures of every possible description, human, human-like, insectoid, batrachian, avian, vegetable, electronic, you name it. Myshkin's version of the cosmos looked like a science fiction illustrator's sample book.

My universe was a lonely place. Only Earth held life, and only human life on Earth was sentient. It was a pessimistic view, I'll admit, but as the mother of the ill-favored baby was wont to say, "It's ugly but it's mine."

Well, Myshkin was right. There were aliens galore. At various times and in various versions of the future—and of the past, as a matter of fact—they visited Earth or we visited their worlds or space travelers of different species met in unlikely cosmic traffic accidents or contact was made by radio or by handwritten notes tossed away in empty olive jars.

One version of posthuman Earth was dominated by a single greenish fungus that covered the entire planet, oceans and all, leaving only tiny specks of white ice at the North and South Poles. Another was sterilized, and thank you, weapons industry, for developing a bomb that could kill everything—*everything!*—on an entire planet. But spores arrived from somewhere later on, and a whole new family of living things found their home on Earth.

I saw all of this and more, and I saw the very fabric of space-time becoming feeble and unsure of itself. I saw it tremble and quake beneath the mighty assault of that accumulated and ever-growing soul-force, and I realized what was happening. The cosmos itself was threatened by whatever screaming demons of chaos cavorted beyond its limits.

At length a rent appeared, and I was able to peer into it, but the black, screeching chaos that lay beyond it I will not describe to you. No, I will not do that. But I peered into that swirling orifice of madness and menace and I mouthed a prayer to the God I had abandoned so long ago, and I swore to that God that if one man, if one soul could counter the malignities who populated the fifth dimension, or the fiftieth, or the five millionth, it would be I.

Did I say that the soul is the immaterial and immortal part of a living, sentient being? And did I say that I had realized, in spite of my lifelong skepticism, that God was a living reality? Perhaps I should have said that *gods* were living realities. I do not know how many universes there are, each one created by its own god, each god behaving like a mischievous child.

And that chaotic void beyond the cosmos—was that in fact part of a higher realm of reality, in which *all* the universes drifted like the eggs of some aquatic life-form, within the nourishing fluid of the sea? If my soul should leave our cosmos and enter that chaos, to face the demons—demons that I now realized were the gods of other universes—would it then forfeit its claim to immortality?

Could those demons be stopped? Could I, one man, stand against this infinite army of insanity? There was a single way to learn the answer to that question. I decided that I would take that way.

I—

The Second Effort

by John Tynes

The tea was sweet, milky, and warm. Jacob swirled the spoon in the cup lazily, staring at the cream-colored liquid. He took a sip, spoon now lying on a paper napkin, and enjoyed the sensation. Putting the cup down, he glanced around the cozy tearoom just off the Temphill town square and decided he was ready.

From the floor he lifted a black canvas case, padded with rubber at the corners and covered in zippers and pouches. He placed the case on the table, carefully away from his tea, and unzipped the top. Reaching in, he gingerly lifted the laptop computer up and out of the case. He kept an eye on the tea, remaining wary of a spill that could damage the laptop. Now more confident, he placed it on the table in front of him and turned it on. Within a minute or so he had the word processor up and started typing.

Jacob remained lost in his work for a minute or so. When next he looked up to take a sip of tea, there was a man sitting across the table from him with a genial smile on his face.

"Hello, Jacob," the man said.

"Afternoon, Dad. I'm glad you could join me."

"Think nothing of it. I haven't been here in quite a while."

"So I've noticed," Jacob replied with a slightly sarcastic note in his voice.

A smiling older woman walked up. "Would you like a cup, sir?"

"That would be fine, just fine," said Jacob's father.

The woman placed a cup on the table and poured hot tea into it. Jacob passed his father the cream and sugar.

"All your stuff is gone, I'm afraid," Jacob said.

His father nodded. "I know. My parents sold it off or burned the lot of it. I'm sorry it's gone, but it's nothing I truly needed."

"I suppose. Still, they even sold your manuscript."

The man waved his hand casually. "That's twenty years' water under the bridge, Jacob. You needn't press the issue."

Jacob nodded, chastened, but couldn't help adding, "Well, I would have liked to have had the original, at least."

"You don't need it, son. Let it do its work in its own way."

"Oh, it is. There's been a printed version only recently, about four years ago. Small press, of course, but still a quality job—it's in a uniform edition with the first twelve volumes. Still as potent as ever, too."

"That's good to hear. It's nice when one's work acquires a life of its own."

Jacob chuckled. "I had no idea you possessed such a dry wit, Father."

"Well, we've never actually met before, have we?"

"No, that's true," Jacob said ruefully. "I really don't remember you at all, just Mother."

His father frowned. "Has she respected my memory?"

Jacob shook his head. "Got married a year after your death. Cecil Bierce, from your old school."

"Cecil? Good god."

"Don't fret, Father. I took care of both of them a while back."

Jacob's father smiled. "That's my boy. It's good to see you take after your old man."

Jacob leaned forward, suddenly intense. "Tell me what it was like. Tell me what writing your manuscript was like."

"My manuscript? A wretched task. I'd spend every night sweating and flailing about, waking up four or five times when the dreams were just too much. Then several hours in the morning trying to get it all down on paper. We serve a powerful lord, Jacob, but he demands much of his servants."

Jacob's face grew cold. "I'm no servant, Father."

"Of course you are, son. Both of us are, and others. You can't deny your role."

"You know nothing of my role, dead man."

"Jacob, why the hostility? Surely you don't reject our part of the great plan?"

"There is no plan, Father. No plan but what we make."

Jacob's father sat back and folded his arms across his chest. He looked at Jacob for a long moment. "What are you on about?"

"Are you familiar with post-modernism, Father?"

"Vaguely. It's been a while."

"Post-modernism postulates that in this modern age, creativity can not be divorced from context. Every writer writes with the knowledge of all the other writers he has read, or even just heard of. Every artist paints with his mind full of all the art he has seen before. The dispersal of information in the twentieth century is such that there's nothing wholly original left to a given individual. You can't write a story that hasn't been written before, in some form or other. And the more you see and read, the more you come to realize the building blocks of the craft. Post-modernism leads to the art that references other art, or society at large. It is intrinsically self-reflective, either on the surface or beneath."

"I suppose I follow you."

"Father, I believe post-modernism is the first crest of the new wave. Not an artistic wave, but a wave of human experience. I believe the widespread dispersal of knowledge and ideas is building a collective unconscious among all of humanity, and eventually a collective *consciousness* that will awaken as an independent life form, the queen bee of the human hive. Post-modernism is just a minor symptom of a mindset that will become the norm rather than the avant garde."

"What the bloody hell has this to do with us and our lord?"

Jacob looked smug. "You were another wave, Father. You and your book and your great bloated lord with the mouths on his palms."

"My lord? My lord? You serve him too, son. Your soul was sworn to him before you were ever born!"

The voice of Jacob's father had risen in volume, and this last declaration attracted the notice of other patrons seated nearby. Jacob glanced about, looking reassuring, and then leveled his gaze at his father.

"You're speaking in metaphors, Father, and you don't even know it. Yes, my soul is his because I inherited your power and the compulsion to use it. You created your own lord, Father, and you wrote your own damned manuscript. Yes, Y'golonac exists and yes, those who read your words become his servants. But it's all because of you. Your manuscript was the first creative work to involve the reader in the work's own self-reflexivity and alter his reality accordingly. It's quite amazing, really."

"What are you talking about? This is gibberish!"

"No, Father. Would you like to see gibberish? Here, look at this!"

With a snarl Jacob spun the laptop computer around so that the screen faced his father. Wary, the older man read the words on the screen: "My late father is sitting across from me, appearing to be in his late forties. He is dressed in conservative but current clothing, and has a demeanor of reasoned intelligence." Jacob's father looked up. "What is this? What am I supposed to think of this?"

"Father, as you've acknowledged yourself, you're dead. You died more than twenty years ago by your own hand, scant weeks after getting mother pregnant. In the time we've been sitting together, has it ever occurred to you that your presence here in this tearoom with me is quite impossible?"

"Nothing is impossible to those who serve Y'golonac!" his father sputtered.

"Oh, please. Father, you're a construct. I wrote this bit here on my computer as a focus, and willed you into existence so we could finally talk. Sadly, you're just as tiring and absurd as mother said."

"Nonsense! I serve lord Y'golonac! In him all things are possible!"

A woman at the next table glanced over nervously. The two men talking intently paid her no heed.

"Do shut up. Father, you wrote a manuscript that, when read, changed the reality of the reader. I've gone beyond that. I can change people's reality all on my own, without their participation. I called you into existence, and made everyone in the room here believe you were present. They all see you, believe in your existence. The waitress brought you a teacup. The people nearby stare when you raise your voice. They are all quite convinced of your presence."

Jacob's father sat back, and said nothing.

"Struck dumb? You really have nothing to say anymore but cliches. I've explained your existence to the point where I can't consciously ignore the fact that you can't be here, and as a result you, hollow man, have nothing more to say."

The man stared at Jacob dumbly.

"I think it's time for you to make your exit."

Without a word, Jacob's father got up and walked across to the restroom. Several patrons glanced at him briefly, curious about the argument they'd overheard.

Jacob turned his laptop back round to face him. He tapped his fingers on the table.

"More tea, dear?" asked the waitress.

"Yes, thanks," Jacob said.

"And your friend?"

"No, I believe he's had his fill."

The waitress bustled off, handing fresh pots of tea to others in the room. Jacob smoked a cigarette. Eventually, he got up and walked into the restroom where his father had gone. He found him inside, leaning against the wall.

"Still here?" said Jacob.

His father stared at him, fighting back tears. "Bastard," he said. "Bastard. You'll wake with no face someday, and choke on your own flesh."

Jacob smiled. "You know, I can see the wall behind you, Father."

The older man grew more transparent, and within moments faded away.

Jacob stood for a moment, wondering what his father's headless god was thinking right now. What would it be like to be aware not just of your mortality, but also of your artificiality? Jacob shook his head.

Soon he was seated back at the table. He looked at the screen of his laptop and then deleted the text. He glanced around the room with the unconscious cruelness to his features he had inherited from his father. Fresh from his recent effort, Jacob decided to try again: "She feels the pains in her chest suddenly, and experiences a shortness of breath. It's the beginning of a heart attack, and the end of the life of—"

Oh damn, thought Jacob. *What was the name of that waitress again?*

The Queen

by Diane Sammarco

Out of the corner of her eye she could see tiny, tinged bubbles of her own saliva reflected in the near dawn light. Consciousness had brought familiar visitors in this wretched place—pain and fear. She lay motionless, cradled by the dead foliage but able to feel the damp, cold sod through the layers. In her stupor she dared not move, fearing the extent of her injuries and fearing more that her stirring might attract it. She would not survive another attack.

Thin, black branches veined the gray sky over her head. The trees of Goatswood Forest slept in their gray tombs of bark. Dead to the eye but really only waiting for the right signal—some temperature or sluggish chemical keyed by the first ray of sun. Later than other valleys in the area, the trees would sprout leaves and compete for the few rays of sun that managed to penetrate the blackness of the woods. Maybe the denseness of the stand accounted for the fact that these trees seemed to lose their leaves sooner in the fall and sprout them later in the spring. And perhaps it also would account for the sparsity of animals and birds in this area. Only the trees stayed, shackled by their roots, silent witnesses to the macabre dramas played out in the shadows of Goatswood.

She became aware of a distant rumbling. It wasn't thunder, but a pulse that throbbed the earth beneath her, matching her own body rhythm but deeper, threatening. She listened. The sound came from the far side of the clearing where she could not see through the mist and the shade. It stopped. Her own ragged breath betrayed her and she held it as best she could. The sound started again, giving her the meager comfort of knowing the other's whereabouts, if only for the moment.

The other was still there in the shadows searching for her by scent or sound, driven by its own fear of her and the need to destroy her. She was the enemy, the threat that made it alert for the smallest sound. Her power was a dark passenger that lay curled inside her, so strong that it threatened her own existence.

The girl had been found in the woods outside Goatswood. A traveler, galloping to speed the trip through these notorious woods, had glimpsed a small, dark shape moving steadily and purposefully away from the trail and toward the center of woods. Frightened and anxious to leave whatever it was to its purpose, he drove the horses harder. The coach thundered through the eerily silent wood, its wheels throwing up leaves and bits of mud. As he came round the next bend, his path converged with that of what he now recognized as a child. Drawing the horses in, he shouted to the figure and it turned. A little girl of no more than five years fixed her steady gaze on him. She was naked and soaking wet even though there had been no rain in weeks and there was no stream for miles. He grabbed a cloak from the seat of the coach, wrapped her in it and scooped the unresisting girl in his arms. He raced back to the coach and continued his frenzied escape, not glancing behind him even though he swore later that he heard the booming crunch of large branches giving way to something of enormous size and strength.

Whatever the circumstances were of the girl's short life before she was placed at the Exham Foundling Home, they were tightly sealed in her memory. From the beginning it was clear that this newcomer was not from the blond-haired, blue-eyed, short stock of the people of the Severn Valley. The child had dark olive, glistening skin, dark brown eyes slanted just enough to suggest some Oriental blood, and very dark brown hair with auburn highlights. She was painfully thin and looked as fragile as a new sapling. Mrs. Sharpels, the housemother to the cottage of the five- to ten-year-old girls, named her Elizabeth. Elizabeth had not spoken the night she was found and it took a year after that before she said her first words. It was as if she were learning the language for the first time. However, once she did speak, her words were well formed and revealed a quick mind eager to learn.

Elizabeth proved to be a compliant child. Given a task, she set about it with fervor, never resting or complaining until it was finished and often doing more than required. She adjusted rapidly to the schedule of the Home but was remote in her relationships with the other children. She often seemed puzzled when the other children sought her out to join in games. The child preferred to explore the perimeter of the buildings and the children's fenced-in play yard and otherwise occupied herself with solitary pursuits.

She grew quickly, eating ravenously and seemingly without pleasure, of whatever meal was placed in front of her. In a year she added two inches to her height, but remained reed thin and extremely agile. Her habit after meals was to retreat to a dark corner of the room and watch with unblinking eyes as the other children played. Or she went to the library, which had an extensive collection for such a small institution, thanks to the generosity of a former resident. Here she would spend hours engrossed in books, especially history books. No amount of coaxing would bring her from her self-imposed exile or elicit more than a terse response.

Mrs. Sharpels grew more fond of the curious little girl as the days went on. She made it her personal crusade to free this unsmiling child from whatever nightmare held her in its grip. She taught her to take sweet oil and polish the dark mahogany on the banister until it reflected her face and to knead great dough loaves for the coarse bread served at meals. The two would spend time in the bakehouse, or sit together at the cabinet piano while the older woman picked out tunes. Her young charge listened intently as if to discern some meaning from the notes. Sometimes Elizabeth would reward her mentor by sliding just a little closer and tentatively fingering the piano keys. Although she rarely smiled, this time together seemed to please the child.

Elizabeth proved also to be a talented artist. The drawings she produced were not like the crude pictures of animals and landscapes drawn by the other children. They were of stark expanses lacking trees but filled with geometrically shaped rocks that appeared to have protrusions at the base that could roughly be equated with legs and to be in purposeful progression across the paper. These visages were also populated by other horrifying creatures unlike any Mrs. Sharpels had ever seen, but drawn with such detail that it was hard to believe they were only products of the small girl's imagination. Malevolent beings most closely resembling insects were the main theme that dominated her pictures. They had grotesquely shaped bodies from which protruded legs like thick, misshapen branches. On what could only be equated with a face were multifaceted iridescent eyes and three mouths. The most prominent things on the creatures were huge wings, and they were often depicted in flight toward a horizon dominated by two gray metallic objects. These beings were also shown engaged in sophisticated tool-using and other purposeful acts that displayed intelligence. She drew other creatures, more humanoid but lacking facial features, shown under the insect's control, tending to rows of cylinder-shaped objects. It was impossible to encourage Elizabeth to use her talents to draw anything but the terrifying pictures. Mrs. Sharpels never ceased to feel icy chills at the sight of Elizabeth's handiwork.

During one reading lesson, Liz seemed particularly taken with a book about the Egyptian pyramids. "What lives here?" the girl asked without looking up from the page.

"No one lives there, dear. Pyramids are for the people who died in Egypt a long time ago. Those people believed that when a person passed on, they still needed things for the afterlife."

Liz looked past her, out the window and suddenly straightened with recaptured memory. "They are there. Out there." So convincing was her exclamation that Mrs. Sharpels turned involuntarily and followed the child's gaze. The autumn sun was low on the horizon and Goatswood Forest was a gaping black mouth across the field. Just at the edge something moved, but the dimness made it impossible to tell what it was—perhaps a trick of the light. The older woman turned back to the book and read a passage about the Nile River to Elizabeth. When she glanced out the window again, the figure was more distinct. It had moved toward them across the field. Elizabeth was watching impassively. It was a man with an odd shuffling gate making steady progress toward the building. With the light behind him, he was only a silhouette growing larger by the moment. When he was thirty or so feet from the window, Liz rose and walked over to the sill.

"Elizabeth, stand back. I think that's Mr. Hurley," but Mrs. Sharpels knew it wasn't the old caretaker. The walk and the shape were wrong. A few feet from the window the figure paused and lifted its head. The light from the house hit it fully and revealed a body shaped like a man with two arms and two legs, but no fingers on the hands. Instead, there were two hooked appendages that seemed to generate from the wrist bones. The legs were bowed and misshapen. Its skin was yellow and parchment thin over a pulsating network of veins. Mrs. Sharpels stared, transfixed by the horror that stood before her. She only started to scream when she realized that it had no face. Where the face should have been was an oval-shaped mass of yellowed skin. Liz pressed her face against the window. The thing outside the window pressed one hand against the glass; the fragile pane was all that prevented it from touching her.

"Elizabeth!" she screamed and grabbed the child by the wrist. Just then the pane shattered and the groping appendage was inside the room. The woman backed up to the fireplace, dragging Liz by the arm as the creature poured over the sill and broke the rest of the glass from the window. As it moved, a vile stench filled the room and it emitted a low-pitched menacing sound. Trapped in the chimney corner, Mrs. Sharpels grabbed a poker and swung it at the beast. The blow glanced off harmlessly and it reached out for Elizabeth, dumping over the coal scuttle. The woman swung again and again. Now both the child and the woman were screaming as the beast picked Elizabeth up in its claw-like hands and held her over its head. It turned back toward the shattered window with the girl clutched in its grip, the muddy light from the gaslamps making its shadow a twisted giant on the wall. Mrs. Sharpels continued her futile efforts to free the child. Just then, it paused and looked up as if hearing some sound that was inaudible to the others. Its attention was riveted on the horizon. It dropped the child and withdrew through the window, moving off west into the gathering night, back toward Goatswood Forest. Assuring herself that Liz was all right, the shaken housemother carried the girl to her room. Her screams brought the others to the room, but by then the beast had disappeared into the darkness and she knew no one would follow it.

The other was still on the opposite end of the clearing. Liz's body ached. She drew her limbs toward her and folded her arms to her chest. They felt like sticks, hard and cold without the warmth of flesh. She tensed and relaxed her shoulders, trying to regain the sense of her body. The bones in her shoulder cracked like dry wood. She licked her mouth with her tongue and felt the roughness of her lips. It was as if all the moisture had been drawn from her. Now she could not see the other, but she could sense that it was near and she knew it could sense her.

A memory came to her of the beginning. It was an awareness that she had been waiting a very long time. Her arms and legs ached to be moved and stretched. She was wrecked with pain. Her joints were stiff with the constraint of her wrapping. Sounds were muffled by the thickness around her. She could hear things moving outside and felt herself being pushed. Shadow beings moved around her half-sensed world, shoving her this way and that, and then moving away only to return to further probe her gauze shell. Thin legs kicked at the walls and her body contorted. She gulped, choking on fluid. She strained to see but vision was useless in the unrelenting whiteness. The suffocating softness held her body in its grip.

The walls began to yield a bit and she hit the sides in a frenzy of spasmodic jerks. This seemed to attract the attention of the shadow beings and they crowded around her, nudging the sac nervously. The attention goaded her to new heights of intensity. Her efforts were rewarded with a tiny rip in the fabric. A pinpoint of light penetrated her world and musty air gushed in from outside. She was carried from the whiteness on a gush of liquid.

Sometimes at night, the plump housemother would find Liz searching for a way out of the locked building, gently but persistently probing at cracks and crevices. Liz's eyes would take on a longing gaze as she peered out through the parted shutters toward the night sky. It was during these times that she seemed to be in some kind of trance, unaware of her surroundings and unresponsive. "What are you looking at, child? You don't want to go out there at night," Mrs. Sharpels advised, pulling the weathered wood tight with sudden urgency.

One night during the summer, she had heard Elizabeth wandering and had pulled her away as the child managed to climb a stepstool and free the shutter latch at an attic window in the back of the house. As the heavy woman attempted to latch the window in near darkness, she glimpsed the corner of a black branch poking through the shutter. When she touched it, it had a hard, cold shell-like feeling and recoiled from her hand. In the next instant it whipped back through the window, cutting her palm. Momentarily frozen with revulsion and terror, she turned to Elizabeth. She was gone. A frantic search found her back in bed. The housemother blamed the incident on her imagination, the wind, and the old black walnut trees that rimmed the house. But the following day she saw that Mr. Hurley bolted locks on all the shutters. Elizabeth couldn't free the shutter on subsequent trips, but Mrs. Sharpels watched from the door of the attic as the child probed for a crack and touched the tip of the thing that returned her touch from outside the window.

In the next year, although Elizabeth could not have been more than eleven years old, she grew another two inches until she was almost as tall as Mrs. Sharpels. Her dark hair was now even a deeper shade of ebony and her skin was tan from frequent trips around the limits of the play yard. She was by far the most agile and strongest of the girls her age. Her obvious physical and mental superiority made the other children jealous and now openly hostile to her. The close bonds that should have arisen over time never formed. Liz remained an outcast. More than once the housemother was forced to intervene in a fight between Liz and another child. Though never provoking a fight, she never avoided one either, and proved to be a fierce opponent.

Once, Liz was found holding a large girl down on the ground with her hands dangerously tight around the other child's neck and her face a dispassionate mask. The conquered child was gasping for breath and covered in dirt and sweat. When released from Liz's grip, she wailed loudly and ran off to join a cadre of others who were shouting at Liz from a safe distance. After that day, it was clear the others feared and avoided Liz. Finally, such was her supremacy that they could only sit and glower when she passed. And she made no effort to seek the other children out. If the situation bothered her, she did not show it. Her only companion was Mrs. Sharpels, who was always watchful and secretly troubled by this little girl's frightening potential. Whatever her reservations, the old housemother loved Elizabeth as if she were her own and tried her best to compensate for the isolation from her peers.

"May I see the book?" Mrs. Sharpels gestured toward the sheath of yellowed papers the librarian was holding.

"I didn't even know this was here, before Elizabeth found it in the back of the stacks." Janet Thorpe turned the handwritten volume over in her hands. "It looks like a diary. But it must have been hidden in one of the huge volumes of material compiled by Dr. Regis."

Mrs. Sharpels recognized the name of a historian and scientist who had lived near the edge of Goatswood Forest in a decaying mansion surrounded by twisted hawthorn trees. Dr. Regis was generally regarded as a brilliant man who became senile in later years and took to raving about things watching him and taking over the Earth. He had died about ten years ago at age 80. Having no family, his huge library of work on the history of the area and other projects both in Great Britain and the Middle East, where he spent much of his adult life, was donated by the local government to the Exham Foundling Home.

Mrs. Sharpels retreated to a table in the corner and opened the diary.

12 January, 1883. I've been to the cone in the clearing. I waited until it was very cold. I know now that they're not as active in the winter. It is the safest time to enter the forest. Even those vile creatures are daunted by the English winter.

I realize the connection now. The carvings on the outside have so much in common with hieroglyphics, I knew it was no coincidence. I think this civilization visited Earth before. I have made tracings and will try to decipher the meaning. I realize on every trip I may be caught and only God knows what they would do. I pray the light and the cold protect me. So far, I've seen no trace of anything.

1 February, 1883. I have discovered how to interpret the carvings. What I read is a sketchy history, but enough to know I was right. The Shaggai enslaved the ancient Egyptians and forced them to build temples that we now know as the pyramids, in much the same way they had controlled the Xiclotl. But the pyramids were not used for worship. I don't know their use yet, but I will. I must go inside the cone to see more. I wonder if my need to find out the answers to this riddle will be enough to overcome my fear.

15 February, 1883. The Shaggai are active inside the temple during the day, so I went last night and my worst fears were realized. Mastering the entrance was not hard. It slid outward with enough force to push the ice and snow back from the portal. As cold as it was, my fear made me perspire as I breached the dark opening in the cone. Although I should have been prepared by my familiarization with the carvings, my first sight of the insects was so horrible that I dropped my lantern and they stirred. I waited for what seemed like an eternity before realizing they were not going to move from their slabs.

To read about the horror of the beings from Xiclotl could not have prepared me for what I encountered when I passed their cells, and the terror of inching along that dark passage, my back almost brushing their groping appendages. They are frightening and menacing in every aspect. Low growls signal their frustration at not quite being able to pull me close enough. Only the cell bars saved me from being torn to bits. But I knew that the answers to my questions lay further on and I marshalled the courage to follow the ever-downward spiral.

In the dim light of the lantern I could barely make out the carvings, but I didn't need tracings, since by now I read the Shaggai language almost as well as English. The immensity of what I learned is made fresh by having to write it now. We cannot survive this. They are among us.

From the beginning of their habitation on Earth, the Shaggai realized that the Earthlings were not as malleable as the Xiclotl. They could be controlled only with great mental strain by their captors and not always then. Rebellion was a constant danger. But since the Xiclotl slaves were few in number, it became necessary for the Shaggai to enter in an unholy alliance with some of the more power-hungry Earth leaders. A few of these leaders had great influence over their fellow beings and could use them to serve the Shaggai's purposes. I realize that it was during this time that the pyramids were built. Not as temples, but as hives to serve as nesting places for the diminishing Shaggai species. Their plan was to build Shaggai numbers to the point where colonies could be established throughout the Earth. Working closely with the Earth creatures proved to be the undoing of this plan.

Experiments took place in laboratories near the hatcheries under the collaborative efforts of scientists from both species. These experiments are so abhorred by the Shaggai that the details were not written, but apparently somehow the two species were interbred. What resulted was a being that lived its pupal stage as one species and upon entering adulthood, metamorphosized into the other. Before the leaders realized what was happening, thousands of cells in the pyramid were implanted with the crossbreeds. Upon hatching these beings resembled humans and as they reached their twelfth year they would change into abnormally large Shaggai. Their reproduction followed the Shaggai. Only certain females could reproduce. Two females would be chosen from the hive and administered the right secretions to function as replenishers of the species. The two females emerged as human children. Upon their metamorphosis, they changed into Shaggai but far larger and superior in strength and intelligence to others of their race. These two fought to the death for control of the hive. Often, the strongest would change first and prevail over her opponent.

The remaining Shaggai that were not crossbred detested the mixed breed. They were looked upon as mutants and lower forms of life. "True" Shaggai often raided the mixed-breed hives and killed all the occupants. In the last carvings, it shows that these true Shaggai realized that Earth was too dangerous a place and transported off the planet, leaving the Earthlings and mutants behind. When the Shaggai later returned to the Earth, however, something in the atmosphere had changed, trapping them here.

These last writings are from the new section I discovered in the cone. One barely noticeable passage leads off into a section that is clearly the nursery area. The carvings here are new. The beings who have found their way here are not true Shaggai. They are mutants who discovered this cone and subjugated the earlier Shaggai inhabitants. That explains why they are so much larger.

I've seen the cells in the nest. It's empty now. There were ten surviving pupa. Two are females, the rest are drones. They were sent out to live among us. The small, weak drones will be easy to kill once they have changed, but the queens are quite a different matter. They are survivors and the progenitors of the mutant race. Once they change, a cycle will begin that will mean the end of our civilization. The new Shaggai are preparing now for her to return. They are waiting for their queen. When she returns they intend to start new hives and plant mutant children everywhere. Where are these children? They must be close by. There's not much time left to find and destroy the mutants. Surely the true Shaggai would hunt them down and kill them. The true insects are still there in the cone, imprisoned somehow below in the dark. But I am an old man without courage enough to go down there and free them.

The volume slipped from her hand and thumped to the floor, attracting the attention of the librarian. "Where is Elizabeth?" Mrs. Sharpels' round face was contorted in fear and horror.

"She went out in the play yard hours ago. You know how she likes to be alone."

Elizabeth stretched and kicked the cluster of dead leaves that had accumulated as she slept on the forest floor. The nap had renewed her. She felt better and opened her eyes. Her vision was much better now and she wiped the side of her head against one rigid, black foreleg. The stiff new hair on her body was still damp as she rolled to right herself. She was feeling stronger by the minute. She turned her new wings to the meager sunshine to dry them.

At that moment, she realized the other was very near. She had barely fought it off before but had managed to knock it unconscious. It was awake now and somewhere very close. At that instant the rock hit the side of her head and split the multi-faceted eye squarely down the middle. Green fluorescent liquid oozed down her antenna from the damaged socket. Elizabeth screamed in agony and attempted to take off. Her wings weren't dry. She heaved off and fell back down just as the rock came down again and rended another portion of eye and cracked the brain cavity. Elizabeth swung wildly and her claw found purchase on the fleshy leg of the other. But it was too late; the last blow neatly separated Liz's head from her neck and killed her.

Mrs. Sharpels straightened, clutching her chest and bleeding heavily from the gash in her thigh. She had to get back to Exham and tend her wounds before she set out in search of the second queen. There was no time to lose.

The Undercliffe Sentences

by Peter Cannon

We are tentatively shooting for a summer 1995 release date, to coincide with NecronomiCon '95 where Mr. Campbell is to be the guest of honor (or is that the guest of horror?).

— Scott David Aniolowski, prospectus for *Made in Goatswood*

Carl Dreadstone, guest of horror at the 1995 Brichester Fantasy Convention, wrapped up his talk about authorship, "Horror: Fantasy or Fiction?", with the usual lies about his childhood. In truth, both his parents had been loving and kind, giving him the sort of enlightened, humanistic upbringing that those raised beneath the blighted yoke of religious superstition can only envy. Nothing had scared Carl Dreadstone as a boy, not even the dark. But what self-respecting horror writer is going to let on that his had been a "normal" family? Certainly not a professional like Carl Dreadstone, who was never one to disappoint the fans.

"Finally, after years of intensive therapy, I succeeded in sublimating my fears into my fiction. Any questions?"

Dreadstone surveyed the sea—no, puddle—of moon-shaped faces hovering above soft, baggy bodies, which lay strewn like discards at a parish jumble sale over the seats of the auditorium. A few flabby arms, like overripe cheese, rose balloon-like in the air.

"Yes, you there with the skull earring."

"I've heard rumors that you weren't the con's first guest of horror. Have you any comment?"

"Yes, that's quite true. In fact, I wasn't even the second choice. Martin Amis had not said no when originally invited. You can imagine how the organizers were practically foaming at the mouth at the prospect of roping in a popular mainstream author—an extract from *London Fields* appearing in a 'new gothic' anthology had given them their opening—but in the end Amis realized he had better things to do. Then they tried to get Jay Ramsey, but he was already booked to go to America. Frankly, I was about the best they could scrape up at the last minute. Next question, please."

"Do you ever write anything but horror?" piped up another lad.

"Yes, I've tried. Lord knows, I've tried. And failed. How I wish I could write literary fiction and be accepted as a real author—like Martin Amis or Gwyn Barry, to name two of Britain's top novelists." While Dreadstone would have loved to bare the soul a bit further, from experience he knew audiences could tolerate only so much self-pity. So after an anguished pause he simply said, "But I must do the best I can within my limits as a mere genre writer."

"Do you mind not being famous?" asked another adolescent.

"Yes, I do. I mind it terribly. But then I realize there's still lots to be grateful for in this life whenever wacks like you ask me questions like that."

"What was Errol Undercliffe like?" came the next query.

"Rather indulgent with pushy and self-centered fans, based on our one encounter. I was in the audience at an author talk just like this one thirty years ago, at the last Brichester Fantasy Con. Afterwards I managed to steer Undercliffe into a corner and grill him at length about Roland Franklyn."

And so the inquisition went on for another half hour. No one could deny that patience—though at times it felt like self-abasement—was Carl Dreadstone's strong suit. For example, his fondness for signing books of his sent from America was legendary in horror circles. These collectors were often considerate enough to include U.S. currency, which he could then change for pounds at the bank before waiting in line at the post to mail the books back overseas. Usually his correspondents provided an envelope and left him a few extra pence for his trouble.

In any event, this one-man performance had been no more an ordeal than the author signing the night before. One admirer had been pushing a handcart stacked with hardcover copies of Dreadstone's last three novels—*The Itching*, *They Who Suck*, and *Alien Turds*—all pasted with remainder stickers. He'd cleaned out the stock of the Lower Brichester branch of a national discount chain, the git had cheerfully confessed, and looked forward to reselling them for a profit to his friends. Most had required personal inscriptions. Dreadstone had been only too happy to oblige. Then there had been the many fans with copies of his current novel, *Vampire?!* A joy, as always, seeing and fingering one's new book for the first time.

In fact, Dreadstone's only real regret was that he had missed the panel scheduled opposite him, featuring S. Hutson and S. Hudson. Like Superman and Clark Kent, Hutson and Hudson had never been seen in the same room at the same time. For years he'd suspected that the author of *Heathen* and the author of *Hounds of Horror* were one person—though he wouldn't put it past the man to hire a double to keep the deception alive. Hutson, or Hudson, as the master of contrived plot and perfervid prose, was more than capable of pulling that kind of juvenile stunt, he was sure.

After a good vomit in the gents, Dreadstone headed for the dealers' room, where he hoped to find Richard Royce, editor of True Lite Press. Royce was bringing out an edition of his tales, *The Undercliffe Sentences: Parodies or Pastiches?*, the sort of stuff his regular publisher wouldn't be caught dead doing but ideal for a small press. Dreadstone wanted an update. A pity the book hadn't been ready in time for the convention, but then Royce had only been holding the manuscript for three years. There had been concerns about money, libel, copyright infringement, bad taste—all the familiar excuses for delay. At last, however, Royce had agreed to shake hands on the deal and the project was pretty much formally under contract.

Dreadstone was in luck. The editor of True Lite Press was sitting alone, free of pesky customers, at a table near the door.

"How's tricks?" asked the author.

"Not bad, I suppose. I've already sold three copies of *Photographed by Lightning*. Undercliffe's always a reliable seller. Even better, one bloke bought a copy each of my two published novels."

Like most specialty publishers, Royce carried a wide range of titles, mainly within the field, but he offered other odd volumes as well—like his own two non-genre novels, *Aforethought* and *Dreams Don't Mean Anything*. Such mention led Royce to expand on his so far unfruitful efforts to place several successor novels. Lately things were looking up, though. The head of the London vanity press where he worked one day a week as Special Director had expressed an interest in issuing one or more of them.

"I see you have copies of *Vampire?!*," Dreadstone finally interrupted.

"Oh, yes. Several potential customers have thumbed through it. Quite the crowd pleaser, from what I hear. Mind autographing my supply?"

"Glad to. 'Til I get my author's copies, this is the next best thing."

As Dreadstone set about this pleasurable task, Royce held forth on his ambitions for True Lite Press, which had had a slightly different name in the sixties, long before his own involvement. He planned to reissue *How I Discovered My Infinite Self*, by "An Initiate", and was busy trying to track down Roland Franklyn's exceedingly rare tome, *We Pass from View*, bound in bright blue.

"Even if we could find a copy, there's no guarantee the text wouldn't writhe and shimmer across the page." Royce chuckled.

Dreadstone recognized the reference, to an episode in one of Undercliffe's homages to Franklyn, and smiled—thinly. He, Dreadstone, after all, knew the tales of these two authors more intimately than any fan, critic, or collector on this planet. Only he could have pulled off such a brilliant send-up as *The Undercliffe Sentences*, simultaneously parodying Franklyn a la Undercliffe and Undercliffe a la Franklyn. Or was it more a matter of pastiching? Given how closely Franklyn and Undercliffe could resemble each other in style and content, the differences weren't always obvious. Well, readers liked puzzles. Let them figure it out.

"Oh, before I forget. I have something for you." Dreadstone set down the last signed copy of *Vampire?!*, while the editor reached under the table and handed him a bulky envelope. "I think you'll be pleased. We took especial care. No rush to return it, of course."

"Dare I ask? What I gave you six months ago, is it, can it really be—"

"Yes, the copyedited manuscript. As I say, whenever you get around to it—"

Eager as he was to check it over, Dreadstone had no immediate opportunity to peruse his manuscript, which he dropped off in his room in college—how economical it had been to hold the convention at Brichester University during the summer vac—since he'd promised to meet Harvey Nadler, of Delta Film Productions, for lunch in the cafeteria.

Usually an important author, in particular a guest of horror, had an entourage at these gatherings. Authors of equal if not greater stature hung out with him, stood him lagers at pubs, shielded him from the unwanted advances of the fans. His editor, his agent, stood by his side like a Praetorian guard. But where was Dreadstone's editor? Where was his agent? Well, it just so happened that they were also Jay Ramsey's editor and agent—and because Jay Ramsey was in America on tour they were also on tour in America. With Jay Ramsey, who'd be signing a four-film deal in Hollywood.

Harvey Nadler was an old friend. Delta Film Productions had considered taking an option on *The Itching*, on *They Who Suck*, on *Alien Turds*—and now they were considering picking up the option on *Vampire?!* Delta Film Productions had yet to pay Dreadstone a penny, but perhaps it would be different this time. Right. And maybe in the New Year he'd receive his knighthood, for services to literature.

Dreadstone joined Nadler at a formica-topped table for two, near the kitchen. It was noisy enough for them to talk without fear of being overheard.

"Please thank your publicity department, Carl," said Nadler, with a thin smile. "A copy of *Vampire?!* was on my desk a month ago. What I've read looks promising—not as allusive as previous novels, I was relieved to find. Readers can't stand that, you know. It makes them feel dumber than the author. Never condescend to your audience, Carl. It's bad form as well as bad business."

"I made a deliberate attempt to be more commercial, Harvey," responded Dreadstone. "Vampires are hot right now."

"Yes, they're hot all right. Very hot. Damned hot. There are more vampire books on the loose today than bats in hell, Carl. Ever try to tell one bat from another? Believe me, Carl, you've seen one bat you've seen 'em all."

"I appreciate your concern, Harvey."

"Ever think about screenwriting?"

"No, I never have."

"Why not?"

"Oh, I don't know. Maybe because my heroes Roland Franklyn and Errol Undercliffe never wrote screenplays."

"Franklyn and Undercliffe, as if I needed to remind you, Carl, had their careers cut prematurely short. If they'd survived to your age, I'm sure they would've moved to Hollywood ages ago."

"What about *Red Dreams*, Harvey? You know, Harry Chang's adaptation of three of Undercliffe's best tales."

"Come on. That arty stuff?"

"Chang's interpretation of *The Drifting Face* is beyond anything we've done or could even conceive of in the West. If an independent Korean film maker were to express an interest in adapting one of my works, why I'd—"

"Carl, is *Red Dreams* part of this weekend's film program?"

"No. In fact, I was rather surprised to learn it wasn't. I mean—"

"Carl, what was shown last night at that special midnight screening?"

"I believe *A Clockwork Orange* and *Child's Play 3*."

"Right. There you have it—the kinds of films the public want to view."

Dreadstone had been sorry to have missed these two movies, as well as the subsequent police raid—he wondered if the organizers now regretted advertising their film program in the *Brichester Herald*—but he'd needed his sleep after the long trip from London by lorry. After debating the genius of Stanley Kubrick versus that of the director of *Child's Play 3*, whose name neither of them could remember, it was almost time for the next big event.

"One last piece of advice," said Nadler as they bussed their trays. "Have you ever considered doing novelizations? I might be able to send something your way in that line sometime, if you like."

"No, I haven't, Harvey, but please do keep me in mind, though."

Next on the docket for Dreadstone was an interview with the editor of a local fanzine called *Spirited*. *Spirited*'s readership may not have been large, but it had circulated around the Brichester region off and on over the years and Dreadstone was never one to turn up his nose at even the humblest of publicity venues. He met the editor, a pubescent fourteen-year-old who'd recently taken over the position, in an empty classroom.

"Should I have heard of you?" the lad asked as he fiddled with his tape recorder.

"Yes, definitely. I'm a professional horror writer."

"Before we begin, I should tell you I prefer fiction to be about real life."

"Well, I prefer fiction to be about real life, too. But it so happens that what I write, what I'm capable of writing, isn't about real life. It's escapist. It has nothing to do with the everyday cares of ordinary existence, like finding and holding a job, or getting married and staying married. Do I make myself clear?"

"Yeh."

"When you reach my age, my boy, you'll recognize your own shortcomings as keenly as I do mine."

"I should hope not—oh, here, the mike's on. Ready for the first question?"

"Fire away."

"Does it bother you that none of your work has ever been turned into a film, especially when others, less talented than yourself, have made a packet on movie sales?"

"Yes, it does. Funny you should bring it up. I was just talking to a producer friend of mine about this very subject. To speak plainly, I'm frightfully jealous of toffee-nosed twits like ———— and ———— who've been paid such obscene sums of money for rubbish like ———— and ————. Very self-satisfied these hacks are, too, I might add. Hate 'em."

There was an extended pause while the editor flipped through the pages of a loose-leaf notebook on his lap.

"Right, second question. Would you care to comment about how your words have been altered in American editions of your books?"

"Yes, I would. Take the word 'randy.' In *They Who Suck* it was turned into a proper name. Yes, believe it or not, there are Americans named 'Randy.' A shift from lowercase to capitals affected a major sex scene—'Tiffany was feeling randy' into 'Tiffany was feeling Randy', with a capital R. I'm afraid some American readers got the impression I sanctioned threesomes. I'm sorry, but I don't."

"What about foreign translations?" asked the editor.

"I've just placed the English translation of the French translation of a story of mine, 'The Revenge of the Curate of Temphill', with another French publisher. Mark Twain did something similar once, with that jumping frog tall tale of his. It's also like that dinner-table game, telephone, where one person whispers a saying to the person next to him and so on round the table. The results can be quite hilarious. I hope to keep 'Revenge of the Curate' going this way between French and English for as long as I can."

There was another lengthy break, until the editor again found his place in his notes.

"Is Carl Dreadstone your real name?"

"As real as the name Roland Franklyn or Errol Undercliffe."

"Where were you born?"

"Clotton."

"So you grew up here."

"Yes and no. My family moved to London as soon as they could afford to get out. I was almost able to go to the loo by myself at the time. As a teen I returned to the area for the occasional pop concert."

It was a comfort to Dreadstone that the editor's questions were beginning to follow in some logical sequence. As he'd done in dozens of past interviews, he covered the familiar biographical ground—ancestry, schooling, jobs, his discovery of the works of Roland Franklyn and Errol Undercliffe—varying the details in subtle and fiendish fashion. "Let future Dreadstone scholars straighten out the mess" was his motto. What could be more boring than plodding and unremitting consistency?

Three hours later Dreadstone looked at his watch. He'd missed the tour of the nearby Undercliffe and Franklyn sites, though to be honest he didn't care all that much, unlike some scholarly types he knew, which drab house or grotty street or blitz-bashed neighborhood had inspired his mentors in a slag heap like Brichester. He would have to hustle to make his next appointment, a reading in the college library of his notorious acrostic tale, "The Letters That Spell."

Written in the second-person plural voice, this ingenious short-short requires you to take the first letter of the first word, the second letter of the second word, the third letter of the third word, the fourth letter of the fourth word, and so on, until you reach a word with fewer letters than the number you were up to. Then you count down to one, whereupon you start to count up again, until, as before, the count exceeds the last number of the series, and you once more descend the scale, as it were, repeating the process to story's end. These letters form an anagram concealing a passage from Robert G. Ingersoll's classic *Some Mistakes of Moses*, a favorite text of his freethinking parents. Dreadstone's explanation of all this afterwards took several times as long as the reading itself. He was glad he'd been allotted a full hour.

Back in his room Dreadstone deliberated whether to smoke a joint or pop some LSD in preparation for the climactic con banquet in the caf, billed as the "Feast of Eihort." No, taking drugs is what he invariably did before writing anything important. The complimentary six-pack of Tetley's beer the organizers had been so kind to place on his pillow was all he required to fortify himself for the feeding.

Dreadstone was accorded a chair at the head table, along with such other dignitaries as S. Hutson and S. Hudson, who sat side by side, like Laurel and Hardy—or was it like Tintin's twin detectives, Thompson and Thomson? In the glow of the tepid beverage he'd swilled beforehand, Dreadstone couldn't decide whether the pair resembled each other or not. At any rate, he passed through the alcohol-free meal in an agreeable stupor until speaker time, when horror m.c. *extraordinaire*, Beavis Lampbeavis, rose to his feet.

"Ladies and Gents, Girls and Boys, Lasses and Laddies, Ghouls and Goys, may I have your attention please," Lampbeavis announced, tapping Dreadstone's head sharply with a spoon. "We have gathered here at Brichester U. to 'honor' one of horror's professionals. Let me say right off the bat that the rumors running round the con are indeed true. He wasn't our first choice, nor even out second—as I'm sure he'd be the first to confess. Right, Carl?" Dreadstone nodded. "But if there's one thing you can say about Carl—some might say the only thing—he's a jolly good sport."

"Hear, hear!" cried a voice in the crowd, possibly Richard Royce's.

"Others would say that Carl Dreadstone is a modest man, of modest achievements. Just think about it. First he made us scratch our skins in horror with *The Itching*; next he made us purse our lips in horror with *They Who Suck*; then he made us wipe our, er, wipe ourselves in horror with *Alien Turds*; and now with his latest novel *Vampire?!*—or is that *Vampire!?* Quick, Carl, which is it?"

"It's question mark first, exclamation second, Beav."

"Yes, right, thank you. With *Vampire?!* Carl Dreadstone will, uh, will, uh—drive his fans batty!"

More cheers from the assembled horror hordes.

"It's been my privilege, Carl, to flip through your new novel," the m.c. continued. "It includes so many characteristic touches. On page fifty, for instance, you describe a *Los Angeles Times* crossword clue as being followed by the numbers four and five in parentheses. Carl, you should know in the United States crosswords don't provide the number of letters and words where there's a multi-word answer, as we do in Britain. Nor is the phrase 'eggs and chips a la mode' apt to appear in an *L.A. Times* cookery column. Chips are 'French fries' in America. As for the word 'cookery', I believe it's not in common parlance across the Atlantic. You get the picture."

"Yes, my ignorance appalls even me at times," answered the author, standing up so the whole room could hear. "Forgive me."

"We forgive you, Carl. I promise to supply you a complete list of your gaffs in time to correct them for the paperback edition."

"Thank you, Beav. Spoken like a gentleman."

"I think you'd agree with me, Carl, that you've already said enough today—at your author chat, at your story reading, at the feast just now. So if you don't mind, why don't we dispense with the customary guest-of-horror speech. Sit down, relax—and get set to enjoy a special personal tribute."

Dreadstone readily complied. He liked receiving accolades. A moment later a young chap appeared beside the m.c., sheets of paper in hand. Lampbeavis introduced him to the audience.

"At the eleventh hour, we on the organizing committee decided that a writing contest would be a smashing idea. As a surprise for you, Carl, we invited your readers to send us stories, no longer than 10,000 words, that mimicked, parodied, or otherwise ripped off your fiction. The response, I must say, was gratifying. The winner will now read his tale in its entirety."

"This is my version of Mr. Dreadstone's brand of 'televisionary' horror," the fellow mumbled into his manuscript. "It's called 'The Curate of Temphill Goes to New York.'"

Dreadstone thanked his lucky stars he was sitting close enough to catch every word of the lad's low, monotonic delivery: the slow introduction with its antecedentless pronouns; the strings of adjectives run riot and metaphors gone mad; the lengthy inward expository passages unrelieved by dialogue; the images out of cheap films and comic books; the blood, the entrails, the animal sacrifices; the climax where the narrator realizes the killer's name spelled backwards is—

The crowd roared its approval as soon as people noticed the amateur had stopped reading. Fan fiction. It was Dreadstone's secret vice. He consumed it the way some addicts stuff themselves with bonbons—or fill their veins with crack—or drown themselves in Tetley's beer. But how much of a good thing can one bear? After the winner departed, Lampbeavis introduced the runner-up, who proceeded to read his Dreadstone offering in full. Then it was the turn of the third-place finisher, and finally of the "horrible" mention.

At the end Lampbeavis announced to the few souls still scattered about the caf that these four stories would be featured in the next issue of *Spirited*. "I'll make sure you get put on the comp list, Carl," the m.c. said in parting.

"Thanks, Beav. I look forward to seeing them in cold print."

Back in his room Dreadstone looked forward to a little light reading before seeking the darkness he craved. Another page or two of Gwyn Barry's best-selling *Stumbling on Melons*? No, there was something waiting for him even more thrilling—how could he have forgotten?—the copyedited manuscript of *The Undercliffe Sentences*.

He pulled it out of the envelope, plopped it on the bed, and dove in. He soon discovered that every page was a veritable Jackson Pollack of editorial markings: commas added and deleted, dashes for semicolons, semicolons for colons, colons for dashes, words italicized and unitalicized, infinitives split and adverbs transposed, big paragraphs minced into little paragraphs, entire passages rewritten to convey their hidden meanings. In short, he found all the usual changes and corrections he'd come to expect from a thorough copyedit job. If he'd wanted to punctuate, paragraph, italicize, or emphasize in the way that the copyeditor had, he reminded himself, he should have done so in the first place. Fair enough. All this he could and did routinely accept.

There was another class of commentary, however, that took him aback. These had mainly to do with content, scrawled in indelible red ink in the margins, odd queries like: "Are you sure the name of the initiate who travels to Tond is Yokh'khim?"; "Did this occur before or after the yarkdao built the city of Derd?"; "Would this character be likely to use a tok'l container for this purpose?"; "What's the true, heirophantic significance of the phrase *xada-hgla soron*?"; and perhaps queerest of all, "As'lak, Sauron, Daoloth, etc.—do you think it safe to use this incantation?" Did the answers to these nitpicking questions—this was a collection of parodies or pastiches, after all—really matter? He fell asleep pondering the possibilities.

In the morning he woke up knowing he had to speak to the woman who had dissected the manuscript, performed the autopsy as it were, given how vividly the post mortem had appeared in a dream. (Dreams can and do have meaning, even if Richard Royce might disagree.) There was something insistent about her queries that brooked no delay in response. Perhaps there was still a prayer the patient could, if not be revived, at least be reanimated.

He located a working phone two blocks from the college, slipped in a 10p piece, and rang the number in Goatswood.

"I say, it's a mite early, Dreadstone. Couldn't this wait 'til the dealers' room opens at ten?" answered the editor of True Lite Press.

"You have to tell me who your copyeditor is, Royce. I must talk to her straight away, see her if possible. I sense she's local. Not at the con, is she?"

"Yes, she does live in Brichester, but fat chance you'd catch her at the con. She's a recluse, has no phone, scarcely ever goes out."

"Sounds like your typical introvert copyeditor—wide knowledge making up for lack of worldly experience."

"We chose her for your book because of her particular expertise."

"You wouldn't mind my calling on her."

"Not at all, not at all. She welcomes visitors, she gets so few of them. You can walk from the university to her place in Dee Terrace, on Mercy Hill."

"I think I can find that." Then, remembering his manners: "Thanks awfully. Sorry to wake you."

"Quite all right, but please remember, there's no hurry on the manuscript."

Dreadstone consulted a city map to make sure he could find his way. The most direct route was through Central Park. At that hour of the morning he had the park to himself, apart from the few furtive figures that flitted like loose sacking through the underbrush and the nasty bits of paper that skimmed across the grass like illicit lovers on a lark. He passed the bandshell where the Titus Groans had played a concert in '66. He had come down from London for that one, just as he had a year later to hear Spinal Tap perform at the island beyond Severnford. Ah, the memories! The horned skulls and the devil masks bobbing and weaving in the strobe lights, the lads leaping and prancing through flaming pentagrams, the night breeze wafting the acrid scent of Wimpy burgers—all now as quaint as druids and Stonehenge. He'd been heavily into the works of Errol Undercliffe at the time and thought it no coincidence that bass guitarist Derek Smalls had gone on record as having read and liked *The Man Who Feared to Sleep*, while the influence of "Through the Zone of the Colossi" was manifest in Nigel Tufnel's lyrics on Tap's *Break Like the*

Wind album. No doubt about it—heavy metal music had helped satisfy his youthful craving to believe in some higher spiritual authority.

From the foot of Mercy Hill he had to climb a dozen or so levels before reaching Dee Terrace. The house was unmistakable—the waist-high weeds in the garden, the cloud of flies above the chimney, the black curtains across every window except a bricked-up one on the ground-floor—each eccentric detail bespoke a copyeditor's domain. He knocked at the front door. From inside a woman's voice screamed: "I'm naked. Wait a minute!"

Five minutes later the door opened. She wore a pink nightgown that clashed with the crimson wallpaper of the hall and the carrot color of her hair. The silky garment barely concealed the flabby folds of her aged flesh.

"Hello, I'm Carl Dreadstone."

"Never heard of you."

"I'm a horror writer. You—"

"A horror writer! Of all the nerve!"

"I'm attending the fantasy convention being held this weekend at the university, and was wondering—"

"Yes, I know all about that from the reports on the telly. Shocking, absolutely shocking it is showing filth like those films. Jail is too good for those degenerates!"

"I was hoping you wouldn't mind my dropping in. I've brought—"

"A present. For me?" The woman eyed the package under his arm containing the copyedited manuscript. "I never get presents anymore. Never. You'd better come in."

He followed his hostess down the hall into a sunken living room, lit by a single red bulb on a ceiling cord and furnished with a bed, a chair, a state-of-the-art home entertainment center. A dark-skinned girl was dusting.

"Bhaji, we have a visitor. We must play something. What would you like to hear, young man, Debussy's string quartet or Beethoven's 'Opus 135?'"

"Either, both. It doesn't matter."

Dreadstone sat down in the chair, the envelope on his lap, while the woman went over to the console and jabbed at some buttons. Nothing happened.

"Miss Arco, the tape player's broke," whispered the girl. "You forget."

"Broke! Why didn't you tell me? Get out, you impudent wog. Out I say. Can't you see I have a guest?"

"Yes, Miss Arco." The girl left quietly, evidently accustomed to such treatment.

"Never mind," the woman said, sitting on the bed. "I shall sing for you. The 'Vissi d'arte' aria from *Tosca*."

"Please don't trouble yourself—"

"Trouble! You talk to me of trouble! I'll tell you about trouble!" Her face took on a scarlet hue that matched neither the pink of her gown nor the orange of her hair. "For years I live alone here. Nobody comes. Then yesterday a busload of those, those *people* turn up at my house. They trample the garden with their clumsy feet. They try to look in windows. They bang on the door. Nobody cares about me—they only care about *him*."

"Him?"

"My late husband. That idiot. If they want *him* they can go to his grave, near the school. That other horror writer did, soon after he died, and look where it got him—worse than the grave! I threw out all my poor little Frankla's books after that, including every copy of *We Pass from View*. Disgusting the way they used to ooze through one's fingers, just disgusting!"

"I'm sorry—"

"You're sorry! What about me, Leda Arco? Yes, I go by my own name now. Only that pathetic failed novelist gives a damn, what's his name, you know the one I'm talking about."

"Richard Royce?"

"That's the one, that's the one. Only he appreciates me. He gives me work—"

"Yes, I know!" Dreadstone shrieked. He'd decided he'd better assert himself if he didn't want to spend the rest of his natural days in that house. "Please listen. That's why I'm here. You copyedited my manuscript. That's what's in the envelope. I wanted to talk to you about your—suggestions."

The woman stared at Dreadstone, as if suddenly recognizing him for the first time. Her complexion shaded into purple.

"You! You! You thief! That's what you are. How dare you steal my husband's stories!"

"I didn't steal anything. I wrote *The Undercliffe Sentences* as a way of acknowledging my debt to the influence of my predecessors. It's perfectly normal and innocent."

"Normal! Innocent! How dare you! How dare you use his concepts when you have no idea, no idea you understand, what you're doing!"

"Stylistic concerns aside, I take it you had some problems, serious problems I'll grant, with some of the text."

"I was his wife! If you knew what I know you wouldn't be so glib about the burrowers beneath the Plain of Sound on S'glhuo or what the elder things kept out of later editions of *Revelations from Glaaki*."

"I'd like to put everything right—"

"Come here." Her tone was gentle again. Amazing how she could shift from one mood extreme to another. "Let Ledasha help you."

Dreadstone hesitated. The woman reached over and pulled him next to her on the bed. He unsheathed the manuscript.

By the glow of the red bulb they went over *The Undercliffe Sentences*, page by page, paragraph by paragraph, sentence by sentence. Bathed in blood, the words seemed to wiggle, to squirm, against the rosy-hued page. They were compelled to read much of the text aloud, including the Daoloth chant, repeating it three times. Discarded manuscript leaves fluttered to the floor, gathering in curiously ordered heaps at their feet.

They had reached chapter four when Dreadstone felt something on his calf, beneath the trouser leg. He scratched the offended area, to relieve the itching of some tiny creature who sucked, depositing its orthographical droppings. He pulled both legs onto the bed, as did the woman breathing heavily at his side. Dreadstone seemed to be viewing the scene through the thin and shifting perceptual haze of an acid trip that was just ending—or just beginning. He closed his eyes as they lay back and embraced, but it did no good. When he opened them he saw her mouth was disappearing—the left side was already gone—for swarming over their limbs and faces like flies were the Undercliffe letters, the Undercliffe syllables, the Undercliffe words, the Undercliffe phrases, the Undercliffe clauses, the Undercliffe sentences.

The Awakening

by Gary Sumpter

True science will not deny the existence of things because they cannot be weighed and measured. It will rather lead us to believe that the wonders and subtleties of possible existence surpass all that our mental powers allow us clearly to perceive.

— William Stanley Jevons, *The Principles of Science*

Ghosts are like termites," Graham called from the landing. "If they're there, you have to disclose them."

At the bottom of the stairs, Christine looked to Wetherby, the estate agent. He set down his briefcase and nodded. "The law says we have to reveal if a house is stigmatized: That is, if a murder or suicide has recently taken place in the home, we must inform the prospective buyer."

Christine shifted uneasily. "What happened to the previous owner?"

"Hanged himself," Wetherby told her, as though he were summarizing the latest episode of *Coronation Street*, not a suicide. "In the attic."

"Do you know why?" Graham asked, joining them downstairs. "I mean, did he leave a note?"

Christine was appalled. "My God, Graham, must you be so morbid?"

"I really wouldn't know about that," Wetherby said. "The note, I mean: Mr. Stark had no immediate family, and the executor—a distant cousin, I believe—lives in Scotland."

Wetherby's beeper went off; he excused himself and scurried into the kitchen to telephone his office. Graham looked at Christine expectantly. "Well? What do you think?"

"What do I *think*?" Christine threw her hands up in desperation. "What am I supposed to think? Graham, it's a *haunted house*. I don't know how I ever let you talk me into this."

"Perfect!" He smiled and kissed her on the forehead. "Shall we put in an offer?"

* * *

The half-timbered Gloucestershire farmhouse was more than three hundred years old, and fairly reeked of antiquity. Surrounded by beech woods, it overlooked the Vale of Berkeley and, on a clear day, one could see the dark ribbon of the Severn River out beyond Brichester—or so the estate agent had assured them. The property itself was expansive; there would be plenty of room for Caesar, their Alsatian, to roam. Best of all, it was only a two hour drive from London on the M4—but a world away from the bustle, the perfect retreat for a writer.

If Graham Beaumont has achieved some measure of success in his literary endeavors, it is due almost entirely to luck and perseverance: He was always the first to admit that he possessed neither the impeccable technique of a Poe, nor the extraordinary imagination of a Lovecraft—yet his career was plagued by often unfavorable comparisons to both. Years of struggling in London had taken their toll; Graham needed a change of pace, and Christine—who grew up in the country—was eager to leave the city behind.

The farmhouse was, quite simply, everything they had hoped for—and more: The previous owner had effected a painstaking restoration of the ivy-mantled house from top to bottom, achieving a complete rejuvenation of the exposed oak beams and the ancient flagstone floors. The splendid mullioned windows had been carefully restored to their former grandeur, and the shutters hand-painted. A refurbished carriage house adjacent would accommodate both the Metro and the MGB. The house came fully furnished, although the unusual mix of styles revealed Stark's rather eclectic tastes. Renovating the place would not be necessary, although Christine—despite her earlier misgivings—had already compiled a notebook full of decorating ideas by the time they moved in.

* * *

Their first project was the master bedroom. By the end of the week, however, it became apparent that they hadn't enough wallpaper: Christine volunteered to drive into Brichester for another roll, while Graham busied himself with clearing away some of the weeds that were encroaching on the drive. He had a bucket full of the unwelcome vegetation when a voice called out: "Hello!"

Graham looked up. Across the way, at the only house within earshot, a middle-aged woman in a floral dress waved from her rose garden. She struggled to her feet as Graham approached.

"I'm Vera Corwin," she said, adjusting her spectacles. "You must be the new owner at the Old Horns."

"I'm Graham Beaumont. My wife and I just moved in this week."

"Keeping busy, I'll wager." She gazed across to the farmhouse. "So much to do. Mr. Stark did a lot of work when he first moved in—renovating and such—but I'm afraid he started to let the place go, toward the end."

"How long had he lived here?"

"Oh, not long. About a year." Vera paused to trim her roses. "It was quite sad, and so sudden. Did you know that Mr. Stark was convinced he was being watched? He said he heard voices."

Graham shook his head; Stark had been a psychotic. "Do you know what he did for a living?"

"Now that's the queer thing; he never said. Although he once told Des—that's my husband—that he was doing research of some sort. What is it that *you* do, Mr. Beaumont?"

"I'm a writer." Graham wanted to find out more about the enigmatic Mr. Stark, but a stout fellow—spanner in hand and coveralls smeared with grease—emerged from the garage. "Vera, have you seen—*Hello!* Who's this then?"

Vera waved him over. "Come and meet our new neighbour, Des. Graham Beaumont, this is my husband, Des." He wiped his hand on his coveralls and extended it to Graham. Vera lowered her voice conspiratorially: "Mr. Beaumont's a writer, Des."

"Oh? Beaumont, eh?" Des stroked his chin, and recognition flickered in his eyes. "Beaumont—*The Howling Man*?"

"That was *Charles* Beaumont—an American," Graham chuckled. "And quite deceased, I assure you. But you have the right genre."

Des brandished his spanner in the direction of the farmhouse. "And *you've* come to the right place if you need inspiration for a ghost story."

"Oh, are you writing about the Old Horns, Mr. Beaumont?" Vera was giddy with excitement. "Am *I* in your story?"

"Well, I—"

A toot of the Metro's horn was Graham's salvation; Christine had arrived home, and not a moment too soon. He apologized to the Corwins for having to dash off, offering as an excuse some important legality or other to which he must attend.

Inside, Graham made tea. "You won't believe what happened today," Christine said. "I was very nearly in an accident."

Graham started, but managed not to spill any of the tea as he filled her cup. "What happened?"

She spooned in some sugar and stirred. Caesar slept comfortably at her feet. "I was coming down Victoria Street, in Mercy Hill; some madman came roaring up on the wrong side of the road!"

"Probably an American," Graham laughed, and offered her a biscuit. "They can't seem to get the hang of it. Everything okay, though?"

"Mmm." She took a bite of the Peek Frean. "No worse for wear. Just a little shaken, that's all."

"I can imagine. Makes my day seem rather mundane, I'm afraid. Though I did meet our neighbours, the Corwins."

"Really? What are they like?"

Graham helped himself to a biscuit. "Oh, they seem nice enough; rather—folksy."

"Give them a chance, darling. It's a different way of life out here." She went off to run herself a bath. Graham lingered in the kitchen and finished his tea. Caesar was soon awake and pawing at the back door; Graham let him out, then went down to the cellar, where the last of Stark's personal effects had been stored.

Graham sorted through a trunk full of old clothes. Not much use going through this junk, he knew; who would want a trunk full of old clothes? One suit had been patched so many times that it was difficult to tell if any of the original fabric remained. Graham lifted it out of the trunk and made a startling discovery. Beneath the threadbare clothing there were books. Graham lifted them out one by one: Ewen's *Witch Hunting and Witch Trials*, Notestein's *A History of Witchcraft in England*, original editions of George Gifford's *Discourse on the Subtil Practises of Devilles*, Matthew Hopkins' *The Discovery of Witches*, and Reginald Scot's *Discoverie of Witchcraft*. The trunk was a treasure trove of esoteric literature; Stark's taste was unusual, to say the least. Had he been practicing witchcraft? It seemed unlikely: The books, though rare, were clearly not akin to the hoary, ill-famed tomes of demon-dreaded lore Graham had once glimpsed at the British Museum.

He noticed a bookmark in *The Discovery of Witches*; opening the book, Graham scanned the yellowed page. A local reference caught his eye: *The Abolishment of the Brichester Coven*. His curiosity aroused, Graham carried the book back up to the kitchen to read.

According to the text, when a number of children went missing in Brichester during the autumn of 1644, authorities began to suspect the existence of a coven. The services of Matthew Hopkins were retained and the results were as rapid as they were alarming: Within a fortnight, the witch-finder and his two assistants had rounded up twelve of thirteen suspected witches. These were interrogated, but refused to divulge the name of the thirteenth—the leader of the coven. Finally, after "great and fatiguing effort", Hopkins managed to extract the sorcerer's identity: Zerobbabel Endicot. The witches were executed, and Hopkins promptly set about tracking the fugitive.

He found him, some weeks later, on a farm a few miles distant from Brichester. Hopkins asserted that Endicot had, a number of months previous, succeeded in calling some kind of demon out of the void: a demon that begat a monstrous child upon his wife. Sussanna Endicot had, apparently, complained to her neighbours "of grievous Torment in her Bowels, as if they were Infect'd and Infest'd with Daemons"—and with good reason: Hopkins recorded their description of the child as "an Abomination to the Lord, an Hellish Blasphemy with Eyes like a Flame of Fire." According to the witch-finder, Sussanna died—mercifully—in childbirth and "the Hobgoblin Monstre fled into this Wilderness by Flying in the Air, as no mortal can, and ye Hills were cover'd with ye shadows thereof."

Hopkins recorded in great detail the apprehension of Endicot, and his subsequent execution on Mercy Hill. The fate of the "Hobgoblin Monstre", however, was preserved with less explicitness: The witch-finder stated only that it was "imprison'd in darkness by prayer and ye Ancient Sign."

* * *

The following week Graham was obliged to visit the offices of his London publisher, under whose imprint his latest hardcover collection, *Odd Postures & Antick Gestures*, was about to be released. He was horrified to learn that someone in the office had shamelessly subtitled the book *Twelve Tales of Terror in the Lovecraft Tradition*. Those eight words had reduced two years of his life to mere pastiche; it rankled, but it was too late to do anything about it. 50,000 copies had been printed and were on their way to the shops. Advance reviews had already been published: The *Times* declared *Odd Postures* "a first-rate collection marking Beaumont's long-overdue return to the field", while the *Daily Mail*—somewhat less charitably—called it "an unmitigated disaster, a pointless and derivative exercise in self-aggrandization." Graham always took reviews with a grain of salt; after all, need the two opinions be mutually exclusive?

Beyond Slough, with the London skyline receding in the rear-view mirror, Graham felt a sudden relief. Out past Reading and Swindon on the M4, he raced the MGB through rolling countryside, flying past a dozen villages and a hundred miles of farms and cottages, to the junction of the M5 north of Bristol.

The trip thus far had taken a little under two hours, but Graham knew that the vintage model could easily have shaved off forty-five minutes—had he been inclined to let it. Instead, he stayed close to the posted speed limit and cruised with the top down and the breeze in his hair.

And why not? Traffic was light, the sun was shining, and he felt alive again. He'd be home in time for dinner. On a whim, he decided to leave the M5 and take the long way home, A.38 through Brichester.

WELCOME TO BRICHESTER, the sign proclaimed. But it was crooked, and the city was dying. Graham wheeled onto the ring road, astonished at the fate of countless old buildings in the city centre, glorious relics of a bygone age that had weathered the centuries, now being torn down to make way for shopping centers, office complexes, and highrises; golden Cotswold stone was being gobbled up at an alarming rate, replaced by slabs of cold grey concrete that quickly fell prey to the aerosol depredations of spiteful delinquents. Brichester, he decided, was almost as bad as London.

Christine had dinner waiting for him. Afterwards, Graham settled into his armchair with the *Brichester Herald* while Christine cleared the dinner plates from the table. "How far back did you say our property extends, Graham?"

"About a hundred feet beyond the shed, I should think." He looked up from his paper. "Why do you ask?"

"Because Caesar chased something into the woods behind the shed this afternoon. I was afraid it might be a skunk, so I went in after him."

Graham sniffed the air. "Lucky for us the skunk escaped."

"Yes, but did you know there's an old well back there?"

"Oh?" He raised an eyebrow.

Christine nodded. "There is. It's mostly covered with brush—and a lot of the wood has rotted away. Do you think it might still work?"

He shrugged. "I'm not sure it would be safe. I've heard a lot about ground water contamination lately; makes you think about where your water's coming from."

Graham aimed the torch down the well. Thirty feet below, something glinted in the light—but it wasn't water. "There's something shiny in the mud down there."

Christine leaned closer for a better look. "What is it?"

"I can't tell. A piece of metal, perhaps."

"How do we get it out?"

Graham shrugged. "Why would we even want to?"

"Well—it might be valuable. An old coin or something."

"Whatever it is, it's bigger than a coin. And the only way to get it is to climb down into the well. It's getting late; I think I'll pass."

* * *

They were awakened by a growl and a sudden yelp that reverberated in the night. Christine switched on the light. "That sounded like Caesar."

"You're right." Graham got up, and stumbled over to the window. He parted the blinds; bars of moonlight fell upon the bed. "I don't see him. The skunk again?"

"Oh, Graham—you'd better go look. If he's cornered something—"

Graham grumbled, but couldn't argue the logic. He put on his robe, stepped into his slippers, and headed downstairs. Christine watched from the window as Graham's torch played across the yard. He appeared on the path, pausing to wave up at the window, then disappeared behind the shed. The light was swallowed by the trees, and Christine felt very alone. What if Caesar *had* cornered something—a fox, perhaps? It might attack Graham, too. She wondered what was taking him so long, wondered whether she should get dressed and go after him—but then the beam from the flashlight reappeared, flashing wildly. Graham emerged from the woods, dashing headlong toward the back door. Christine ran to the landing and heard the door open.

"Graham, what is it? What's wrong?"

"It's Caesar," Graham panted. "He's fallen in the well!"

The Brichester Fire Department arrived within forty-five minutes, but Graham knew that Caesar was dead. Thirty feet is a long way to fall, and the dog hadn't moved at all since Graham had discovered him. The torch had revealed the grotesque position of Caesar's body, legs splayed at a crazy angle; nearby, something glinted.

"Sorry, mate." The fireman who carried Caesar's limp form up from the well shook his head. "If it's any consolation, he probably died instantly."

Small consolation, Graham decided; he's still dead.

"Oh—and I found this down there, too. You must have dropped it."

Something glinted in the fireman's hand as he passed it to Graham. Perhaps Christine had been right—maybe it was a coin after all. No, it was too big; more like a medallion of some kind—but whatever it was, it needed a good cleaning. He shoved it into his pocket and took Christine inside.

The next morning they buried Caesar. Graham dug a small grave behind the shed and carefully lowered the dog in; a low mound of earth and a flat rock marked the spot. Christine wiped away a tear and placed Caesar's favorite toy—a well-chewed rubber ball—beside the stone.

Afterwards, Graham found some wood in the shed and set about boarding over the well.

* * *

Graham cleaned the metal object as best he could; it looked like bronze. It was a medallion, Graham decided; there was even a small hole, for a long-lost chain. One side was engraved with the symbol of what appeared to be a pentagram; the other bore a Latin inscription: *CAVE LUSUS NATURAE. TERRIBILIS VISU. INIMICUS HUMANI GENERIS. MDCXLIV.*

Christine leaned closer for a better look. "What does it say?"

"My Latin's a little rusty," Graham replied. "Something about a freak of nature: 'terrible to see, inimical to humans.'"

Christine traced her finger over the inscription. "Not very flattering, is it?"

"No, but I shouldn't worry; the date is 1644."

* * *

Somehow, Beaumont knew he was dreaming; he could see himself quite plainly, walking out the back door, down the path and around the shed. The phenomenon was disturbing, but Beaumont found himself powerless to stop it. Into the woods he walked, until he came at last to the well where, with his bare hands, he pulled at the boards that covered it. An opening was soon made; Beaumont leaned closer and peered into the blackness—and gasped in horror at the huge, glistening eye that blinked at him. There came the sound of moist movement, and a pair of groping appendages—tentacles?—flailed up from the darkness to latch onto the edge; the thing was trying to climb out of the well. When Graham awoke, he was shaking.

That morning, Christine decided to go shopping in Brichester. After the Metro passed from view at the end of the lane, Graham made his way back behind the shed and into the woods, dreading what he might find there. Breathless, he approached the well. The boards were intact; the dream had been just that—a dream, and nothing more. What had made him think otherwise? Everything was falling into place: Mr. Stark, and his "research"; the medallion, with its curious inscription; Hopkins' account of the Brichester coven. It suddenly occurred to Beaumont that he and Christine might well be living in what once was Zerobbabel Endicot's house. When Hopkins wrote that Endicot's monstrous offspring was "imprison'd in darkness", was he referring to the well? Beaumont shuddered involuntarily at the notion and returned to the house.

There was a touch of frost on the window panes that night, and Graham threw another log onto the fire. "I don't think Caesar's death was an accident," he said suddenly.

Christine turned her gaze from the flames. "What do you mean?"

"Think about it: How did Caesar end up at the bottom of that well? He couldn't just *fall* in; it's three feet high."

Christine considered this for a moment. "Then how?"

He cleared his throat. "What if he was chasing something that went into the well?"

"You think there's an animal living in the well?"

Graham contemplated telling her of his suspicions, but said nothing; through no fault of her own, Christine's life was too prosaic. She wouldn't understand, couldn't grasp the significance.

"What's the big mystery, Graham? Whatever it is, you've boarded the well up. It'll have to find another home."

* * *

The voice sounded far-away and dream-like—but Graham knew he wasn't dreaming. He was wide awake; Christine lay sound asleep beside him. The words were too muffled to understand. He sat up, listened, and *heard*. RELEASE ME. Yes, there was no mistaking it. But where was it coming from? RELEASE ME—IN THE WELL—RELEASE ME. The voice began to throb. Beaumont threw his hands over his ears, but it did no good: The voice was in his head. THE OTHER WAS TOO WEAK—HE FAILED ME—YOU ARE STRONG—I CAN FEEL YOU—RELEASE ME. The voice buzzed and reverberated; it drowned out all sensation.

And then suddenly the voice was gone. Beaumont was alone with the silence, which he now found almost unbearable. It was too quiet, too oppressive; he felt drained, exhausted, and fell back onto the bed.

He was awakened by a sudden flash of light. Christine had opened the blinds. She scowled at him. "Graham, it's nearly noon. Are you planning on sleeping all day?"

* * *

DON'T TRUST HER—SHE WANTS TO STOP US. The frying pan fell from Graham's quaking hands and clattered to the floor, startling Christine. "Clumsy!" she teased. "I asked you to help with the dishes, not frighten me half out of my wits!"

Graham was paralyzed by the voice. He stared, his jaw slack, while Christine bent to pick up the frying pan.

THE KNIFE—. Graham blinked, and glanced over at the gleaming steak knife in the sink.

THE KNIFE—. *No.* He swallowed and stood his ground, nerves straining.

SHE KNOWS—THE KNIFE. "*No!*" Graham shrieked, flinging a plate to dash against the counter. He stumbled blindly out of the kitchen. The voice pursued him down the hall and into the bathroom.

SHE STANDS BETWEEN US—SHE BLOCKS OUR DESTINY—KILL HER. Graham could no longer resist; he was oblivious to everything but the voice, pounding like a drum. KILL HER.

And then it was gone, as suddenly as it had appeared. Christine knocked tentatively on the door. "Graham? Are you alright?"

He paused to catch his breath. She'd want some sort of explanation of course, but how could he even begin to explain? "Yes, I'm fine now."

"Was it a migraine?"

Yes, of course it was. "A migraine. But it's gone now."

"Can I get you anything, darling? A drink?"

"Some water, perhaps."

He heard her footsteps padding toward the kitchen. Graham got to his feet and stumbled down the hall after her. Christine had her back to him, reaching up to retrieve a clean glass from the cupboard. The knife beckoned. He seized it; Christine turned, startled to see him in the kitchen. Her gaze fell upon the knife clenched in his hand. Graham hesitated; the moment was lost.

"Graham? What on earth—"

KILL HER KILL HER KILL HER

Graham shrieked; he had to make the voice go away. Metal flashed, gleaming in the light; the blade plunged, again and again, over and over. The kitchen was slick with blood and Christine's tortured cries. She struggled, but in vain. The cries stopped; she fell to the floor with a thud, followed by the knife—but the blood continued to flow until Graham could see nothing but red.

* * *

He stood at the well and drew a deep breath. The crowbar bit into the boards, splintering them, until there was a small opening, big enough to see through. He dropped the crowbar, leaned forward, and peered into the darkness below.

Graham Beaumont took hold of the remaining boards with his hands and pulled.

Random Access

by Michael G. Szymanski

I knew something was wrong with Ann Compton the minute she pulled open the sturdy door of her Brichester flat. Even though we hadn't seen one another since she'd left the States for college in England, I wasn't expecting to greet anyone other than the same cheery tomboy with whom I had hiked and biked and wrestled—losing more often than not, and through no lack of effort on my part.

When that door swung open, I found myself facing both my childhood friend and someone else, an overlay personality which gave the impression of a strange and not entirely welcome double image. I assumed it was my imagination assisted by twelve cups of airport coffee and the drive up from Bristol, but that first impression was hard to shake.

There was a subtle physical difference as well, and if I had tried to describe it to anyone, they would've laughed in my face; but I'm going to try it here and hope for the best.

For one thing, Ann had always favored relatively loose clothing, right to the time she stepped onto the plane for her overseas flight. Well, the woman who stood in that doorway had by some mysterious means unfathomable by the male of our species poured herself into a pair of stretch jeans and a minuscule exercise top which revealed more detail than I had ever been aware of, and I am admittedly no slouch when it comes to those matters.

For another thing, her entire vocabulary of body language was suggestive in some undefinably blatant manner. Maybe it was the way her free hand stroked the bare skin of her stomach as if she was in some way aroused by the sensation of touch; not of merely touching herself, mind you, but of the touching itself. And the way she stood, as if she were daring me to—what? Damned if I knew.

But of more significance was her face, that familiar, open, sparkle-eyed face, which now bore an expression of such heated intensity that it could have knocked me to the floor if she'd stepped forward too quickly. Her features seemed more pronounced than I remembered, making her more Ann than the girl I'd grown up with.

I remember one time in high school a friend of mine in photography class took a picture of me for an experiment. While developing the film he printed one photo normally, but printed another one reversed. Cutting the two prints in half vertically, he took the left half of the normal image and placed it with the right half of the reversed image, putting the remaining two halves together the same way.

The result: One depiction of me was angelic, open and childlike in its innocence. But the other—the other was dark, brooding, even cruel, a mirror of the darker half of our personality. As I stood there in that Brichester hallway looking at my longtime friend and confidante, it occurred to me that I was looking at the living embodiment of exactly that sort of photograph. And the worst of it was, I really don't think she even knew who I was.

"Ann?" I spoke hesitantly, absolutely uncertain of her response. But something clicked behind those challenging eyes, and some of the old Ann Compton asserted itself—but even then, not completely.

From there on, our reunion proceeded with reasonable normality, my old pal returning to joke and tease and exchange excruciatingly bad puns over a bottle of wine. For a while, my disturbing first impressions were forgotten.

About two hours into our mental slugfest, Ann's roommate, Sharon Dale, came home, and I was properly introduced. We hit it off well, which is no surprise because Ann and I share a similar list of qualifications for friendship. Sharon joined our impromptu party, and as she sat I couldn't help but notice she seemed surprised, although pleasantly so, by Ann's joviality. I waited until Sharon and I were alone together in the kitchen making coffee, then attempted to ease my way into the subject that was gnawing at me.

She was a bright, intuitive woman, and she realized where I was heading right off; in fact, she met me at the station.

"I'm worried about Ann," she told me. "Something isn't right with her and hasn't been since she came back from spring holiday. It was supposedly a quiet backpacking trip through the Cotswolds, but I think something happened there—." She paused, obviously uncomfortable expressing these thoughts to a relative stranger. "Look, Steven, you're her closest friend or I wouldn't have said as much as I have, but I think you should know, I believe Ann was—assaulted. And I think she's trying to suppress it."

As I look back on it, I think I can safely say this was my first real confrontation with the harsh realities of life, and I didn't like it any better then than I do now. My first response was a cold silence which Sharon misinterpreted.

"I spoke out of turn. I'm sorry I said anything." She started to leave, and that pulled me out of my sulk.

"No, no, you did the right thing. But are you sure? I mean, Ann can take care of herself pretty good—." I trailed off, realizing just how stupid that sounded.

"No, I'm not sure, but how else do you explain the way she's acting? She was as you remember her when she left. When she came back from the Cotswolds—." She inclined her head toward the living room.

We talked a bit more, taking some solace in our mutual ineffectiveness, but at least we determined to get the truth out of our friend, and to help her in whatever way she needed.

It was 2:00 a.m. when the coffee and the conversation ran out, and we all decided sleep was essential if we were going to salvage any part of the next day. The couch in the tiny living room was a pull-out; I pulled it out, took off my shoes, pulled on an old pair of pajamas, and crashed into the pillow.

I came awake sitting bolt upright, the heat wash of sudden fear coursing through my body and stepping up my heart into a doubletime rhythm that rattled off my rib cage. My disjointed thoughts passed through a number of possibilities. Nightmare? Burglar? The cry from Ann's room cut through the haze even as it made me jump out of the bed, hitting the floor at a dead run. I was vaguely aware of Sharon coming out of her room; she was asking me something in an urgent voice, but damned if I can tell you what it was. I hit the door to Ann's room and thundered in, not knowing what I'd be interrupting.

It was a nightmare, and a bad one at that. Ann, still fully dressed, was tossing around on the bed as if locked in a struggle with some invisible attacker—or maybe an attacker out of memory. I was crossing the room to shake her awake when she started speaking.

"The trees—which way? Silver trees—moving in the shadows—the buzzing in my head—want to leave, get away from the trees, away from this place once more into the great void beyond the planetary envelope. Chasing—herding—the cone in the woods—the buzzing in my head!"

Two things happened simultaneously, though at the time I thought I'd imagined the second. Ann sat bolt upright in the bed, eyes wide and pupils dilated, yet I got the firm impression she wasn't seeing me at all.

The second, less certain occurrence, which stopped me from speaking to Ann right off, was a high-pitched, exceedingly irritating buzzing sound which was so intense it could have been generated inside the cavities of my skull. It was a harsh, brutal sound, its only mercy being that it was abruptly gone, leaving me to try kidding myself into believing I hadn't actually heard it.

Ann was out of the bed and shuffling towards the French doors that opened onto a small garden behind the apartment building. I said, "Hey, Annie," or something of the sort as I started to intercept her, but Sharon's cautioning voice stopped me.

"Be careful, Steven, I think she's sleepwalking. It might be dangerous to wake her."

"So what the hell do we do?" I was growing more and more anxious the closer Ann got to those doors. "Looks to me like she's going for a walk."

"Stay with her. I'll get dressed and catch up to you with the car." God bless Sharon and her cool head.

It was a good thing I'd bought a trenchcoat my first day in the city, because I'd have looked awfully stupid traipsing around Brichester in a pair of pajamas of questionable taste. As it was, I barely had enough time to grab the coat and dive into my sneakers before Ann turned a corner and was momentarily lost to sight.

I caught up with her before she reached the next corner; I have to say, for someone who was sound asleep, Ann had some definite ideas about where she was going.

If you ever have the opportunity to take a walk with someone who isn't there, I wouldn't recommend it. Ann was a husk—unspeaking, unaware of her surroundings, yet she moved with a clear purpose and some hidden goal in mind. I know we're only rarely in control of our lives despite all our pretensions to the contrary, but that lonely walk with Ann was a study in cold helplessness.

I couldn't talk to her, didn't dare try to wake her—the only thing I had to be grateful for was the fact that traffic was sparse at that hour, because Ann never once stopped at a corner, no matter what the crosswalk signal advised. *Did this relate to the assault?* I wondered. Well it had to; Ann had never sleepwalked in the entire time I'd known her, and I knew if Sharon were here she'd say the same.

Whatever was happening to Ann, it had its roots in that place; the Cotswolds, Sharon had called it. Watching that vacant-eyed lump of animated flesh that was my friend, I told myself that I would find the bastards who were responsible for this if I had to tear apart the entire valley to find them.

Being unfamiliar with the city, I had no idea where we were heading, if in fact we were heading anywhere; but I don't think it was coincidence that we ended up on the campus of Brichester University. Once we hit the campus, Ann picked up the pace and managed to get a little ahead of me again before I pulled myself out of the haze of unreality I had fallen into while following my friend through the sleeping streets of Brichester.

The crash and clatter of broken glass dragged me back and pushed me into a quick sprint which brought me to the front steps of the campus library just as Ann stepped through the slide-panel door she had shattered with a conveniently placed landscaping rock.

Tiptoeing across the shards, I followed her into the near solid gloom of the building's interior. What kind of navigation system she was using I've no idea, but for myself the groping around blindly method allowed me to shuffle along behind the sound of her retreating footsteps.

Shortly, the footsteps were replaced by a new sound: a rapidfire clattering that was somehow familiar yet unidentifiable then and there. I found Ann silhouetted in the flickering backwash of a computer monitor before which she was seated, fingers flying over the terminal's keyboards with a speed I will never believe was natural.

Images played on the monitor in rapid succession, appearing and vanishing even as they registered on the eye. A vague overview was intimated in that visual abundance; visions of starfields, galaxies, and gas clouds vied with portions of educational programming, all of which was in some way related to astronomy—a subject in which Ann had never once expressed the slightest interest.

Caught up as I was in the frenetic display of images, I wasn't immediately aware of that same incessant and irritating buzzing which filled the room to its capacity, threatening then to squeeze right into my brain. I turned to locate the source of the sound—and was confronted by oblivion.

* * *

I have vague memories of being alone in that room, with police sirens wailing in uncomfortable proximity. Then Sharon was there with someone else I didn't recognize, who helped Sharon drag me hastily to her car; I didn't seem capable of walking at the time, and I recall Sharon speaking to me in an urgent tone, like you would to someone who'd suffered a concussion, to keep them from falling asleep.

My first clear recollection was the softness of my pullout bed back at the flat, and of Sharon holding a cold cloth to my forehead. I sat bolt upright before my brain could send any signals, and I found myself confronting a haphazardly dressed guy about my own age who looked up from the book he'd been leafing through, a vaguely cheerful expression on his narrow features.

"There you are," he told me, then to Sharon: "See? I told you the shock was only temporary."

After we had established the fact that I was all right, Sharon introduced me to John Baker, a college friend she'd bumped into enroute to her car. "I explained what was happening," Sharon told me, "and John offered to help; as it turned out, I'm rather glad he did. I could never have gotten you out of the library before the police arrived. What happened to you, anyway?"

"Damned if I know. There was a buzzing sound, and then—nothing." I noticed John perk up a little at that, but I wasn't in the mood to press the point at the moment. Besides, something more important had occurred to me. "Ann! What happened to Ann?"

"She's all right," Sharon assured me. "Apparently after you—passed out—she left the library and came straight back here; when we got back with you, there she was, asleep in her own bed as if nothing had ever happened. It's all a bit frightening, Steven; I'm not certain how to deal with it."

"Well I daresay we'll have to deal with it," John informed us, "or the situation will only grow worse."

"And what makes you the expert of the hour?" I groused, still not in the mood to play the perfect host.

"Only the fact that I have a little more knowledge than you," he replied, not the least offended. "While we were tracking you down in the car, Sharon explained the situation to me, but it wasn't 'til she mentioned Ann's trip to the Cotswolds that something clicked. Look, you're both concerned that Ann was assaulted at some time during that trip, and I have to tell you you're right—but not in the way you think."

Well that explained everything; I looked to Sharon for a little help, and she shrugged at me. "John has an interest in the out-of-the-ordinary," she said, uncertain of her approach. "He's something of an expert in the area of—well—"

"The occult," John helped her. "The paranormal, the supernatural, the strange forces that sometimes inflict themselves on our lives—as in Ann's case." My blank stare must have given him a clue as to what was on my mind, because he held up a hand to hold me off. "I know, I know, but let's not go through that tired routine of disbelief; listen to what I have to say, and make an informed decision."

"I've heard some of this," Sharon piped in. "You really should listen."

That was enough for me, for the time being. "All right. What have you got?"

John held up the book. "I have this: an annotated history of the folklore of the Severn Valley, complete with legends, lore, and a few tidbits the local residents would much rather have kept to themselves. One of those tidbits concerns a tract of land known as Goatswood.

"According to this book, Goatswood has been considered an unhealthy place since folk first settled in the valley. There's a vague and lurking fear connected with the place, and all sorts of weird tales have been told about it.

"Travelers go in but they don't come out, or the ones who do are never quite the same again. There are documented incidents of men staggering back into town stark, raving mad after a night in the Wood. And judging from Ann's itinerary, her route would've taken her very near if not directly through the place."

I was having serious difficulties with this, and I can imagine what you're thinking right about now. "So you're saying she had some kind of close encounter with an evil tree or something?"

"Among other things," John responded enigmatically. "But most importantly, I believe Ann encountered something that has dwelt in Goatswood since before the existence of humanity; and I firmly believe that it was still with her when she left the Wood—and that it is with her even now."

He was brief and succinct, telling us about an alien race which fled a dying world in vast temple-ships which struck out into the universe to locate a new home, and of how one of these craft eventually found its way to Earth, where it was stranded by some unidentified property of our world that effectively sabotaged their mode of propulsion.

These insect-like creatures and their slaves were supposedly confined to the proximity of their temple-ship, but that didn't stop them from drawing in the indigenous lifeforms and subjecting them to their own particular brand of cruelty. As an example, he let us read the suicide letter of a guy named Shea, who apparently went mad while in the Wood, and became convinced that one of these creatures had actually, physically, *entered into his brain* to show him what horrors a cold and uncaring universe has in store for us.

It was John's theory that one of these insects had assaulted Ann in the same way but, unlike the case of Mr. Shea, who felt the creature was influencing him from afar, Ann's assailant *had entered her mind and remained there*, a psychic parasite controlling Ann's actions as she slept.

The obvious eventually occurred to me. "Why?"

The question disturbed John, altering his entire demeanor. "When we found you," he began, "you were lying in front of a computer terminal; I assume Ann had been using it when you found her." He waited for my assenting nod before continuing. "When we arrived, the monitor was displaying an educational program about space technology, in particular America's space shuttle program. I think the creature is looking for an escape route, a way to break free of Earth and roam the universe freely again."

"So what do you suggest we do?" I said to fill the uncomfortable silence that followed.

John shrugged. "You read the Shea manuscript. At any time, that thing could subject Ann to visions of such horror that she'll never recover. What do we do? We have to expel that compassionless abomination before it has no further use for Ann and drives her totally mad."

* * *

Of course, that didn't tell us what we could actually do about the situation, even presuming we in fact believed what John was telling us, which I have to tell you I didn't; not a word of it. All I knew for certain was that something had happened to Ann, probably in Goatswood, and that she was going to need our help to sort herself out. That's where we left it that night, after deciding not to tell Ann about her midnight walk, reasoning that she was troubled enough without adding to her burden.

The days that followed were uneventful. Ann, completely unaware of her midnight stroll, behaved more or less normally, but I could tell she was still distracted, though I don't believe even she knew by what. The only strange occurrence during that next week was a second visit from John Baker.

He asked about Ann, if there had been any further sleepwalking incidents, or if she'd been experiencing nightmares. When he was satisfied, he handed over a small plastic computer disk with the word "Mobius" scrawled on its label. "Keep this in reach at all times," he told me. "Take it with you if Ann has another incident. If she's at a terminal, put this disk in, type 'Mobius' at the prompt and hit Enter. The program is self-booting. That's all you'll have to do, and I believe you of all people will know the right time to run it."

Honestly, I didn't know what the hell he was talking about or how it could possibly apply to Ann's problem; not then, and not for the next couple of days, until the night Ann had another incident.

It could have been a replay of that first night, except that Sharon and I were slightly more prepared but no more organized as Ann retraced her steps to—and yes, through—the campus library doors and to the bank of terminals in the reference section. I had a flashlight this time, so it was easier to follow after her; and in my other hand, scooped up almost unconsciously as I dove out of the flat, was the Mobius disk.

There was no real reason for me to have picked it up; I had no belief in John's ridiculous story, or any faith that the disk could help Ann in any way. During the days following that first incident Sharon and I had discussed the possibility of seeking psychiatric help for our friend; but, cowards that we were, we never made a decision, putting the matter off until now, when it was too late.

She went to the same terminal, switched it on, and began playing the keys with that disturbing velocity which made all of John's bizarre theories seem just the least bit plausible. Again the blurring of images, clips, and charts played over the screen, and this time I couldn't doubt that some sort of search was taking place in front of me, but when I asked myself who was doing the searching, the coward in me took over again and refused to consider the possible answers.

The double slam of car doors announced the arrival of Sharon and John outside. I turned around to send the beam of my flashlight back the way I'd come as a signal to them—and that's when the buzzing hit me again.

Damn, it was a godawful sound, a fingernails-on-chalkboard rasping that ignited a miniature nova in the center of my brain, and I knew without looking where it was coming from. Despite myself I turned, screaming silently at my idiot self even as I looked at Ann to see a mercifully blurred form flash across the gap between her and the terminal in front of her.

It was true. Every insane, impossible word John had told us was true, but I doubt even he realized the full extent of the vileness we were—I was—facing in that flickering cathode glow. Insectile, yes, but more; and less. I caught the impression of wings, of multiple eyes and mouths, a misshapen body at home in more than the normal three dimensions and the voids between them. It was a winged atrocity, a multiplanar perversion—*and that filth was living inside Ann's brain, polluting it with its poisonous presence and bending her to its alien will!*

But it wasn't there now, I reminded myself. It had leapt from her brain and gone—my God, it had gone *into the computer!* Its search was no doubt hampered by the restraints of its human host, and so it had taken a more direct route to the information it sought.

Freed of her puppet master, Ann slumped in her chair and fell sideways against me, startling me out of the shock which must have caused me to pass out the first time I had witnessed this transfer. I could hear the sound of running feet in the library behind me, and John's voice cutting through the deceiving quiet of the night.

"The disk, Steven, the disk!"

I know what Ann must have felt like all those weeks since that thing had raped her mind in Goatswood, what it was like to have your body move in response to commands other than my own. My hand reached out, inserted the disk, haltingly typed out the word MOBIUS, and punched the Enter key.

The utterance which came next should have been left in the cold heart of space, or in the shattered ruins of a dead planet which had so truly deserved its extinction. What my mind translated through a near unbearable carrier wave of agony was an amalgam of frustration and rage; oh yes, the rage. Then came the images.

They hit the screen in a visual bombardment, and if you think I'm going to describe to you what I saw in those few eternal seconds you, my friend, are truly insane. For a moment I saw what *it* had seen, viewed scenes of *its* experiences and encounters with things that made itself seem gnatlike by comparison. Even now, after all this time has passed, the only way I can preserve my sanity is to keep telling myself those images were not real.

And then they were gone and I was vomiting up the contents of my stomach onto the keyboard.

* * *

The police caught us that time, arrested and duly charged us with a wide assortment of crimes against which we had no plausible way of defending ourselves. It didn't matter; Ann was free, and thankfully retained no memory of that thing's presence within her mind. And that little alien bastard was trapped in a loop program designed by one of John's friends.

At the station and out of Ann's earshot, John explained to us his suspicions concerning the parasite. In order to pass through so-called solid matter, the creature would by necessity have to alter its own molecular structure, traveling, as it were, on a different wavelength. It was John's theory that the insect assumed a configuration having many of the same characteristics as energy, most likely in the form of electricity and, once inside the rigid configuration of the computer's programming, it would have been converted into a string of raw data.

In such a form—and this was total guesswork on John's part—the creature would have to obey certain laws of physics and programming, and so could be channeled in some way. The Mobius program was a channel of sorts, except that it looped back on itself, sending any data it accessed into an eternal loop from which it had no chance of escaping without outside assistance—and it wasn't about to get that.

We told Ann only that she had had a couple of sleepwalking incidents which had ended up at the library, and since she never had a repeat performance after that night, she seemed willing to let it go at that.

We weren't able to take the disk with us when the police came, but John's friend went to the library the next day and asked about its whereabouts. He was told that, since it wasn't a library disk, it, along with several other disks, had been wiped clean with a bulk magnet. Whatever that disk held—or whatever it imprisoned—was gone, magnetically erased from existence, banished to oblivion where it could never inflict itself upon some other innocent who might come under its influence.

But what about the others? What about the rest of those things still hiding out there in Goatswood, biding their time till another hiker blunders in—and maybe takes something out as Ann did.

They should be wiped out; hell, they should never have existed. They're evil and they wallow in it; they violated someone I care for more than I would have admitted before those events in Brichester, and that demands vengeance.

There are still occasional nights when I hold my wife tightly as she struggles against a dream assailant, thanking whatever passes for God in this world that she never remembers any of it the next morning. The nightmares are fewer and farther between these days, but each time one grabs her a rage builds inside me until it doesn't seem I can hold it in any longer. That rage goes out to Goatswood and the alien disease that infects it.

There has to be something that can be done.

I *will* make them pay.

Free the Old Ones

by C. J. Henderson

3 MARCH—2:15 a.m.

"Mr. Clarke, I know that you're tired, but if you could give us the facts just one more time—"

I stared up into the long face of the district magistrate and sighed. I wasn't sure what was wrong, but I was getting damn tired of trying to figure it out.

My name is Jordon Clarke. I'm a private investigator. Not the kind from the American cinema—I'm not much of a drinker, I don't smoke, and the cases I accept don't call for a detailed knowledge of weaponry or the martial arts. I'm a basic nook-and-cranny man, chasing down information for Brichester's solicitors, giving the shadow to errant husbands and wives—the usual.

I had thought that night was part of the usual. Seeing as how the district magistrate didn't agree, however, I pulled down a deep breath and started the whole story over again.

"For the benefit of those with severe learning disabilities, I will repeat—I was on the job. Mr. Jonathan Cleveland wanted to know where his wife was spending so much of her time. She'd been going out once a month for the last several years, meeting with her group. The last few months, however, the meetings had gotten more and more frequent. Lately she was going out almost every night—sometimes not coming back until morning."

"What kind of 'group' was it, Mr. Clarke?"

"Mr. Cleveland didn't know."

"He didn't know—?"

"That's his story," I growled, no longer able to contain my growing fatigue. "She'd led him to believe it was a church group. When he started to get suspicious, he popped round to see the vicar. He wasn't comfortable about it, seeing how he hadn't attended services for a good while. That was when he discovered that his wife was in no groups their church offered."

I was talking faster, spitting the words out.

"He confronted her. She said it was none of his business. He simmered for a few days, then came and hired me. I followed her tonight. She went to some type of deserted ruin outside of Severnford—her and quite a lot of other folk. Of course, you know this, because you swept the lot of them up in your raid—along with me!"

I slammed a fist against the table that separated myself from the magistrate. My voice went up several octaves, hovering near the shattering point as I practically screamed, "Now, will you please—please—contact Mr. Cleveland and verify my story. Unlike the lot of you civil servants, my livelihood depends on me being out and actually doing my job."

The officer to the left of the magistrate asked, "And you didn't see anything?"

"For the tenth, bloody time," I shouted, "I never got close enough. You lot pinched me before I could get near. But, Lord's sake—you know that. You were there! What kind of—"

The magistrate put up his hand. He turned to the officer who had just spoken and, for a long moment, neither of them said anything—simply staring at each other instead. Then, finally, the uniform broke the silence, saying, "He doesn't know."

"No, I'm sure you're right, Hastings." The magistrate turned back to me then, saying, "Mr. Clarke, I beg your apology. A woman of quite notable personage was in those ruins tonight. You are correct in surmising both that Mrs. Cleveland was not there to meet with a lover, and that she is not the woman to whom I am referring."

The magistrate propped his elbows on the table, then steepled his fingers, finally letting them thread through each other. Resting his nose on his thus-locked hands, he stared off wearily into his own future, telling me, "The incarceration of that woman is going to create a considerable flap—indeed, the vid and tear sheet crowd are chattering in the main staging area already."

The magistrate moved his fingers apart, then let his face fall into them. Holding his head with gentle self-pity, he said, "All involved are going to be quite popular with the media for the next few days. So, Mr. Clarke, if you're the type willing to sell your story—go ahead, get what you can. England is still a free country, despite what the Labor Party might think. But sir—"

The weary official paused, pulling his hands away from his face. Staring me in the eye, he told me, "My advice to you would be to leave here and to forget what little you know. Forget about Mrs. Cleveland, forget about the ruins off Cotton Row. Go back to your life, Mr. Clarke," he said, standing up out of his seat.

As the officers with him also rose, he turned his back on me and walked for the door. Then, just as he was passing through it, he threw over his shoulder, "If you can. If you can."

5 MARCH—3:25 p.m.

Three days later and I still couldn't get the magistrate's warning out of my head. At first I'd thought he'd been giving me a touch of bluff—trying to keep me from muddying the waters. I thought about approaching the reporters but squelched the idea.

First off, I didn't have very much of an angle to sell them. Second, after the magistrate's warning, whatever small amount of fame and business I might have generated by getting my face on the BBC I decided most likely wouldn't have compensated for crossing him. I knew that long after the chattering faces had hurried back to the safety of their studios in London, I'd still be in Brichester trying to eke out a living—with the local constables all feeling I didn't deserve to.

That decided, I had contacted Mr. Cleveland instead, given him the scoop and my bill. He didn't want to pay at first. Said I should have kept his wife out of jail. I told him that was his job and threatened to go to the papers with the story of what I'd been doing there if he didn't cough up.

He did. I left.

On the way back to the office, though, I couldn't help but speculate on what I'd brushed up against. The district magistrate hadn't been exaggerating. The reclusive Lady Allison Shelington-Thorn being swept up in a police raid was an open call to the smirking press. And oh, how they'd answered.

The swill the papers and the nightly broadcasts were reporting was something out of a Quatermass movie—witch cult practicing in Severnford—old castle cite of suspected blood sacrifices—police raid nets celebrity—Lady Allison requests solitary confinement to avoid the press—leading Oxford dean comes to practitioners' defense—not the first time the Severn Valley has known such antics—

It was a circus—but each to his own amusements, I supposed. For me, none of what had happened seemed very entertaining. Pulling up in front of my building, I thought about that night. I had been honest with the magistrate—I hadn't *seen* anything. But the things I had heard—smelled—the entire fetid feel of the grim, brooding area—it hadn't affected me at first—not until later, until I'd had time to dwell on it. Then, surprisingly, it had left me shuddering. The sight of the ruin kept coming back to me—the glow of the fire shimmering inside, lighting the sparse, gray, diseased grass, the few pathetic, bloated oaks—

I closed my eyes to the memory. Taking the steps to my office two at a time, I hurried inside and then slammed the door behind me. I felt quite the idiot, panicked by a memory—sweat gathering under my collar, despite the cold outside and in. Turning to my work, I scooped the mail up from the floor then headed in for the answering machine and my e-mail.

Stop playing the fool, I told myself. Halloween's still eight months away.

Just another of my mistakes, I suppose.

13 MARCH—5:30 p.m.

A part of my brain could not believe I was doing it. Another was screaming that it was about time. I had gone to London to deliver a report to the chief operator at Smythe, Gardener, and Goldman. Report delivered, check gathered, I had been on my way up the A.38 back to Brichester when suddenly I took the left onto the Berkeley Road, the road to Severnford.

A nagging worry cursed me the entire way. Something in the pit of my brain had been quietly terrorizing me since that night at the ruins. Each little thing I had seen there—every speck of fungus parasitizing the rocks, hanging from the trees; the barren patches of lifeless ground; the broken stone of the place, the black streaks seared into its shattered bricks—all of it had kept coming back to me, warning me away from the site I had never wanted to see again, dragging me back to the place that had captured the curiosity of the world.

As I drove, I could not believe how our little corner of the nation had become the focus of so much attention. Witch groups from around England and a score of other countries had voiced their support for the imprisoned cultists. A few professors were saying they weren't rightly "witch" cults since it wasn't Satan they were worshiping, but they were filler, not big press.

The big press was dwelling on a number of the story's other themes. First there was the celebrity angle. Lady Allison was the most recognizable of the number, but it turned out that more than half those swept up by the police were notables of some sort—doctors, physicists, writers, executives, and, of course, the bored wives of executives. So far, their only connection to each other seemed their belief practices.

The second were those practices themselves. The arrests had been for trespassing and endangerment. They were small charges in the large scheme—most likely ones that would have been dropped if a reporter who haunted the Brichester station hadn't tagged along behind the magistrate and his party and started the whole hoopla rolling. There were all sorts of excited rumors being bandied about a blood sacrifice of sorts, but no one had been charged with murder, so I'd been discounting those. No, what was interesting about their practices were not that they were sensational, but that they were—what word would fit best—bizarre. Ancient. Even mystical.

The incarcerated and their supporters were laying out the story of trying to bring spirituality back to the world. The short of it seemed to be that God and his angels were somehow cut off from the world millions of years ago and that what we tell as the story of the Garden of Eden to the cult was something completely different.

God did not banish man; man chose to banish God. Of course, the cult did not use any of the proper Biblical names anyone knew. To them, God was Cthulhu—or Q'talu, or Cootad'lu, or any of a dozen others. The press was having as hard a time agreeing on proper spelling there as they were over the names of most Arab terrorists. There were a thousand other names floating, however, figures identified as Y'golonac, Daoloth, Shub-Niggurath, Glaaki, Eihort, Byatis, and the like. My personal favorite was "Gol-goroth, the forgotten Old One", more for the lurid title he had been gifted with than anything else.

Be all that as it may, however, the further the press dug into the background of all these characters, the more unbelievable the stories became. It was soon made apparent that the Severn Valley had been the site of such worships as far back as the available records went. Many of the spots where stories centered were of Roman building. Others were even older.

The third point was the most disturbing, though. The newly discovered religion was sweeping through the press mainly because it claimed to come with a guarantee. Unlike Christian, Moslem, or the Buddhist-style philosophies, this one came with a deadline. According to its newly found spokespeople, God was coming back—soon. If the proper words were spoken in the right places when the stars were correctly aligned, et cetera, then snap—the doors would open, or the clouds would part, or whatever, and God would be here. Next month, they promised. April 2, actually.

The thought had a lot of people excited. Unemployment had hit the twenty-three percent mark. Thirteen minor wars were raging in the world. The country's murder rate was something like one person every forty-five minutes. Not nearly as bad as the Americas, but bad for us. People were living in the streets, under bridges, in mass shantytowns like never before in the nation's history. There would be few better times for God to come to town, and the public bulk was beginning to roll toward the notion of taking a closer look at Lady Allison's personal savior.

For some reason, however, I couldn't share their enthusiasm. And I knew why. It was the nagging memory of that night at the ruins. It throbbed in my brain like a splinter too far under the skin to dig out, and yet painful to even the slightest touch. No matter how I tried to dismiss the thought, I found myself drawn back to it again and again—only then to be repelled anew by something within it which I could not understand.

"And now," I whispered to myself, driving down Mill Lane once more, "you've got nothing better to do than go back."

Why? my brain asked me in an urgent, frightened tone. *What do you think you're doing? What can you accomplish?*

As I pulled at the wheel, turning my car onto Cotton Row, terror began to bubble within my stomach. It surprised me at first. Quickly, however, my anger forced it down and away, leaving me to wonder just what was happening to me. It was only another tale of the same poor, sorry types we've all seen again and again—unable to deal with their own world and looking to something from beyond to cure everything for them. If it wasn't God it would be space aliens.

And yet, for the first time, I'd been affected myself. There was a feeling in the very air that the doors should be opened and the clouds parted—that what was going on was right and good and necessary. That the world needed Glaaki and Byatis and all the rest of them down here among us, sorting the wheat from the chaff.

The castle came into view as I turned the corner. I left behind the same row of untenanted cottages I had days earlier, driving on toward the three walls and the lone tower still standing on the crest of their hill. There was one difference this time, however—the large crowd gathered at the base of the hill. Parking my car among all the others strewn along the roadway, I got out and moved forward, pushing my way through the pressing mass.

The size and the look of the crowd shocked me. There were maybe six hundred people altogether. Many were gathered around the various catering trucks buying hot dogs and toffeed almonds. Others were taking pictures, buying souvenirs from the vendors. *How?* I wondered. *How did anyone come up with souvenirs so quickly?*

But there they were—toy angels, lead figures looking more monster than prophet, edible spiders and millipedes and the like, plastic saints with pencil sharpeners built into the rocks at their feet—and T-shirts. Two different stands were already competing. The one with fewer patrons seemed the more serious, if such a word could be applied—detailed etchings in black and gray showed torturously hellish creatures done up in Renaissance poses. Vaguely humanoid figures with octopi-like heads were dressed in Christian raiments, their crowns lit by brilliant haloes.

The other stand had gone the novelty route, cartoon pictures with catchy phrases—things like:

Don't be at odds
With the Elder Gods

or

My folks touched the Savior's mantle in Severn
And all I got was this lousy T-shirt

There were a score of others, but the most popular one of all seemed to be simplest, one with but a four word motto:

FREE THE OLD ONES

It seemed as if every tenth person were wearing one, pulling them on over their coats. The police had roped the ruins off, of course, leaving two men there to keep the curious away. I was in the process of observing the crowd when a hand touched my shoulder. I did not start outwardly—my nerves were not that raw yet—but inside a dozen voices screamed within my head, all demanding opposing actions. Turning about perhaps a shade too quickly, I found the district magistrate.

"So, Clarke, here to do some shopping?"

"I only tithe Anglican, sir," I told him.

"Better make some stiff donations in the next few weeks," he answered. Then he stared at me for a long moment, inspecting my face more closely than a man might his own in the mirror before an important engagement. He locked his eyes with mine, searching for something. After a moment, though, he blinked, then touched his hat, saying simply, "Well, see you later, Clarke."

I mumbled something inane to him, watching him walk off into the crowd. Not the gawking tourists, but those pressing the police barriers, those who had come—seeking. I watched them part as he walked. They backed away from him as if afraid. They were a weak bunch, purposeless, wanting, unable to do anything except wait and hope and dream. Their eyes were vacant, often rheumy. Many of them moved with a half-paralytic gait, as if normal, upright motion were foreign to them.

I shuddered to see them—helplessly staring up at the ruins, waiting for Lady Allison's cartoon God to come and deliver them a world of milk and honey. And then something in the look of one of them caught my attention. He had not done anything in particular—neither moved in any exaggerated way, nor failed to move.

But something unregistered in his visage had caught hold of my eye. Then, just as suddenly, that same something repelled me. Before I could contain myself, I had turned back for my vehicle. At first walking, I then found myself running, throwing myself through the crowd, shoving aside all in my way. My keys in my hand by the time I arrived, I fumbled at them, forcing them at the door with unreasoning hurry. The key missed the lock again and then again. I could feel tears welling in my eyes—horrible, frightened tears. As they washed over my face, I stabbed at the door with my keys, cursing them, cursing the lock, cursing myself and God and all in between.

Then, suddenly, blinded by a fear and pains I couldn't identify, I smashed at the door with my fists, kicking it, throwing myself against the car. I hit with such fury that I knocked myself backward to the ground, tearing my jacket and my knee. My hand closing on a loose paving stone, however, I saw my means of salvation. All I needed was to regain my feet, smash the window, and I would be in control again—inside and safe.

Lurching madly to my feet, I was but a moment from shattering my window when a hand caught my wrist. I spun on my restrainer like an animal, my every thought to kill the interloper who would force me to stay in the tainted foul reek that was calling to me—screaming to me—

It was the district magistrate. Calmly, he removed the block from my hand and then dropped it back to the ground. Without a word, he fetched up my keys, placed them in my hand, and then moved me back to the driver's door, guiding my fingers until the lock was safely open. Then he stood back as I pushed myself inside. I grabbed at the wheel clumsily, needing to wrap my trembling fingers around something.

Outside, the magistrate moved my door over to close it. He stopped a few inches from shut, however. Looking in at me with a sad understanding, he whispered, "It only gets worse, Mr. Clarke."

And then he shut the door gently and walked away. I stayed where I was for a long while, frightened and cold. My eyes never stopped tearing. It seemed the least of my problems.

20 MARCH—11:10 p.m.

I sat in the British Museum, rubbing at my eyes. I had spent the last few days there, from morning until as late as they would permit. Flashing my license and giving the matron a winning tale about trying to get my degree at nights and, "Oh, please, please, couldn't I leave with the custodial staff?" had gotten me the extra hours I seemed to need to torment myself completely.

As always, there was a voice in my mind whispering to me about how obsessed I had become with the whole Elder Gods nonsense. I had turned down a score of cases, almost lost some of my standing ones. I was a week or two from dipping into my savings, and those were not extensive. But still, no matter how many times I told myself how foolishly I was acting, the overwhelming part of me would just agree and keep on reading.

Relaxing for the moment, knowing old Frank would soon come to tell me it was time for the lock-up, I let my tired eyes run over the mound of books with which I'd surrounded myself. The titles whisked through my head—*Legendry and Customs of the Severn Valley*; *De Vermis Mysteriis*; *The Vale of Berkeley*; *Book of Eibon*; *From Magic to Science*; *Beyond the Occult*; *Notes on Witchcraft in Monmouthshire, Gloucestershire and the Berkeley Region*; *Witches: Investigating an Ancient Religion*; eleven volumes of an abomination named *Revelations of Glaaki*; and a worn and greasy edition of a hideous thing named the *Necronomicon*. Frank swore in a conspiratorial whisper that the feel of the volume came from its having been bound in human skin. After much of what I'd read, I was afraid to call him on the notion.

The librarian had provided me with other relevant texts as well—local histories of the Berkeley area set down by clergymen, not the usual stuff of black cats and cows gone dry through the evil eye, but tales of prowling daemons. Crawling, crab-like beasts, elephant-headed things with serpent-like growths for beards, great flying beasts, dozens more. So eager to help a poor, middle-aged duffer struggling to get through school, she brought me every noxious bit and piece the library had, even called other stations to get their vilest stock on loaner.

I appreciated her efforts and told her so, thanking her as best I could, trying hard to suppress my sense of irony. When old Frank came that night, I staggered out of the museum in a daze, went to my car and somehow made my way home. Again, too sickened to eat, I fell into bed in my clothes. I was not sure how many days I had been wearing them. I didn't care, either.

21 MARCH—2:15 p.m.

Part of my reading the day before led me to Scotland Yard and what the police morbidly label the Perfidy Files. The first parts I inspected consisted of unpublished, handwritten texts which were the last known words of people who have perished or disappeared under bizarre circumstances. I was only allowed to see those which were over twenty years old. Nothing more recent could be released to the public. I didn't mind. Those were disturbing enough.

I read one in which the author told of a house guest being drawn into a pattern on the beach beyond his bungalow—how he knew he would be next. He disappeared without a trace. Another was the quite lengthy suicide note of the late fantasist Ronald Shea, an unbelievable tale of insects from outer space which—I find I can not even begin to sum up his mad tale—suffice to say he was found next to the manuscript with his wrists slashed. To his mind, it was the only action he could take to save the human race. Another, a story written by a newsman named Ingels before his own suicide in a sanatarium, rivaled anything I'd seen so far for sheer madness.

The second section to which they allowed me access was a simple pair of audio tapes. The first was an interview between a Dr. Linwood and a most bizarrely obsessed man. The patient told an incredible tale of being trapped by the inhabitants of nearby Goatswood so they could use him in a ritual sacrifice to a thing named Shub-Niggurath. He claimed to have escaped, but that their ritual had transformed him into a monster. The doctor asked him to remove his great layer of coats, but switched off the tape at that moment. The accompanying police report stated that the tape was found in the doctor's office at the time of his complete mental breakdown. Gibbering incoherently, he had to be restrained by his colleagues. The report quoted a Dr. Whitaker, who was listed as first on the scene. He had seen Linwood's last patient and swore to the ridicule of the other doctors that the man was so incredibly deformed he barely seemed human.

The second was made during a sort of black mass during which a man named Fisher murdered one named Gillson, then killed himself by leaping out a window. They had thought their ritual would rend the veil of reality and show them something beyond all common knowledge. Judging from their screams at the end of the tape, I was willing to believe they'd gotten just what they wanted.

As I sat in the Yard's public examinations room, I listened to that tape again, wondering at what the loud dry rustling sound in the background was. Police notations put it down to mechanical trouble—but the sound did not occur until after Fisher and Gillson had finished with their invocations. I shut the machine off as the pair began their pitiful screams again.

Fine, I thought, *they got just what they wanted. So, now—what is it you want?*

Sadly, I had no answer for myself.

22 MARCH—8:30 p.m.

A lead at the Yard the day before took me to an art dealer, far up-country in Leeds. He possessed the last known work of a Thomas Cartwright. The name meant nothing to me, but the officer who dropped me the hint swore the artist had been murdered by "an instrument that doesn't officially exist." When I simply stared at him, he whispered me the dealer's name and told me to go see Cartwright's last painting. I did.

I wished I hadn't.

The dealer took me to the far rear of his storage area. There the painting stood on a free-standing easel, a small overhead lamp lighting it for best effect. He left me alone with it, promising to return when he could. I stared at the canvas, drawn toward it but also forced away at the same time. The conflicting emotions raged within me, setting a boundary line between myself and the painting I could not cross. It was a violently somber work—and a thing of madness if ever I had seen one.

The center of the picture featured an oval body from which protruded countless thin, pointed spines of multicolored metal. At the more rounded end of the oval a circular, thick-lipped mouth formed the center of a spongy face from which rose three yellow eyes on thin stalks. Its underside was a ring of white pyramids—presumably used for locomotion.

In many ways, it looked like nothing more than a rock and roll album cover, or some 1960's Hollywood idea of a horror to end all horrors—as if a few anatomical abnormalities could bend a person's mind. And yet, I could not raise my arm to touch the dead man's work—could not stop the trembling that had buried my hands in my pockets lest I see their spastic twitching. The dealer, finally coming back with a tray laden with a steaming pot, cups and the necessary rest, said, "How about a hot one, then?"

"Oh, sorry," I answered, sweat gathering around my ears, a tightness wrapping itself around my throat. "You shouldn't have bothered doing anything special. I'm not a customer."

"Of course you're not," he said with a knowing sadness. Setting the tray down on a worn, thin-legged table, he added simply, "You came to see the Cartwright."

Pouring me a cup of dark, steaming amber, he extended it to me by its saucer. I could see in his eyes that it was taking all his strength to keep his hand rigid. Chastising myself mentally, I somehow found it within my will to brace my own nerve to match that of an art dealer. Accepting the cup without slopping more than a few drops, I thanked him as graciously as I could.

Taking a sip, I felt the warmth forcing its way down the dry passage my throat had become. Suddenly I wondered when I'd last had anything to eat, or drink. I couldn't remember. Desperate to chase the troubling thought away, I attempted a bit of humor with the dealer. I reminded him just how much the Cartwright was worth, pointing out that I could have easily made off with it.

He smiled for a long moment, set his cup down—and then he laughed. It was a hollow, self-pitying sound, a thin, desperate titter that made my skin crawl. Looking up suddenly from his doubled over position, he asked, "Would you, Mr. Clarke? Would you—please?"

A tear ran down his haggard face. I made to offer him my handkerchief, but he pulled out his own, telling me politely, "Save it, sir. I'm sure you'll be needing it."

I managed to get halfway back to Brichester before I was forced to pull off the road and prove him correct.

28 MARCH—12:05 p.m.

"Free the Old Ones, free the Old Ones, free ...."

I muted the sound from the news broadcast. As usual, it centered on the debate over the Old Ones. The public seemed up in arms, demanding the cultists be allowed to complete their ritual. The churches were opposing, of course, most of them quite strenuously. But they were a small voice against the frothing tide of public opinion. The nation had rallied behind the notion of permitting the Glaakies, as they were now known, access to the Severnford ruins to do whatever they had to.

Many were fanatics about the idea, but most people simply didn't seem to care. What harm could there be in it, they asked. What difference did it make? All they want to do is open a doorway to let God come down and make everything better. What's the harm in that? Let them try, we couldn't be any worse off than we are now—could we?

I stared at the chanting images on the screen, wondering how long I had been in my bed—not really caring. I watched the footage of the picket walkers, thrusting their signs at the cameras: *Shub-Niggurath Knows Best*, *Christ Is Guilt—Glaaki Is Love*, *Don't Spurn Their Return*, *Gimme That Old One Religion*. The most prevalent by far, however, was the slogan that had been there from the beginning: *Free the Old Ones*.

I turned the sound back up as the newscaster prepared to take us to outside the courtroom, where the big question was supposed to finally be settled. As I waited for the answer, my mind drifted back to the art dealer I'd seen in Leeds. He had given me another lead—a story about a catatonic murderess who was shown the Cartwright painting.

It had somewhat matched the description she had given of a "thing"—the supposed seeing of which had forced her to act in, as she interpreted it—self-defense. The hope had been that seeing the painting might get her talking. He told me of her reaction. She had screamed at her initial glance, the first sounds she had made in three years. Then she had lunged for the piece, her only goal surely its destruction.

"She didn't reach it, though," he sighed. "The fact she hadn't moved in so long slowed her down—saved it." He paused for a moment, then added bitterly, "Lucky me, eh?"

At first I had thought to try and find her, but it seemed like so much effort. And, I asked myself, to what end? So she could tell me another hideous tale that would send me somewhere else? So I could further ignore my business and the rest of the world? Why, why bother? Why do anything? What did it matter? What could it matter? I knew what was coming. I knew. I—

My thoughts ceased as a sudden impulse rushed my fist upward, crashing it against my head brutally.

"Shut up!" I heard myself screaming—felt my fist strike again and again. "Shut up, shut up, shut the bloody Hell up!" My skull ringing, I pushing myself toward the mirror.

"Look at yourself," I growled. When I merely glanced at the glass without focusing, the part of me desperate to reverse the course I had been sliding along moved my lips, making me scream—

"Look at yourself, Goddamnit! Look!"

I did. My face was heavily stubbled—drawn and weary—its skin a sickly, sallow shade. My eyes were hollow, the pits beneath them dark and enormous. My hair was unwashed, matted and straggly, my eyes crusted over, barely open. Snot encrusted my nostrils. My lips hung apart, stupidly agape. I was repelled by the image—sickened.

And then a thought struck me—hadn't I seen such a sight recently? Hadn't it affected me in much the same way? I didn't have to torture my brain to recover the memory of when I had last seen such a face. It had been the man in the crowd at Severnford, the one so repellant that simply viewing him had sent me stumbling off half crazed.

And before I knew it, I was in the shower. Hot water scalded me, forcing the layers of filth up off my skin, the smell gagging me. I lathered my head and body with bar soap, rinsed it all away. Then I did it again. And then again. My eyes stung, but I didn't care. I rubbed at them repeatedly—better the pain than the blindness.

Steam billowing out of the open bathroom, I listened to the news as I stepped out of the shower. Chuckling as he read the report, the empty, facile puppet in the tube gleefully announced, "And so all charges have been dropped, and the state has rendered its verdict that the Glaakies will be permitted to conduct their service. What do you think of that, Nancy?"

"I guess, ha ha, it means a new age for all of us, eh?"

"Guess again, bitch," I said, grabbing up my razor. Scraping my neck, I cut away the unwanted, repeating, "Guess again."

31 MARCH—7:20 p.m.

"June, June," the nurse said gently, barely touching the middle-aged woman sleeping in the chair. "You have a visitor."

She opened her eyes slowly, as if every contact with the world outside her head was to be dreaded. She was only forty-five at best, but she sat in her rocker as if they had been carved from a single piece. I looked at her and a sadness welled up within me. She had a small, attractive face, a small body with large, still quite shapely breasts. I almost laughed to think that if I were anywhere else I would be trying for her phone number.

And maybe she'll give it to you, if you can wake her from her coma, snickered a sarcastic voice in my head. *You might make a proper future together, considering you're both loopy.*

I forced myself to concentrate on why I was there. Not noticing anything amiss with me, the nurse brushed a strand of still radiant auburn hair from the woman's face, urging her to wake. She moved slowly—resentfully—not caring that she had her first visitor in some eight years. Not caring that I was present or that the world still existed. As far as she was concerned both conditions would cease soon enough.

She had fallen in love in her late teens with a boy named Michael. He had promised her a new life—and almost delivered. The record hinted that the boy's parents were cultists of some sort. They had disappeared under mysterious circumstances. June claimed the father had "absorbed" the mother, and that Michael had intended the same fate for her. She battered his head in with a spanner the first chance she got. During her trial she slipped into a catatonic state, where she remained for three years until the incident with the Cartwright painting—and from then again until I came to see her.

By the time I arrived at the Wolverhampton sanatarium, her past had been mostly forgotten. She was Quiet June—no trouble, no bother. The nurse turned to me with an apologetic look. I asked her to leave us—said I would just sit with my "aunt." As soon as she departed, however, I leaned forward, taking June's hand. It was cold—nearly bloodless. Stroking it, I whispered, "June. It's almost time. *They* are coming."

There was a stirring in her eyes—a reaction made completely to the emphasis I'd placed on the word "they."

"You were right," I told her. "Michael and his parents were monsters. You held them off—but it wasn't enough. There are more of them now than ever. And they're coming back. Soon."

I watched her eyes moving—darting back and forth. Something inside her was kicking back into gear. Part of me pitied her, cursed me for leading her on. Voices in my head reminded me that she had suffered enough already. I dismissed them, however, putting my needs—the world's needs—first. I had to hear her story. Suddenly what she had to say and how she said it mattered more than anything in the world.

"June," I whispered, still half-certain I'd taken leave of my senses. "I don't have any proof. For all I know I might be as mad as they say you are—but I don't think so. I think something monstrous is coming—something you've seen." I was shaking so badly by that point I found I could no longer stroke her hand. I felt her fingers moving in mine, trembling as well.

"But you're the only person still alive in the world who's seen whatever in Hell it is that's out there," I told her, "whatever it is that's trying to get to us—to everyone."

Her body shook with pain. Her shoulders moved spasmodically, her head turning slowly—twitching. The nervous shaking spread throughout her body. Foam began to fleck along her lower lip. Desperately, I whispered, "I need you to tell me your story. I need you to listen to mine—to tell me I'm not crazy." Desperation clogged my throat.

As the same fear wracking June spread down her arms and into mine, I summoned all the strength I had remaining and hissed, "Help me. Oh, dear God—help me."

And then, June's eyes cleared. Suddenly she fell into a graceful calm, her jerking tremors fading. As she looked around the room, really seeing it for the first time, she said in a dry, hollow voice, "You're not crazy."

I leaned over and kissed her on the cheek. We stared into each other's eyes for a moment, and then identical smiles cracked open our faces.

We were only a quarter of the way to Brichester when the radioman told us I was being sought in connection with her kidnaping. I'm not sure which of us laughed the harder.

1 APRIL—11:35 p.m.

Having abandoned my car the night before, June and I were slower getting to Severnford than I would have hoped. We spent the night with a friend in Cirencester, Jack Saner, an old mate from my service days who'd discounted the news of my criminal abducting as soon as he'd heard it. He made us comfortable and listened to both June's and my stories with rapt interest.

When we finished, he had only one question.

"So, what you proposin' to do, then?"

After a long silence, June answered, saying, "Same thing I did last time, I suppose." I smiled. So did Jack.

Leaving the room, he came back with a trio of automatics and a bag of spare clips. Passing them around, he said, "The bloody mongrel government is so keen to see these Elder Gods, let's send some of 'em on to 'em, eh?"

June accepted the weapon as if it were the most natural thing in the world. That bothered me for a moment. But then I thought, after what she'd seen in her time, the playthings of an IRA man like Jack must have seemed rather tame—maybe even quaint.

After that we had checked our ordnance, slept, and then set out for Severnford in his car. We'd had to abandon it some ten miles from the ruins, the roads all blocked by the press of vehicles pouring into the area. It was the typical carnival bag of thrill seekers and the curious, the cynical and the true believers and those willing to exploit the lot of them.

Setting off on foot an hour after sundown, we were just sighting the ruins a handful of minutes before midnight. That was the last moment, of course, the time the courts had decreed the ancient castle should be turned over to the Glaakies.

We pushed our way through the milling, humming crowd, making our way for the police lines. I did not know what we were going to do—what we could do. My most conservative estimate put the crowd in the thousands. And even if only a tiny fraction of them were seriously there to usher in the new age—people like Gillson and Fisher, like Shea and Cartwright and June's crazed Michael—what, I asked myself, did I think we could do?

Free the Old Ones, free the Old Ones, free the ....

Trying to ignore the low chant all around us, I realized there was no doubt we would be three against an army. The closer we got to the front barriers, the more of the crowd gave over to the obsessed and the obscene. A putrid smell hung over them, oozed out of them, letting us know that hundreds of those around us had already given themselves over to whatever it was that was coming.

And, if that were not enough, when we did reach the police lines it was fair positive they would be more interested in taking me into custody than anything else. Still, we walked on, shoving our way forward, not knowing what else there was to be done. Then, several yards still out from the barriers, a familiar voice sounded.

"Mr. Clarke—over here."

The district magistrate stood in front of the lines, waving us on. Gambling that everything I had felt about him was true, I urged my companions on. The magistrate offered his hand to June as did his man Hastings. As Jack and I scrambled across the substantially reinforced barrier, I said, "You don't seem surprised to see me."

"We both knew you'd be here, Mr. Clarke," he answered. "Though I admit it's a pleasure to see you ready to stand this side of the wall."

Free the Old Ones, free the Old Ones, free ....

I looked around as he spoke, noticing for the first time that aside from the magistrate and Hastings, there were few official types in sight. The grand majority were just folks, men and women, some perhaps grandfathers and mothers, all bound to the cause as were we.

Free the Old Ones, free the Old Ones ....

Then, as the magistrate turned away for a moment, a girl no more than fourteen approached our position. She had a field rifle in hand, and a look about her that said she knew how to use it. And then, looking down at her, something brittle snapped inside me. What kind of a game were we playing at, I wondered. We had no proof for what we felt. It was just a religion—just another lot of scared, superstitious people telling frightened stories.

Suddenly I wondered if all of us on both sides of the barrier might not be mad. Tapes and paintings and suicide notes? That was my evidence? I had had to go to the bughouse to find someone to tell me that what I was thinking was sane. And then I'd stolen her out, given her a gun, and taken her to the object of her insanity.

Free the Old Ones, free the Old ....

I wanted to believe, to find some kind of shoring proof to justify the absolute faith I so desperately needed. Wondering at how I could have come so far without yet truly believing, I closed my eyes, trying to squeeze out all around me, searching for one clear moment to think.

Free the Old Ones, free the ....

Opening my eyes, I could see a line of vehicles making their way forward through the crowd. Knowing they had to contain the cultists, knowing the moment of their precious alignment was but minutes away, I turned to the girl with the rifle and asked her, "Isn't this a school night?"

"I did my homework." When I only raised an eyebrow in response, she told me, "Think of this as extra credit."

I moved my head from side to side. The lead car had stopped at the front of the barrier. Robed figures came swarming out of every vehicle. The magistrate broke off to confront them.

Free the Old Ones, free ....

Turning to the girl, I touched her on the shoulder, then asked, "Tell me—please—why are you here?"

She stared at me, her head at an angle, her expression one as if I'd asked her what color the sky was. Finally, deciding that I might simply be blind, she told me, "Because I don't want to go to Hell."

Free the Old Ones, ...

Beyond, the cultists demanded entry to the ruins. It was plain to see from his stance alone that the magistrate had refused them. I looked down at the girl and smiled, telling her, "No. No, I guess I don't, either."

The leader of the Glaakies reached beneath his robes, pulling forth very official looking papers. The district magistrate summoned all the formidable presence he had and refused them again, papers and all.

Free the Old ....

June and Jack appeared at my sides. I shook Jack's hand, traded quips, and then watched as he raced up the hill to take his place amid the broken stone of the ancient castle. Touching my arm, June turned me to her.

Free the ....

"Thank you," she whispered. She kissed me on the cheek and then moved close, hugging me. I could feel her tears on my shoulder.

"Thank you, so very much."

Free ....

And then a struggle erupted near the front barrier. The robed figures swelled forward, followed by a thousand others. I squeezed June's hand, and then we both pulled our weapons. Shots rang out, and the night sky went black.

The Music of the Spheres

by Kevin A. Ross

disaster, *n.* 1: *A baleful aspect of a planet or star.* 2: *Sudden and extraordinary misfortune; a calamity.*

A cold rain lashed at the windows of his office, but Neal was oblivious to it. He was totally absorbed in the array of computer printouts spread across the desk before him. Tangles and clots of numbers vied for his attention, and he studied the figures with increasing excitement, still unable to believe what the last few days' data indicated.

Yes, there could be no doubt: This must be Nemesis. Everything fit. The size of it. Its distance from the Earth. The trajectory of its orbit.

Fourteen trillion miles away, soaring through the constellation of Bootes, the Herdsman, was the most sought after body in all the heavens. The murderer of the dinosaurs. The so-called "death star" which scientists had dubbed Nemesis.

The Americans had come up with the theory over a decade ago. Alvarez had discovered what had killed the dinosaurs: 65 million years ago a comet or asteroid had struck the Earth and triggered a tremendous climactic upheaval. This radical theory had spurred others to look deeper into the mystery. Raup and Seposki had suggested that the Earth was subject to such mass extinctions at regular intervals of about 26 million years. Originally denounced as preposterous, this hypothesis had led Dr. Richard Muller to seek the cause of these regular decimations of terrestrial life.

What he had found—or rather, hoped to find—was that a companion star to Earth's sun existed, and that its unstable orbit took it through the Oort comet cloud at regular intervals. Its presence would "shake loose" comets from the cluster, sending them raining down through the solar system, pummeling moons and planets in an eons-old cycle of celestial destruction. Such disasters were believed to trigger the demise of nearly all life on Earth at that time. It was, almost literally, an Earth-shattering theory.

Muller and his colleagues had sought in vain for their death star for several years. And now Brichester University's Cruciform Array of radio telescopes had detected an anomalous body which fit Muller's data to a "T."

Stewart Crossley, Neal's clever young protege, had been the first to notice the anomalous signals emanating from what he had decided was a brown dwarf star. Neal had used all his influence as a Fellow of the Royal Society to convince the Royal Greenwich Observatory to undertake a series of observations and photographs of this object.

The data had come back confirming Neal's and Crossley's wildest hopes: No proper motion was detected in the object's orbit, and there was a decided lack of lines in its spectrogram. All this, combined with its dim magnitude, seemed to indicate it was a small but relatively close star. In sum, it could be nothing other than the so-called "death star."

Neal ran his hand over his high forehead and into his thinning hair. Closing his eyes and leaning back in his chair, he smiled, triumphant with the thought that his discovery would assure him a place in the annals of astronomy not just in Britain, but throughout the world. It would be perhaps the most important astronomical achievement since Clyde Tombaugh's 1929 discovery of Pluto. Neal frowned at this, however, for he mused that Tombaugh had used the late Percival Lowell's data to find the lost world at the rim of the solar system—and hadn't Neal and his colleagues just done much the same thing using the Americans' data?

It was a trivial notion, and one Neal dismissed, rubbing his eyes. He and the others had put in too many hours in their Nemesis investigation to worry about how legitimate their claim to fame would be. Tempers were on edge, arguments were common, and more than a few mistakes had been made due to fatigue and frayed nerves. For Neal, the worst had been the headaches. He suspected that his married colleagues would be having a worse time of it, considering how many extra hours they were spending at the remote radio observatory. Little wonder everyone was so testy.

Satisfied that the arrangements for the official announcement could wait until morning, Neal rose and headed for the control room, and then for Crossley's office. He would have to ring Talbot at the University's Public Affairs Office this evening, to tell him the news. Talbot would no doubt want to be on hand for the news conference, though Neal smiled wanly at the thought of letting that smug young bureaucrat learn of the find along with the rest of the world. That would set him right off.

There was also Dr. Davies at the Royal Observatory at Herstmonceux: It didn't seem fair to put his old friend through his paces on Neal's behalf without sharing the secret—and part of the credit, of course—with him. He could almost picture old Davies' reaction: sputtering out questions, his face turning redder and redder, his eyes and smile widening, his pipe clenched precariously in his teeth and bobbing up and down as he spoke. He would be so excited he'd probably smoke a whole pouch of that foul tobacco of his by bedtime.

But no one else would be told for now. That would wait until the official announcement later this week. Everyone here had of course been sworn to secrecy, so there was little chance of the news reaching the public or the scientific community before then.

Neal walked silently into the control room. It was late, and only Gilmour and Wright were on duty. Or supposed to be: Wright was slumped over on his desk, his head down on his arms. Neal cleared his throat loudly, and when he had the attentions of both men, he dismissed them for the night. Wright muttered a half-comprehensible thanks as he left, and Gilmour immediately flew to his feet, grabbed his jacket and headed for the door. No doubt his wife had been after him about his excessive hours at the observatory.

When both were gone, Neal backtracked through the abandoned halls. Stewart's light was still on, and Neal frowned at the familiar harmonic rumbling sound coming from within. Crossley had made audio translations of the radio signals received from the Nemesis star, and had played them incessantly ever since the staff had realized the significance of their source.

This was a common conceit among radio astronomers: that somehow these signals would mean something, or produce an actual audio message. And every radio astronomer wanted to be the first one to receive and recognize such an alien transmission.

At least Crossley didn't take it too seriously. He had made several different recordings from various angles, times, frequencies, and wavelengths, but had found nothing out of the ordinary. He had, however, annoyed the blazes out of nearly everyone in the building with his constant playing of those rumbling low-register notes. Sometimes he even played them at ear-shattering volumes, but thankfully only for short periods.

Neal knocked softly at the door, then went in. Crossley looked up from his desk, where several books and magazines had been haphazardly stacked.

Stewart Crossley was an eager, energetic man, some thirty years younger than Gerald Neal's 59 years. In many ways, he was in fact Neal's opposite. Where Crossley's frame was thin and wiry, Neal was stout and large-featured. Neal could not even claim to have once shared the younger man's energy in his own youth: He had always been physically sluggish, and not overly friendly with others. He had never married, having devoted his entire life to studying what lay far outside the reach and sight of man. He recognized this shortsightedness in himself, but did nothing to check it.

Crossley, on the other hand, had a lovely young fiancee, a graduate student in History at Brichester. Neal had joined the couple for lunch on more than one occasion; he had found Catherine to be quite attractive and bubbling with intelligence and wit—the perfect match for the equally effervescent young radio astronomer.

"What can I do for you, Gerry?" asked Crossley. He pushed past a cold cup of coffee to turn down the volume on a portable cassette player from which warbled the grating tones of the death star.

"Just popped in to let you know I'm going to go ahead and set up the news conference for later this week."

Crossley grinned, pushed a lock of straggly black hair off his forehead. "I suppose the Public Affairs people will insist on scripting our statements?"

"I doubt it. Talbot can fox his way through enrollment reports and grant announcements, but I think he leaves the scientific departments to their computers and laboratories. He'll definitely be out of his element with radio interferometers and brown dwarf stars."

Crossley sat back down, not particularly amused. He had been worried that the University wouldn't realize the importance of the discovery, and would delay the announcement so that someone else would beat Neal's team to the punch.

The past couple of days Neal had noticed Crossley's growing anxiousness to announce the Cruciform Array team's discovery. Stewart had been especially vexed when Neal asked Gilmour to recheck all the data and run diagnostics on all the equipment. The young astrophysicist had argued long and hard to make the find public immediately, and had finally thrown up his hands and stalked away. By the next morning he had cooled off from his tantrum.

"I had Catherine do some digging with regard to historical reports of comets—you know, Edmund Halley and so forth. Thought it might be good background for the press release. She came up with some interesting bits." He turned around the book which had been in front of him, so that Neal could read it.

From the look of it, the book Crossley proferred was an illuminated medieval treatise of some kind. A brightly-hued picture adorned one leaf of the old tome, its colors still vibrant after—what? 300 years? More? A dark spherical shape streaked across a star-filled night sky painted a deep blue; beneath the hurtling body several pale human figures lay prostrate on the ground, as if dead. Neal noted that several similar upright figures stood ahead of the sphere's progress, as if watching the thing pass overhead.

Crossley pointed to a passage below the illumination. "Catherine says this dates back to the Black Plague, and talks of how just before the outbreak there were reports of a dark star sighted in the sky over France. Wish I could read this stuff, but my Latin's plenty rusty."

"Mine too," muttered Neal. The exquisite calligraphy covered nearly every inch of space not taken up by the illustrations.

Crossley spread open another book. Another drawing, this one much more primitive than the previous, showed an even more crudely drawn figure atop a building; the man was dressed in a simple robe, and appeared to be a Red Indian. Above him, a star-like shape crossed the sky, a black cloud trailing behind it.

"Montezuma, the Aztec king. Legend has it his people saw what they called a 'smoking star' just before Cortez arrived. You know what happened then—"

Neal frowned, uncertain of what Stewart was after here. The recording of the radio emissions still groaned on the tape player on the desk, and it was beginning to annoy him.

"Yes, yes. The Spanish subjugated them in the course of a few years. This is all old hat, Stew. Comets have always been considered bad omens. This is nothing new, and not the type of thing I think we need to dwell on before the press. God knows they'll be dredging up enough of that business as it is without our encouragement."

Undeterred, Crossley dragged a magazine from between two books, and set it atop the books while he thumbed through a stack of manila folders. Out came one of the photographs taken at Greenwich. This he laid beside the copy of *The Annual Review of British Astronomy and Astrophysics*.

"Look at this." He opened the magazine to an article on Greenwich's study of a recent supernova. Neal didn't have to read the article, as he and Davies had worked together to record the event with their respective radio and optical apparatus; both were, in fact, mentioned prominently throughout the article.

Before Neal could respond, Crossley held up a finger and turned the pages until he came to a small sidebar piece titled "Son of Supernova?" A small photo showed the large bright angry red of the exploding star at center, with a much smaller and dimmer dark blue object below it. Neal vaguely recalled that Greenwich had tried out a new speckle camera while observing the supernova; this device was used to minimize atmospheric distortion to aid in distinguishing separate celestial objects when they appeared close together. The small object had appeared at about the same time the Royal

Observatory had begun its survey, but had disappeared without a trace within days. It was decided that this was merely some unstable fragment of the star that had quickly burnt itself out.

"Yes, I remember all this, Stew. What—"

Crossley placed the latest photo of the "death star" alongside the much smaller magazine picture.

Neal stroked his chin, then picked up both pieces to view them more closely. Yes, there were some similarities. Both were oddly flattened, yet still spherical, and both gave off the same burnt orange luminescence.

"Stewart, the supernova was nowhere near where we've got—"

While Neal had been examining the other photos, Crossley had been rummaging through his books again. When Neal looked up from the photos he found himself faced with yet another variation of the spherical image. The younger astronomer held a thin, folio-sized book in both hands, opened toward Neal. The pages were covered with a text printed in an ugly brown ink that actually hurt the eyes to look at.

But it was the illustration which nearly made Neal gasp. It was the familiar slightly flattened sphere, only viewed close up. It was a relatively crude painting or drawing, he had no idea which. It reminded him of an illustration he had seen for an old H. G. Wells book: a great dark sphere, its surface crisscrossed by ugly red cracks, like scars or blood vessels. This was much the same, only it brought to him not a tug of nostalgia for his boyhood reading, but a shudder. This was somehow unwholesome, creepy. The eye-burning brown text surrounding it didn't help matters.

Crossley had laid the book down on the desk as he spoke. "This dates back to the mid-1800's. Catherine ran across this when she was working on that article on the lake. It's supposedly the collected writings of some weird cult. Most of it's utter gibberish. But look, this nineteenth century British cult—these aren't superstitious medieval peasants or aboriginals—they believed in this comet-god who sang to the stars and planets as it passed by them in its orbit. They said it destroyed those worlds it passed, by waking up demons or ancient gods or what-have-you who slept on each world."

Neal followed Crossley's finger as he traced the lines of brown ink across the page while paraphrasing the text. No doubt about it, he had a great whacking headache now. And his tolerance for this superstitious claptrap had reached its end. He reached in front of Crossley and closed the book.

"Go home, Stewart," he said, frowning. "We've all been at this too much the past couple of weeks. We're all tired." Crossley started to protest, but Neal gently cut him off.

"And you know, I think I'm going to delay the announcement until next Monday. Give everyone a few days' rest before the press starts hounding us. Sound okay?"

Crossley started to speak, stopped, looked down at the book sheepishly, and seemed to shrink in on himself. "You're right, Gerry. This is all pretty wild, but it's really nothing new. I just thought it was odd that this fellow was able to toss off such a close approximation of what it's taken us years to see with much better equipment."

Neal nodded. "And you'd do us both a great favor," he started, reaching for the tape deck, "by not playing this bloody infernal noise anymore. It's got everybody in the place gnashing their teeth." With an unwittingly patronizing smile, Neal stopped the tape, ejected it, and put it in his coat pocket.

With this chore accomplished, he waited until Crossley had left, then locked up the building, said goodnight to the long-haired nightwatchman, and began the long drive to his house in Brichester. It was still raining, and between the hypnotic slap of the windshield wipers and the chaotic "Uranus" movement of Holst's *The Planets* which played on his car tape player, he was growing very tired. His eyes and head ached, and even his fingers felt stiff. The phone calls to Davies and Talbot would have to wait until morning. Hang it, perhaps he would just let Talbot set up the whole bloody circus after all—

He blinked rapidly and jerked the wheel, for his wandering attention had let the car swerve into the oncoming lane. Luckily, this late at night there was little or no traffic on the A.38. The rush of adrenalin kept him alert for the remainder of the drive, but once home he found himself barely able to get out of his clothes and into bed before falling into a restless, dreamless sleep.

* * *

Neal was awakened by the insistent chirping of the phone; pulling himself around in the dark bed, he noted that it was either 4:30 in the morning, or his LED clock was wrong. Still in his undershirt and boxers, he managed to reach the phone on the sixth ring.

The voice at the other end wavered wildly between mumbling and sputtering hysteria, as if a radio dial were being whirled from station to station. It took several seconds for Neal to realize that it was Catherine's voice. It took him a few more moments to calm her down.

"Stewart—Stewart's dead, Gerry." Though he had been half-asleep moments before, he was now suddenly wide awake.

"He came home last night very—depressed." Catherine's voice had become calm, almost robotic. Neal suddenly felt as if he had inherited her earlier panic. Stewart dead?

"Wha—What happened last night, Gerry? He said he felt like he had let you down. He wouldn't—wouldn't tell me about it." Catherine gasped out a wracking sob before continuing. "He took a bunch of pills, Gerry. He c-came home and locked himself in the study, t-turned on the music, and wouldn't come out."

Then suddenly there was fury in her voice. "Dammit, Gerry, were you going to cut him out of the news conference? Take all the credit for finding your bloody Nemesis?"

Neal sat too stunned by her vehemence to reply. Did she really think of him this way? Had he misjudged her this much? He hoped it was merely grief fueling this fury.

"What the hell did you say to him, Gerry?!"

Neal jerked the receiver away from his ear, barely fumbled it back in its cradle. He sat with his head in his hands for several minutes. *Jesus, Stewart. What we were on to, what we were almost ready to show the world—why would you do such a stupid thing?*

Now the triumph of the fabled death star's discovery would be Neal's alone. It might even be tainted somewhat, if Crossley's suicide were taken in the wrong light. Neal threw off such trivial worries, embarrassed that he should be so concerned with the effect Crossley's death would have on the research, rather than on the loss of his friend and the bitter reaction of Crossley's fiancee. My god, was this what Catherine really thought of him?

He would be unable to sleep now. He didn't want to stay home and brood, which he knew he would do. Better to go to the lab. He could figure out how to break the news of Crossley's death to the others, start making arrangements for the press conference—immerse himself in work so that he wouldn't think about Crossley, and Catherine—

He dressed quickly, mentally recreating last night's talk with Crossley, searching for a reason. Had he said something to him to cause this? Had he been too condescending with him? He searched his jacket for his car keys, found that he had thrust them into his pants pocket.

Once in the car, he turned on the ignition and leaned back and closed his eyes. Calm yourself. There is nothing to be done here. Stewart let the work get the better of him. Mustn't do the same. Neal jammed the car into gear and wheeled out of the parking garage to enter the outside world, where the first pre-dawn commuters were themselves just rising.

The drive through Brichester was dreary, and the previous evening's rainshower had become a fully fledged electrical storm now. The streets were wet and dark, almost slimy-looking. He almost regretted leaving the concrete shelter of the parking garage, for the dark, storm-filled sky felt oppressive, omniscient and omnipotent above him.

Neal shuddered. Crossley and Catherine's delirium had taken root in him. He fumbled in the glove compartment for a cassette tape, punched a button and ejected *The Planets*, and slid in the new selection. The wooded river valley rushed by as he sped down the A.38 towards the site. Far below on his left he could just make out the glassy bends of the Severn occasionally shimmering as the lightning streaked across the sky.

Suddenly the music throbbed out of the speakers. The familiar rumbling bass of the dark star's radio signal.

"How did that get in here?" Neal muttered aloud. He glanced into the glove compartment for the tape case, but saw only a jumble of empties; he didn't want to risk searching among them while driving.

The notes of the music crooned, warbled, rumbled. He thought of whales coupling in the inkiest depths of the ocean, vast dark shapes emitting these sounds. But there was something else here. Something darker. Pain? Rage? What?

Was that a voice? He thought he had heard a faint wordless voice wailing amid the static and against the background of throbbing low-register notes. A dull ache began to pulse behind his eyes in rhythm to the alien "music."

Neal stabbed at the rewind button on the tape deck, watching the LED panel as it glared back at him with an angry red "TAPE/REWIND." After a few moments he punched the Play button so hard he hurt his finger. "TAPE/PLAY."

The Nemesis music again rolled out of the speakers, and Neal stared dumbly at the cassette player as if he expected the ethereal voice's lyrics to scroll across the LED panel. But where was the voice this time? Had he even heard it at all?

If he had looked up, Neal would have noticed that he had again drifted into the other lane of traffic. He would have seen that he was directly in the path of a petrol truck hurtling down at him from London.

But Neal was so engrossed in the music that he didn't look up.

* * *

In the wake of Dr. Gerald Neal's tragic death, the board of Brichester University appointed Dr. Charles Bloom as his successor. Bloom, an unassuming—and some would charge unimaginative—member of the Astronomy and Astrophysics Department, was surprised to learn the nature of his predecessors' research.

In the weeks following Neal's death, Bloom carefully studied the results of Dr. Neal's and Dr. Crossley's research, and came to the conclusion that he was well out of his league. With the approval of the University, he contacted Drs. Richard Muller and Luis Alvarez, the two California astrophysicists who had worked so diligently on the Nemesis theory. Bloom sent Muller and Alvarez all the data accumulated by Neal and Crossley, under the condition that the initial Brichester findings be fully credited should the theory actually pan out.

At the University of California at Berkeley, Muller and his team immediately set to work to verify the Brichester data. In the California deserts countless telescopes—both optical and radio varieties—trained their attentions toward the portion of the heavens where Bootes, the Herdsman, trod the starways. Soon Muller contacted other astronomers around the world to verify the findings. Hundreds of radio telescopes aimed their dishes at the "death star" and began receiving its alien transmissions.

Three days after the Californians joined the investigation, a massive earthquake rocked northern California. Reportedly a 7.8 on the Richter scale, the quake killed over thirty people and injured hundreds more. The epicenter was just outside Stockton, less than sixty miles from Berkeley.

Two days later, a similar tremor devastated nearly a hundred square miles in North Africa, near Addis Ababa. Over a hundred people were killed outright, and the resultant loss of food and shelter in the already drought-stricken area was expected to bring the death toll well into the thousands. Within hours local bandit-chieftains armed with automatic weapons had confiscated most of the available food and fresh water supplies in the region.

At about the same time as the African disaster, seismologists reported yet another quake, this time in the South Pacific. Centered several hundred miles due west of the southern tip of Chile, in an unpopulated stretch of boundless ocean, this quake caused no fatalities. Nevertheless, shipping was suspended for several days while tidal waves and fierce storms lashed the area.

* * *

The music grows ever louder, though we do not hear it. It is not intended for us. Does the cockroach comprehend the casual whistling of the man who crushes it underfoot?

But the Earth hears. The Earth and those who rest within her drowned cities, lightless burrows, and ancient crypts. They hear. They understand. They begin to shake off eons of of deathlike dormancy. They begin to move toward wakefulness.

Growing Pains

by Richard Watts

Warren Anderson didn't like queers. He didn't like blacks either, but he really didn't like queers. There was a queer in the office where he worked. Mincing bloody poof. Hunter his name was, plump and soft and delicate, not hard like a man should be. Himself, Warren worked out in the gym almost every day, lifting weights until he saw red. His figure was that of a man half his age. No one would know he was pushing forty, were it not for the tracery of broken capillaries across his puffy cheeks, his thinning hair, and the sharp lines anger had scored across his face.

Warren didn't want to go to work tomorrow. Never did on a Sunday night. Licking his dry lips with a suddenly thick tongue, Warren poured himself another glass of thin red wine. He gulped half of it down before refilling his glass and settling back in his chair. He stared at the television with bloodshot eyes, watching the flickering figures without really seeing them.

Outside he could hear someone staggering home down the street, the crunch as they walked through the broken glass on the pavement outside Warren's door. He had dropped his first bottle on the steps as he turned his key, and had had to go back to the wine bar for another, or face a dry and sleepless night. The man in the bottle shop (probably a poof, Warren thought) had leered at him when he asked for another bottle.

"You drank that one fast," he had tittered. "You must be thirsty."

Trying not to shout, Warren had coughed out a response, snatched up the change and the wine bottle, and fled home. His skin had crawled as he ran, and sweat inched its maddening way down his sides. God, but he hated poofs. Why, the whole wine bar was probably full of them, staring at him with their cold insect eyes, chittering and sniggering behind his back. It was a bad thing when a poofs' wine bar opened in Lower Brichester.

A few blocks from home Warren had slowed his pace, wiped his brow and proudly noted that he was barely out of breath. Evening was coming on, the western sky bleeding over streets still clotted from the afternoon's rain. Sodden newspapers gagged the mouths of drains. Snail trails glistened upon the cracked pavement, delicate traceries of silver threading between the dog turds. Thin, gray houses lined the street, each identical to his own. Only the occasional cracked window pane or bright curtain marked them apart. At least this suburb was still free from the yuppie plague creeping down from Mercy Hill: childless couples with their sleek cars and smart houses, compact disc players and, mobile phones. Real people, like Warren, were being forced out. There were so few of the old families left. In his street, only a few of the people Warren had grown up with still remained. More than half the houses had foreign cars parked in front of them now.

Just as he had been opening his door the second time, half-heartedly kicking away the wine-stained paper and broken glass from his step, the girl next door came out of her house. She had moved in only a week ago. No boyfriend had helped her, Warren had noticed, only an older woman, most likely her mother. The little tart was living alone. Probably brought a new man home every night.

Warren called out a greeting, asked her if she'd like to come in for a drink and a bit of fun. "Piss off, Neanderthal," she called over her shoulder as she opened the door of her BMW and slid into the driver's seat. The engine drowned Warren out as he angrily shouted at her.

"Bitch!"

She didn't hear him. Swearing, he let himself in, and began to get drunk.

* * *

Monday began like every other, with a sore head, a dry mouth, and a sinking feeling as Warren realized that another gray week lay before him. It was a week like any other, empty and endless. That Friday was his office's social night. Everybody stayed back after work for a few drinks, and then a few drinks more. Sometimes, Warren knew, things got out of hand. He had heard more than one story about what went on when the secretaries had a couple of drinks too many. There were always stories. It was only to be expected in a building with this much history. Warren had heard tales told by those staff who worked night shift, tales of pale spiders the size of kittens scuttling out of sight behind the filing cabinets in the basement, tales of ghosts. It wouldn't have surprised Warren to discover that the building was haunted. He knew at least three people had died here. One of them he had found himself.

Old Mr. Haldane, who had worked in Personnel for as long as anyone could remember, had committed suicide in his own office. Apparently his wife had left him after thirty years of marriage; no one knew why, nor had it seemed polite to ask. Haldane had taken to sitting in his office, not speaking, silently filling in forms, working back late, long after everyone else had gone home. Eventually he shot himself. It was Warren who found the body the next morning, still sitting stiffly at its form-strewed desk, the papers before it splattered with a final scarlet signature.

People had been conceived here too, of that Warren had no doubt. It was only a year or two ago that there had been a major scandal on the 14th floor. The Claims Department's supervisor Mr. Weedal had been transferred, along with another man and a woman. Something about outrageous behavior on the fire escape, rumor had it. Warren wasn't surprised. Nothing surprised him any more. He had heard about fun on the photocopier, even seen the grainy A4 copies of coupling as they were handed around the office the next day. People were having sex here all the time. At the last social Warren had noticed that young Parker, the young lad in his department (a cricket player, wasn't he?), had managed to lock himself in the storeroom with a typist, Shelly. The two of them didn't come out for half an hour, and when they did both of them were red-faced and panting.

Warren had never had such luck at an office party himself, in all the twelve years he had been working at the Walton Street Tax Office, but there was always the chance someone would proposition him. As long as it wasn't the poof.

Warren felt himself growing flushed, his hands sweaty at the disgusting idea. Men's bodies, touching, thrusting. The mere thought made him nauseous. To make himself feel better, Warren forced himself to imagine screwing one of the three secretaries in his department. Which of them did he fancy the most?

There were actually four secretaries, but the fourth girl was a pale, bloated troll of a woman, all loose rolls of white flesh and idiot, staring eyes. Darlene, her name was. It was a pity really. She had been quite attractive until she put on so much weight. He definitely didn't want to fuck Darlene, Warren decided, although he might have before she got fat. Must have been all the junk food she ate, working the night shift, down in the labyrinthine basement where the furnace grumbled and muttered to itself like a jealous god. There had been a lot to catch up on after Weedal had been transferred.

Of the three sexy secretaries, Warren didn't want to fuck Shelly. He didn't really fancy blondes, although the idea of having Parker's seconds somehow unspeakably excited him. Nor Marg either, although her Irish accent was a bit of a turn-on. She was too thin for him, too awkward and bony. No, it was Kathy he liked the most, with her boyish curves, her bright laughter and her short black hair. She reminded him of his favorite model in the well-thumbed copy of *Fiesta* that always sat beside his lounge-room chair. He definitely wouldn't mind a piece of Kathy.

Parker, blond, athletic, his nose permanently sunburned and peeling, interrupted Warren's reverie, barging into the conference room, his arms weighed down with a crate of beer. Warren helped him carry it to the table, and eagerly accepted his offer of a drink. Soon Shelley and Kathy came in, Shelley giving Parker the cold shoulder. He winked at Warren, and Warren smiled back, feeling good. Feeling like a man. Kathy set up a radio; Mr. Wilson arrived, Singh and Powell trotting behind him. Soon the room was a hive, abuzz with conversation.

Warren, refilling his glass (how many times now?), looked up to see a plump, dapper figure standing on the opposite side of the table.

Thinning blond hair swept neatly back over a pale forehead, crisp suit, gold earring. It was Hunter. The queer. He simpered at Warren, and raised his glass in a silent toast. Resolutely Warren turned his back and strode blindly into the crowd, temples pounding. Fucking poof. Several more drinks did nothing to cool his temper. He could feel Hunter watching him, smiling that cruel queer smile, probably the same smile he used on young boys as he asked them to take off their school uniforms. He was watching him. He probably fancied him. God, what if Hunter thought he was a poof? Warren knew he wasn't that way, but he had to show Hunter, had to show them all. A girl. He had to have a girl. With grim determination, Warren staggered drunkenly towards the small clump of secretaries. The crowd parted as he came.

* * *

The taste of cheap wine and stale lager. A tongue, probing, trying to crawl down his throat. Filing cabinet digging into his back, his hands fumbling, fingers digging into something soft and yielding. Heavy bulk, smell of sweat and perfume, a fetid warmth embracing him, swallowing him. This was not what he wanted. This was not how it should be. He tried to cry out, but something was stuck in his throat. Something warm and squirming. Reflexively he swallowed. There was a satisfied sigh. He opened his eyes to see Darlene's bloated face gloating over him, her lipstick smeared, her heavy jowls flushed with pleasure as her tongue, dripping ropy strands of saliva, withdrew back into her mouth. Without a word she stood, straightened her dress, and went to rejoin the party.

* * *

"You're awake. Good."

Warren opened one eye. A blurred impression of dark streets rushed past him. He felt dizzy. He felt dirty. He needed to clean himself, to scrub away the memory of what had happened to him at the party.

"If you're going to throw up again, do let me know. Maybe you could do it outside the car this time."

It was Hunter's voice. This was Hunter's car. Warren couldn't move.

"I looked up your address in your wallet," Hunter went on. "You were in no state to drive home. Made quite a mess of yourself, didn't you? Turns out you're on the way to my place, so I said I'd drop you home. No bother." He looked over and smiled. Blearily, Warren tried to smile back, although his cheeks were locked tight. His throat hurt, and it felt like something had used his tongue as a shroud.

Hunter prattled on, something about opera. Warren wasn't listening. He was looking at Hunter, at the open collar of his shirt, tie loose and dangling, at his thick neck, and a glimpse of tufted hair. Warren caught himself wondering if Hunter was that hairy all over. The thought horrified him. Blood rushed to his cheeks, and to other parts of his body. Inside him, something stirred. He groaned.

Hunter looked over, face creased with concern. "Almost there, old fellow," he said.

They pulled up outside Warren's narrow house. Hunter killed the engine, and went around to open Warren's door. The street was silent. The full moon hung low in the sky like a skull. Long arms of cloud reached out tremulously to cover its pock-marked face, as if it could not bear to witness what was about to occur. Warren looked up to see Hunter smiling at him. "I've seen you watching me," Hunter said. "Aren't you going to ask me inside?"

Warren did.

* * *

Sunlight speared into Warren's brain as he opened his eyes, waking from a dream of darkness where blind figures wrapped in rags crawled over a bloated shape made more terrible because it could not be clearly seen. Hunter was long gone, although his scent still lingered. Warren convulsed as he remembered what he had done last night, what he had allowed Hunter to do to him. He bit down on his knuckles to stop from screaming and drew blood. It tasted of illicit pleasure. He shut his eyes, but he could not erase the memory that replayed itself in his mind: a dance of fingers and tongues, a symphony of gasps and moans, the soft slap of flesh against flesh.

Naked, Warren staggered to the bathroom, feverishly fumbled with the shower's hot water tap. He stood under the scalding spray for more than an hour, attacking his flesh with the scrubbing brush until he was raw and bleeding. He had wanted to blot out the memory of the office party, but had not realized how much he needed to forget the experience. To wipe out the memory of one obscenity, he had committed another far worse.

Warren could not wash away the stain of his sin. He felt gravid with guilt, weighted down with wickedness. He felt sick. He felt monstrous. Bile rose in his throat, and he bent over in the shower, gagging, but could not vomit. His stomach convulsed. Sobbing, Warren dropped to the tiled floor, the shower spray beating down endlessly upon him. Even as he wept, great wracking sobs, tears whirling away down the drain, he felt the seed planted within him by last night's lust begin to grow.

* * *

He couldn't go back to work. After more than two weeks, the telephone had stopped ringing. Mail had piled up on the carpet before the door, falling through the slot in silent recrimination. He had almost stopped eating, save for occasional sudden cravings for horrible foodstuffs. Mostly he drank, creeping out of his house after dark to bring home bottles of wine and lager. His loungeroom smelt like a brewery, yeasty and faintly rotten. So did he. His stomach had long since stopped complaining, and now swelled in silent reproach, the only witness of his aberration.

On the rare occasions Warren managed to meet his own shame-filled gaze in the bathroom mirror, he saw that he had lost weight. His face was gaunt and unshaven, his skin dull and blemished, the corners of his mouth cracked and bleeding. Without exercise, he felt as if his whole body was slowly turning to jelly. His swollen stomach ached, a hard knot of protestation, the only thing about him still solid and resolved. Barely moving from his armchair, no longer looking at the bright pile of glossy magazines which lay invitingly beside him, Warren sat, and drank, and dreamed.

* * *

He was climbing the outside of a building, a tower made of green stones, which shone slick beneath the light of a dim and swollen sun. Higher. He had to climb higher, before the storm. The air tasted humid and salty when he breathed. Warren didn't know how he was climbing; there were no fingerholds. Then he looked down, and saw that his multiple arms no longer had fingers—

Pale dancers whirled about in a grove of filing cabinets, among the concrete roots of a forest whose trees were glass and steel. They sung something as they cavorted and swirled, a title, a word. Warren could not be sure if it was his own name they shrieked with such intensity, or that of something much more horrible than he—

The cavern walls recoiled at his touch, and the air rang with distant breathing. A viscous, milky fluid dribbled down the ribbed membranes through which he crawled. Somewhere ahead of him was the well. He would throw himself into it and be swallowed by the darkness. When at last he found its gaping aperture, a liquescent something with fleshless segmented legs and eyes without sockets rose up before he could kill himself. Horribly, even as Warren screamed, the thing reached out as if to cradle him, as if he were its child—

* * *

Warren lay in his chair, hands loosely clasped over his swollen abdomen. Something kicked, and pressed its approximation of a face against his distended stomach's tautly stretched skin. There was a knock at the door, and a woman's voice. Not Hunter then. The poof had tried to visit him two or three times, whispering through the letter-flap about guilt and closets and long-repressed urges. Warren had paid no attention. Now there came the splintering sound of locks bursting.

Darlene wobbled into Warren's view. She was not dressed for the office. Other figures crowded behind her. Like Darlene, they too wore stained robes and expectant expressions. Dimly, Warren heard their admiring voices. Darlene surged closer, caressed his sweat-slicked forehead with plump, boneless fingers.

"Behold," she said proudly to those other figures Warren could not clearly see, "behold the Mother."

The Beard of Byatis

by Robert M. Price

The blustery autumn afternoon found Mr. Batchel on one of his rare trips away from his accustomed Stoneground parish. Clerical colleagues had often joked how that when Mr. Batchel was installed as rector of the parish the bishop had used screws and bolts. And thus he considered it something of a quiet victory whenever he ranged any distance from home. In this instance his holiday coincided with an archaeological conference held at the venerable Brichester University in the Severn Valley. An amateur expert in the archaeology of his own beloved Stoneground region, he had been invited to speak on avocational archaeology in one of the morning sessions. He had amply demonstrated, he hoped, that one might yet be a scholar without holding a professional post in the field. He could not deny that the occasion to address an audience mostly composed of young students in the department, budding scholars who might well already exceed his own knowledge, was more than a little daunting. He caught himself feeling once or twice that he was in the position of defending his amateur status before a skeptical audience, though in fact the subsequent question period revealed no such thing.

At any rate, now, after a hardy lunch in the University Commons, he felt nicely relaxed. Strolling about the stately grounds with young Mr. Barlowe, a seminarian in the Divinity School of the University, and as it happened his own temporary assistant, Mr. Batchel held his program leaflet close before his eyes and deliberated aloud as to which of the afternoon symposia he might choose. Young Barlowe persisted in interrupting the older man's concentration as he seemingly felt compelled to play the tourist guide and indicate every point of interest on the grounds of the Divinity College.

"Now there's a difficult choice! 'Recent Excavations of Megiddo' simultaneous with the report of the Prussian Palestine Exploration Fund. How's the knowledge-hungry scholar to decide? Eh? What's that, Barlowe? Yes, of course. I've seen it more than once, y'know. Didn't I tell you I'm no stranger to your campus? Past years have brought me to Brichester on more than one occasion. I might even be able to fill you in on a detail or two. But back to the matter at hand. What do you think of this lecture on the Assyrian Monuments and the Old Testament? After all, it's to be given by one of your Old Testament men. Do you know him? I'm afraid most of the faculty these days are new to me."

Barlowe knew him all right. "Oh him! The story is that Professor Thistleton's primary qualification for his post is that he's quite the fossil himself! It's said he's able to take the most interesting topic and give it all the excitement of a sealed tomb."

"I see," mused Mr. Batchel, trying to seem disapproving of such levity at the expense of an esteemed scholar, yet scarcely able to repress a grin in memory of the jokes he himself had long ago circulated concerning his own divinity professors. "Then how about the presentation on 'Near Eastern Numismatics and the Gospels'? Is Professor Lampton any more inspiring? Seems I may be acquainted with one or another of his books—"

When no quip was forthcoming from the garrulous Barlowe, Mr. Batchel looked up from his creased brochure to discover that he was alone. He had left his assistant a yard or two behind. There he stood transfixed before a niched statue. Catching "up" to him, Reverend Batchel registered recognition as he, too, saw the statue's unusual aspect. The subject depicted appeared to have posed in an attitude of complete startlement, a highly unconventional design to say the least.

"I see they've moved it again," he mumbled.

Barlowe's eyes had now transferred themselves to his mentor. "So you know it, do you? I can't imagine why I've never seen it before now."

"That doesn't surprise me, my young friend. It's never been one of the proudest possessions of the school, I'm afraid, yet in view of certain factors, the administration have never felt free to dispense with it altogether. There are few left who even remember Professor Ashdod. I fear I am one of them." He knew he was now in for a bit of explaining, so he took the younger man's arm and guided him to a bench in the shade of a nearby oak.

"Many years ago, when I was fresh out of Cambridge, my interest in archaeology already keen, I took the opportunity to come over to Brichester for a symposium I'd read of in the *Ecclesiastical Circular*. The subject was the myth of the Gorgon and new light brought to bear by Mycenaean excavations. I'd heard of the great Dr. Ashdod during my days at Cambridge and had read an article or two he had written. So I felt I couldn't pass up the opportunity. The statue, as peculiar as it is, represents him at just that time, which also happens to be the time he disappeared."

"So there's a mystery attached to it, is there?" asked Mr. Barlowe, whose startled curiosity of a moment before had now passed into genuine interest. "Was there foul play? Some professional rivalry? A jealous colleague did him in? It wouldn't be the first time, from what I've heard."

Shaking his hoary head in distaste at such a blatant display of salaciousness, Mr. Batchel replied, "Not a bit of it, young man! And yet now I suppose I must tell you the whole story." With a sidewise look at his companion, as if sizing him up, he continued, "But I can't say I'm persuaded you are, as the Writer to the Hebrews says, mature enough to graduate from milk to solid food."

"Why, what can you mean, Mr. Batchel?" came back the stung reply.

"If I am not mistaken, young Barlowe, you confess yourself under the baneful influence of the Rationalist critics of the Continent, do you not?"

Here the younger man drew himself up straight and ventured, "I am not ashamed to say I have read Strauss and Baur, a bit of Kuenen and Schleiermacher. I find in them many things that are praiseworthy. I like to think I am forward-looking in my sympathies, yes."

"As I thought. Let me remind you, young man, one must have one's bearings straight before one will know where 'forward' points. Well, I am going to tell you a tale that your German pundits would scorn, and I can only hope you will be more open to certain possibilities than they. 'More things in heaven and earth,' you know.

"This will seem a digression, but bear with me. I well remember my anticipation on the morning of that lecture, filing into one of the great auditoriums, Handley Hall, I believe it was, borrowed from the Chemistry Department for the day. Professor Ashdod was putting his papers and charts in order with the care of a Hindu priest preparing the grass square for his Vedic mummery. He seemed visibly annoyed at having to work around the collection of nozzles and spouts built into the lab lectern he had been assigned. I quickly made my way to the front and greeted the great man, mentioning how I had been intrigued with his work. This he seemed to appreciate. I noticed how in the presentation which followed that he often appeared to be directing himself to me, as if he were unsure of more than one interested listener.

"His thesis was a fascinating one. He ventured the singular theory that the legendary Medusa was at first a sun symbol, a symbol for the eclipse, at which one dare not look straight on. Her snaky locks, of course, were the rays of the sun, as in the Ninety-first Psalm. The noonday devil, you know. And behind this lay a deeper significance, that of the terrible power of the divine whom none may see and live.

These symbols came to be coarsened and ill-understood until all that remained was the nursery tale of a woman whose visage could turn the viewer to stone.

"All this was quite ingenious. But the most exciting thing was what he had pieced together from his extensive digging in these English hills. Various remains, barrow carvings, a ritual artifact or two, a fragmentary bas relief, of which he proceeded to circulate rubbings and photographs, had led him to the conviction that the Gorgon cult had reached these shores, perhaps on the fabled trading ships of Tarshish, and that the worship of Medusa had survived longer here than anywhere else. The data allowed for a hypothetical reconstruction of a further stage of mythic evolution than had been traceable in Classical sources. It seemed that in Britain, Medusa's cult had been combined with that of a local fertility god, one of Frazer's 'corn-kings', if you will, called 'Byatis.' Medusa was made his consort, no doubt because of the familiar pattern of the widespread Phrygian Mysteries of Mother Cybele and her consort Attis, of whom Professor Ashdod judged Byatis to be a local variant. I'm sure you are aware of the rumored practice of the grim rites of Cybele in nearby Anchester, for instance.

"This Byatis began to be assimilated to his new bride, taking on some of her traditional iconography. For instance, where Medusa possessed a mane of serpents, Byatis sported a full beard of the revolting creatures. And, like his better half, the old man's gaze was petrifying. There was more, but this will suffice for our purposes.

"Well, I can tell you, as a budding archaeologist I sat spellbound. After the lecture I made my way again to the front of the hall and waited impatiently as others asked their questions. As they gradually dispersed, Professor Ashdod recognized me and seemed pleased to see me. As I would soon learn, he had no living family, and preoccupation with his researches had permitted him little in the way of a social circle. He was a lonely man. I could sense this and so summoned the great effrontery, youngster that I was, about your age, as I say, to invite him out to a local pub to continue our discussion. This he seemed gratified to do.

"We repaired to a private table and the professor bore with my eager queries. It is not often one has the opportunity to speak with a genuine authority, much less to share the personal speculations he hesitates to commit to paper. At length, Dr. Ashdod, seeming somehow satisfied, as if I had managed to pass some test I was unaware of taking, gave me the greatest surprise of the afternoon when he invited me to join a local dig he was planning to mount in the nearby Berkeley-Camside area.

"'There are ruins there, young sir, that I believe may well have a connection with the worship of Medusa and Byatis. They seem relatively undisturbed, mainly because, if I am correct, the exposed section appears to be the covering of an underground tomb, and your casual delver hasn't the fortitude to move the massive slabs. To the untrained eye it probably looks like no more than a Roman foundation stone, and there are plenty enough of those around. Actually it was a cycle of local legends that first put me on to the place. As confused as they were, the stories suggested at least that there might be something under the visible stonework.

"'And there was the serpent motif. That's what makes it a bit more than a hunch. But I admit it's speculative. I'm asking you because so far I've been able to hire only manual labor to move the outer stonework. We've surveyed the site. The next step is to gather a small group of educated colleagues such as yourself. You see, young Mr. Batchel, I need people who have some idea of what we're looking for, and with a sensitivity to the careful nature of what we're doing. Not just diggers.'

"I can only say I was speechless. But at length I assured the savant that I was certain I could take the time from my new parish duties (meanwhile hoping it was so!) and learned from him the details of date, place, and necessary preparations. That night on the train home I had much to consider.

"At that time I was a young apprentice as you are now, and it was fortunate for me that I served under a man with scholarly interests of his own. He understood something of the importance of the mission I sought to undertake, at least that it was important to me, and he gladly agreed to excuse me from my parish rounds for a week, longer if necessary. Thus it was that with a clean conscience I found myself packed and eager to join Professor Ashdod and to meet the small coterie of students he would have assembled.

"My train pulled into the Camside station in the late afternoon. I found the professor in the tap room of the local inn where we would be staying. I sat down as we exchanged pleasantries, and soon we were joined in the cool darkness by three other young men, graduate students from Brichester University, as I was soon made to understand, each engaged in thesis work under Dr. Ashdod's supervision. I have followed the careers of those young men in the intervening years, and each has repaid their mentor's faith in them.

"With all of us assembled, the professor shared the dismaying news that the workmen we expected to aid us had missed their train and that no locals sufficiently familiar with the requisite equipment might be found on short notice. We would be unable to start work till sometime on the morrow. This, however, was no serious blow to any of us, as it was unseasonably warm for the late spring afternoon, and we were as happy to pass the time in convivial company.

"It was not long before our discussion left trivial matters and focused on our common task. The professor had gathered a modicum of fresh information from the morning's informal scrutiny of the surface masonry, as well as from conversation among the Camside villagers he chanced to encounter while making arrangements and securing the necessary permissions for digging. It seemed that our purpose was known to the local rumor mill. The usually tepid business of archaeology, of interest only to the specialist, was here attracting a good deal of popular attention. Dr. Ashdod was everywhere met with suspicious questions and mumbled replies. About all he could extract by way of explanation was a muttered 'Best to let sleeping dogs lie.' This riddle he presented for our exegesis, but no solution was forthcoming from our amused company of smug sophisticates.

"But someone else in the smoky recesses of the tap room must have heard him. Over shuffled an aged form, carrying something in one hand. Without looking, without really noticing at the moment, I assumed he held a pint as we did. Later I had cause to wonder whether it were perhaps something else. At any rate the wizened form looked down at us with blazing eyes, so intimidating that we by tacit consent thought it best not to offer him a seat in our circle. He said, in accents I cannot now repeat, a dialect I knew must be peculiar even in rural Camside, something to this effect: '"He catcheth the clever man in his cleverness," saith the scripture. Ye with your vaunted science are wise in your own conceit. Take care what ye will do!' And with that the man turned like a soldier on his heel and strode back into the obscurity of the tavern. And at the last moment it occurred to me that his dark dress, which seemed to merge with the shadows of the place, looked for all the world like a clerical habit of an earlier generation.

"My companions had a good laugh over this intrusion, but I will confess that I found myself strangely sobered by it. And then, I need not tell you, the others had a second laugh at my expense. I joined them in the merriment then, as several of us took out our pipes and began to pack them.

"The long afternoon drifted imperceptibly on into evening, and I begged to be excused and made for my room for a bath and a quiet evening of reading. As I finally dozed off I reflected how lucky I was to have a rector of enlightened temper and not one of the sort who had rebuked our party earlier.

"We were up early and gathered at the site to await our workmen, who were not long in arriving. I noticed a local man or two drifting about the periphery of the site for the first half hour, but after that we were left to our business. As the sun rose, it became uncomfortably warm. Some removed their shirts, others made a makeshift head dress from their handkerchiefs. Now, I remember thinking, we looked the part indeed. One might have transferred us bodily to the sands of Egypt or the plains of Sumer with no incongruity. So again we waited as the powerful winches lifted the hindering stonework out of the way. In all this Professor Ashdod let nothing escape his supervision, as the stonework itself was something of a relic, even if it paled by comparison to what we hoped to find. And what was that? I don't suppose any of us, except perhaps the professor, had any specific notion.

"At length the path was clear. It was by now no surprise that the slabs had indeed covered a passage underground. It was, however, quite a relief to see that the passage itself was not seriously clogged by boulders or collapsed masonry. And yet the danger existed that our very efforts might be the cause of a collapse, so we proceeded carefully, the professor of course in the lead. There was precious little leeway to navigate the shaft, so one of the students stooped at Dr. Ashdod's side as he sought with lamp and magnifier to decipher what carving remained on the striated wall surfaces. The rest of us busied ourselves with examining the now-revealed underside of the cover slabs. These held little of interest, one or two fossils trapped in the limestone, signs of chiselwork here and there. We grew anxious for news of whatever the professor might be discovering and perked up at each morsel he or his assistant might call back to us.

"As the sun sank, we could see that the two of them had made a great deal of patient progress toward the inner recess. There was no sign that the chamber would prove to be very deep, and we all knew it might have been breached in a single hour or two, but the professor had over many years and many expeditions learned that painstaking work is least likely to damage what is not at first seen.

"He now called in the rest of us to see what little we might of an inner door, that which might be expected to open upon the tomb proper, if that should indeed be what it was. The sun was by now faint, and the lamp light was insufficient to gain more than a hint of the outlines of an inscription. So, like children sent to bed on Christmas Eve, we reluctantly packed up and returned to the town, leaving behind our crew of workmen who doubled as a night watch team, happy to do it for the generous compensation Professor Ashdod offered.

"Hot and tired, we all made for the comfortable tap room again, abuzz with excitement, eager to hear from the professor's own lips what finds he had made. He seemed as ready to tell as we were to hear. He opened a napsack and began to spread out for our examination a collection of small broken artifacts he had recovered from the scattered rubble of the shaft. Our eyes strained for details in the cozy but frustrating gloom of the place. He took up each one as he explained what he made of it. I knew we were getting the oral version of what would be a major scholarly paper, and my ears missed nothing. The inside of the pub had become a seminar room.

"In short, it seemed the professor had already found ample corroboration of his theories at several points. The walls of the shaft harbored votive tablets dedicated to the divine pair Medusa and Byatis. Of these two worthies themselves no likeness was found, though perhaps this was because of the legendary danger of seeing their visages. Might the superstitious mind (as we then viewed it) not fear that even the second-hand depiction of the pair could prove petrifying in its own right? There were new relics, also some which paralleled the evidence already collected from other British sites, a few of which confirmed his conjectural restorations of fragmentary earlier items. The few inscriptions, mostly the prayers inscribed on votive plaques, were in Koine Greek or monkish Latin. It would be difficult to date the find, but this linguistic evidence suggested a date somewhere in Late Antiquity.

"From these scholarly ruminations we were rudely recalled by the sudden reappearance of yesterday's dour intruder. This time none of us had even noticed his approach, so preoccupied were we. His peculiarly accented declamation was punctuated by the flashing of his eyes in the lamplight: 'Woe to them that heed not even after the second warning! Their conscience is seared, and they wot not the evil that they do!' With that his knobby hand, protruding from the black sleeve of his cassock, made to descend like a hammer on our table. I braced for the clatter sure to result, but there was no impact, no sound. My eyes had strayed for an instant to the alarmed face of Professor Ashdod, who little fancied this old man scattering his precious relics by a clumsy blow. When I looked back, the old priest was gone.

"The professor was the first to speak: 'Science must always make its way in the face of superstition, gentlemen. Let us hope our watchmen are alert against this man's compatriots. Let us turn in so as to be ready for a great day tomorrow. We will see what awaits us within.' With that he drained his mug and began to collect the artifacts he had spread out on the table, rather like, I thought, a player at cards cradling his winnings.

"I saw one item he had neglected, gingerly lifted it by a corner, and passed it to him. I was surprised at his reply. 'Not one of ours, Mr. Batchel. Keep it for a souvenir.' I did just that and have always carried the stonework fragment upon my person as a keepsake to this day.

"The night was full of dreams, some ominous, anticipations no doubt of what ancient heathen remains we might discover on the morrow, others depicting our own imagined future fame as partners in a great discovery. Quite silly in retrospect.

"The morning began with a surprise. Doctor Ashdod did not appear to meet us in the breakfast room, nor did he answer to a knock at his door. Growing worried, we finally decided he must have risen earlier than the rest of us and preceded us to the dig. It was a relief when this surmise proved out. As we approached the site over the clover fields separating it from the town, followed again by suspicious village eyes, we were relieved to see Professor Ashdod emerging from the shaded mouth of the shaft.

"'Welcome, young men! To tell the truth, I just couldn't wait. I never managed to fall asleep, so I decided to be up before dawn and ready at the first light. The workmen were surprised to see me,' he chuckled, 'and I found a rifle barrel greeting me as I approached. But soon the men recognized me. They reported no trouble. I half feared some of the locals might try to close up or damage the site, though I still haven't the faintest idea why.

"'But here's the news: I've managed to pry loose the barrier. You'll find it propped against that rise.'

"We gathered round the stained slab, the workmen moving back from their surveillance as we did so. It was they who had deposited it there after the professor had dug round the buried edges so as not to damage the thing. We studied it in silence for a moment, and I don't mind admitting I was the first to venture a translation. It was ecclesiastical Latin, and it was the Vulgate text of Exodus 33:20, 'Ye cannot see my face, for man shall not see me and live.'

"'Obviously,' someone pontificated, 'it wasn't placed there by the worshipers of the god. It's a warning to stay away. Perhaps placed there by church authorities after having closed down the shrine and persecuted the devotees. What do you think, Professor?'

"'Likely enough, Mr. Bainbridge, but don't forget that some of yesterday's inscriptions were rendered in the same Latin. We shouldn't be too quick to rule out a secret worship of pagan deities by nominal Christians. It wouldn't be unparalleled. And even they would have sufficient reason to warn people away from looking at their gods, given what they believed about their deadly powers. Anyway, I'm going in. I want the rest of you to wait out here. Oh, don't worry, you'll soon enough have your turn. Shipley, be a good lad and fix me up a couple of torches. The sun doesn't help much in there. It seems to turn a corner and to open into a small grotto, much like a Mithraeum.

"'I can tell from the echoes that we've not been so lucky here as in the shaft: Much of the inside must have collapsed long ago. So quarters are tight, and until I see for myself what's in there, my clumsy feet are the only ones that will be trampling the floor, understand?'

"We all saw his wisdom, though that hardly lightened the burden of frustration. Shipley tied handkerchiefs onto a couple of fallen branches, dipped them into our lamp oil and set them ablaze. He passed them one by one to the professor who must have hollowed out makeshift brackets or holes for them. Then all alike, we waited and listened.

"His familiar voice began to take on an eerie quality as he passed further along the hidden recesses of the underground structure. No obstruction so far, that was obvious. His voice drifted up as if from the underworld.

"'I'm able to stand erect here, and I believe I've reached what was the altar area. What luck that it survived the centuries! And this— Good Lord! It must be the likeness of Byatis himself!' He laughed in exultation. His efforts were now rewarded, his theories confirmed, his lasting fame assured. Back on the surface we began to applaud him. Our excitement rose like a fever as we awaited his momentary reappearance and our own turns to retrace his path one by one. But there was no sound of bootfalls, no further word of discovery. Was he so lost in deciphering some inscriptions? We called, but still there was no answer.

"Genuinely worried for our mentor for the second time that morning, we argued over who ought to go in after him. These deliberations were cut short by the sudden eruption of a figure from the mouth of the shaft. He sped into us, knocking us aside like so many ninepins. What could have so panicked the professor?

"As we picked ourselves up we were dumbfounded to see the figure, now clearly naked, run with blinding speed past us and on into the hills opposite the village. This could hardly be the sturdy but middle-aged form of Professor Ashdod! Frankly I doubt that any of us, hardy young specimens as we were, could have caught up with the fleeing figure, but none of us thought of that just then. Once we realized our leader must still be inside the tomb, more than likely injured by this lurking enemy, we decided we must throw caution to the wind. Shipley shouldered the rest of us aside and began to crawl inside.

"Fearing more mischief, we waited with bated breath. Only a moment later, Shipley's voice came up: 'Rum thing! He's not here! And I can't see any image he might have been describing, either! Wait, here's something—no!'

"Blood chilling, we looked at one another, and this time it was Bainbridge who took the plunge. Moments later, his voice came back, rather too calmly: 'Listen chaps, there's enough room on this end. Come on down. But get a grip on yourselves first.'

"With the help of our stolid workmen we were able, an hour or so later, to trundle into a borrowed wagon what we had found in the shrine of Byatis. We knew we would have to remain in Camside long enough to arrange to have the thing shipped back to the University. That much was easy to figure out. The difficult thing was trying to come up with a tale to tell the University authorities, one that they might believe. What we finally decided on was this: Poor Professor Ashdod, on the eve of our planned excavation, sought relief from the unusual heat with a dip in the

River Cam. From this seemingly innocent amusement he had not returned, overcome with a cramp and drowning before any of us understood his peril. Nor was his body to be found. We would say we had commissioned the statue of the professor as a commemoration of our beloved mentor and donated it to the University. Once we returned to the campus, we waited a plausible length of time before presenting the statue, and there it stands today."

The patient Mr. Barlowe seemed at first not to understand that Mr. Batchel had concluded his story. Then: "But, if you please, what *did* happen to the professor? And what was it you shipped back to the University from Camside? Surely not the statue?"

"I had thought you took my meaning, Barlowe. Don't you see, it was no statue, but the professor himself. The ancient power of Byatis had not faded with the ages."

The younger man was silent in disbelief. He stared at Mr. Batchel as if the latter had suddenly sprouted a second bald head. "Surely you don't mean to tell me that he was turned to stone by the statue of a Gorgon? You're not, are you?"

"I needn't. To quote our Lord, thou hast said it. But I don't expect it to sink in all at once. No indeed. It took me some years of further investigation to come to the conclusions I now hold on the matter. One of those conclusions is that the stone image of Byatis which the professor stumbled upon was no more a true statue than the one we have just seen. Think back to the naked running figure. My first thought was that he must be one of the hostile Camside villagers who had lain in wait for the professor to do him ill. But the more I considered it the more mysterious the matter became: How could such a one have entered the sealed tomb ahead of us and contrived to reseal it from within? Were the workmen, too, in on the scheme? They weren't even native to the area. At length our naked runner seemed fully as puzzling as the naked man who fled away when our Lord was arrested in Gethsemane. But in recent months I have, shall we say, formed a hypothesis. And I want you to help me test it."

"Me?" protested the nonplussed Mr. Barlowe, as if afraid he was being reeled in like a fish on the older man's mad hook. "Really, it's fine for you to believe whatever you please, but—"

"Why, Mr. Barlowe! You disappoint me! I should think a rationalist like yourself would welcome the opportunity to debunk the supernaturalist delusions of a medieval relic like me. I was so sure you would rise to my challenge that I invited you along for this conference in the first place. You see, it was no accident that we ran across the 'statue.' I knew we would sooner or later, and I counted on your healthy curiosity. It did not fail me. I hope it will not fail me now."

After a few moments, the two men rose and returned to the Refectory. The afternoon seminars had passed without benefit of their attendance. They chose a table and continued their conversation, employing hushed tones as the seats around them began to fill.

"There is a man here at Brichester I wish to question. He is a faculty member, in the Classics Department. Perhaps you know him or have studied with him." Here Mr. Batchel mentioned a name that is perhaps best withheld. "I believe he may hold our answer. You say that you do know him? Good. What I wish is that you may request an appointment to see him. Say that you wish to introduce me, that I wish to pursue the possibility of offering a lecture course at Brichester. It will not sound outlandish; you may know that I am retained by my own alma mater to examine prospective graduates."

Still looking as if he had been made the dupe of a joke that had not finished tightening its bands about him, young Barlowe stammered his agreement. "I suppose that couldn't do any harm. But please remember, Mr. Batchel, I am not yet through this institution. I will trust you not to say anything that might prejudice the faculty against me."

Mr. Batchel smiled and took his assistant by the shoulder. "Rest assured, my young friend, you will have nothing to regret. And soon all things shall be made clear. It's been a long day. Let us retire."

As the professor in question was himself participating in the archaeological conference, it was no great matter for Barlowe to locate and arrange to see him in his office the following afternoon. The baffled divinity student stayed close to Mr. Batchel for the duration of the morning and afternoon, attending this and that lecture, but retaining little of what he heard. He could not cease turning over Mr. Batchel's cryptic half-explanations in his mind. And still no light came.

Beside him his older comrade rose and clapped. As they made their way through the thick crowd of those filing out of the lecture hall, Mr. Batchel exclaimed, "Well, it seems that even I am not yet too old to learn. But I do wonder how those Aztecs and Incas are to be reconciled with the Table of Nations in Genesis chapter 10. Leave it to the theologians, I suppose. They'll come up with something. They always do. Why, what troubles you, Mr. Barlowe? Oh yes, of course, we have an appointment across campus, don't we? No time for tea. We'd best hurry along."

The secretary was waiting for them in a thickly carpeted, well appointed office. "I believe you are the professor's last appointment for the afternoon. Please do try to keep in mind he has had a busy day with the conference. You may go on in. He's expecting you."

It was quite a study, a private library to envy. Mr. Batchel could scarcely keep himself from devouring the exotic rows of bindings with covetous eyes. Young Mr. Barlowe could not hide his timidity as he addressed the imposing figure before him. Though he had been a student in one of the professor's classes only the previous year, he knew it was not likely he would be remembered among scores of university and seminary students. After a few fumbling words, Barlowe introduced Mr. Batchel to the professor. The tall, broad, bearded man would, save for the cut of his suit, have suggested more the successful London financier than the erudite academic. He greeted Mr. Batchel, though he made no move to shake hands. Nor did the smiling Mr. Batchel. All three sat down, as if on signal.

"Yes, Professor, it is just as our young friend has said. I would much enjoy piloting a lecture course in some upcoming term. Local archaeology has long been a specialty of mine, and I should like to develop some of the theories of one of Brichester's own esteemed faculty, now sadly deceased. He had certain speculations, not unsupported by evidence of a striking character, as to the immigration of the cult of Medusa to these very shores, and the fusion of that cult with a local mystery religion, the religion of—"

The deep, vaguely accented voice interrupted him: "Yes, I have heard of the work of the man you speak of, a Professor Ashdod, I believe. I regret to have to tell you that his work has been long ago surpassed, discredited really. I am afraid some of the most recent work in the field may have escaped your notice, busy as you must be with parish duties. And yet I do not mean to denigrate your scholarly gifts, sir. I attended your own lecture yesterday morning and was quite impressed. I take a dim view of this Medusa business, but it is not impossible we might be able to arrange something for you in the next spring term on some other subject." He rose to signal the interview was at an end.

The Stoneground rector and his apprentice made for the door and were called back a moment later. The study door was now closed, but the secretary hailed them. "The professor has asked me to have you meet him tonight after the final convocation behind the main library building. By then he may have had the opportunity to speak to the Dean about the matter you discussed."

"Splendid!" said Mr. Batchel. Young Barlowe's eye's remained empty and expectant. As the two men left the building, their long shadows pouring down the steps they slowly descended, Barlowe could contain himself no longer.

"I'm sorry that proved a cul-de-sac, though you may get your lecture course."

"Tush tush, my boy. My duties at Stoneground would never allow it. And your professor may yet have our answer for us. We must be patient. As Professor Ashdod knew, that is the only way not to overlook crucial bits of evidence."

"But he never even let you finish your question about Medusa and Attis! That can hardly be what he wants to discuss with you!"

"The trained archaeologist learns how to read even the smallest and least obvious signs. And I believe you mean 'Byatis.'" At this, Barlowe gave up and resigned himself to wait for the outcome later that night. He only thought it odd that the professor should choose so recondite a meeting place. Perhaps he simply thought it best to avoid the crowd of those attending the convocation.

The convocation came and went, ringing down the curtain on another scholarly conference, each enough like the others that Mr. Batchel invariably found them assuming the monotony of a stack of old neglected journals on the dusty shelf of memory. But each in its hour was conducted with the pomp of a state occasion. As one of the conference speakers this time he himself was entitled to don his academic regalia and join the processional. From the front line of pews in the Brichester University Chapel, he had one of the best seats in the house for the seemingly endless round of invocations, testimonials and finally the keynote address.

Later he could not recall the identity of that final speaker or even his theme. He was busy reviewing in his mind what he might have to say an hour or two later when he had his much anticipated meeting with the professor. The professor himself Mr. Batchel noticed up ahead in the line of march and marked it when he briefly ascended the dais to introduce one of the speakers who was to introduce yet another speaker.

The moment finally came to march back out of the chapel and disperse. As he again took his place among the grandly vested faculty and visiting scholars, Mr. Batchel could not help but reflect how one might be inclined to have a bit of sympathy after all for those old scribes and Pharisees whom our Lord rebuked for lengthening their tassels for acclaim among men. But enough of that. There was young Mr. Barlowe waiting for him.

After a brief return to their assigned rooms to shed his academic gown, Mr. Batchel led the way to the appointed meeting place. Many hours had passed and the moon was high, and by its light they had no difficulty finding their way to the main library, then circling its vast girth. The rear of this building was whiskered with rows of trees and hedges, and the professor's presence among all these standing shapes was not immediately apparent.

"Professor?" called Mr. Barlowe hopefully, yet not without a note of intimidation. Almost like a distant bird call came the response at once.

"Here, gentlemen."

The two companions followed the voice, arriving in a few moments' time at what seemed an artfully contrived portico of ivied arches rising from a thick bank of shrubs. Within the arch stood the shadowed form of the one whom they sought. His silhouette was vague, almost shapeless, implying he had not taken time to doff his academic regalia.

"Ah, the Reverend Batchel, and of course, Mr. Barlowe. I trust you enjoyed the convocation. Always a great stimulation for scholars to gather for their mutual enlightenment, don't you think? And now to the matter at hand. I must confess that I have had cause to give your unique theories further consideration. And it may surprise you to hear that I have experienced something of a change of heart on the question. Indeed, I now find myself very much convinced that you and your late friend Ashdod were correct. Further, I would like to supply you with an irrefutable bit of evidence—"

Drifting clouds slid off the face of the full moon, and by its light Mr. Batchel believed he could behold an odd *shifting* among the hair of the professor's full beard. As the clergyman's hand went to his pocket, his gaze remained fixed and he believed he saw, as he had expected to see, the slow emergence from that stirring hair of something like slugs, their tips sickly white in the moonlight.

"Barlowe! Look away, if you value your soul!" exclaimed the Reverend Batchel with uncharacteristic urgency. Withal did he close his own eyes, flinging toward the third man some object he had palmed a moment before.

As the frightened and obedient Barlowe swung round, his eyes caught sight for a brief moment of that which his mentor made ready to pitch at their enemy. It was a stone star-shape, possibly bearing a central sigil of some sort. But then he clenched his eyes as if he planned never to open them again and he dropped to the ground.

"Now I believe it will be safe to look," came Mr. Batchel's again unperturbed tones. "More than likely the University will have to find space for another commemorative statue."

But Barlowe was not looking where the professor had been standing. Rather his eyes followed a small shape scuttling crab-like into the cover of the shrubbery. He thought it resembled a living starfish, though fleshy in texture, surmounted by a single, disproportionately large, unblinking eye. But then it was gone, and who could say?

For the first time Mr. Barlowe found himself greatly relieved to be leaving the rare atmosphere of the University and returning to the provincial gravel-ground parish. At length he ventured to interrupt Mr. Batchel, sitting opposite him in the train car, absorbed in a biblical monograph he had purchased at Brichester University two days before.

"Mr. Batchel, I really must ask you something."

"Yes, my young friend? Some theological matter? Or archaeology perhaps?"

"Neither, or perhaps both! You must tell me what happened at the last. How did you dispatch the professor? And, well, *why*?"

Closing his book, Mr. Batchel leaned forward and said, "Now I should have thought that obvious. But perhaps a word of explanation might be in order. Let me take you back to that tragic day many years ago, after the loss of Professor Ashdod, as we, his young proteges, were on the point of dispersing. One evening, as I strove to make sense of all that had transpired, rather in your state of mind at the present, come to think of it, I took a long walk. I found myself on the road leading from Camside to the nearby village of Severnford. As I looked up, my eye fell upon a quaint chapel. At once I veered from my path to seek a place of prayer within.

"As I trod the moss-covered pathway and passed between a pair of blackened pillars, I could not help but notice, with my eye for rare church architecture, a striking piece of stonework adorning the arch over the garth. It depicted something I first took for the familiar St. George and the dragon motif, but a closer scrutiny revealed an unusual variation on that theme. The dragon had more the shape of a gargoyle and seemed to be bearded, a detail found on Chinese dragon sculptures, but never on their European cousins. And its nemesis was a winged angel holding aloft no conventional cross or sword, but a great five-pointed star from which the monster seemed to recoil. I entered the church with renewed interest but found no one of whom I might inquire. Hoping someone might yet appear, I resolved to pursue my first design of quiet prayer amid the empty pews.

"It was not long before a worried-looking verger appeared, hoping it was not a prowler whose tread he had heard and relieved to see that it wasn't. I rose and followed him down the nave, as he had generously agreed to give me a brief tour. I am, as you know, always curious to see the nooks and crannies of country churches for whatever antique wonders they may afford, but that day I was really only concerned to know of the peculiar stonework piece. And yet that fled my thoughts completely once I laid eyes on the first framed portrait we passed. It was the likeness of the old priest who had accosted us in the taproom!

"'Is this your present rector?' I asked, as nonchalantly as I could.

"Here the man chuckled and replied, 'Hardly! This is old Doctor Raines, and him a century gone!'

"I cut the tour short at that point, for I knew then what I needed to know. I knew who had visited us in the inn, and, recalling the star held aloft by the carven angel, I also knew what he had brought us. The extra relic on the taproom table had been a miniature replica of that star, and it was that which I learned too late could counter the baleful influence of Byatis, who escapes his stony confinement by luring the unwary to take his place. But as you saw last evening, the star retained its power."

Mr. Barlowe did not again disturb the silence which recaptured the compartment. For the rest of the rail journey only the chugging of the train was to be heard. We will not follow either the train or Mr. Barlowe further, save to mention that his remarkable experience was not without its effect upon his developing theological convictions. From that day forward there existed a greater commonality of spirit between him and his mentor. And it may not be out of place to divulge the fact that many years later, when Mr. Batchel went on to his reward, it was none other than Reverend Barlowe who succeeded him in the pulpit of Stoneground Church, which he served well. Nor would it be unduly surprising if, on some future visit to his old divinity school, he should pause with a curious seminarian before a peculiar statue depicting a robed and bearded scholar. One might speculate whether Mr. Barlowe would venture any sort of explanation.

The Horror Under Warrendown

by Ramsey Campbell

You ask me at least to hint why I refuse ever to open a children's book. Once I made my living from such material. While the imitations of reality hawked by my colleagues in the trade grew grubbier, and the fantasies more shameful, I carried innocence from shop to shop, or so I was proud to think. Now the sight of a children's classic in a bookshop window sends me fleeing. The more apparently innocent the book, the more unspeakable the truth it may conceal, and there are books the mere thought of which revives memories I had prayed were buried forever.

It was when I worked from Birmingham, and Warrendown was only a name on a signpost on a road to Brichester—a road I avoided, not least because it contained no bookshops. Nor did I care for the route it followed a few miles beyond the Warrendown sign through Clotton, a small settlement which appeared to be largely abandoned, its few occupied houses huddling together on each side of a river, beside which stood a concrete monument whose carvings were blurred by moss and weather. I had never been fond of the countryside, regarding it at best as a way of getting from town to town, and now the stagnant almost reptilian smell and chilly haze which surrounded Clotton seemed to attach itself to my car. This unwelcome presence helped to render the Cotswold landscape yet more forbidding to me, the farmland and green fields a disguise for the ancient stone of the hills, and I resolved to drive south of Brichester on the motorway in future and double back, even though this added half an hour to my journey. Had it not been for Graham Crawley I would never again have gone near the Warrendown road.

In those days I drank to be sociable, not to attempt to forget or to sleep. Once or twice a month I met colleagues in the trade, some of whom I fancied would have preferred to represent a children's publisher too, for a Balti and as many lagers as we could stay seated for. Saturdays would find me in my local pub, the Sutton Arms in Kings Heath. Ending my week among people who didn't need to be persuaded of the excellence of my latest batch of titles was enough to set me up for the next week. But it was in the Sutton Arms that Crawley made himself, I suppose, something like a friend.

I don't recall the early stages of the process, in his case or with any of the folk I used to know. I grew used to looking for him in the small bare taproom, where the stools and tables and low ceiling were the color of ash mixed with ale. He would raise his broad round stubbled face from his tankard, twitching his nose and upper lip in greeting, and as I joined him he would duck as though he expected me either to pat him on the head or hit him when he'd emitted his inevitable quip. "What was she up to in the woods with seven little men, eh?" he would mutter, or "There's only one kind of horn you'd blow up that I know of. No wonder he was going after sheep," or some other reference to the kind of book in which I traveled. There was a constant undercurrent of ingratiating nervousness in his voice, an apology for whatever he said as he said it, which was one reason I was never at my ease with him. While we talked about our week, mine on the road and his behind the counter of a local greengrocer's, I was bracing myself for his latest sexual bulletin. I never knew what so many women could see in him, and hardly any of them lasted for more than an encounter. My curiosity about the kind of girl who could find him attractive may have left me open to doing him the favor he asked of me.

At first he only asked which route I took to Brichester, and then which one I would follow if the motorway was closed, by which point I'd had enough of the way he skulked around a subject as if he was ready to dart into hiding at the first hint of trouble. "Are you after a lift?" I demanded.

He ducked his head so that his long hair hid even more of his ears and peered up at me. "Well, a lift, you know, I suppose, really, yes."

"Where to?"

"You won't know it, cos it's not much of a place. Only it's not far, not much out of your way, I mean, if you happened to be going that way anyway sometime."

When at last he released the name of Warrendown like a question he didn't expect to be answered, his irritating tentativeness provoked me to retort, "I'll be in that square of the map next week."

"Next week, that's next week, you mean." His face twitched so hard it exposed his teeth. "I wasn't thinking quite that soon ... *"

"I'll forgive you if you've given up on the idea."

"Given up—no, you're right. I'm going, cos I should go," he said, fiercely for him.

Nevertheless I arrived at his flat the next day not really expecting to collect him. When I rang his bell, however, he poked his nose under the drawn curtains and said he would be down in five minutes, which, to my continuing surprise, he was, nibbling the last of his presumably raw breakfast and dressed in the only suit I'd ever seen him wear. He sat clutching a small case which smelled of vegetables while I concentrated on driving through the rush hour and into the tangle of motorways, and so we were irrevocably on our way before I observed that he was gripping his luggage with all the determination I'd heard in his voice in the pub. "Are you expecting some kind of trouble?" I said.

"Trouble." He added a grunt which bared his teeth and which seemed to be saying I'd understood so much that no further questions were necessary, and I nearly lost my temper.

"Care to tell me what kind?" I suggested.

"What would you expect?"

"Not a woman."

"See, you knew. Be tricks. The trouble's what I got her into, as if you hadn't guessed. Cos she got me going so fast I hadn't time to wear anything. Can't beat a hairy woman."

This was a great deal more intimate than I welcomed. "When did you last see her?" I said as curtly as I could.

"Last year. She was having it then. Should have gone down after, but I, you know. You know me."

He was hugging his baggage so hard he appeared to be squeezing out the senseless vegetable smell. "Afraid of her family?" I said with very little sympathy.

He pressed his chin against his chest, but I managed to distinguish what he muttered. "Afraid of the whole bloody place."

That was clearly worth pursuing, and an excuse for me to stay on my usual route, except that ahead I saw all three lanes of traffic halted as far as the horizon, and police cars racing along the hard shoulder towards the problem. I left the motorway at the exit which immediately presented itself.

Framilode, Saul, Fretherne, Whitminister—old names announced themselves on signposts, and then a narrow devious road enclosed the car with hedges, blotting out the motorway at once. Beneath a sky clogged with dark clouds the gloomy foliage appeared to smoulder; the humped backs of the hills glowed a lurid green. When I opened my window to let out the vegetable smell, it admitted a breeze, unexpectedly chill for September, which felt like my passenger's nervousness rendered palpable. He was crouching over his luggage and blinking at the high spiky hedges as if they were a trap into which I'd led him. "Can I ask what your plans are?" I said to break the silence, which was growing as relentless as the ancient landscape.

"See her. Find out what she's got, what she wants me to." His voice didn't so much trail off as come to a complete stop.

I wasn't sure I wanted to know where his thoughts had found themselves. "What took you there to begin with?" was as much as I cared to ask.

"Beat ricks."

This time I grasped it, despite his pronouncing it as though unconvinced it was a name. "She's the young lady in question."

"Met her in the Cabbage Patch, you know, the caff. She'd just finished university but she stayed over at my place." I was afraid this might be the preamble to further intimate details, but he continued with increasing reluctance, "Kept writing to me after she went home, wanting me to go down there, cos she said I'd feel at home."

"And did you?"

He raised his head as though sniffing the air and froze in that position. The sign for Warrendown, drooping a little on its post, had swung into view along the hedge. His half-admitted feelings had affected me so much that my foot on the accelerator wavered. "If you'd prefer not to do this—"

Only his mouth moved, barely opening. "No choice."

No reply could have angered me more. He'd no more will than one of his own vegetables, I thought, and sent the car screeching into the Warrendown road. As we left behind the sign, which appeared to be trying to point into the earth, I had an impression of movement beyond the hedge on both sides of the road, several figures which had been standing absolutely still leaping to follow the car. I told myself I was mistaking at least their speed, and when ragged gaps in the hedge afforded me a view of oppressively green fields weighed down by the stagnant sky, nobody was to be seen, not that anyone could have kept pace with the car. I hadn't time to ponder any of this, because from the way Crawley was inching his face forward I could tell that the sight a mile ahead among the riotous fields surrounded by hunched dark hills must indeed be Warrendown.

At that distance I saw it was one of the elements of the countryside I most disliked, an insignificant huddle of buildings miles from anywhere, but I'd never experienced such immediate revulsion. The clump of thatched roofs put me in mind of dunes surmounted by dry grass, evidence less of human habitation than of the mindless actions of nature. As the sloping road led me down towards them I saw that the thatch overhung the cottages, like hair dangling over idiot brows. Where the road descended to the level of the village it showed me that the outermost cottages were so squat they appeared to have collapsed or to be sinking into the earth of the unpaved road. Thatch obscured their squinting windows, and I gave in to an irrational hope that the village might prove to be abandoned. Then the door of the foremost cottage sank inwards, and as I braked, a head poked out of the doorway to watch our arrival.

It was a female head. So much I distinguished before it was snatched back. I glanced at Crawley in case he had recognized it, but he was wrinkling his face at some aspect of the village which had disconcerted him. As the car coasted into Warrendown, the woman reappeared, having draped a scarf over her head to cover even more of her than her dress did. I thought she was holding a baby, then decided it must be some kind of pet, because as she emerged into the road with an odd abrupt lurch the small object sprang from her arms into the dimness within the cottage. She knotted the scarf and thrust her plump yet flattish face out of it to stare swollen-eyed at my passenger. I was willing to turn the vehicle around and race for the main road, but he was lowering his window, and so I slowed the car. I saw their heads lean towards each other as though the underside of the sky was pressing them down and forcing them together. Their movements seemed obscurely reminiscent, but I'd failed to identify of what when she spoke. "You're back."

Though her low voice wasn't in itself threatening, I sensed he was disconcerted that someone he clearly couldn't put a name to had recognized him. All he said, however, was, "You know Beatrix."

"Us all know one another."

She hadn't once glanced at me, but I was unable to look away from her. A few coarse hairs sprouted from her reddish face; I had the unpleasant notion that her cheeks were raw from being shaved. "Do you know where she is?" Crawley said.

"Her'll be with the young ones."

His head sank as his face turned up further. "How many?"

"All that's awake. Can't you hear them? I should reckon even he could."

As that apparently meant me I dutifully strained my ears, although I wasn't anxious to heighten another sense: our entry into Warrendown seemed to have intensified the vegetable stench. After a few moments I made out a series of high regular sounds—childish voices chanting some formula—and experienced almost as much relief as my passenger audibly did. "She's at the school," he said.

"That's her. Back where her was always meant for." The woman glanced over her shoulder into the cottage, and part of a disconcertingly large ear twitched out of her headscarf. "Feeding time," she said, and began unbuttoning the front of her dress as she stepped back through the doorway, beyond which I seemed to glimpse something hopping about a bare earth floor. "See you down there later," she told Crawley, and shut the door.

I threw the car into gear and drove as fast through the village as I reasonably could. Faces peered through the thick fringes over the low windows of the stunted cottages, and I told myself it was the dimness within that made those faces seem so fat and so blurred in their outlines, and the nervousness with which Crawley had infected me that caused their eyes to appear so large. At the center of Warrendown the cottages, some of which I took to be shops without signs, crowded towards the road as if forced forward by the mounds behind them, mounds as broad as the cottages but lower, covered with thatch or grass. Past the center the buildings were more sunken; more than one had collapsed, while others were so overgrown that only glimpses through the half-obscured unglazed windows of movements, ill-defined and sluggish, suggested that they were inhabited. I felt as though the rotten vegetable sweetness in the air was somehow dragging them all down as it was threatening to do to me, and had to restrain my foot from tramping on the accelerator. Now the car was almost out of Warrendown, which was scarcely half a mile long, and the high voices had fallen silent before I was able to distinguish what they had been chanting—a hymn, my instincts told me, even though the language had seemed wholly unfamiliar. I was wondering whether I'd passed the school, and preparing to tell Crawley I hadn't time to retrace the route, when Crawley mumbled, "This is it."

"If you say so." I now saw that the last fifty or so yards of the left-hand side of Warrendown were occupied by one long mound fattened by a pelt of thatch and grass and moss. I stopped the car but poised my foot on the accelerator. "What do you want to do?"

His blank eyes turned to me. Perhaps it was the strain on them which made them appear to be almost starting out of his head. "Why do you have to ask?"

I'd had enough. I reached across him to let him out, and the door of the school wobbled open as though I'd given it a cue. Beyond it stood a young woman of whom I could distinguish little except a long-sleeved ankle-length brown dress, my attention having been caught by the spectacle behind her—at least half a dozen small bodies in a restless heap on the bare floor of the dark corridor. As some of them raised their heads lethargically to blink big-eyed at me before subsiding again, Crawley clambered out of the vehicle, blocking my view. "Thanks for, you know," he muttered. "You'll be coming back this way, will you?"

"Does that mean you'll be ready to leave?"

"I'll know better when you come."

"I'll be back before dark and you'd better be out here on the road," I told him, and sped off.

I kept him in view in the mirror until the hedges hid Warrendown. The mirror shook with the unevenness of the road, but I saw him wave his free hand after me, stretching his torso towards the car as though he was about to drop to all fours and give chase. Behind him a figure leapt out of the doorway, and as he swung round she caught him. I could distinguish no more about her than I already had, except that the outline of her large face looked furry, no doubt framed by hair. She and Crawley embraced—all her limbs clasped him, at any rate—and as I looked away from this intimacy I noticed that the building of which the school was an extension had once possessed a tower, the overgrown stones of which were scattered beyond the edge of the village. It was none of my business whether they took care of their church, nor why anyone who'd attended university should have allowed herself to be reduced to teaching in a village school, nor what hold the place seemed to have over Crawley as well. They deserved each other, I told myself, and not only because they looked so similar. Once they were out of sight I lowered the windows and drove fast to rid the car of the stagnant mindless smell of Warrendown.

Before long the track brought me to an unmarked junction with the main road. I wound the windows tight and sped through the remains of Clotton, which felt drowned by the murky sky and the insidious chill of the dark river, and didn't slow until I saw Brichester ahead, raising its hospital and graveyard above its multiplying streets. In those streets I felt more at ease; nothing untoward had ever befallen me in a city such as Brichester, and nothing seemed likely to do so, especially in a bookshop. I parked my car in a multistory at the edge of Lower Brichester and walked through the crowds to the first of my appointments.

My Christmas titles went down well—in the last shop of the day, perhaps too well. Not only did the new manager, previously second in command, order more copies than any of her competitors, but in a prematurely festive mood insisted on my helping her celebrate her promotion. One drink led to several, not least because I must have been trying to douse the nervousness with which Crawley and Warrendown had left me. Too late I realized my need for plenty of coffee and something to eat, and by the time I felt fit to drive the afternoon was well over.

Twilight had gathered like soot in cobwebs as wide as the sky. From the car park I saw lights fleeing upwards all over Brichester, vanishing home. The hospital was a glimmering misshapen skull beside which lay acres of bones. Even the fluorescent glare of the car park appeared unnatural, and I sat in my car wondering how much worse the places I had to drive back through would seem. I'd told Crawley I would collect him before dark, but wasn't it already dark? Might he not have decided I wasn't coming for him, and have made his own arrangements? This was almost enough to persuade me I needn't return to Warrendown, but a stirring of guilt at my cowardice shamed me into heading for that morning's route.

The glow of the city sank out of view. A few headlights came to meet me, and then there were only my beams probing the dim road that writhed between the hills, which rose as though in the dark they no longer needed to pretend to slumber. The bends of the road swung back and forth, unable to avoid my meager light, and once a pair of horned heads stared over a gate, rolling their eyes as they chewed and chewed, rolling them mindlessly as they would when they went to be slaughtered. I remembered how Crawley's eyes had protruded as he prepared to quit my car.

Well outside Clotton I was seized by the chill of the river. Though my windows were shut tight, as I reached the first abandoned house I heard the water, splashing more loudly than could be accounted for unless some large object was obstructing it. I drove so fast across the narrow bridge and between the eyeless buildings that by the time I was able to overcome my inexplicable panic I was miles up the road, past the unmarked lane to Warrendown.

I told myself that I mustn't use this as an excuse to break my word, and when I reached the Warrendown signpost, which looked as though the weight of the growing blackness was helping the earth drag it down, I steered the car off the main road. Even with my headlight beams full on, I had to drive at a speed which made me feel the vehicle was burrowing into the thick dark, which by now could just as well have been the night it was anticipating. The contortions of the road suggested it was doing its utmost never to reach Warrendown. The thorns of the hedges tore at the air, and a gap in the tortured mass of vegetation let me see the cottages crouching furtively, heads down, in the midst of the smudged fields. Despite the darkness, not a light was to be seen.

It could have been a power failure—I assumed those might be common in so isolated and insignificant a village—but why was nobody in Warrendown using candles or flashlights? Perhaps they were, invisibly at that distance, I reassured myself. The hedges intervened without allowing me a second look. The road sloped down, giving me the unwelcome notion that Warrendown had snared it, and the hedges ended as though they had been chewed off. As my headlights found the outermost cottages, their long-haired skulls seemed to rear out of the earth. Apart from that, there was no movement all the way along the road to the half-ruined church.

The insidious vegetable stench had already begun to seep into the car. It cost me an effort to drive slowly enough through the village to look for the reason I was here. The thatched fringes were full of shadows which shifted as I passed, as though each cottage was turning its idiot head towards me. Though every window was empty and dark, I felt observed, increasingly so as the car followed its wobbling beams along the deserted lane, until I found it hard to breathe. I seemed to hear a faint irregular thumping—surely my own unsteady pulse, not a drumming under the earth. I came abreast of the church and the school, and thought the thumping quickened and then ceased. Now I was out of Warrendown, but the knowledge that I would be returning to the main road whichever direction I chose persuaded me to make a last search. I turned the car, almost backing it into one of the overgrown blocks of the fallen tower, and sounded my horn twice.

The second blare followed the first into the silent dark. Nothing moved, not a single strand of thatch on the cottages within the congealed splash of light cast by my headlamps, but I was suddenly nervous of what response I might have invited. I eased the car away from the ruins of the tower and began to drive once more through Warrendown, my foot trembling on the accelerator as I made myself restrain my speed. I was past the school when a dim shape lurched into my mirror and in pursuit of the car.

Only my feeling relatively secure inside the vehicle allowed me to brake long enough to see the face. The figure flared red as though it was being skinned from head to foot, and in the moment before its hands jerked up to paw its eyes I saw it was Crawley. Had his eyes always been so sensitive to sudden light? I released the brake pedal and fumbled the gears into neutral, and saw him let his hands fall but otherwise not move. It took some determination on my part to lower the window in order to call to him. "Come on if you're coming."

I barely heard his answer; his voice was indistinct—clogged. "I can't."

I would have reversed alongside him, except there wasn't room to pass him if he stayed put in the middle of the road. I flung myself out of the car in a rage and slammed the door furiously, a sound that seemed to provoke a renewed outbreak of muffled drumming, which I might have remarked had I not been intent on trying to wave away the suffocating vegetable smell. "Why not?" I demanded, staying by the car.

"Come and see."

I wasn't anxious to see more of Warrendown, or indeed of him. In the backwash of the car's lights his face appeared swollen with more stubble than an ordinary day could produce, and his eyes seemed dismayingly enlarged, soaking up the dimness. "See what?" I said. "Is it your young lady?"

"My what?"

I couldn't judge whether his tone was of hysterical amusement or panic or both. "Beatrix," I said, more loudly than I liked tc in the abnormal silence and darkness. "Is it your child?"

"There isn't one."

"I'm sorry," I murmured, uncertain whether I should be. "You mean Beatrix—"

I was loath to put into words what I assumed she must have done, but he shook his blurred head and took an uncertain step towards me. I had the impression, which disturbed me so much I was distracted from the word he'd inched closer to mutter, that he couldn't quite remember how to walk. "What are you saying?" I shouted before my voice flinched from the silence. "What's absurd? Never mind. Tell me when you're in the car."

He'd halted, hands dangling in front of his chest. His protruding teeth glinted, and I saw that he was chewing—seemed to glimpse a greenishness about his mouth and fattened cheeks. "Can't do that," he mumbled.

Did he mean neither of us would be able to return to the car? "Why not?" I cried.

"Come and see."

At that moment no prospect appealed to me less—but before I could refuse he turned his back and leapt into the dark. Two strides, or at least two convulsive movements, carried him to the doorless entrance to the church. The next moment he vanished into the lightless interior, and I heard a rapid padding over whatever served for a floor; then, so far as the throbbing of my ears allowed me to distinguish, there was silence.

I ran to the church doorway, which was as far as the faintest glow from my headlights reached. "Crawley," I called with an urgency meant to warn him I had no intention of lingering, but the only response from the dark was a feeble echo of my call, followed by a surge of the omnipresent vegetable stench. I called once more and then, enraged almost beyond the ability to think, I dashed to my car. If I had still been rational—if the influence of Warrendown had not already fastened on my mind—I would surely have left my acquaintance to his chosen fate and driven for my life. Instead I fetched my flashlight from under the dashboard and having switched off the headlamps and locked the car, returned to the rotting church.

As the flashlight beam wavered through the doorway I saw that the place was worse than abandoned. The dozen or so pews on either side of the aisle, each pew broad enough to accommodate a large family, were only bloated green with moss and weeds; but the altar before them had been levered up, leaning its back against the rear wall of the church and exposing the underside of its stone. I swung the beam through the desecrated interior, and glimpsed crude drawings on the mottled greenish walls as shadows of pews pranced across them. There was no trace of Crawley, and nowhere for him to hide unless he was crouching behind the altar. I stalked along the aisle to look, and almost fell headlong into a blackness that was more than dark. Just in time the flashlight beam plunged into the tunnel which had been dug where the altar ought to have stood.

The passage sloped quite gently into the earth, further than my light could reach. It was as wide as a burly man, but not as tall as I. Now I realized what my mind had been reluctant to accept as I'd heard Crawley disappear into the church—that his footfalls had seemed to recede to a greater distance than the building could contain. I let the beam stray across the pews in a last desperate search for him, and was unable to avoid glimpsing the images scrawled on the walls, an impious dance of clownish figures with ears and feet so disproportionately large they must surely be false. Then Crawley spoke from the tunnel beyond the curve which my light barely touched. "Come down. Come and see."

A wave of the stench like a huge vegetable breath rose from the tunnel and enveloped me. I staggered and almost dropped the flashlight—and then I lowered myself into the earth and stumbled in a crouch towards the summons. The somnolence audible in Crawley's voice had overtaken me too, and there seemed no reason why I should not obey, nor anything untoward about my behavior or my surroundings. Even the vegetable stench was to my taste, because I had inhaled so much of it since venturing back to Warrendown. Indeed, I was beginning to want nothing more than to be led to its source.

I stooped as far as the bend in the tunnel, just in time to see Crawley's heels vanishing around a curve perhaps fifty yards ahead. I saw now, as I had resisted hearing, that his feet were unshod—bare, at any rate, although the glimpse I had of them seemed hairier than any man's feet should be. He was muttering to me or to himself, and phrases drifted back: "... the revelations of the leaf ... the food twice consumed ... the paws in the dark ... the womb that eats ... ." I thought only my unsteady light was making the scraped passage gulp narrower, but before I gained the second bend I had to drop to all fours. Far ahead down the increasingly steep tunnel the drumming I'd heard earlier had recommenced, and I imagined that the models for the figures depicted on the church walls were making the sound, drumming their malformed feet as they danced in some vast subterranean cavern. That prospect gave me cause to falter, but another vegetable exhalation from below coaxed me onward, to the further bend around which Crawley's heels had withdrawn. I was crawling now, content as a worm in the earth, the flashlight in my outstretched hands making the tunnel swallow in anticipation of me each time my knees bumped forward. The drumming of feet on earth filled my ears, and I saw Crawley's furred soles disappear a last time at the limit of the flashlight beam, not around a curve but into an underground darkness too large for my light to begin to define. His muttering had ceased as though silenced by whatever had met him, but I heard at last the answer he had given me when I'd enquired after the child: not "absurd" at all. He'd told me that the child had been *absorbed*. Even this was no longer enough to break through the influence of whatever awaited me at the end of the tunnel, and I crawled rapidly forward to the subterranean mouth.

The flashlight beam sprawled out ahead of me, doing its best to illuminate a vast space beneath a ceiling too high even to glimpse. At first the dimness, together with shock or the torpor which had overcome my brain, allowed me to avoid seeing too much: only a horde of unclothed figures hopping and leaping and twisting in the air around an idol which towered from the moist earth, an idol not unlike a greenish Easter Island statue overgrown almost to featurelessness, its apex lost in the darkness overhead. Then I saw that one of the worshiping horde was Crawley, and began to make out faces less able to pass for human than his, their great eyes bulging in the dimness, their bestial teeth gleaming in misshapen mouths. The graffiti on the church walls had not exaggerated their shapes, I saw, nor were they in costume. The earth around the idol swarmed with their young, a scuttling mass of countless bodies which nothing human could have acknowledged as offspring. I gazed numbly down on the ancient rite, which no sunlight could have tolerated—and then the idol moved.

It unfurled part of itself towards me, a glimmering green appendage which might have been a gigantic wing emerging from a cocoon, and as it reached for me it whispered seductively with no mouth. Even this failed to appall me in my stupor; but when Crawley pranced towards me, a blasphemous priest offering me the unholy sacrament which would bind me to the buried secrets of Warrendown, some last vestige of wholesomeness and sanity within me revolted, and I backed gibbering along the tunnel, leaving the flashlight to blind anything which might follow.

All the way to the tunnel entrance I was terrified of being seized from behind. Every inhabitant of Warrendown must have been at the bestial rite, however, because I had encountered no hindrance except for the passage itself when I scrambled out beneath the altar and reeled through the lightless church to my car. The lowered heads of the cottages twitched their scalps at me as I sped recklessly out of Warrendown, the hedges beside the road clawed the air as though they were determined to close their thorns about me, but somehow in my stupor I managed to arrive at the main road, from where instincts which must have been wholly automatic enabled me to drive to the motorway, and so home, where I collapsed into bed.

I slept for a night and a day, such was my torpor. Even nightmares failed to waken me, and when eventually I struggled out of bed I half-believed that the horror under Warrendown had been one of them. I avoided Crawley and the pub, however, and so it was more than a week later I learned that he had disappeared—that his landlord had entered his room and found no bed in there, only a mound of overgrown earth hollowed out to accommodate a body—at which point my mind came close to giving way beneath an onslaught of more truth than any human mind should be required to suffer.

Is that why nobody will hear me out? How can they not understand that there may be other places like Warrendown, where monstrous gods older than humanity still hold sway? For a time I thought some children's books might be trying to hint at these secrets, until I came to wonder whether instead they are traps laid to lure children to such places, and I could no longer bear to do my job. Now I watch and wait, and stay close to lights that will blind the great eyes of the inhabitants of Warrendown, and avoid anywhere that sells vegetables, which I can smell at a hundred yards. Suppose there are others like Crawley, the hybrid spawn of some unspeakable congress, at large in our streets? Suppose they are feeding the unsuspecting mass of humanity some part of the horror I saw at the last under Warrendown?

What sane words can describe it? Partly virescent, partly glaucous—pullulating—internodally stunted—otiose—angiospermous—multifoliate—. Nothing can convey the dreadfulness of that final revelation, when I saw how it had overcome the last traces of humanity in its worshipers, who in some lost generation must have descended from imitating the denizens of the underworld to mating with them. For as the living idol unfurled a sluggish portion of itself towards me, Crawley tore off that living member of his brainless god, sinking his teeth into it to gnaw a mouthful before he proffered it, glistening and writhing with hideous life, to me.

CALL OF CTHULHU® FICTION

THE SHUB-NIGGURATH CYCLE

Among the most familiar names in the Lovecraftian litany, Shub-Niggurath, the Black Goat of the Wood, the Goat with a Thousand Young, is never met personally in Lovecraft's stories, but is often referred to in rituals and spells. This deity mutated and was adapted as Lovecraft crafted and revised tales spawned by other authors. Here for the first time is a comprehensive collection of all the relevant tales concerning Shub-Niggurath.

5½" x 8½", 256 pages, $9.95. ISBN 0-56882-017-8; available from bookstores and game stores or by mail from Chaosium, Inc., 950-A 56th Street, Oakland, CA 94608-3129.

THE HASTUR CYCLE

The stories in this book evoke a tracery of evil rarely rivaled in horror writing. They represent the whole evolving trajectory of such notions as Hastur, the King in Yellow, Carcosa, the Yellow Sign, Yuggoth, and the Lake of Hali. Writers from Ambrose Bierce to Ramsey Campbell and Karl Edward Wagner have explored and embellished these concepts and thereby created an evocative tapestry of hypnotic dread and horror. Here for the first time is a comprehensive collection of the thirteen relevant tales; several are rare and (almost) impossible to find. Selected and introduced by Robert M. Price.

5½" x 8½", 320 pages, $9.95. ISBN 0-56882-009-7; available from bookstores and game stores or by mail from Chaosium, Inc., 950-A 56th Street, Oakland, CA 94608-3129.

CALL OF CTHULHU® FICTION

MYSTERIES OF THE WORM

New Second Edition, Revised and Expanded. At the end of H. P. Lovecraft's life, the young Robert Bloch was an enthusiastic member of Lovecraft's literary circle. This is a new edition of the long out-of-print volume that collected most of Bloch's early work concerning the Cthulhu Mythos. The new edition includes three additional tales from the period—"The Brood of Bubastis", "The Sorcerer's Jewel", and "The Creeper in the Crypt", previously available only in scarce fanzines and anthologies. Bloch also has slightly revised the texts of three other stories. Seventeen tales, introduction by Robert M. Price, the original afterword by Bloch, and a supplementary essay by Lin Carter.

5½" x 8½", 272 pages, $9.95. ISBN 0-56882-012-7; available from bookstores and game stores or by mail from Chaosium, Inc., 950-A 56th Street, Oakland, CA 94608-3129.

CTHULHU'S HEIRS

Tales of the Mythos for the New Millennium. Nineteen new stories of the Cthulhu Mythos, never before printed. These range from an ironic tale of a cultist's conversion, to a first-person narration of possession by the thing from beyond itself, to what amounts to a retelling of the Lovecraft classic "The Dunwich Horror" from the inside out. These stories are by turn deft, horrifying, and hilarious, and give new life to the notion of the Mythos. Also, two rare stories are reprinted, one the definitive version of Ramsey Campbell's "The Franklyn Paragraphs." Selected and with an introduction by Thomas A. Stratman.

5½" x 8½", 288 pages, $9.95. ISBN 0-56882-013-5; available from bookstores and game stores or by mail from Chaosium, Inc., 950-A 56th Street, Oakland, CA 94608-3129.